Remembrance

by

Nathan Smith Hipps

Tallahassee, Florida

Inquiries should be addressed to:
CyPress Publications
P.O. Box 2636
Tallahassee, Florida 32316-2636
http://cypress-starpublications.com

lraymond@nettally.com

Library of Congress Cataloging-in-Publication Data

Hipps, Nathan.
    Remembrance / by Nathan Smith Hipps.— 1st ed.
       p. cm.
    ISBN-13: 978-0-9672585-9-1
    ISBN-10: 0-9672585-9-6
    1. Georgia—Fiction. 2. Domestic fiction. I. Title.
    PS3608.I67R46 2005
    813'.6—dc22
    2005030089

ISBN 10 0-9672585-9-6
ISBN 13 978-0-9672585-9-1

First Edition

For my mom

from whom all my blessings flow

Preface

I never met Leola Cowan Smith, my great-grandmother. All I know of her are the many stories shared with me by her daughters, my grandmother and great-aunt. I remember one day asking my grandmother to tell me about her mother, what kind of person she was, and the kind of life she led. The first thing grandmother said was, "My mother had such a hard life. She had so many obstacles to overcome, and she made it through each one of them. She was a very strong woman."

It is from these words that I wrote about my great-grandmother, Leola Cowan Smith. From the few pictures I have of her, I can see what Grandmother was talking about. Leola had the look of someone who had taken all life had to offer and survived to tell about it, none the worse for wear. The only picture I have of her as a young woman shows a pleasant, pretty girl who seems to be looking forward to life with the hope that it will be filled with love and happiness.

In December of 1900, she married Luther Monroe Smith in Newton County, Georgia, about fifty miles east of Atlanta. Luther was indeed a handsome man who, based upon his daughter's striking resemblance to him, was probably quite the charmer. I have no doubt that Luther was the love of Leola's life. Only four years after their marriage, Luther died suddenly from an outbreak of measles that swept through the tiny hamlet of Porterdale and its surrounding communities such as Rocky Plains, where Luther and Leola lived after they married. Luther contracted a virulent form of measles, which quickly led to pneumonia, the disease that ultimately took his life. From the newspaper accounts of the time, I found that the outbreak most likely started at the local high school before insinuating itself into the community. In this particular article, there was one reported death. Undoubtedly, due to the date of the article, this was Luther.

With two young daughters to support, Leola had to make some quick and difficult decisions. She really had no other option at the time than to move in with her parents. This was a tough living situation because, at this time, her parents were elderly and in need of care. Leola's father was an invalid, and her mother died four years later, which left Leola to care for her father. It was Leola's sister who took on a job and supported the family while Leola ran the house. These were lean years for all of them; they had very little money and had to work hard to keep food on the table and clothes on their backs.

v

Nearly eleven years after Luther died, Leola remarried. Luther's brother John had recently become a widower, leaving him with five young children to raise. The marriage was one of convenience, providing stability for their children as well as support and companionship for Leola and John. From what my grandmother and Aunt Ethel told me, John often compared Leola to his dead wife. He would point out things that he felt Leola was doing wrong and would contradict her on matters of the children. I can only imagine what Leola was feeling at this time, the sense of loss not only for her husband, but also for what their lives together would have been like.

The other half of the story is centered upon my grandfather's parents, John Harbard Smith and Susie Rebecca Carter Smith. As described by my grandmother, John Harbard was a "determined" man who liked to get his way. Though he was a gruff man who was at times very tough on the children, especially my grandfather, he had a tender side that displayed itself to his wife. My mom told me that John Harbard and William (Dewey, as he liked to be called) often clashed, each as stubborn as the other. The confrontations between the two of them were fierce and finally reached a point where they could no longer live together in the same house. My grandfather was, for all intents and purposes, on his own as a teenager.

Following his heart's desire to search beyond the borders of his life, Granddaddy became a railroad man. It was a job he loved, and well into the latter stages of his life he always attended the annual railroad fish fry where he could reminisce with his old buddies from long ago. Railroad life brought excitement into his life as well as satisfied his desire to explore the world around him. After he left the railroad and settled down into family life, my grandfather worked as an auto mechanic.

My grandparents met at a church social in the early 1920's, surprising to me because at that time, Granddaddy was not a churchgoer. But, with influence from his mother, he attended the social. The eligible young women of the church prepared box dinners, and the eligible young men picked the dinner they liked. The two young people would then spend the dinner hour together, getting to know each other and assessing whether or not there were any "sparks" between them. I am certain that Granddaddy was glad he went on that particular Sunday when he met my grandmother. She had matured into a very beautiful young woman and could have had her pick of boyfriends.

They married in 1923 and remained together until my grandfather's death in 1972. My grandfather strained the early years of their marriage; I don't think he had quite sowed all of his wild oats before becoming a husband and father. He would often go out with his buddies and drink quite heavily, returning home late at night with a buzz and, at times, a nasty disposition. Despite this, he turned his life around in his later years and became one of the most dedicated, loving, and wonderful fathers and grandfathers I have ever known. In 1926, my grandparents moved to Homestead, Florida, where Granddaddy went into business with his cousins. Having only been there for six months, they faced an event that nearly cost them their lives.

The Great Miami Hurricane of 1926 nearly destroyed everything in its path: buildings, bridges, and people. At the height of the monstrous storm, with wind gusts exceeding one hundred seventy-five miles per hour, my grandparents had to evacuate their house and drive to Granddaddy's uncle's house. It was pitch black, nearly midnight, when they drove toward safety. Both of them were sure that they, along with their two-year-old son, would die. It was an experience they would never forget. They moved back to Georgia and re-built their life together.

Remembrance is a novel based upon the stories my grandmother and great-aunt told me. In writing this book, I took the liberty of artistic license to create some characters and events to fill in gaps and add depth to the notion of hardship that many people faced at the turn of the Twentieth Century. I consulted newspaper accounts, county records, family records, and church records to document names and facts as they were available.

—Nathan Smith Hipps
March 16, 2005

Acknowledgments

I owe a debt of gratitude to several people for their help and inspiration in writing this book. Mere words are not nearly enough to express my thankfulness for their kindness, patience, and encouragement. However, since words are all that are available to me, I will give it a try.

This book would never have been written if not for my grandmother, Lucy Margaret Smith, and her sister, Ethel Leanice Smith. Ever since I was a young child, I have been fascinated by history, both in the worldly sense as well as the familial sense. I repeatedly asked my grandmother and great-aunt to tell me stories about their family, in particular, their mother and the struggles they faced while growing up. I am grateful that they never tired of telling me these stories, sometimes the same stories, over and over again.

I would also like to thank and acknowledge my grandfather, William Dewey Smith, for sharing his accounts of the great hurricane of 1926 and for just being the person he was, a lovable, unique character who loved all of his grandchildren dearly.

Also, I'd like to thank my aunt, Margaret Anne Smith, and my uncle, William Dewey Smith, Jr., for their remembrances of their family life, especially the murder of their grandfather and the ensuing trial.

I tried finding a publisher for this novel for ten years without any luck. To those agents and publishers who gave me encouragement, I do appreciate your kind words. When I decided that I would no longer try to find a publisher for this novel, I finally found someone who was willing to publish it. To Leland Raymond, I say a special "thank you" for giving this story a chance.

As always, I thank my family for their continued love and support to a son, brother, grandson, nephew, cousin, and uncle who could be as moody and forlorn as he could be witty and happy.

Most of all, I thank my mom for being my biggest fan in this life and the person who encouraged and loved me more than anyone else. It is from my mom that I inherited my love of history and my mom who exemplified the qualities that made her family so special to me. I am truly blessed to have had such a wonderful and loving mother. I thank you, Mom, for being the best mother a kid could have. I love you and miss you terribly.

ONE

L EOLA SAT ANXIOUSLY next to the bed, watching helplessly as her husband gasped for air. The sound was haunting, almost like the moaning of a restless spirit unable to find its way through the light into the afterlife. She stared at him, heartbroken, knowing there was nothing she could do to ease his pain. Every now and then his desperate breathing was interrupted by a deep, hacking cough as he tried in vain to clear the mucus accumulating in his lungs.

His condition had worsened since yesterday. The texture of his skin was coarse, its color a fiery red, his eyes blank and weary. He looked nothing like the vibrant, handsome young man she fell in love with and married four years ago. Suddenly, he sat straight up, springing forward as if yanked by a heavy rope. The acute movement startled Leola. She tried to comfort him as he thrashed about the bed, his agonized face turning the slightest shade of blue. Terror-stricken, she screamed for the nurse.

Gwen burst into the bedroom from the hallway that connected to the kitchen. She was a large woman who moved with surprising ease despite her size. She ordered Leola to bring her a hot towel that was soaking in a mixture of camphor and menthol next to the wood-burning stove in the kitchen. She held Luther as upright as she could.

"Breathe, Luther! Breathe!" Gwen pleaded.

He shook his head violently, rocking his shoulders from side to side, angrily attempting to shake the insidious disease from his ravaged body.

"Leola! I need the towel now!" Gwen ordered.

Leola squeezed the excess liquid from the towel. The combined smell of camphor and menthol reeked through the back of the house, seeping into her skin and hair and clothes. The pungent odor worsened the throbbing headache that had plagued her since Luther became sick.

She raced to the bedroom and handed the towel to Gwen, standing over her, numb, defeated by her husband's pain. The last few days had been a nightmare for her. She loved Luther more than life itself, and watching him die was more than she could bear.

Gwen wrapped the towel around Luther's head, pressing it against his face, forcing the medicinal fumes into his lungs. She held firmly to his back, keeping it as straight as possible. He breathed as best he could, but the coughing was relentless, causing him to wrench in pain with each stultified breath as if someone was sticking a dagger deep inside his lungs.

"Leola! Look in my bag and hand me that rubber tube!" Gwen ordered again as Luther's life slipped between her fingers.

Leola scanned the darkened room, the curtains having been pulled together since Luther took to his sick bed.

"Where is it?" she asked in panic.

"Over by the dresser!"

Leola stumbled over a footstool in her haste, nearly colliding with the pine dresser that stood next to the window. Her hands shook so uncontrollably she had trouble opening the worn fabric bag. The seconds ticked by like shots from a rifle. Luther's life lay in the balance. Silently, she screamed at herself as she rifled through the bag, unable to locate the lifeline that could temporarily save her husband. The tube was coiled in a circle at the bottom.

"Quickly, Leola!" Gwen instructed.

Leola uncoiled the long tube and handed it to Gwen. Standing away from the bed, she pressed herself against the wall, thankful that her two young daughters were with Rachel, their grandmother. She did not want them to see their father in such agony.

"Hand me the bag!" Gwen snapped. Leola moved in spite of the paralysis enveloping her body.

Gwen removed the towel from Luther's head and threw it on the floor. She reached inside her bag and pulled out a bottle of alcohol and a small scalpel. Leola felt faint as the room closed in on her. Gwen swabbed Luther's neck with the alcohol. Her hands steady, she made an incision at the base of his throat then opened the wound and inserted the tube into his windpipe.

The rattling sound of air-stirred mucus made Leola nauseous. She'd seen and heard all she could take. Covering her mouth with both hands, she bolted from the room, running through the back porch into the yard.

The sweet, crisp February air calmed her stomach. She breathed it in deeply. A cold wind blew through the barren limbs of the sycamore trees, sweeping down the road toward town. Impulsively, Leola followed the wind, chasing after it as if it had stolen her last hope for happiness. Tears streamed down her face. A fine, soft mist fell gently upon her. She ran blindly, neither knowing nor caring where she was going.

Her legs cramped as she ran, but she continued running, distancing herself from the realities of the disease that was arrogantly killing her husband. She passed Elm Street and Washington Avenue, past the livery stable and feed store, her lungs on fire from the sharp air. A horse-drawn wagon carrying bales of hay approached in the distance; a family of cows feeding in a meadow stared blankly as she rounded the curve on the old dirt road that led to a wooden bridge spanning the Yellow River. Exhausted, she came to a stop.

Doubling over in pain, only now did she realize how far she had run in the freezing mist. She leaned against the railing, unable to catch her breath. The cries she had buried deep inside her came rushing out with the force of a stampeding herd of wild horses. Her body heaved uncontrollably, so deep was her pain. One thought occupied her mind . . . *why!*

If it would ease Luther's pain, she would gladly jump into the cold waters below, anything to save the man she loved. It was too soon to lose him. The cold mist intensified, turning into a steady drizzle. The river moved swiftly below her, curving past the cotton mill into the horizon. As she looked out over its murky waters, she felt as alone as she'd ever been.

TWO

BORN A DECADE AFTER the end of the Civil War, Leola knew little of the world outside her home. She had never even traveled the ten miles into Fitzgerald, the nearest town, a small settlement founded by Union and Confederate soldiers too weary and battered to make the long trek back to their own homes. Though the community boasted five hundred settlers, Leola had never seen or met any of them, only the few farming families who attended the same church she did and whose children were her classmates at the one-room schoolhouse.

The longing to change her way of life became unbearable as she grew older. Days turned into weeks, which in turn gave way to months and years, all the same, one blending into the next. The need for something different turned into desperation: a new experience, a friend, a young man whom she could love, anything other than the constant companion of loneliness.

Circumstance, however, dictated otherwise for most rural residents of southern Georgia in the decades after the war. The agrarian society upon which life was built set an unyielding course for those who lived there. Families relied upon solitude, stoicism, and self-preservation for their survival. Hard work filled their lives; there existed little time for anything else.

Leola grew up in a home without the luxuries of parental love or nurture. Her father was a tyrant who rarely let her out of his sight, and her mother an unemotional and distant woman unable to express love. Leola spent many hours staring through the panes of glass in her bedroom window, forlorn, lonely, imagining a place out there, somewhere, in which she could find happiness.

In the summer of 1900, she made the decision to begin her life anew. Fueled by the excitement of the new century, she left her father's house and, against his vehement warnings, traveled north to visit an elderly aunt in Covington, Georgia, fifty miles southeast of Atlanta. Her father went into a rampage the day she left, grabbing her by the arm, his eyes wild, his voice biting into her skin as he warned her against the evils of the outside world. His anger, however, failed to sway her.

When the train pulled from the station, a tremendous burden lifted itself from her shoulders. She was exhilarated to be free of him, like a songbird let loose from its cage. Her spirit soared higher than it had ever dared to travel. In the deep recesses of her soul, she slowly envisioned a life she controlled without her father's influence. The thought pleased her. For once, she was glad to be alive.

With a population approaching fifteen hundred, Covington was a big city in Leola's eyes. Its wide, dirt-packed roads stirred with activity, horse-drawn buggies passed at a leisurely pace while scores of children raced alongside them, laughing and taunting as they outraced the huge, lumbering beasts. Leola commissioned a surrey to take her to Aunt Rosalie's house. The ride in the black, fringed buggy enchanted her.

She'd never seen so many stores and shops and people all gathered together in the same place. Her eyes darted from one side of the road to the other, stopping long enough to marvel over one brick building that towered three stories over the dusty thoroughfare. The wonder of it all gave life to the imaginations of her childhood. The feel of city life was just as she'd expected, compact and condensed, a large number of people confined to a small area, their hustle and bustle electrifying the air.

A hammock of sycamore trees majestically brushed the eastern side of City Hall, their three-pointed leaves just beginning to show a hint of autumn. As the surrey rounded Town Square, the clock tower's resonant chime ushered in the five o'clock hour. Early diners were making their way to The Station Restaurant for a steak dinner. The Covington Bank and Loan promptly shut its doors while "Closed" signs popped up in storefront windows. A flurry of businessmen and shoppers poured onto the street. The city's energy infected Leola with the desire for change.

She accompanied her aunt to a Wednesday night church service and on the following afternoon to a tea with Aunt Rosalie's sewing circle. The ladies giggled and gossiped and, by the end of the afternoon, encouraged Leola to attend the Sunday worship service where she was sure to meet several eligible young men. Blushing delicately, Leola acknowledged the women's interest but made no promises one way or the other. If her own will had brought her this far, then fate was duty-bound to make her journey complete.

She met Luther while making a five-dollar deposit for her aunt at the local bank. Her attention was instantly drawn to the handsome teller; her face flushed with embarrassment when his eyes met hers. His gentlemanly manner and beautiful smile won her heart, and in this chance meeting she could see her future.

Luther called on her the following evening, sitting with her on the porch swing while Aunt Rosalie kept a watchful eye through the curtains, which she had surreptitiously pulled apart. Leola fidgeted unconsciously, worried that Luther would find her boring, a country girl who knew little of life beyond the confines of her family's farm.

"How long do you plan on staying in Covington?" Luther asked.

"Only through next week. I have to get back home," Leola answered softly.

"What's your hurry? You'll miss the Fall Festival when the leaves turn. It's a big deal up here. People come from miles around to see the sycamore leaves turn colors: bright red, yellow, and orange. You've probably never seen so many people as come here."

Leola blushed. "I don't get to see many people at all. We live on a farm way out in the middle of nowhere. The only time we go anywhere is to church on Sunday. Daddy doesn't let us go much further than that."

This intrigued Luther. "How come?"

Leola spoke softly. "He doesn't put much trust in other people. He's afraid they'll change us somehow if we get too close."

Luther felt Leola's embarrassment. "How close is too close?"

He inched over on the swing. Aunt Rosalie pressed her nose to the window, not at all happy that the space between her niece and this young man was narrowing. Luther flashed his winning smile at her and waved his hand innocuously.

Leola giggled, softly, yet mischievously. "I don't mean that kind of close."

"So I can move closer?" Luther grinned.

"You know what I mean."

"No I don't. Tell me."

Leola thought carefully about her words. "Daddy doesn't want other people to change us, to change the way he's made us. He's a very peculiar person. He believes in doing things a certain way and only that way. He's suspicious of other people and thinks that everyone's out to get him."

"Or you."

Leola blushed again, more intensely, her hands trembling. She felt as though Luther could look right through her, that she didn't possess the sophistication of mystery.

Luther noticed her discomfort. "Why are you so nervous?"

"I'm not a city girl like you're used to, Luther. I'm just a simple farm girl. I'm not smart like city girls or sophisticated in the ways of life like they are. I appreciate your interest. It was so nice of you to stop by for a visit, but I'm afraid we're two different people from two different worlds."

"You think so? I grew up on a farm just a few miles from here, lived all my life in a stop in the road called Snapping Shoals. I bet you never heard of that place before."

Leola nodded her head.

"I lived there all my life until I went to work for the bank. I didn't want to be too far from my family so I settled in Porterdale. The only sophisticated thing about me is the tie I wear to work every day, and that's only because I have to. I grew up barefoot and in overalls. We have a lot more in common than you think, Leola." Luther looked directly at her. "Why don't you stay in Covington a little while longer? I'm sure your aunt won't mind."

Leola lowered her head, staring vacantly at her trembling hands. "I can't. I have to get home. It'll be harvest time soon, and I have to help Mama put up vegetables and preserves." Leola was torn. Luther's sincerity and charm played with her heart.

"Then come back after you're finished," Luther begged.

"Daddy would never allow it. He forbade me to make this trip; we had an awful fight about it. When I left home, I knew there'd be a price to pay when I got back. Going anywhere else is out of the question." Leola's increasing sadness gave way to tears.

"Then stay, Leola. There's no sense in putting yourself through that when you don't have to. I'll take care of you."

The earnestness in Luther's eyes dissolved Leola's fears, prompting her to remain in Covington awhile longer. He called on her every evening thereafter, much to Aunt Rosalie's concern, and proposed two months later. They married the first week in December at the Presbyterian Church, surrounded by Luther's family. As Leola spoke her vows of matrimony, the memories of the past faded into obscurity.

They settled in a small, two-bedroom house inside the southern boundary of Porterdale. Leola loved her new house and took to the chore of making it a home with determination and pride. Luther amused himself with her attention to detail. She would arrange a shelf with books and knick-knacks, step back to eye her accomplishment, and then completely rearrange the entire shelf.

She was happy, a fact that warmed Luther's heart. Seeing the joy in her eyes made him complete. He loved her more than he had loved any other; she was the other half that made him whole. Their souls, he felt, were destined to be together. True love has a way of finding its way no matter the obstacles or journeys it must make. And his love for Leola was true.

On Sunday afternoons, they had dinner at Rachel's house, Luther's mother. The entire family gathered for a sumptuous meal of fried chicken, ham, mashed potatoes with gravy, corn on the cob, and freshly made cornbread. Rachel insisted on doing all of the cooking herself and no one objected; she was the best cook for miles around.

Those who knew Rachel admired her strength of character and the infinite fountain of love within her for her family and friends. Her soft features were rarely touched by the deceptions of indecision or worry. Though her burdens in life were many, she never complained. When her husband was returned to her a crippled man from the war, she loved him even more; his sacrifice became hers.

Luther's family wrapped its arms around Leola, claiming her as one of their own. Rachel became the mother she'd always wanted, and Luther the man who loved her more than she could ever imagine. Nothing, it seemed, could bring them any harm.

Until that gray January day in 1905.

THREE

It started as a day no different than any other Saturday. Leola left the children with Luther while she walked to the market in town. It was a cold day, colder than she could ever remember. Heavy frost covered the ground, and patches of iced-over puddles from the freezing rain the day before dotted the road. She was careful not to slip, maneuvering as if she were traveling through a minefield. A heavy shawl covered her neck and chin; the long, woolen skirt she wore buffeted the sudden blasts of icy wind that swept in from the north. The cold, heavy air draped itself over her like an unwanted embrace.

When she entered the market, Leola bumped into Mrs. Henley, a matriarch of the Presbyterian Church. Her hasty entrance and quick greeting seemed to catch the older woman by surprise. With mouth agape, Mrs. Henley left the store in a nervous run, disappearing down the sidewalk in a swirl of plaid-colored pleats and white lace. Puzzled, Leola turned to the storekeeper.

"I guess you haven't heard," Gerald spoke softly.

"Heard what?" Leola asked.

"Walter Seagrove died last night . . . it was measles."

Leola steadied herself; a silent gasp of air exited her lungs as she braced herself against the counter. She had heard the terrifying stories of the outbreak twenty years before that wiped out one-quarter of Porterdale's residents.

"It's 1885 all over again. Everyone's afraid that whoever they come into contact with might be infected. Fear will make a person do strange things. I've seen it turn brother against brother and neighbor against neighbor. Lord help us if this one's as bad as the last." Gerald stacked the last crate of winter squash on the floor.

"I can't imagine anything with that kind of power," Leola stammered.

Wearily, Gerald shook his head in remembrance. "I've lived in this town all my life, and I can truthfully tell you that I've never seen anything like it before or since. I thought it was the end of the world, expected to see the Four Horsemen of the Apocalypse ride down Main Street and take up residence in the courthouse. It was like the devil himself had come to Porterdale."

Leola could not speak, her words constricted by the growing fear inside her.

"Nobody knew what to do about it, not even Doc Pritchard. We had community meetings and prayer services, but nothing worked. They still kept dying, one by one, awful deaths, too. From what people said, it was like their skin was on fire, burning right off their bones. Some scratched themselves so bad they got infections that turned their skin green. Something had to be done about it or all of us would have surely died. A group of men got together and ran it out of town by fire, burned down the houses where it had been."

The proprietor's tale reawakened the fear Leola felt when she first heard the stories of pestilence and the town's desperate fight against evil while trying in earnest to appease a wrathful God. She hurriedly made her purchases and left the store, running for the safety of home, knowing why Mrs. Henley was so afraid.

"What's wrong, Leola? You look like you've seen a ghost." Luther followed Leola as she rushed into the kitchen.

"I have. A ghost from a long time ago." Leola caught her breath.

"What are you talking about?"

"Where are the girls?" Leola whispered. "I don't want them to hear this."

Luther moved closer, placing his hand upon Leola's shoulder. "They're playing in the front room. What is it, Leola? What has happened?"

"Measles! Walter Seagrove died last night from measles!"

The mere mention of the word sent chills down Luther's spine. "Are you sure?"

"That's what Gerald said. It's been reported near Rocky Plains, and at the high school several students and teachers have it. I'm scared, Luther. You were here the last time it broke out. You saw how it turned people against each other." Leola cried.

Luther pulled Leola into his comforting embrace. "Don't worry, Leola. It won't be like that again. We're not the same people we were back then."

Though his words soothed his terrified wife, Luther was not sure whether he believed them himself.

He remembered the outbreak of 1885 with chilling clarity. Though a youngster of ten, the image of the hooded men lived just inside his memory. They carried torches up and down the streets and alleyways dissecting the town. In the beginning, only a few men braved the unknown, venturing into the streets to combat the scourge. But their numbers increased as the plague spread. They went from door to door tracking the disease.

When they reached his house, Luther hid behind his brothers. The hooded inquisitors frightened him, their eyes peering through small holes cut in the burlap sacks. When they spoke, the fabric moved back and forth in front of their mouths like the beating of a heart.

"We need to search your house, ma'am," one of the men addressed Rachel.

"There's nothing here you're looking for," Rachel replied.

The men did not move. "We have the authority to do a search of the premises, with or without your permission."

"By whose authority? Your own, I suspect." Rachel's composure remained intact.

"Ma'am—" the man interjected.

"How can you be so lacking in compassion? Turning on your neighbors in a time of need and burning them out of their homes!" Rachel pleaded.

"We gotta do something. You got a better plan?"

"Pray. Pray that we are delivered from this plague. And pray that God in heaven forgives you for your cowardly deeds." Rachel shook her head in resigned defeat.

"We don't have time for God to act. We've got to take care of this problem ourselves before we all die."

The men brushed past Rachel and her sons. Though terrified, Luther refused to cry. He wanted to be strong for his mother's sake.

Rachel maintained her dignity as the motley gang of men moved from room to room, checking under beds and in closets for any sign of the disease's presence. She held her youngest son close to her side; a cry penetrated from the back of the house. One of the men rushed into the room, alarming the others that he had found a man confined to his bed.

The men huddled together, whispering amongst themselves. Rachel broke into their circle, glaring into the cutout eyes of the burlap sacks. The indignity of the situation compelled her to protect her family.

"That man you're so afraid of is my husband. He's no danger to you or anyone else in this town. He is crippled, an invalid of the Confederate Army. He can no longer walk or get out of bed without needing help. But even in his condition," she sneered, "he's more of a man than any of you cowards! Now, get out of my home!"

One of the men knew Rachel was telling the truth and apologized for the group. Undaunted, they continued with their mission toward the next house down the road.

The houses that were infected had a red marking placed upon the front door, the inhabitants given three days to pack up and abandon their home. Luther watched the uncontrollable hysteria from his bedroom window, horrified at the sight of his neighbors' homes burning to the ground.

Leola panicked, overcome by an intuitive feeling that something terrible was going to happen. Luther did his best to hide his concerns from her, but he, too, was afraid. He had come into contact with Walter Seagrove at the bank the week before he died: a simple transaction for cattle feed that ended with a handshake.

Walter's family buried him at Hopewell Cemetery the day after his death, hoping the quick burial would take the disease with him. But even with his body in the ground the townspeople still worried, wondering who would be next, who'd had contact with Walter Seagrove while he was ill.

Luther felt feverish as he stood by Walter's grave, his throat scratchy and sore. He was careful not to cough near Leola or the girls. Subtle chills raced down the backs of his legs. He felt dizzy and lightheaded. When the interminably long service mercifully ended, Luther rushed home and went directly to bed. For days he kept up appearances, believing, while also praying, that the act of living normally would make him better.

As he walked home from work one evening, Luther found that he could hardly move. His muscles were sore, the lower part of his back in extreme pain, every step slow and deliberate. He checked his pocket watch: nearly nine o'clock, two hours late getting home.

Leola kept his dinner warm, constantly looking through the kitchen window for any sign of him, unable to imagine what was keeping her husband. She busied herself with menial chores that had already been done, washing dishes that were clean, dusting furniture that was polished. She paced back and forth between the dining room and the back porch, at the mercy of each passing moment. Finally, the back door opened and closed. The sound of footsteps awakened her heart.

She quickly set the table, positioning the plate and silverware then repositioning them. Her nerves were on edge as she waited impatiently next to Luther's chair, expecting him to walk in at any moment. The minutes sluggishly ticked by on the mantle clock, increasing her agitation.

"Luther! Dinner's on the table!" Her words echoed down the empty hall without reply.

The back door was slightly ajar. Perhaps he went back outside, she thought, finding some chore that needed immediate attention. She looked into the shadows of darkness but saw nothing stirring except a swirl of leaves caught up in the heightening wind.

Uneasiness penetrated her soul, her intuition strong with dread. She tapped quietly on the bedroom door.

"Luther? Are you in there?" she whispered quietly, almost as if she didn't want him to hear her.

"Yes, I'm here."

His weak reply startled her. She entered the room and found Luther lying on the bed with a quilt pulled up to his chin.

"Luther, what's wrong?"

"I don't feel good, Leola. I think I need to rest here for a while. Kiss the girls goodnight for me, will you?"

Instinctively, she felt his forehead and ears.

"You're burning up with fever. I'm going to put a cold compress on your forehead." She gently caressed his face, his skin awash in a pallor of gray that made him look older than his twenty-nine years.

As she unbuttoned his shirt to swab his chest, she noticed several red spots dotting his torso. Her mind suddenly went blank, freeing itself of thought, insulating her emotions against the brutal reality staring at her. She could not breathe or cry, feel or scream, a prisoner inside a room without windows or air, locked in darkness, victimized by circumstance.

The night was as long as it was unforgiving. Leola sat in an uncomfortable straight-back chair watching Luther's every breath. His sleep was restless. At times he pushed the covers away from him as if he were on fire, yet in the next moment sought their warmth from the penetrating chill. He was nauseous, wrenching in pain as his body purged itself again and again. She held him when he was quiet, and spoke softly to him when he writhed in pain.

The sun rose without notice; a blanket of gray clouds and heavy fog obscured its presence. Though exhausted, Leola still watched over her husband, counting every breath he took. He had lain still for the past hour, a sign that did not comfort her. She tried to gently waken him, nudging his arm while calling his name, but he was either unwilling or unable to wake up.

Gripped by the fear of losing him, Leola raced out of the house, running to Doc Pritchard's as fast as her feet would carry her, every second a possible difference between life and death. She stumbled on the rocky, dirt road, her tie-button shoes twisting her ankles on the scores of red-clay rocks that covered the surface. The cold, Georgia clay ate into her hands, skinning her palms each time she fell and lifted herself up.

She made the distance in a matter of minutes, pounding upon the doctor's door as she leapt upon the porch.

"I'm sorry to bother you so early, but it's Luther! He's very sick! He has a fever, and it won't break! I don't know what to do!"

Doc Pritchard grabbed his bag and headed out the door. The sincerity of Leola's request told him the situation needed immediate attention.

The examination took only a matter of minutes. Doc Pritchard knew right away it was measles. The disease had developed rapidly and spread with fury. A sudden chill surged through Doc's body. He closed his eyes and whispered a quick prayer. After twenty years of relative calm, he was not prepared to battle the deadly enemy once more.

The scars of the last epidemic were fresh on his mind. The hysteria that swept the town rang in his ears with renewed intensity. The fingers of blame had been pointed in his direction; townspeople accused him of quackery. His mind spun out of control, sweat streamed down his face, his mouth as dry as a ball of cotton.

"I don't know how to say this without coming right to the point, Leola." Doc Pritchard dreaded confronting her.

Leola took a deep breath, a breath so deep it raised her posture and stiffened her neck. Her eyes focused upon Doc Pritchard with a fear that pleaded for mercy.

"Luther's got the measles. It's an advanced case, and it's spreading quickly. I fear his lungs are filling with mucus. He could be developing pneumonia as well."

Leola interrupted Doc Pritchard in the hopes that his diagnosis might somehow change if she stopped it soon enough. "Well, he did say the other day that he had a sore throat, so I fixed him some tea with honey and lemon, and he said it helped."

She searched for other things to say, other straws to grab onto, but the look on Doc Pritchard's face told her everything she feared.

"I'm sorry, Leola. There's not much I can do at this point but pray for a miracle."

He reached out to Leola, but she could not respond. Her body shut itself down automatically, as if someone had turned a switch and cut off her flow of life.

For days afterward, Leola went through the motions of living in a stupor—expressionless, void of emotion. Her movements were sluggish and tired, her thoughts blank and dark. She was neither alive nor dead, but in that area in between where spirits go when they become too overburdened by the hardships of life and living.

Doc Pritchard sent Gwen to care for Luther in his final days, acting as both his nurse and interim mother to his children. The daunting tasks rested squarely upon her, the family's survival dependant upon her fortitude. The girls worried her constantly, both too young to fully comprehend the seriousness of their father's condition, wondering why they couldn't see him.

Lou, the younger of the two, seized an opportunity to enter Luther's room while Gwen hung clothes out to dry in the back yard. Though her tiny hand barely reached the doorknob, she opened the door and peered into the room. Her father was laid out on the bed, unconscious, gray, struggling for air. He looked like one of her porcelain dolls, dressed in his nightclothes, prepared for sleep. Slipping inside the room, she gingerly stepped to the side of the bed.

"Daddy," she whispered. "Daddy," she whispered again, impatiently tugging at the sleeve of his shirt. His lack of response puzzled her; why didn't he speak to her? Why didn't he smile and take her in his arms and kiss her on the cheek like he always did?

Gwen watched from the hallway, the hand-woven basket still in her hands. Her eyes filled with tears as Lou patted her father's arm and whispered into his ear. "It's okay, Daddy. You don't have to talk to me if you don't want to. We can play tomorrow when you feel better."

The overcast sky held the promise of rain; the smell of precipitation thickened the air as Leola took the girls into town, unaware that the growing paranoia put her family directly in harm's way. The few people they encountered looked at them with fear, most of them turning away or instinctively covering their faces. An elderly man Leola did not know followed them down the street yelling "unclean" before disappearing down an alleyway.

Quickening her pace, Leola held tightly to her daughters' hands. The general mercantile store stood at the end of Main Street, two buildings down from the telegraph office. They would be safe there; she knew the proprietor well. He was one of Luther's best customers at the bank.

As they passed the telegraph office, two teenage boys approached from behind and threw large rocks of hardened clay at them. The dirt-encrusted missiles shattered against the wooden posts lining the covered sidewalk. The crashing sound ripped through the air like gunfire. Leola jumped. The girls screamed as the splintered pieces pelted them. Leola pushed them into the general mercantile store as fast as she could.

David Reese, the proprietor, bolted past them, racing after the teenage boys. They scurried down an alleyway and ducked into the back door of the feed store, seeking refuge in the upstairs loft. Unfazed, David walked back through town, his manner direct and unafraid, the look on his face reflecting the disdain he held for those who stood idly by. The townspeople looked at him in silence, turning their backs, continuing on their way.

Two women from Leola's Sunday school class were inside the store, witness to the event yet seeing nothing. They pulled away, terrified, afraid to touch Leola or breathe the same air that she breathed. Clutching shawls across their faces, they scurried outside. Leola stood in the middle of the floor, holding tight to her daughters, wondering where she would find the strength to carry on without Luther.

"I've seen better examples of Christian behavior from atheists." David spoke with a decided Georgia drawl as he glimpsed the two women fleeing from the store.

Leola shook her head. "It's all right, David. I should have expected this, but I just didn't think people could be this afraid."

"They're scared, that's for sure. It doesn't excuse their behavior any, but it sure explains it. When it comes down to a matter of life or death, a person will always side with himself, unfortunately." David gave each of the girls a piece of candy. "How's Luther?"

Leola sent the girls to look at material before answering. "He's not well. Gwen Baldtree is taking care of him. Doc Pritchard said it's just a matter of time . . . " Leola's voice broke with emotion.

"I'm sorry, Leola, I really am. If there's anything I can do, you just let me know. Why don't you and the girls pick out whatever you like? My treat. My granddaddy wouldn't let anyone walk out of this store with more burdens than they walked in with, and neither will I."

Leanice picked out material of pink gingham chambray while Lou grabbed the brightest blue lace fabric she could find. For herself, Leola chose a simple silver broche with engravings of little hearts around the sides. She bought a pair of cufflinks for Luther that matched his best suit.

The barren sidewalks did not comfort Leola as they left the store. She circled to the back of the building and went down Johnson Street to avoid Town Square.

The house was quiet when they arrived home, too quiet Leola thought.

Gwen was in the living room, sitting in the mahogany rocking chair that once belonged to Grandma Malinda. The diminishing light of day cast a softened film over her face as it filtered through the sheer curtains. She stared out the window, her eyes penetrating the view before her as if she could see beyond this life and into eternity.

"Luther's gone, isn't he?" Leola stopped in the doorway.

Gwen simply nodded her head, tightening her grasp on the Bible that lay in her lap, her eyes filled with tears.

"I'd like to see him." Leola softly stroked the top of Leanice's head, which was buried in the pleats of her skirt.

For a moment the room was still, as if this were a painting of four people captured in an eternal second, frozen in time forever. Quietly disrupting the portrait, Lou walked into the center of the room, looking first at Gwen, then at Leanice and, finally, at her mother.

"Mommy, why aren't you crying?"

All at once Leola was faced with the brunt of her own emotions, as well as those of her children. Though devastated, she managed a smile.

"I'm not crying because Daddy's on his way to heaven, and I know he's very happy."

Lou sat in the middle of the floor, folding her hands in her lap and bowing her head away from the others. She thought of the trips into town for ice cream with her father, sitting on his lap as he rocked her to sleep, and his strong hugs that made her feel safe. She wondered where heaven was.

Leola stood at the door to the bedroom, nearing collapse, unsure whether she had the strength to see her husband's lifeless body.

Gwen lit two candles after Luther died, placing one on either side of the headboard, a tradition taught by her mother, who explained that the flames would take away the scent of death. The amber glow of the burning candles gave the room a strange sense of inviting warmth. When Leola looked at Luther, she knew he was at peace and that the struggle was finally over.

Sitting beside him in the same straight-back chair from which she held her nightlong vigil, she spoke through tears, her voice constricted by the emotions coursing through her.

"I don't know how to let go of you, Luther. I don't know if I can. You rescued me when I was drowning . . . and now I feel like I'm drowning again, but you're not there to rescue me this time. How can you leave me like this, Luther? I need you! I can't go back to the way things were before I met you . . . I just can't," she broke down briefly, regrouping herself by the memory of Luther's love. "Thank you for loving me, Luther; thank you for breathing life into me and making me feel wanted. Thank you for giving me such a happy home and two daughters whom I love with all my heart."

She reached for his hands, which were folded atop his chest, and gently raised his right hand to her cheek.

"I love you, Luther Smith, don't you ever forget that. I will see you again one day, and what a glorious day that will be."

She caressed his cheek, for the last time feeling the softness of his skin. Though death now separated them, she knew that she would always belong to Luther, a thought that both comforted and saddened her. Before leaving the room, she kissed his forehead and blew out the candles that masked the scent of death.

FOUR

THE DARKENED SKIES THAT lingered over Porterdale were at last blown away by a blast of wind that ushered in brilliant sunshine. The plunge in temperature did not deter the family from giving Luther a proper funeral. A large crowd of mourners circled the gravesite, their faces sad, some even wracked with grief. Leola looked through them, recognizing the ones who a couple of days before had turned from her, incapable then of simple compassion.

They were hypocrites, she thought. She could not bring herself to forgive them, not at this moment anyway. The man she loved more than life itself was gone. There was room in her heart for nothing more than an unrelenting pain. One day, far in the future, when the shock of Luther's death subsided enough, she might find forgiveness. But not this day.

A bitterly cold wind blew throughout Reverend McElmurry's eulogy. Leola stood next to Luther's oldest brother John, who was shouldering the brunt of Rachel's weight. She had fainted once that morning and her legs were unsteady, but Rachel insisted upon attending her youngest son's funeral.

The girls faced the wooden box that contained their father, neither of them aware that the cold wind burned into their faces. Leanice held her mother's hand as it rested upon her heart. Lou stood to the side, independently, her arms folded across her chest, the petulant look etched on her face, defiantly attempting to wrestle her father from the clutches of death. She didn't want anyone touching her or consoling her or trying to make her feel better. She wanted her father to be alive.

The reverend's words of sympathy were picked up on a stream of air and scattered by the winds to the far corners of the earth as far as Leola and Rachel were concerned. Leola's thoughts were transfixed upon an uncertain future, while Rachel's turned to the distant past and a little boy with sandy-colored hair and eyes the purest of blue. Words held no meaning, comfort nothing more than a temporary distraction from the pain of loss and love.

It was all Leola could do to leave Luther's side. She remained at the gravesite alone, pleading, beseeching, silently screaming that all be returned to normal, that time reverse itself, allowing them the luxury of starting over. Her pleadings unanswered and with a heavy heart, she turned to walk away. In front of her, encircling her, bold and callous, stood a committee of city elders, their faces stern and unsympathetic.

"We know this is a bad time, Leola, and we apologize for that, but we've got to get a handle on this situation. We can't take a chance on this thing spreading any further. We drove it out of this town once, and we'll do it again. We want to be fair about this, so we're going to give you some extra time—five days—to leave your house."

The bluntness of the man's decree struck Leola as crass, but she did not cross them. They were serious and their ranks large. A tinge of fear settled over her, alone on a hostile planet. Ferociously, out of a gust of wind it seemed, John pushed his way through the group of men and took his place at Leola's side.

"What's up, fellas?" His voice was blank.

"We just have a little business here with the Widow Smith," the smaller man spoke with a half-smile.

"Any business you have with her, you have with me." John's patience ran thin.

"We don't want any trouble, John, but we've got to think about our community and our families. You should know what we have to do."

John took a step forward, his large frame blocking the sun from the old man's face. "If any of you so much as sets foot on my brother's property, I will not hesitate to start shooting."

The man rebuked John's anger. "You remember what it was like last time, John. People dying left and right!"

Others added their support.

"It's not worth a whole town dying!"

"Don't make us fight you, John. You're outnumbered!"

John's voice thundered through the air. "Don't threaten me!" Fire burned from his eyes. "We should be pulling together as a community right about now, not ripping apart the lives of those who have fallen victim to the plague! If this is your way of showing compassion, then go to hell! All of you!" John stared the men down.

"Thank you, John," Leola tried to quell the situation. "But there won't be any need for violence because of me. We'll leave here as soon as I can figure out what to do."

"Don't let them intimidate you, Leola. They're just a bunch of scared jackasses without a sturdy backbone between them." John eyed the group as they sidled away.

"That may be. But there are a lot of them out there, and they're scared, more scared than we are. At least we've faced the devil, seen him for what he is. They haven't, and that makes them all the more dangerous."

Leola had to make decisions and be quick about it; times were hard for everyone, her options few. She had no means of supporting herself and her children. Though it sickened her, there was only one thing Leola could do, the last thing she ever thought about doing after marrying Luther: return to her father's house, if he would let her.

Susie Floyd, John's wife, kept the girls while Leola went to the telegraph office to wire her parents. She stood at the counter for the better part of an hour trying to find the right words. She'd not had any contact with them in years; knowing what to say was difficult, if not downright impossible. She made the message short and to the point, precluding any need for sympathy, knowing none would be given.

She visited the telegraph office the following afternoon shortly before five o'clock, hoping, if not dreading, to find a wire from her parents.

The clerk carefully looked through the stack of received transmissions.

"I don't see anything in here, Mrs. Smith, but it still might come through. We don't close until six o'clock."

The news prompted little in the way of reaction from Leola. The elderly official returned his attention to the stack of telegrams waiting to be sent to destinations far and near. Leola sat on a bench and waited.

The methodical tapping of the telegraph machine lulled her into a hypnotic trance, transporting her back to the last time she saw her parents, the last time she felt like an intruder in her own home. It was after she'd accepted Luther's proposal, traveling to her parent's house to collect her belongings.

Luther insisted upon accompanying her to a place he knew little about, to meet people of whom he knew even less. Leola warned him that her parents were much different than his own; their reception could be uncomfortable, if not brutal. They arrived at the train station without accompaniment or familiar face.

"I'm sorry, Luther. I didn't expect them to be here; I should've told you that. I don't even know if they'll let me on their property. It's a far piece from here."

"I'm used to walking, Leola. I walk home from the bank every afternoon. It's a good eight miles from Covington to Porterdale." Luther took Leola's hand.

It was a pleasant autumn day, skies deep blue, the sun's fading warmth resting upon their shoulders. The walk down Ten Mile Road gave Luther an appreciation of Leola's world. It was not much different from what he had known growing up, a farming community dotted with small A-frame houses, large pecan trees, and wild chickens running loose. The surrounding countryside was flatter than that of North Georgia, but the endless fields of cotton and corn were the same.

As they neared the halfway point, Leola became silent, her face lined with worry. Abruptly, she stopped in the road as if she'd hit an invisible brick wall.

"Luther, I can't go through with this . . . I can't put you through it." She looked at him with desperation and fear.

Luther put his arms around her. "It's all right, Leola, there's nothing to be frightened of. I'm here. Whatever happens, will happen. We're in this together."

"Promise me you won't leave without me, Luther, just promise me that."
"Of course I won't." He looked into her eyes. "I love you, Leola. Always remember that I love you." He kissed her gently on the forehead then on the cheek.

The remainder of the walk down Ten Mile Road was as timeless as the future that lay in front of them. They passed a few neighbors harvesting their fields and waved with a familiarity that was returned in kind. In the distance, a small house with a neatly kept exterior emerged on the side of the road.

Elizabeth Cowan answered the door with a look of astonishment and inconvenience. She was a petite woman, slightly over five feet tall, with a manner that suggested arrogance rather than animosity. Her hair was pulled straight back, revealing a face that, while not beautiful, was remarkably youthful for a woman her age. After a moment of awkward silence, she invited the couple inside as if they were strangers who had asked for a drink of water.

Leola held tight to Luther's hand, defying the unwritten code of the house that forbade any display of affection.

"Mama, this is Luther Smith . . . my fiancé."

Elizabeth managed a slight nod in Luther's direction. She seemed nervous, anxious to get them out of the house as soon as possible. "Here are your things; I took the liberty of packing everything myself, just to save time." She presented Leola with a small bag.

Though shocked by the meager belongings her parents allowed, Leola did not protest, afraid of creating just the kind of scene she'd hoped to avoid. Reluctantly, she accepted the bag, easing the tension with an unfortunate change in subject. "Where's Daddy? I thought I'd at least . . ."

Her statement trailed off before it was completed. The sense of aggravation emanating from Elizabeth signaled that the visit had already reached its conclusion. Luther, however, would not allow his fiancée to leave under such circumstances. "Where is Mr. Cowan? I'd like to meet him myself." He looked with intent at Elizabeth.

"He's out in the fields. I doubt he'll come in at this time of day, but you can try if you like."

She gave Luther a stern glare before excusing herself to the kitchen. Leola cringed, dreading even more what her father might do. Her shoulders sank as she looked apologetically at Luther. He responded with a quick wink and sly grin.

Leola felt her mother's stare piercing through her as she looked over the fields, but she stood her ground, unyielding, refusing to let Elizabeth deprive her of this one last act of independence. She caught sight of her father working with a hired hand near the west boundary of his property. At first stifling a wave, she waved again, catching the old man's attention.

Zach looked up but did little more than wipe his brow and continue working. To him, he had no daughter, only a wife and his work to keep him occupied.

The rude action insulted Luther, and he dismissed the desire to meet his future father-in-law. Picking up Leola's belongings, he led them back to the train station.

"Leola, I don't mean to pry, but why do your parents—" He stumbled for a moment, unable to find the right phrasing.

Leola finished the thought for him. "—Treat me like an unwanted house guest? Because that's what I am to them. It'd be different if I were a boy, or even if I had brothers. Mama had a lot of difficulty when I was born. The doctor told her she couldn't have any more children. And Daddy was counting on a large family, with lots of sons, to help him work the farm. I put an end to all of that, so they blame me for their misfortune."

Luther pulled her near. Leola turned and looked at the only home she'd ever known for what she thought would be the last time.

"Mrs. Smith. It's six o'clock. Your wire didn't come in." The clerk gently nudged Leola. "If you like, I could send someone over to your house if it comes in tomorrow."

Leola awoke slowly, lethargic. "Thank you, but that won't be necessary. I'll stop by in the morning."

Two days passed without any word from her parents. Fear slowly crept into Leola's veins. The warnings to burn down her house rang in her ears as the deadline to evacuate rapidly approached. A hand-scrawled note was left on the front door, threatening to set fire to the house whether they still lived there or not.

A small band of men approached at nightfall, carrying torches. They banged upon the door.

"We warned you to get out! The hour of decision has passed!"

The men held their torches high, the flames tickling the roof.

A single gunshot screamed into the darkness, quickly followed by another.

"Get the hell off this property!" John yelled at the men.

"Back away or the next shot won't miss!" Bob, his younger brother, backed him up.

The hooded men scattered, ditching their torches, seeking the safety of darkness.

"Damn cowards!" John sneered.

John's sentiments were shared by his brother, Bob. "I'd like to see them in broad daylight without those sacks over their heads. Then we'd see what kind of men they are!"

Luther's brothers stood watch over his property while Leola and the girls sought refuge in John's house. The realization of violence ended Leola's dreams for happiness once and for all. As much as she loved Luther and the home where they shared their lives together, she had to leave.

Another three days passed before the wire finally came in. Leola breathed deeply, balancing a sense of relief and dread. Her hands trembled as she opened the message.

RECEIVED YOUR WIRE. LET US KNOW WHEN ARRIVING.

Short and to the point, the message was unsigned.

The last day of February was as cold and blustery a day as the day Luther was buried. Faces were grim and the mood somber as the train pulled into the station to take Leola and her children away. The cold, dry air intensified the steam that poured from the locomotive, creating a vision that this was only a dream shared by all the participants from which they would awake with unified relief.

There was little in the way of conversation; embraces and tears replaced words as Luther's wife and daughters boarded the train. Rachel kissed her granddaughters tenderly, reminding them how much she loved them. She embraced Leola, holding tight to the last earthly reminders of her little boy.

"I wish things could work out differently, Leola. I will miss you terribly; you're the daughter I never had. I love you. You were so good to my son, and for that I am eternally grateful. You made him so happy . . . thank you, Leola. Thank you for taking such good care of my son."

Rachel again leaned on the supportive shoulder of her eldest child.

As the train pulled from the station, Leola recalled her last train ride, one filled with nothing but hope and promise. Never in her wildest imagination did she think her next train ride would be filled with so much despair and uncertainty. With the girls already asleep, Leola closed her eyes in search of that precious peace that had somehow eluded her.

FIVE

I'D LIKE TO GO TO Hopewell and visit the cemetery if you don't mind." Rachel's sudden request surprised John as he helped his mother into the horse-drawn wagon. She had not said a word since the train departed.

"It's rather cold for that, Mother, don't you think? Why don't you wait until a more fitting day?"

Rachel sat rigidly in the wagon, her eyes focused upon something only seen by those who knew her loss. Susie Floyd silently protested this idea to her husband.

"I'd like to go now, but if you don't want to take me you don't have to. I'll find a way to get there."

Susie Floyd again glanced at her husband but John merely shrugged his shoulders. Nothing could stop his mother from making this pilgrimage.

"Aren't you going to stop her?" Susie Floyd whispered. "She'll catch her death of cold in this wind!"

"Don't blame John for this, honey. He knows me, and he knows that I'll get to the cemetery one way or another. I have to. There's no worse pain in life than to have a child die before you. I can't let my baby think his mother doesn't miss him. He knows I'll be there."

Against her better judgment, which she always considered astute, Susie Floyd nodded in approval.

As the slow-moving wagon pulled up the hill toward the church, Rachel tightened her shawl against the biting wind, the icy cold penetrating the marrow of her bones. When the cemetery came into view, her eyes brightened, her soul revived.

She had picked out the plot of land in the church's cemetery when her husband died two years before. Surrounded by a grove of crepe myrtles and dogwood, the idyllic spot blossomed with color during the spring and summer months when purple meadow beauties covered the sloping terrain. In the early morning hours, before the sun's arrival burned away the remaining patches of fog, the field was awash in a purplish mist that looked as if a velvet covering had been draped over it.

Rachel walked through the barren field, the meadow beauties in hibernation, the crepe myrtles and dogwood stripped bare by winter's fury. But the longing to be near her son overshadowed the harshness of the season.

For a few precious moments, Rachel allowed herself to dote on the fair-haired boy who ran through the fields behind his grandmother's house gathering wildflowers for her. He placed the most brightly colored ones on the crown of her head before scampering off to a meandering stream in search of pebbles and stones to add to an already substantial collection.

He was smaller than his brothers, not as stout as they were but not thin either. Quiet and thoughtful, he only spoke after giving deliberate thought to his words and the repercussions they might inspire. He was a seeker, a philosopher, a peacemaker. He was different. He was Rachel's son.

She stood against the elements in a place outside this world, far removed from the wind and cold, the pain and grief.

With a deep and somewhat prolonged breath, emerging from the cocoon of remembrance, Rachel left her little boy and returned to the cold, hard concrete slab that marked his grave. The penetrating chill returned, the longing to see her son returned, the feelings and emotions and finality of death returned. The burden of loss wrapped its menacing tentacles around her, squeezing the lifeblood from her body. Slowly, painstakingly, she walked away.

SIX

Leola awoke with a start, having slept deeply, longer than she intended, the events of the past month at last finding refuge. The girls slept soundly; Lou's head rested on her sister's shoulder. Leola stared at them, almost as if she were trying to enter their dreams and escape with them into another world.

"They're very pretty little girls. You must be quite proud."

An elderly woman seated across the aisle interrupted Leola's trance. She had a kind face, much like Rachel's, and wore a beautiful hat that tied below her chin.

"Yes, I am." Leola nervously ran her hands through her hair, attempting to improve her appearance next to the impeccably dressed woman.

"My name is Virginia Roan. I'm traveling to Thomasville to see my brother and sister-in-law. I've visited them once a year for the past thirty years, but the trip is getting more difficult the older I get, you know, what with rheumatism and all."

Leola nodded slightly though she did not respond.

"I live in Tennessee, Chattanooga to be exact. Where are you from? I'm sorry, dear. I didn't get your name."

"Leola, Leola Smith, and these are my daughters, Leanice and Lou. We're on our way to Fitzgerald."

"Oh, how nice. Visiting family?"

"We're moving down there." Leola pulled the lap of her dress uncomfortably, not really wanting to pursue this avenue of conversation any further.

"You must be meeting your husband there. I'm sure he's anxious to see these darling children."

Leola answered quietly, "My husband recently passed away."

Virginia's face dropped in embarrassment at having pushed the conversation this far. "I'm sorry, dear. I lost my husband at a young age, too. He was killed during the Great War, you know, in the Battle of Shiloh in Western Tennessee."

Struck by the sincerity of the woman's voice, Leola looked across the aisle into the old woman's eyes. They were a brilliant shade of green, like two sparkling emeralds set in an oval pin. As she spoke, the old woman slowly turned an elegant parasol made of black lace that sat in her lap.

"He was such a handsome man, tall and sturdy. He courted several young women before he called at my father's house. I was intrigued from the moment I laid eyes on him, beguiled even. I knew right then and there that he was the only man for me, and he felt the same."

Virginia raised the parasol to her right shoulder, as if she were about to open it against the bright sunshine in front of a large estate.

"We married exactly one year later, May 19, 1852, and our son was born the following year. He looked just like his daddy, except he had my eyes. Eugene was so proud of that boy; it was such a happy time." She paused momentarily, smiling lovingly in the distance.

"I didn't think they would ever end, the happy times that is, but they did. The war broke out and came to our doorstep. Eugene volunteered for service and was killed. Plunderers came into our home, stole anything of value and then burned it to the ground out of pure spite. Barbarians are what they were, nothing but inhuman, spiteful barbarians."

The old woman's story captivated Leola. If only for the time being, she felt somewhat relieved of her own burdens. Virginia stared into the distance for several moments, lost in the emotions of something never forgotten.

"He died on a Wednesday, two weeks after our tenth wedding anniversary. I never remarried. I so adored that man. Two years later, Christian, our son, died after being thrown from a horse. I had not even accepted Eugene's death when Christian died, and I have yet to recover from that. And now I visit my brother every year in Thomasville. He's the only family I have left."

She looked directly into Leola's eyes. "Be thankful that you have your children, Leola, and pray that God grants them long and happy lives."

Virginia placed the parasol back in her lap and rolled it unconsciously in her hand. The air was silent, broken only by the train wheels spinning over the tracks.

Leola stared as intently at Virginia as she had the girls, entering the memories that lived just inside the old woman's soul. In studying her, feeling her pain, Leola found peace, knowing why she had met Virginia Roan, and her message stayed with Leola always.

Leanice stared out the window of the moving train, expressionless, anticipating the uncertainties that lay ahead. The rolling hills had given way to flat farmland, and withered stalks of summer corn covered the ground as far as the eye could see, each row as perfect and straight as the next.

In her wakening state, Lou was momentarily confused by the surroundings. The woman across the aisle from her mother looked like one of the church matriarchs, all dressed up in her Sunday finest with a glorious hat to match. If she were in church, however, the preacher would be hollering and perspiring and yelling at the congregation, but all she heard was something quiet and rhythmic that she couldn't identify.

"Where are we, Mama?"

"We're close to Grandma and Grandpa Cowan's house."

"Will Grandma Rachel be there?"

"No, honey, she's at her house." Suddenly, Lou remembered everything, as if a door had opened and ushered in all the memories. She yawned deeply and stared glumly at Mrs. Roan's hat.

Leanice had been deep in thought. "Mama, what are Grandma and Grandpa Cowan like?"

"Well, honey, they're like any other grandparents. They work hard, they go to church on Sunday, they're just people."

"Are they like Grandma Rachel?"

Leola paused for a moment. "Some people are like Grandma Rachel. They like to give lots of hugs and kisses to their grandchildren and show them just how much they love them. And other people don't give many hugs or kisses, but it doesn't mean they don't love them, they just have a different way of showing it."

The porter called the next stop, Fitzgerald, arriving in twenty minutes, at three o'clock, giving Leola little time to remember things as they were. She said a quick prayer for patience and understanding.

Lou sat sideways in her seat with her back against Leanice's shoulder, her thumb stuck in her mouth. She stared long and hard at the feathered hat Mrs. Roan wore; the brightly colored pattern of peacock feathers stood proudly next to a turquoise pin.

"Hello, there," Virginia spoke with a glowing smile.

Lou returned Virginia's smile with a smile of her own, complete with thumb and fist.

"How old are you?" Virginia asked.

Lou held up four, then five fingers on her right hand, the one not stuck in her mouth. "This many," she replied through her thumb. "How old are you?"

Virginia thought for a moment before holding up five fingers on each hand. "Oh, I guess I'm about this many."

Lou laughed in spite of her thumb. It was the first time she had laughed since her father died.

"That sure is a pretty dress you have on," said Virginia. "It matches the color of your eyes perfectly."

"I picked it out myself," Lou replied proudly. "Mama said we could have anything we wanted."

"Well, you certainly did a good job of choosing such a becoming color. Did your mama make the dress for you?"

"Uh-huh. She made it while my daddy was sick. He got real sick, and we couldn't see him. He died."

"I'm sorry," replied Virginia. "I had a boy a few years older than your sister, and he died, too." Virginia smiled sweetly at Lou then looked at her mother, who gazed at the old woman as if she were a saint.

As the train pulled into the station, Virginia dug into her purse and pulled out two shiny nickels. She handed one to Lou and one to Leanice. "You are two sweet girls. Enjoy your new home and buy something you like with your nickels."

Lou hugged the old woman's neck and kissed her on the cheek, as did Leanice.

Leola looked into Virginia's face and smiled, clasping the older woman's hands. "I'm very glad I got to meet you, Mrs. Roan. You've helped me more than you'll ever know. I guess we're not as alone in this world as we sometimes think we are."

She kissed Virginia on the cheek, as her daughters had, and departed the train. Virginia smiled gently, rolled the parasol in her hand, and drifted into another time and place where happiness surrounded her.

SEVEN

ZACH COMPLAINED ALL THE way into town. The thought of missing his Sunday afternoon nap did not improve his surly attitude. He held tight to the reins, tighter than he had to, but not tight enough to ease the tension boiling inside him. He hated being thrown off his daily schedule for any reason, especially if that reason had something to do with his daughter.

Elizabeth turned a blind eye to Zach's mood, something she'd learned to do long ago. She had a way of insulating herself from his fits of anger, her mind retreating to the happier times of her youth. Though she wouldn't dare admit it, Elizabeth anxiously awaited the arrival of her granddaughters, secretly longing to hear the sound of children's laughter filling the empty rooms of the old house. She was lonely, having lived many years with a man she did not love.

Elizabeth met Zach at the small Baptist church they attended, though she scarcely paid much attention to him. He always looked angry, like he was about to hit somebody. It could have been that his face was naturally made that way, but she thought he helped it along quite a bit. He was tall and thin, with closely cropped hair around the sides of his head and a full patch on top. His deep-set eyes and brushy eyebrows gave him a gaunt look that made him appear even more sinister.

Elizabeth's mother and Zach's father were distant cousins who had both married within their extended families. The custom was an old one, ensuring that family possessions were kept within the family. Elizabeth feared her parents, more so her mother, Isabel, who kept her young daughter on a short leash, watching over her like a hawk defending its dead prey. Isabel demanded that Elizabeth conform to her wishes, but the young girl did not want to marry Zach Cowan.

The thought of spending her life with someone so dour depressed Elizabeth. There were other boys in the church she could date but none whom her mother deemed appropriate. She was especially fond of Hank Myers, a boyish-looking eighteen-year-old with the hint of a grin always underlying his expression. His zest for life, the way he carried himself, the infectious laugh that charmed her heart, swept Elizabeth into an upward spiral of young love.

At church socials, Hank was always in the middle of a large crowd, either telling tall tales about the one that got away, or balancing a variety of plates and glasses on his head. He embodied what Elizabeth lacked, the spontaneous and fun side of life. She glowed in his presence, enamored by his complete abandon and joy of living. His charm brought her to life, and her love awakened his heart.

Elizabeth's sixteenth birthday was a turning point in her young life. Her mother and uncle decreed that she and Zach would marry one year hence, on her seventeenth birthday.

Word of the engagement spread quickly, raising more than a few eyebrows within the church. The mismatch was obvious. Zach stood six-foot-four, while Elizabeth barely topped five feet. His features were stark, while hers were soft; his personality aggressive, hers docile. His view of the world dark and oppressive; hers reserved and innocent. He was abusive, she was silent.

Elizabeth begged her mother to keep the engagement a secret, but Isabel made it common knowledge to all who mattered within a day of the announcement. She went to extreme lengths to let others know, as if to say that her daughter was no longer free to socialize with her peers. She wanted to keep Elizabeth away from the temptations of single men, particularly one single man.

Elizabeth did not see Hank until a month after the engagement, hearing through the grapevine that he was visiting family in South Carolina. In her heart she knew he left to escape the pain. When he returned, he was different. The spark in his personality was gone, replaced by a somber and more serious imposter. Elizabeth sensed the change immediately. His pain increased hers one-hundred-fold.

She felt a pair of eyes staring at her throughout the church service, imploring her to notice him. When her mother wasn't looking, she returned the gaze with an expression that conveyed all the hurt and anger and despair and longing she felt. She wanted to reach through the distance between them and touch his face, that angelic, joyous face that possessed her soul.

After a lengthy sermon, the couple met outside. Elizabeth slipped out of the foyer while her mother became engrossed in conversation with the women of her social circle. Hank stood underneath the giant pecan tree as he had many Sundays before, waiting for Elizabeth to join him. As she approached, the air thickened with tension. Hank's face was blank, his eyes welling with tears. Elizabeth thought she would be sick to her stomach.

He managed a forced smile; the moment lingered in awkward silence. His feelings exposed, he broke out with a pained laugh. "I guess I got another story to tell about the one that got away, don't I?" He forcibly hit the side of his leg. "Congratulations, Elizabeth. I hope things work out for you, I really do."

Elizabeth cleared her throat and looked away into an empty meadow overgrown with weeds and dandelion. She stared at the horizon, wishing that she could run to it and jump over the edge into the deep, bottomless pit of despair. The life ebbed from her body, the spirit drained from her soul.

"Thank you, Hank. It means a lot to me to hear you say that." She continued looking into the distance, unable to take the pain on Hank's face.

He looked at her deeply, knowing this was not what she wanted, that she had no choice in this matter. He wanted to embrace her, to assure her that everything would be all right, to sweep her into his arms and carry her away from the unfair restraints of time and tradition. "Why does it have to be like this, Elizabeth?"

She looked down, drying the tears that fell from her eyes. "Don't, Hank. You know why, there's nothing either of us can do."

"It's not fair! Two people who love each other shouldn't be kept apart like this!" He grabbed her shoulders, pleading with her to look into his eyes and tell him she didn't love him.

She quickly looked at him, as if the acknowledgement of his love was something unexpected. For a split second she was free, free to run across the meadow and beyond the horizon with the man who loved her. "You love me?" Her face glowed as the knowledge of Hank's love made her more beautiful than she had ever been.

"Of course I do." He gently touched the side of her face. "I always have. I love everything about you. You make me feel like I have a reason for being here, that there's a purpose for my life. With you I'm a whole person, without you I'm nothing."

Elizabeth's soul burned with renewed life. A rebellion built itself deep within, propelling her to run away right then and there, following Hank wherever he went.

"I was wondering where you were, young lady." Isabel suddenly appeared, pulling her daughter away from Hank and to her side. "I suppose you were telling Mr. Myers the good news of your engagement. I'm sure he's as happy with the news as you are, Elizabeth."

Hank looked at Elizabeth, unable to break the unspoken embrace that bound them together. "Yes, she told me about it, and I wished her all the happiness in the world." He then turned his attention to Isabel. "I was also telling her that I'm moving to South Carolina. My aunt has a rooming house there, and she needs help running it. I'll be leaving in a few days."

Elizabeth looked sharply at Hank, as if everything he had just confessed to her was a lie. The color drained from her face.

"Well, I wish you good luck and success in your endeavors, Mr. Myers. And I know Elizabeth does, too." Hank shook Isabel's hand before extending his hand to Elizabeth. She could not move.

"Aren't you going to shake his hand, Elizabeth?" Isabel's tone was subtly victorious.

Nearing collapse, Elizabeth embraced Hank and kissed him on the cheek. Their love for one another united them in this one, brief moment. Isabel pulled her daughter from the embrace, wishing Hank well as she sent him on his way. As he walked down the dirt road, Elizabeth's soul died.

If Zach Cowan had complete and sole control over his life, he never would have married. He had no use for people, unable to relate on a human level. His personality was basic, almost animalistic, purposefully marking his territory and expecting others to abide by the rules of nature. Emotions and feelings meant very little to him; life was nothing more than a hard journey in which only the fittest survived.

He depended on no one but himself, learning self-sufficiency early in life and clinging to this trait with all his mental and physical might. He worked the fields with his father and brothers and pulled his weight, even though he was the youngest. If his brothers could work two acres per day, then he could work two acres per day.

He had something to prove, something that would make him stand out in his father's esteem. His mother worried that he spent so much time by himself, but his father said it built character, just what a rural farmer needed to survive during the lean years. "A man must develop a bleak outlook on life from the start. That way he won't be surprised when failure or misfortune come knocking at his door."

This was the motto the elder Cowan lived by, one that he indoctrinated into his household at every opportunity. He wanted his children to be realists, if not pessimists, even if it meant sacrificing their souls.

Zach embraced his father's philosophy as if it were the philosophy of God. He never let himself enjoy anything for fear that enjoyment bred disaster. His classmates kept their distance, some afraid by his angered look and others amused by his disheveled appearance. He didn't fit in with the group, which suited Zach just fine.

When his father informed him of the impending marriage to Elizabeth, Zach glumly stared ahead and simply asked, "Do I have to?"

"Yes, you have to," replied his father. "It's important to both families that we protect our land and continue the traditions begun by our forefathers. It would be wise of you to have a large family, fill your house with sons who will help you with the work to be done. Do as you are told, boy. Honor thy father and thy mother, that thy days may be long upon the land which the Lord thy God giveth thee."

Zach followed his father's advice reluctantly, still unwilling to accept the belief that he couldn't be whole unless he had a wife and family. But he couldn't break tradition, and he certainly couldn't disappoint his father. He would marry Elizabeth next spring.

Zach knew of Elizabeth's relationship with Hank, oftentimes observing their meetings under the pecan tree after church. He couldn't comprehend the attraction between the sexes, perhaps because of his own unattractiveness or, more likely, his disdain for the human race. He pitied the foolish couple for their lack of individualism and self-sufficiency. In his mind, they were weak, unprepared to survive the lonely battle of life.

His courtship of Elizabeth met with disaster; his clumsy attempts at conversation only made him more resentful of everyone and everything around him. He hated being the fool, and in this case, he was the ultimate fool. Trying to fill the shoes of the man Elizabeth loved was a task Zach refused to undertake. He would make her obey the obligation of wifely duties, even if he had to force her into compliance.

Elizabeth's depression eventually gave way to complacency. She accepted what life offered her with an expressionless facade under which she hid all emotion. The wheels of matrimony had been set in motion and nothing could stop their progress.

EIGHT

Zach and Elizabeth waited next to their wagon as Leola and the girls stepped off the train, neither making the effort to approach their estranged daughter. With her children and remaining possessions beside her, Leola quietly panicked. It had been years since she'd last seen them, years removed from their abusive ways. The floodgate of painful memories re-emerged with intensity.

Her parents had aged. Zach looked much older than his fifty years, and Elizabeth had lost the youthfulness of her face. Zach stood with his hands in his pockets, the permanent scowl etched on his face. Elizabeth's expression stiffened when she looked into her daughter's eyes. For a fraction of a second, however, her face gleamed when she saw her granddaughters.

The train's whistle blew fiercely, reminding Leola of her encounter with Virginia Roan. No matter the consequences one faces in life, there is always someone who has suffered more. With Virginia close to her heart, Leola picked up her belongings and led her daughters to meet their grandparents.

"Hello, Daddy, Mama. Thank you for taking us in and giving us a home."

Zach gruffly replied something that neither Leola nor the girls understood.

"I'm sorry about Luther," Elizabeth replied. "I know that was a terrible shock." On the surface, Elizabeth's words seemed flat, expressionless, but she remembered all too vividly the feelings of losing someone once loved.

"These are my daughters, Leanice and Lou. Say hello to Grandpa Zach and Grandma Elizabeth."

Leanice sensed the tension between her mother and grandparents, making her shyness even more profound. She whispered a reply then cast her eyes to the ground. Lou belted out a loud greeting that startled even her mother.

"Lou has her father's spirit in her." Leola smiled at her youngest daughter, prompting Lou to laugh and bury her face in Leanice's overcoat.

Elizabeth was immediately drawn to this vivacious little girl. She had a sparkle of life that attracted Elizabeth much the way Hank had many years before. The engaging laugh, the clear blue eyes, even the angelic face reminded Elizabeth of the man she loved to this day.

Zach tossed Leola's bags into the back of the wagon and took his seat holding the reins, leaving Leola and the girls to board themselves.

The trip through town and down Ten Mile Road brought back many memories, some good but most of them bad. Leola pointed out the one-room schoolhouse she attended through tenth grade, the clapboard building with two windows facing the road. With the exception of the fresh coat of paint, it had changed little over the years.

"Is that where I'll go to school, Mama?" Leanice looked at the building as if she could see her mother on the grounds as a little girl.

"Uh-huh. And Lou will start there next year."

At this statement, Lou perked up, looking at her mother with a sly grin. "Uh-uh. I'm not going to school, Mama!"

"And why not?"

"Because! I don't have to!"

"Who said that?"

"Daddy."

"When did Daddy tell you that?"

"He said I was already a smart aleck, and I couldn't get any smarter!"

Leola laughed heartily at the seriousness with which Lou believed her father. "Well, I think your daddy was just teasing you, honey. No one is smart enough for her own good." Leola embraced her daughters warmly.

Elizabeth turned her head slightly, glimpsing her daughter's family from the corner of her eye. In this all-too-brief moment, she allowed herself to feel something she'd denied for many years, the feeling of pure, innocent, unconditional love. Lou caught her grandmother's gaze and returned it with a smile. Perhaps, Elizabeth thought to herself, just perhaps, she could reclaim some of the past.

Zach steered the wagon into the side of the yard. The house had not changed much over the years. A few extra vines snaked their way up the side, but, other than that, things were much the same. Lou bolted up the steps ahead of the others, anxious to see the house where her mother grew up.

The interior was tidy, with everything neatly put in its proper place, a trademark of Elizabeth's housekeeping. A brown sofa draped by a yellow and white afghan lined the interior wall next to the fireplace. A side chair of the same brown color created a semi-circle on the side of the fireplace with a rocking chair. Four windows looked into the living room from the front porch, two on either side of the front door.

The living room opened into a large dining room initially constructed for a bigger family. The long table looked strangely out of place with only two chairs placed at one end. A small hallway led to the kitchen in one direction, and into a larger hallway in the other that led to three bedrooms. Leola took a deep breath, inhaling the faint smell of ammonia-scrubbed walls and floors.

"I sort of feel like I never left, everything looks so much the same." Leola picked up her bags and walked toward the long hallway, followed closely by Leanice and Lou, with Elizabeth not far behind.

"I wasn't sure how you wanted to work out the sleeping arrangements, but both bedrooms up front are clean. Your room is much the way you left it."

"The girls can have my room, and I'll take the one in front. I'll rest easier if they're in the middle."

Elizabeth excused herself to the kitchen while Leola and the girls unfolded and stored away their lives in their new home. Of all her possessions, Leola's most prized was a photograph of Luther encased in a silver frame, which she put on the nightstand beside her bed.

Dinner was served precisely at six o'clock, lamps extinguished at nine in the evening, and breakfast at five the next morning. The household schedule ran according to Zach's schedule. He was a man of unbreakable habit.

Three additional chairs were set along one side of the table, facing Elizabeth. The girls were setting the table when Leola rushed in, embarrassed at having slept through the preparation of her first meal at home.

"I'm sorry for sleeping so long; the train ride took more out of me than I thought. I'll clear the table and do the dishes after dinner." Nervously, Leola took the bowl of applesauce from her mother's hand and set it on the table in front of Zach's plate.

"You don't have to do that, Leola. I've been washing dishes well over thirty years, I think I can manage one more sink full." Elizabeth pushed aside the bowl of applesauce, replacing it with a plate of ham.

"I insist, Mama. We're not here for charity. We'll earn our keep the best we can."

Without a word, Elizabeth shrugged her shoulders and breezed out of the room. Leola's heart beat furiously; the patterns of the past reappeared too quickly.

"The table sure looks nice. I'm proud of you both for helping Grandma with dinner."

"Leanice said one of us should sit next to Grandma Elizabeth, but I want to sit next to you, Mama. And so does Leanice."

"You can take turns sitting next to me, and eventually you might want to sit by Grandma, when you get to know her better." Leola kissed both her daughters.

"Is Grandma Elizabeth mean? She never smiles like Grandma Rachel."

Lou's question bothered Leola. "Lou, remember what we talked about on the train? How some people don't smile as much or talk as much as other people, but it doesn't make them mean, remember that?" Lou nodded in agreement, though it was clear she had forgotten.

"Grandma and Grandpa Cowan are different than Grandma Rachel, but they're giving us a home to live in, so they must love us, right?" Leola tweaked Lou's nose, evoking the impish squeal that delighted her mother.

Elizabeth entered the room with a more pronounced scowl on her face, having overheard the conversation in the dining room. She set a bowl of corn on the table along with a plate of freshly baked biscuits and a jar of maple syrup. Her manner was brisk, almost rude, the hopes for redemption dashed. On matters of emotion, Elizabeth saw things in black and white, the gray area of compromise lost the day she married Zach. She responded to adversity by retreating into a world of silence. As far as Elizabeth was concerned, Lou, like her mother, would live to despise her.

At the stroke of six o'clock, Zach entered the dining room from the long hallway. His arrogant manner frightened the girls; they didn't dare breathe until their grandfather took his seat at the head of the table. Zach graced the dinner with a short prayer that did not include the new members of his household.

A conspicuous silence invaded the room throughout the course of the meal. Leola desperately searched for any common ground that might lead to conversation, but abandoned the idea halfway through dinner. There existed too wide a gap between her life and that of her parents.

"Can I be excused, Mama?" Lou asked. "I have to feed my baby doll before her bedtime."

"Of course you can, sweetie."

Zach suddenly looked up.

"Where do you think you're going, little girl?" Zach growled.

Frightened, Lou peered through the spaces in the back of her chair. "To feed my baby doll. She's hungry and she has to eat before bedtime." Lou turned away from the old man, afraid to look into his beady eyes.

"This is my table, and you will not be excused until you've eaten everything on your plate! And you left a slice of ham and a spoonful of applesauce—waste not, want not! Now sit yourself down and finish that up. If you don't, then your baby doll will have to go to bed hungry!" Zach's face contorted with anger.

"But I don't want it! Please let me go feed my baby doll!" Tears welled up in Lou's eyes.

"Daddy—"

"I will not allow anyone to challenge me in my own house! She will clean her plate or sit there until breakfast!"

Lou started crying. Leola clenched her jaw, determined to reason with her father, when Leanice quickly emptied Lou's plate onto her own.

"Her plate is clean now. Can she be excused from the table?"

Zach stared at his eight-year-old granddaughter with a look he might give a merchant who overcharged him for supplies. With a wave of his hand, he dismissed Lou from the table.

The tension that enveloped the room grew in proportion, spilling into the hallways, kitchen, and living area. The joyful sounds that Elizabeth looked forward to evaporated into the walls and floors, aging the wood that framed the house beyond its years. The walls cracked with fear, the floors separated with anger.

Zach pushed himself away from the table and walked outside to check the animals, completely oblivious to the turmoil he caused. To him, humans were like the animals in his barn, possessions that could be kept under lock and key.

Leola washed dishes as fast and furiously as Leanice brought them in, both anxious to finish the chores at hand and retire to their rooms. The events of the day clouded Leola's mind, the encouragement given her by Virginia Roan splintering into delicate pieces. With each dish and pan she scrubbed, Leola reminded herself that someday, somehow, she would again see the light of promise.

NINE

The days and weeks passed with the same familiarity Leola knew as a child. The patterns of behavior within the house were as rigid and unforgiving as ever, stealing the souls of those who lived there like a thief in the night. She spent her days in long stretches of silence completing household chores, while the evenings provided the only relief when she took her daughters on long walks down Ten Mile Road. The moments of togetherness made the days bearable.

As Thanksgiving passed into Christmas, and winter into spring, she found herself with a small circle of friends and on Sunday afternoons would visit with neighbors from her church.

One of her newfound friends was Sarah Garber, a woman two years older than her mother. The roundness of Leola's face and her smooth complexion reminded Sarah of Elizabeth, her long lost friend, a friendship she still missed thirty years later.

Sarah enjoyed reminiscing about old times, but she hesitated when the topic turned to Elizabeth and Zach Cowan. Though Leola had no emotional reason for asking, she was, nonetheless, curious about her parents as young adults. Sarah weighed her words carefully.

"Your mother and I were very close growing up. We were practically sisters. She was a very different person then, though still quiet and thoughtful; she loved being around people. It seemed to fascinate her, the differences in people, their ways and manners. She loved to sing—had the most beautiful voice you could imagine—but I haven't heard her sing in many a year."

This tidbit of information stunned Leola; her mother rarely spoke, let alone sang. She pushed Sarah further.

"Your parents have always known each other, they're related, distant cousins, you know. The marriage was arranged by their parents, that's what changed Elizabeth. She didn't want to marry your father. She was in love with another boy, my brother, Hank Myers."

Leola's shoulders lifted slightly. "Mother was in love with another man?" She could not imagine her mother with anyone other than her father.

Sarah repositioned herself in the chair, looking out the window as her husband pulled Leanice and Lou around the yard in a small hay wagon he'd built for his own grandchildren. "Don't think that I'm just gossiping for the sake of it. This doesn't have to go any further than this room, but I've always felt that you should know about your mother, why she is the way she is. I know she may not be the kind of mother you wanted, but then, she hasn't had the kind of life she wanted either."

"Nothing will leave this room, I promise. But I do want to know more about her."

Sarah thought long and hard, looking out at the smiles on the girls' faces. "She was such a pleasant girl, almost childlike in her manner, wide-eyed, impressionable. That's why she was so taken with Hank. He was a spitfire, always in the middle of things, the center of attention. Mama said he was full of the devil because he was born during a full moon." Sarah chuckled to herself before continuing. "He was like a magnet, and Elizabeth was drawn to him so strong there was nothing she could do to stop herself from being pulled in."

"Did Hank love her, too?"

Sarah nodded her head. "He adored her. They complimented each other's personalities beautifully. If ever two people were meant for one another . . ."

Leola suddenly felt ashamed of herself for pushing the conversation, sensing from Sarah's demeanor that there was more to the story than she'd imagined. "What happened to Hank?"

"After the engagement was announced, he went away; we have an aunt and cousins who live in Edgefield, South Carolina. But he came back here, just to see your mother one last time. I think he just wanted to know if she loved him the way he loved her."

A single tear traced its way down Sarah's cheek. "He left for good after that, packed up everything and moved to Edgefield, just across the state line from Augusta. Our aunt owned a boarding house there and he helped her out for a while, but the pain of losing Elizabeth was more than he could handle. He killed himself on a Monday afternoon, put a gun to his head and pulled the trigger."

Leola sat motionless. The explanation made things so clear, yet complicated matters even more. She finally reached an understanding of her mother that could pave the way for a better relationship, but she couldn't express this knowledge without betraying Sarah's confidence. The irony of the situation baffled Leola, as if destiny had been moved beyond her reach.

Leanice and Lou ran to their mother's side, both of them exuberant after the ride in Mr. Garber's hay wagon, their cheeks rosy from the excitement of the ride and the cold February air.

Mr. Garber warmed himself by the fireplace, catching his breath after the marathon journey around his yard. "I hope your father can get along without Cale."

"Excuse me?" Leola asked, puzzled.

"My oldest boy Cale, he works with your father. He broke his arm last week, won't be able to help Zach plow the fields for spring planting. I said I hope your father can manage without him."

"He'll figure something out, he always does." Leola said.

Sarah stared out the window, transfixed by the glorious blue heavens that claimed her brother. The fireplace logs crackled noisily before sliding into new positions, the bright orange glow of warmth burning its way to the outside.

The following weeks were marked by change and conflict, a restructuring of boundaries and a fusion of alliances. Leola saw in her mother a pathetic figure who had little control over a life built upon possession and betrayal.

Zach was in a nastier mood than usual one spring day, complaining endlessly about the lack of a field hand and his inability to find another one. He plowed the earth with a maniacal vengeance, screaming at the old mule to work harder and faster. He pushed his own body to the limits, not to mention his temper.

He worked himself into a fiery state of agitation until noon when he took his lunch, mumbling to himself throughout the meal. From what Leola could interpret, he was angry that he could not find a field hand, which, to him, was an outright insult. There were plenty of able-bodied men who could fit the bill, but none chose to work with Zach Cowan.

By nightfall, a burning rage devoured him. He stood at the back door of the house, his head pounding from the millions of thoughts having passed through his mind over the course of the day. His breathing was deep yet inconsistent, his face reddened by the angry sun. "How come dinner's not on the table? You know I want it on the table when I walk in that door!" He stared blankly at Elizabeth as if he were looking at a spot on the wall.

"It's not quite six o'clock yet, you came in a little early tonight. It'll be ready shortly." Elizabeth nervously quickened her pace.

"I know what time it is, I can read a clock! Don't call me stupid, woman!"

"I didn't call you stupid. I merely pointed out that you came in early tonight."

Leola entered the kitchen, immediately sensing her father's volatile mood. She quickly reversed her steps in an attempt to get the girls into their room before it started.

"What the hell do you think you're doing?" Zach addressed Leola without removing his gaze from Elizabeth. Leola froze; skeletons from the past danced around her.

"Nothing. I was just going to sit down for dinner."

"Don't lie to me, girl! I can always tell when a woman is lying! Ask your mother, she's been lying to me for nigh on thirty-five years!"

Elizabeth paused briefly, her body stiff with fear, and then continued filling a bowl with white acre peas. "Don't start that, Zach, not now, not in front of the children."

Elizabeth handed the bowl to Leola, ending the confrontation as far as she was concerned. Leola turned to walk into the dining room when a thunderous crash stopped her cold. She quickly turned around. Zach was standing in the midst of broken dishes, seething with rage.

"You don't want the children to hear what? That you never loved me? That you're still in love with that high-steppin', tongue-waggin', good-for-nothin' fool from a no-account family? Those people would stop at nothing to make me look like some sort of carnival freak. I bet that boy's arm ain't even broke!" Zach accentuated his anger by pounding his fist into the wall.

Leola did not move. The bowl of hot peas burned her hands.

"Just once I'd like to get ahead, just once I'd like things to go my way! You start giving me your lip, and then she comes in here with her ready-made family looking for a handout. I wish all of you would go to hell!" Zach's eyes bulged from their sockets, his face contorted in anger.

Elizabeth took a deep breath and walked silently past him. He grabbed her arm with such force she let out a scream. Pushing her against the wall, Zach put his face inches from hers, his breath burning her skin.

"I do not like you, and I do not like your family, I do not like your daughter, and I do not like your grandchildren. I'm tired of being burdened by everything you represent. I'm tired of being played for a fool." Zach loosened his grip on Elizabeth's arm and stormed out of the house.

The moon shone brightly, its tentacles of light passing through the brilliant scattering of stars dotting the darkened skies. The invading quiet contrasted starkly with the outburst that occurred earlier. Leola could not sleep; the peacefulness of the evening hours belied the restless turmoil sewn into the fabric of her family. She turned on her side and stared at Luther's picture in the silver frame. If ever she could use his strength, it was now.

Elizabeth set the table for breakfast with a setting of older dishes given to her by Zach's mother. She set a place for each family member, including Zach, even though she had not seen him since the previous evening. The girls followed Leola into the dining room, nervously looking around for their grandfather.

Leola could not remember a time when her father missed breakfast, or any meal for that matter. She did not ask of his whereabouts. Instead, she promised the girls another trip to the Garber's house if they minded their grandmother and helped with the Saturday chores.

The ground was still cool, moist and pliable, not yet warmed by the bright, spring sun. Zach started on the front acreage nearest the barn at daybreak, having spent the night on a bed of hay. The fury he unleashed found an appropriate outlet in the dark, rich earth. He plowed the field feverishly, his concentration eventually broken by an approaching figure.

He thought that Cale had, at last, decided to confess his charade and return to work. But the figure, dressed in overalls, was smaller and delicate, feminine looking. Zach squinted, focusing upon the figure as it slowly emerged from the darkness. His eyes widened and his jaw dropped.

"What in the name of heaven do you think you're doing?" His question was more incredulous in nature than accusatory.

"You said you needed a field hand. I'm a field hand." Leola stated matter-of-factly.

Zach turned his back to her and resumed his chore. "Go back in the house and help your mother. This is no kind of work for a woman."

Undaunted, Leola pursued. "It is when no one else is available. Where do you want me to start? Here or on the back acres?"

Zach ignored her. Leola put on her work gloves as she surveyed the back property. "I'll start on the south side by the property line and work my way north."

"You don't know what you're doing!" Zach hissed at her.

"I've watched you do this enough to know what I'm doing. Besides, two pair of hands are better than one at this point. I'll get the other plow and start on the south side."

Zach called after her as she walked away. "I'll not have anyone see my daughter working like a common field hand!"

Without breaking her stride, Leola called back to him, "And I'll not be a burden on anyone, especially if that anyone is you!" As she disappeared into the barn, Zach resigned himself to the inevitable.

The clashing of wills brought with it a tenuous calm. The family was forced into a maturing process that exposed and conquered their own weaknesses. From crisis often arises respect, a respect for oneself as well as a respect for others. Though he would never admit it, Zach begrudgingly appreciated Leola's help. The plowing of the earth, discarding the old to make way for the new, united them as a family, as it did for all the families who depended upon the bounty of the land and the grace of God for their survival. Once the seeds of peace had been planted, all that was needed were the rains of forgiveness.

TEN

For most of the farming families who lived and worked in the rural areas of Ben Hill County, the few miles of dusty, dirt lanes that separated them from town could easily have been roads that led to the other side of the world. Other than venturing into town prior to planting season or bringing crops in after the harvest, the farming community mostly stayed to themselves. The only news they had from Fitzgerald came from the weekly trips Sheriff Fountain and his deputy, Ezra Smith, made to the outlying areas.

It was during these routine runs, checking up on folks, settling the infrequent disputes of property, that the farmers learned the changes taking place in town. A successful petition had been presented to the state legislature to incorporate the town of Fitzgerald as the county seat, which in turn necessitated the building of a town hall and courthouse directly in the center of town, as well as a bigger jail for the incarceration of the county's more prolific chicken thieves and growing number of moonshiners.

During the last week of May in 1902, as Deputy Smith was making the rounds to Bowen's Mill and Queensland, the rural families heard the most surprising news of all, Deputy Ezra Smith, the mainstay of law enforcement since the end of the war, had decided to retire. The news came as such a surprise because most folks figured Deputy Smith would die while on the job with his silver star still pinned upon his chest. He was a proud man, too proud to even consider the notion that anyone of any merit could replace his years of meritorious service, which included an arrest record that stretched from one end of the county to the other.

The only blemish in his thirty-year tenure, the fly in the otherwise perfect ointment that marked a stellar career in the opinion of many of those in the know, was the one event that tarnished Deputy Smith's legend. It followed him wherever he went, the unwanted shadow that peered over his shoulder, the breath of wind that whispered in his ear, the constant reminder of one moment's vulnerability, the lack in judgment that cost a man his life.

No matter the many successes of his long career, he would always be known for the death of his best friend. And, as fate would have it, his successor would be the constant reminder of Ezra's one failing, his own son, Harbard.

There was never a doubt that Harbard would follow in his father's footsteps of law enforcement. Ezra made the decision that his first-born son would become a lawman the day he laid eyes on him, not even ten minutes after his child's entry into the world. It didn't matter to Ezra what Harbard would think about the path his life would take when he was old enough to form opinions of his own. When Ezra Smith made up his mind, neither hell nor high water could change it.

Ezra pushed Harbard relentlessly, never praising his son for any achievement, yet always pointing out his failings. He expected more than perfection from his son; the man who succeeded him as one of the county's protectors had to be damn near perfect.

As a youngster, Harbard perfected his shooting skills by knocking tin cans off fence posts and piercing mistletoe out of oak trees for his mother's Christmas decorations. Eventually, as he grew into his teen years, he accompanied his father on quail hunts. His eye was quick and his aim deadly.

Harbard married the daughter of Ezra's best friend and hunting buddy. She was a wisp of a being, sparrow-like in her appearance and movements. She seemed to hop from place to place, her nervous energy taking her in many directions at once. Her father, J.W. Carter, named her after his mother, Rebecca, whom she favored.

In the early years of their marriage, they were inseparable; where one went, the other followed close behind. Some were amused by the couple's constant companionship, others warmed by their steadfast devotion. Harbard wanted nothing more than to provide for his wife the best he could.

While his father held a firm grip on the position of Deputy Sheriff, Harbard worked as a mechanic at the rail yard, repairing cars that were temporarily pulled from service. The job was physically exhausting, oftentimes forcing Harbard and his fellow workers to take longer breaks during the course of the workday, especially on hot summer afternoons. Grease and perspiration covered his body when he came home at day's end, but the joy in his heart upon seeing Rebecca made any discomfort worthwhile.

Harbard's mother visited often, helping Rebecca maintain the large garden next to the house. They enjoyed each other's company. Rebecca longed for maternal closeness since her mother died and Nancy respected her daughter-in-law for the joy she brought into Harbard's life. Mostly they talked of little more than neighbors, friends, and church. But, on occasion, they ventured into more intimate matters that concerned them both.

"Ezra's not the easiest person to live with," Nancy slowly began as she dug at a group of stubborn weeds. "He has a certain way of doing things and expects everyone else to follow suit. My daddy warned me not to marry a stubborn man, because if we had children they'd be twice as stubborn."

Nancy's remark puzzled Rebecca as she loosened the soil around the onion plants.

"The student always learns more than the teacher, he'd say. And if the teacher really knew what he was doing, the lesson was learned even better," Nancy explained as she tossed the handful of weeds into a small pile.

"Are you trying to tell me that your sons are stubborn?" Rebecca looked at her mother-in-law with a wry grin.

"If I said they weren't, I'd be lying; if I said they were, I'd be admitting my failure as a mother." Nancy looked up at Rebecca, who had abruptly stopped digging.

"If stubbornness is the worst of their qualities, then consider yourself a good mother. My daddy always told us that it's the bad things about a person that others remember most, so if someone doesn't remember you, take it as a compliment. Besides, your sons learned their stubborn ways from their father, not you."

Nancy smiled at Rebecca's insight and returned her attention to weeding. "So you noticed?"

"I don't mean to sound disrespectful but . . . yes."

"He's not an unkind man, really, he just doesn't know how to show affection. His family was dirt poor, and he started working as soon as he started walking. He's known nothing else in his life but hard work, and it can turn a person's soul to stone in due time. I was always afraid that Harbard would end up like him." Again Nancy put the weeding aside and looked up at Rebecca, feeling the other woman's eyes upon her.

"Why do you say that?" Rebecca swatted at a mosquito buzzing around her head.

"Just a feeling I have. Ezra was tough on Harbard, much tougher than he was on the other boys. They fought constantly, and some of the fights they had . . ." Nancy blushed at the recollection, prompting Rebecca to pursue another way of looking at the situation.

"But a man can change, can't he? I mean, he doesn't always have to be just one way or another."

There was a hint of concern in Rebecca's voice, which Nancy noticed. "Oh, I agree. Ever since Harbard has known you, he's changed tremendously. I see flashes of that little boy I tried to reach many years ago. He appears every now and then but never for too long; that wall he built around himself is so strong."

"You don't think he'll stay this way? The way he is now?"

"Harbard's a good boy, and he loves you more than he loves life itself, don't ever doubt that. But where his father is concerned, he'll stop at nothing to prove Ezra wrong. It changes his entire being, like he's consumed by the need to show his father up. I hope he stays with the railroad after Ezra retires. It could start the whole ball to rolling again."

Rebecca could not imagine Harbard being anything like his father, especially toward his own children.

At dinner that evening, Rebecca looked at Harbard with a bit of trepidation, almost fearful that he would turn into his father before her eyes. In her heart, she knew it was foolish to feel this way, but Nancy's words lingered. She stared at him as if she were studying the shape and outline of his face for the first time. He looked no different than he had the day before, but something was different, a feeling, an implication of doubt.

Harbard sensed the uneasiness in his wife almost immediately but waited until they were sitting on the swing in the breezeway before approaching the subject. "How come you've been studying me like a school book all evening?" Harbard asked.

"What are you talking about?" Rebecca tensed slightly.

"You've been acting as skittish as a cat in a washtub ever since I got home. Is there something I did that I should know about?" Harbard looked directly at Rebecca. She turned away nervously.

"I don't know what you're talking about, Harbard. I'm acting no different today than I do any other day." Her voice was flat, though edged slightly with defensiveness.

"There you go again."

"What?"

"You're stiffening up, and you've got that tone in your voice again."

"What tone?" Rebecca became increasingly defensive, which made Harbard press even more.

"The tone that says something's up but you're afraid to tell me . . . that tone." Harbard guzzled down the remainder of his iced tea and wiped his mouth with the back of his hand.

"For goodness sake, this whole conversation is infuriating. You're trying to make something out of nothing." Rebecca again looked away.

"All right, if you say so. But everything's telling me otherwise."

They sat in silence, neither knowing quite how to act after their first quarrel. The tension between them was ridiculous, even comical. Harbard reached over and held Rebecca's hand. "What'd you do today?" His voice was calm and soothing.

"Your mother and I worked in the garden. The onions and turnips are looking good, but something's getting into the snap beans."

"Sprinkle 'em with some sulfur; that'll take care of whatever's eating them."

"Daddy came by for a little while this morning. He said he and Ezra were going to take care of some business this afternoon. Do you know what that's about?"

"Knowing my father, he probably needed a volunteer to help bring someone in. Or they could've gone quail hunting, ya never know with Daddy."

The thought of her father playing lawman made Rebecca uneasy. The frequent hunting trips he made were one matter; the most threatening game he went after was a nine-point buck. But bringing in an uncooperative thief or, worse yet, a moonshiner, was something altogether different.

"Why would Ezra ask Daddy to go with him on something like that? Where's Sheriff Fountain? That's his job, isn't it?" Rebecca's voice was more fearful than antagonistic.

"He's over in Blackshear this week, had a death in the family. What are you getting yourself all worked up about? I didn't say for sure that's what they were doing. I just said that, knowing my father, he's going to put work before pleasure."

"I don't like it, I don't like it one bit. Daddy's not a . . . well, he's not an observant man like your father. He's trusting, he wouldn't think twice about turning his back on someone. Ezra should know that; Daddy's not cut out for this." Rebecca's concern showed on her face.

Harbard put his arm around her shoulders. "It's okay, Rebecca. Chances are they're doing nothing more than giving some poor ol' chicken thief a good talking to, that's all." Harbard's reassurances did not dissuade Rebecca's feeling of doom.

She twisted and turned in bed, finding no position that comforted her. Finally, lying with her hand over her eyes, she had managed to drift off into a fitful rest when a frantic knock at the front door awakened her. She nudged Harbard awake and followed him to the front door.

"What are you doing out this late?" Harbard motioned his father inside.

"I'm not here on a social call. I came over to speak with Rebecca. There's been an accident involving her father." Ezra's words were sterile.

"Daddy's dead, isn't he?" Rebecca worked herself into a state of near-hysteria.

"He's been shot, but he's not dead."

"What happened?" Harbard put his arm around Rebecca, all the while looking sternly into his father's eyes.

"We went down to Bowen's Mill where Wallace and I ran some 'shiners out a couple of weeks ago. I just wanted to make sure they hadn't opened up for business again, and J.W. said he'd go with me, but when we got there, they ambushed us."

"Where's J.W.?"

"I took him straight over to Doctor Robert's house. I'm sorry, Rebecca—"

As Ezra offered his regrets to Rebecca, she fled the room, only to return in her bathrobe and slippers.

"Harbard, take me to my daddy, please." She opened the door and walked out, dismissing the presence of her father-in-law.

Ezra grabbed Harbard's arm. "I'll take you over there. It's the least I can do."

"I think you've done enough already." Harbard broke from his father's grasp.

Rebecca stayed at her father's side until he regained consciousness, though he rarely stayed awake for any length of time; delirium culled him into a nether world of hallucinations. The bullet entered his left side above the hip but did not exit, lodging itself next to his spine, pinning J.W. inside a body that couldn't move. He ran a high fever for days, the threat of infection a death sentence. If it did not break soon, Doctor Roberts would have to operate, an equally threatening task.

The emotional turmoil took its toll on Rebecca; her tiny body withered from the stress of losing her remaining parent. She was too young to become an orphan, too young to find her way through life without a parent's guiding hand. In many ways she was still a child, still dependent upon a father's strength to comfort her, to bestow the knowledge that she belongs to someone and that all is right with her world.

J.W.'s deteriorating condition showed on Rebecca. Her skin barely covered the protruding bones of her face and arms, and her eyes appeared to have sunk deeper into the contours of her face. The bullet lodged in J.W.'s body pierced her soul, poisoning the flow of life, infecting the will to live.

J.W. died the day after Christmas. Rebecca never again spoke to her father-in-law.

ELEVEN

The week after J.W.'s death was as gloomy outside the house as it was inside. A chilly drizzle persisted for several days, waxing rooftops and alleyways with a thin veneer of rain and sleet. At first nothing more than a fine mist that hung like tiny dewdrops in the air, the wintry precipitation gave way to a downpour of cold, hard rain.

The torrent created havoc, strangling the tiny community with impassible lanes of thick, brown, icy mud. The various creeks that twisted through the county overflowed their banks, inching closer to the nearby homes and farms, threatening livestock, not to mention the farmers themselves. To some it was akin to the Biblical flood, the heavens above cleansing the Earth for a new, fresh beginning.

Harbard gave thanks for the interruption in his work schedule so he could stay home and look after his wife. Rebecca's listless, even catatonic condition had not improved. She remained in bed, staring out the window, her eyes not fixed on anything in particular. Harbard sat next to her and gently stroked her long, auburn hair. His concern for Rebecca, though honest and pure, eventually, logically, transformed itself into an increasing rage aimed at his father. Ezra, he felt, was responsible for Rebecca's pain.

The storm clouds that hovered over the area at last rolled away, awakening the town from its temporary slumber. Harbard returned to work, remorseful for having to leave Rebecca alone in her grief. Her condition overwhelmed him. He was powerless, unable to force his will over the grief that consumed her. Confused and desperate, he slowly, stubbornly knelt beside the bed. He was a hypocrite for praying, and he knew it. He'd never acknowledged the existence of God, opting instead to rely upon his own resources to fulfill whatever spiritual needs might arise. The thought of subjugating his will to that of a higher power made him feel weak.

Humbly, however, he asked for help in whatever form it could be delivered. His prayer was selfless, and when he finished, he kissed Rebecca on the forehead.

The following morning, a knock on the back door startled him. Nancy whisked into the kitchen carrying two large bags on either side of her, filled with peas, turnips, and corn, along with a ham from her uncle's smokehouse.

"I came as soon as the rain let up. I would've been here sooner, but the roads were too bad for travel. How's Rebecca?" Nancy rested her hand on Harbard's arm. He lowered his head and nodded.

"She's not doing well at all, Mama. I've never seen her like this before. She does little more than lie in bed all day and look out the window. It's like she's taken off somewhere, and I can't bring her back. I don't know what to do." Tears streamed down Harbard's agonized face. Nancy wiped them away.

"You go on to work and try not to worry too much. A hard day's work is good for the soul. I'll look after Rebecca."

Harbard kissed his mother's cheek, realizing his prayer had been heard. An incredible burden released itself from his shoulders, his lungs filled with the breath of hope.

Nancy quietly opened the bedroom door, staring at her daughter-in-law for some time, noticing that even in sleep Rebecca's face was troubled. Her skin was pale and her features drawn. She'd lost weight, too much for her own good. Nancy set about to make Rebecca a solid meal; the sounds and smells and stirrings of the kitchen would, hopefully, uplift her spirits.

When she awoke, Rebecca was aware that someone was in the house. The thought of an armed intruder was not alarming. Instead, it calmed her in a macabre fashion, an unknown assailant sent from the bowels of depression to end her misery.

She rose from the bed and looked out the window at the barren garden, where a stubble of winter grass emerged from its hiding place below the soil. She imagined her father working in the lot, all the while explaining to anyone who would listen about the importance of conserving the topsoil with winter grass. Her hand touched the window as she tried to reach out to him.

The sound of singing momentarily broke Rebecca's preoccupation with her sorrow. She listened for a moment, recognizing the familiar hymn as one of Nancy's favorites. Rebecca joined in on the second verse, barely singing above a whisper.

'Twas grace that taught my heart to fear
and grace my fears relieved
how precious did that grace appear
the hour I first believed.

As she returned her focus to the vacant lot, a quick, faint knock rattled upon the bedroom door.

"I put some peas and turnips on the stove, and I sliced some ham to go with it. It's freshly smoked. Uncle Jack sent it to you with his condolences." Nancy slowly approached her daughter-in-law.

"When did it stop raining?" Rebecca's voice was weak. She leaned against the window for support.

"A couple of days ago. When I got up this morning, the wind had already picked up and the sky was beautiful and clear."

"The winter grass is starting to come up. I can just hear Daddy telling us everything we need to do before the next planting season." Rebecca laughed briefly to herself, though tears welled in her eyes.

"Your father was a good teacher. Between the two of us I think we can raise a good crop this year."

Rebecca looked at Nancy's reflection in the window. "You'll help me with the garden?"

"Of course I will. I want us to try our hands at tomatoes."

Nancy extended her arms toward Rebecca. The love in her eyes penetrated the walls of alienation. She held Rebecca tightly, stroking her hair while she cried. At last Rebecca had someone to lean on, someone to shoulder her pain.

"Come into the kitchen and let me fix you a plate for lunch."

"I'd like that."

Nancy led Rebecca into the kitchen and saw to it that she ate a good meal. Her mere presence soothed Rebecca's troubled mind, the act of kindness a blessing that saved her from the clutches of grief.

"I never thought I'd lose both Mama and Daddy like this. When you're younger, you see your parents as invincible. You think they'll always be there to pick you up when you fall down. You don't think of losing them."

Rebecca's eyes filled with tears, which she tried to wipe away before Nancy saw them.

"It's okay, honey, don't hide your feelings. If you need to cry, then cry. Get it all out, don't let anything build up inside you so much that you lose the joy of living." Nancy put her hands on top of Rebecca's, and the warmth of compassion flowed into the younger woman's soul.

"When Mama died, my grandmother told me that love would see me through the pain, and it did. But now I don't feel I have that love, or that kind of love, one that's sympathetic. Harbard tries, and I know he loves me, but it's not an understanding or patient love. Sometimes I get the feeling he's more angry at his father than he is concerned for me."

This revelation did not surprise Nancy. She knew that, in time, Harbard would blame his father for J.W.'s death. "Harbard means well, but he's never been one to show much in the way of emotion. And this thing between him and his father is something they'll have to work out. I don't really blame Harbard for feeling the way he does. I expected as much. But the concern here needs to be on you, and how you're doing." Nancy squeezed Rebecca's hand.

Again, tears welled up in Rebecca's eyes. "I need someone to lean on."

"Then lean on me. I'll be more than happy to help you share the load. Tell me anything you need to; don't be afraid of being honest." Nancy looked deeply into Rebecca's eyes. "Whatever it is you feel toward Ezra, talk it out, it won't upset me."

Rebecca sighed, relieved. The one thing she feared most was no longer at issue. "I'm not putting all the blame on Ezra for what happened. Daddy knew the risks and went anyway. What angered me the most was Ezra's attitude about the whole thing. He didn't appear to be very remorseful when he showed up at the door that night. He acted annoyed at having to come by the house to tell me what happened. He was very matter-of-fact, very cold."

Rebecca looked away, afraid that she had hurt Nancy's feelings after all. But her conscience was clear, she had told the truth.

"That's just the way Ezra is. I'm not making excuses for him, mind you, I'm just saying that's the way he is. Whatever you feel toward him will not come between you and me."

For a moment, the image of Rebecca's grandmother sat across the table from her. She was embraced by a feeling of unconditional love. "It feels good to have a parent again."

When Harbard came home that evening, Nancy was busily preparing dinner. The smell of baked ham and sweet potato pie greeted him as he entered the back door. The sight of Nancy cooking his dinner reminded Harbard of his upbringing, how it was his mother who was always there for him. Next to Rebecca, she was the only person he truly loved.

"How's Rebecca?"

"She's doing a little better. I got her to eat a pretty good lunch and she stayed out of bed most of the afternoon, but then she took a bath and decided to lie down again." Nancy basted the ham.

"I'm glad you were here. I know it meant a lot to Rebecca . . . and to me."

"It meant a lot to me, too, son. Rebecca needs all the support we can give her right now, and if that means I need to be here every day for however long it takes, then so be it. Go wash up, dinner will be ready soon."

Harbard smiled to himself. He had heard those very words spoken by his mother when he was a child. For a moment, it was as if nothing had ever changed in his life. He was the child who needed nurturing, and his mother was there to provide it.

Nancy appeared distracted over dinner, running her fork through the peas and corn over and over again. It was somewhat comical to him, a sign he had learned over the years that she was troubled. It used to irritate his father enormously, which, to Harbard, made it all the more comical.

"You're not walking home this late, are you?"

Nancy shook her head as she took a bite of sweet potato pie. "Mr. Jackson next door said he'd give me a ride in his cotton wagon if I'd share some of the onions and turnips with him next year."

"Good, I don't much like the idea of you on the road by yourself after dark." Harbard reached for a piece of pie.

"Well, heavens, Harbard, who do you think is going to bother me if I did walk home?"

"You never know. Some of those 'shiners might be out there looking to hurt somebody after what happened, losing one of their own, or some of J.W.'s family might be angry enough to get back at Daddy."

Harbard's words hit Nancy squarely in the face.

"What do you mean?" Nancy's voice rose sharply.

"It's nothing to get overly concerned about, Mama, but I've heard that some people are holding Daddy responsible for J.W.'s death. You know how people are, it's probably just talk. And I don't think anybody in this county has the nerve to stand toe-to-toe with Daddy."

"I should hope not. What your father did might have been careless, but it wasn't intentional. And that's something I want to talk to you about, Harbard. This feud between you and your father has got to stop, at least until Rebecca is back to her old self again."

Harbard knew his mother was serious. She had a habit of tapping her hand on the table to accentuate her words.

"I can't make any promises, but I'll try. It's my feeling that Rebecca wouldn't be in this fix if it weren't for Daddy. He was so damn arrogant when he came over that night. He talked to Rebecca like he was telling her about a complete stranger." Harbard's face turned red.

"Be that as it may, son, you've got to let go of it for Rebecca's sake. You need to concentrate on her needs, and she needs sympathy, understanding, and a whole lot of love. Now, you think about what's more important to you, a fight with your father or your love for your wife."

Darkness crept over the road as the late December sun settled behind the horizon. Ezra stood on the front porch, his arms folded, a scowl on his face. He could not imagine where his wife might be.

Mr. Jackson's wagon made its final turn onto the Old Church Road. Nancy glanced toward her house and saw Ezra's silhouette against the twilight. She'd seen him in that position enough times to know he was angry.

"Where have you been?" Ezra's tone was cold.

"I spent the day with Rebecca. She's been having a tough time since J.W. died." Nancy breezed past Ezra and into the house.

"Where's my dinner?" Ezra followed closely on her heels.

"It's in my hands, Ezra. I brought you a plate."

"I suppose you told her it was my fault that J.W. got killed."

Nancy turned quickly to face Ezra, anger emanating from her eyes. "I did nothing of the sort. I went over there to be of help to someone who's been forced to her bed because of grief. I went over there to be a friend and a mother, to show her that somebody cares."

"And to take your son's side as always!"

Ezra's comment tore at Nancy's spirit. "Think what you will, Ezra, at this point I really don't care. I wish the two of you would settle your differences behind the barn and leave everyone else out of it."

Nancy stormed out of the kitchen, leaving Ezra in a state of dumbfounded confusion. She returned almost as soon as she had left, carrying a set of fresh linens in her arms.

"Where are you going with that?" Ezra's patience ran thin.

"To the guest room. That's where I'll be until your attitude changes."

"Have you lost your senses?"

"What I've lost is my patience with an arrogant, insensitive man. If you must know, Ezra, I told Harbard that he should set aside his feud with you and look after his wife. I'm not taking sides with anyone except Rebecca."

True to her word, Nancy moved into the guest room and remained there. She had lived with Ezra's shortcomings for years, but never had she seen such a callous side of him. As she stood in the middle of the room holding the set of linens, she realized that she was entering a new phase of her life, one that relied heavily upon knowing her strengths and sticking to her convictions.

TWELVE

Life did not live Ezra Smith. He lived life, always in control, always fearless. If a mountain had to be climbed, he climbed it. Worry was as foreign to him as the distant planets spinning in the universe. Nothing or no one dared confront him, let alone challenge him. Only something beyond his sphere of control could hint at intimidation.

There was a growing resentment directed at him, and he felt it like the wind blowing against his back. Many blamed him for J.W.'s death, a knowledge that made him moodier than usual, more on edge. The questions about his wisdom and integrity gnawed away at his psyche like a mound of termites on a wooden frame. Nancy let him alone, passing it off as another one of his mood swings. Only when she heard the rumors herself did she understand Ezra's mood.

Nancy chuckled aloud when she finally reached Jack's store. She'd become so preoccupied with her thoughts she completely forgot about purchasing flour and yeast and had to backtrack from the old clapboard building where the season's cotton was weighed. She entered from the breezeway at the back of the store where the feed was kept. What she heard made her stop dead in her tracks.

"I tell ya, it's gonna happen. Someone is going after Ezra," Claude, J.W.'s cousin, whispered to the others.

Wesley echoed his older brother's warnings. "There's a lot of angry people out there, and those that aren't angry are being made angry by David. He won't let his father die without some kind of revenge."

Jack was alarmed but not altogether surprised. "Well, seeing that you two are in the family, I'd think someone would have a talk with that boy. You just don't go around threatening to kill someone, especially if that someone is a man of the law. I'll admit, what happened was tragic, but it doesn't call for another life."

"I think it's too late for that, Jack. Things have already been set into motion. It's gonna happen."

Claude's words were definite. Jack shifted uneasily from one foot to the other. Idle threats were one thing, but an actual plan to kill someone was criminal. "Fellas, this is crazy. Something's got to be done, someone should warn Ezra!"

"He probably knows it. You know how he is, always one step ahead of everybody else."

"Yeah, but still–" Jack pleaded.

"You can tell him if you want to, just don't tell him who told ya. I don't want to get caught up in the middle of this."

"I won't mention any names, Claude. I just think the man deserves to know what's up so he can defend himself."

"Do what you gotta do, Jack. Just be careful. David's crazy, you know."

The words knifed through the air, pinning Nancy against a wall of fear. Jack's sudden presence startled her.

"I stopped by to get some flour and yeast." Nancy caught her breath.

"Irene will help you. I've got some business to attend to out back." Jack hurriedly excused himself.

Nancy left the store in a state of near panic, the sack of flour and yeast dragging along the ground. *How many people knew of the plot? Would David really carry out his threat? Should she tell Ezra what she learned?*

Rebecca awoke with a start, a strong feeling of doom fresh on her mind. She couldn't put her finger on it, but things were definitely not as they should be. She'd dreamed wildly that night, her mind racing at the speed of light from one thought to the next. She felt her spirit leaving her body and traveling down a long, dark path. At the end was a gateway of brilliant light.

She marveled at the intensity of the beautiful, white light. It covered and embraced her, surrounding her with bright colors, especially green, that were unlike anything she'd ever seen. She traveled through an archway and saw her father sitting next to a flowing fountain. He motioned for her to sit next to him.

He was dressed in what appeared to be a long, white robe and leather sandals, his face full of love and peace, his beaming smile engaging Rebecca to smile in return. As she sat next to him, she found herself mesmerized by his hair. It was a perfect, pure white.

"Don't be sad, Rebecca. It's time you stopped grieving for me." His voice was loving and compassionate.

"I can't help it, Daddy. I miss you so much. Every day I think about you, and it makes my heart sad. I wish you were with me again." Rebecca started to cry.

"I am with you. I'm always with you; when you wake up in the morning, when you watch the sun set, when you're working in the garden, when you sleep. I'm very happy where I am, Rebecca, this is where I want to be."

The sincerity and warmth from J.W.'s message calmed Rebecca's emotions.

"I'm happy for you, Daddy. And as long as I know you're happy, then I won't grieve so much. But I will always miss you."

Suddenly, Rebecca had the feeling that time was running short, that her visit into the other side, while seemingly timeless, was ending all too soon. She wanted to cling to this moment, to transcend dimensions and remain in this place. As she slowly drifted toward consciousness, J.W. left her with a parting request.

"David needs guidance. He's a ship lost at sea with no direction. Watch over him, Rebecca, be his anchor in life."

J.W. looked tenderly into his daughter's face, smiling proudly before drifting away. Rebecca quickly re-entered the tunnel, as if drawn by a vacuum. Her spirit traversed the darkness like a lightning bolt. She awoke as if she'd been asleep for days, but the impact of the experience was fresh on her mind.

She knew David, her younger brother, was high-strung, but he'd always been able to take care of himself. He did things his way, regardless of societal acceptance. He wouldn't take advice from her, or anyone else for that matter. He marched to the beat of a different drummer. From the day he was born, he did what he wanted, whether his parents approved or not. It was as if he was born with an innate set of morals and principles, his own code of behavior.

As he grew older, David's reliance upon the unexpected grew to extremes. He reveled in his bizarre behavior and the increasingly severe punishments his father meted out. When he was eight years old, David startled his teacher and classmates by sneaking a loaded pistol onto the playground and shooting birds and squirrels out of an oak tree. He was suspended for his actions and beaten by his father, but the controversy only seemed to fuel the fire inside him.

Many of those who knew David were afraid of him. His eyes made them uneasy. Hazel in color, though sometimes turning an eerie shade of bright yellow, they lacked feeling and compassion. When he looked at someone, it was like he was looking at a dying tree or a weather-beaten fence. He could not distinguish between what was human and what wasn't.

After J.W.'s death, David grieved more for the insult than for the loss of his father, convinced that his father's death was an act of purposeful neglect, an act indirectly aimed at himself. He retreated into a world of suspicion and anger, vindictiveness and revenge. He had only one purpose, avenging his father's death.

David familiarized himself with Ezra's routine, watching his every move, knowing where Ezra was from the time he rode into town in the morning until he entered his house after sunset.

The strange dream bothered Rebecca all day, occupying her thoughts well into the late afternoon. She peered out the kitchen window, the pane of glass still covered with frost, creating patterns of tiny lines that looked like intricate stitches of lace. She looked through them, wondering what could be happening.

The walls of the kitchen closed in upon her, the air stagnant from the heat of the wood-burning stove. She choked on the heavy-laden air. Despite the chores awaiting her, she donned a heavy coat and walked outside into the brisk morning air, standing in the brightness of the sun, admiring the winter sky and wisps of cold-weather clouds that danced upon the atmosphere.

The bright green mattress of winter grass blanketed the garden. A sense of peace settled over her as she strolled down the vacant lot. Her father's voice, giving instruction, echoed down the rows of mounded dirt, his strong face sweating in the heat of the late spring sun. She felt as close to him here as she did in the dream the night before.

She closed her eyes and listened to the sound of the wind blowing through the naked limbs of the pecan trees that bordered the alleyway behind the house, hearing in their rhythms the sound of angels speaking. In the midst of the brightness, she again saw the figure of her father, bathed in the glorious light. He reached out to her, the aura from his hands caressing her face.

"Rebecca?"

The sound of her name pleased Rebecca. "Yes, Father."

"Rebecca, it's me—Nancy." She touched Rebecca's shoulder from behind.

Slowly, Rebecca opened her eyes, the tranquility lingering in her heart. "I'm sorry, Nancy. I must've been daydreaming." Rebecca hugged her mother-in-law.

"You looked like you were a million miles away."

Rebecca smiled to herself. "I think I was."

"It's good to see you outside the house again."

"It's good to be alive again. I can't wait for spring to get here. It'll be nice to work in the garden again, I feel close to Daddy here."

Rebecca surveyed the field, finding irony in the bright green of the winter grass, the only sign of life in the otherwise decayed garden.

Nancy stayed with Rebecca all day, choosing to walk home before the sun made its last descent into the western sky. She found herself looking over her shoulder as she walked home, feeling that hundreds of eyes were watching her every step from the face of the woods.

The empty house provided her with little comfort or security, accentuating her vulnerability, defenseless against the faceless phantom that haunted her thoughts. She latched the door behind her and peered warily out the front window, certain that someone was watching her.

She waited nervously at the table, unable to eat until Ezra was safe at home. The minutes ticked by like hours, the waiting tested her sanity. *What if something had already happened? What if this would-be assassin had carried out his plan?*

Suddenly, a loud knock erupted at the back door. Her body froze. The knocking sounded again, this time louder than before. Her mind raced furiously. Ezra had several guns in the house, but she had no idea if they were loaded or where she would find the ammunition. The knocking sounded again, this time from the front door, followed by Ezra's booming voice.

"What the hell you got the house all locked up for? Didn't you hear me banging on the door back there?" Ezra practically barked at his wife as she let him inside.

"I got scared so I locked the doors." Nancy locked the door again as she closed it behind Ezra.

"Scared of what?" Ezra's voice was tinged with condescension.

Nancy shrugged her shoulders. "I don't know, maybe nothing at all, maybe something."

He turned to Nancy as he washed his hands in the sink. "What are you talking about?"

"I heard something in town today that scared me." She sat next to Ezra.

"What'd you hear?" Ezra nonchalantly filled his plate.

She couldn't find the right words to explain the incomprehensible evil that lurked around them. She spoke in as low a voice as she could, as if someone else was in the house listening to her. "I overheard two men talking to Uncle Jack this morning at the store. They were telling him that . . ." She lost her nerve, much to Ezra's growing impatience.

"Telling him what, for Christsakes!"

Ezra's outburst stung her. "Telling him that someone had put a price on your head, that's what!"

Ezra stopped cold, at first stunned by Nancy's knowledge of the threat, but unwilling to show any fear he might harbor. He chewed his food slowly, taking deliberate care to swallow normally.

He drank the remainder of his tea and wiped his face before responding. "You can't believe everything you hear. Most threats don't amount to a hill of beans, especially against someone in my position. Going after the law is suicide, everyone knows that."

Though his words courted bravado, Ezra stayed awake for hours, worried, compiling a mental list of those he thought capable, and willing, of coming after him. The long list included a great many members of the Carter family. The short list included his own son.

THIRTEEN

Harbard awoke earlier than usual, the frigid air invading his sleep, the bed-spread a sheet of patterned ice. He fired up the wood-burning stove and brought in a stack of logs for the fireplace, intending to warm the house before Rebecca arose.

As her emotional condition showed signs of improvement, Harbard's moods followed suit. The sparkle returned to her eyes as well as the nervous energy that kept her busy. It warmed his heart to see her doing the things that made her happy. He vowed to do all within his power to keep things this way.

Rebecca woke from a deep sleep in which she had once again heard her father's pleas about David and, again, was puzzled by its meaning. J.W.'s voice haunted her, so sincere was its concerns, so urgent the cry to action.

The sizzling sounds of frying bacon and ham greeted her as she entered the kitchen. Harbard poured her a cup of coffee.

"Have you talked to your father lately?" Rebecca asked, hesitant.

"No. What do I have to say to him?"

"I just wondered how he was doing." Rebecca sat across the table.

"Who knows? The old buzzard always keeps things to himself. Why are you concerned about Daddy?"

"I didn't say I was concerned." Rebecca already regretted the line of inquisition.

"So what is it then?" Harbard backed off.

Rebecca collected her thoughts. "I have the feeling your father's in some kind of trouble."

"If Daddy's in trouble, he'll find a way out." Harbard dished out the hot, crispy bacon strips.

Again, Rebecca paused. "Just hear me out on this, okay?"

Harbard nodded.

"Daddy's been appearing to me in dreams recently, very intense dreams. He's been trying to warn me about something, and he keeps telling me to watch over David."

Harbard listened intently as he ate breakfast, intrigued by Rebecca's experience.

"You know how David is, and I just get this feeling that he's in some way connected to this warning about Ezra." The implication embarrassed Rebecca.

Harbard analyzed the situation, giving credence and respect to his wife's story. "I'll be honest with you, Rebecca. I've heard that somebody might be out to get Daddy. Some people are real upset about what happened. And David's right in the thick of things."

Rebecca sighed heavily. "I can't take any more of this, Harbard. I'd talk to David myself if I thought he'd listen to reason, but he won't." She lowered her eyes. "I've found my peace with Daddy's death. I don't want to lose that."

The energy ebbing away from Rebecca's soul reached out to Harbard. He grasped it with all his might. "I'll have a talk with David. If anyone can make him see the light of day, it's me." He held Rebecca's hand in his and looked deeply into her eyes. "Don't you worry yourself, everything's gonna be just fine."

David camped out across from the county jail, a position he'd held every morning for the past two weeks as Ezra made his ride into town. Leaning against the hitching post outside Jack's feed store, David eyed the corner of Main and Central, peering under the brim of his hat, his hand resting upon the holster that housed a six-shooter, the hint of a maniacal grin, waiting and watching. Harbard sidled up to the younger man.

"Cold enough for ya?" Harbard stood next to David, his presence ignored. "What're you doing in town so early?"

"I got my reasons," David answered gruffly.

Harbard stood closer to him, close enough to whisper in his ear. "Listen to me and listen good. Any score you feel you need to settle with my daddy has to go through me first. I don't like what happened any more than you do, but this whole thing has torn your sister—my wife—apart. I'll be damned if I'm gonna let anything else torture her like that. If anything happens to my daddy, I'll come after you. And anybody in this county can tell you that I don't miss what I aim at. If you think my daddy's life is worth your own, then go for it. But I'd advise you to watch your every step, and breathe every breath as your last."

Harbard walked away as quietly and unnoticed as he'd appeared. David watched him with a smirk on his face, almost laughing at the threat.

Ezra rounded the corner in time to see Harbard walking away from David. Pulling his horse to a pause, he thought perhaps he had interrupted a meeting of conspirators. He glanced over at David, intentionally making eye contact with him. David facetiously tipped his hat at the older man before jumping astride his horse and arrogantly making his way down the center of town.

Undeterred, Ezra carried out his daily duties, refusing to be intimidated by David's antics. He made his rounds to each of the downtown merchants, his senses on full alert, watching the surroundings carefully, growing eyes in the back of his head as the morning wore on.

Before making his visits to the outlying farms that stretched the length of the county, he made an unplanned stop at the rail yard, speaking briefly with the foreman, Bobby Faulk, while inconspicuously looking for his son. Having eyed Harbard in the office, he excused himself and continued on.

On Tuesdays and Thursdays, Ezra checked on the families down Ten Mile Road, and then followed Willacoochee Creek to the farms near Bowen's Mill on the county's southeast side. He did the same on Mondays and Wednesdays on the west side from Queensland all the way to the Alapaha River. As he completed his run down Ten Mile Road, Ezra turned his horse into the woods that bordered Willacoochee Creek.

Normally, he would ride the edge of the shallow creek up to Bowen's Mill, but the recent rains had filled it all the way up to the embankment, forcing Ezra to ride a trail through the heavily forested woods. His encounter with David earlier in the day flashed through his mind.

Though he was less than a mile from Bowen's Mill, Ezra felt uneasy. His sixth sense alarmed him to potential danger. Instinctively, he slowed his horse. A heavy breeze blew through the thick pines, swirling through the woods like winding fingers poised to grip Ezra from the saddle of his horse. He listened for sounds of danger: footsteps, breathing, the click of a trigger.

His breathing rate dropped, his body on shut-down as if he had become one with the forest, as if he was a part of every tree around him, able to see all that was inside the woods. As he searched the area with his senses, he heard a faint noise, the snapping of a small twig. From the direction of the noise, he determined that it was to his right and behind him about thirty to forty feet. One hand held tightly to the reins while the other slowly gripped his rifle.

He heard a second faint noise, the crunching of leaves or dead pine needles. A pair of eyes burrowed into his back and the aim of a gun pointed directly at him. Suddenly, a shot rang out. The noise pierced the air like a hysterical scream. The bullet shattered a small limb less than six inches from his head.

The precision of the shot scared Ezra to his bones. Anyone with that kind of marksmanship could have easily killed him. He kicked the horse violently, the nimble beast shot through the woods as if out of a cannon. Within minutes he was at Bowen's Mill, out of danger, safe in the warmth of the noonday sun, leaving the incident, as well as the identity of his potential assailant, in the confines of the forest.

Harbard checked his pocket watch. The afternoon was crawling along at a snail's pace. It had been a strange day. He wanted to go home.

When the six o'clock bell rang, he wasted no time getting his things together. Some of his buddies joked that he had a woman on the side, poking fun at their quiet, faithful buddy. But Harbard wasn't in a joking mood. As he scrubbed the worst of the grease from his hands and forearms, he noticed his father wrapping up a chat with Bobby.

"In a hurry to get out of here, are ya?" Bobby chuckled to himself.

"It's been a long day." Harbard remained expressionless.

"I was talking to your father. He said the rains we had pretty much flooded Willacoochee Creek. It was all the way up into some of the pines." Bobby signed the daily log as he spoke.

"Is that what he came over here to talk about?" The sarcasm in Harbard's voice belied his real interest.

"Yeah, that and who stole two chickens from Renfroe's hen house. Say, you weren't out there last night, were ya?" Bobby poked Harbard in the side.

"Can't say that I was, unless I've taken to sleepwalking." Harbard paused for a moment. "What else did Daddy have to say?"

"Not much; asked how things were around here today, if there was anything out of the ordinary." Bobby finished off the log sheet and started to lock up.

"Wonder why he asked that?"

"I couldn't tell ya, Harbard. He's probably just checking on things, you know. He likes to know what's going on."

"I reckon. See you tomorrow, Bobby." Harbard strode out of the office and hurried home, still perplexed by his father's visit.

The sun was setting against a brilliant sky, mixing shades of pink and gold into a spectrum of glorious colors. Rebecca watched the spectacle from the back porch, mesmerized by the beautiful sight.

"Sure is a pretty sight, isn't it?" Harbard spoke quietly as he approached the porch.

"Makes a person's problems seem awfully small. It's seeing something like this that reminds you what life is all about: beauty, serenity, love. And it surely lets us know what's waiting for us when we pass over to the other side."

They stood in the glow of the sunset for several minutes.

"Did you happen to see David today?"

"Yep." Harbard offered little in reply.

"What did you say to him?" Rebecca's face bathed in the light.

"I told him I felt bad about what happened, that you had suffered enough because of it, and that if he had anything to do with getting even with Daddy, I'd come after him."

Harbard's words gave Rebecca solace. She knew her father had intervened and made things right. She wrapped the heavy shawl tightly around her neck and walked inside.

Nancy nervously paced back and forth between the front window and back door, waiting for Ezra. It was long after dark before he got home, and he didn't explain his tardiness. His entire demeanor looked different, his shoulders hunched, his stride unsure and meek, his face as pale as a picket fence. Having no appetite, he stretched out on the bed until sunrise.

The incident in the forest remained unknown to all but its two participants. Ezra never spoke a word of it to anyone, he didn't have to, he knew who did it and why. If he suspected anyone other than David Carter, he'd confront that person and bully a confession. But in this case, it was wiser to leave things as they were, no harm done. But he never knew that it was Harbard who had saved his life.

Shortly after the attack on Ezra, David headed west, lured by tales of fortunes made on discovered gold. He drifted from town to town, usually stirring up trouble in his wake. No one in the family knew where he was or what he was doing, if he was in jail or six feet under. It was two years after his departure that Rebecca learned of his death, shot in the back during a barroom brawl.

For his years of dedication and service, Ezra received a gold pocket watch, which he carried with him until the day he died. He spent his retirement in virtual solitude, alienated by those who held him accountable for J.W.'s death and distanced from others whom he felt unworthy of his time. His one outlet in life, the seeming reason for existence in his twilight years, was an almost daily venture into town to berate his successor.

"Mr. McInnis said he hasn't seen you around lately. What've you been doing with yourself?" Ezra's voice boomed through the front door as he entered the Sheriff's office.

"Workin'," Harbard answered without looking up as he continued cleaning his rifle.

"You gotta keep up with people to know what's going on, son. Circulate in the community, visit with the merchants, chat with your neighbors. Some of your best leads come from idle conversation. That's how I cracked many a case in my time. You gotta be aggressive, get out there and stir up the fire!" Ezra's face turned red as he whipped himself into a frenzy.

"I got the fire just how I like it, simmering away just fine. If it starts dyin' out, I'll add another log." Harbard inadvertently pointed the rifle at his father.

Ezra grabbed the barrel and swung it away. "So now you're aiming your weapons at innocent people! Good God, boy, if you don't know the difference between innocent and guilty, this county's in a heap of trouble! Why, Old Lady Purvence would make a better lawman than you . . . and she's practically senile!"

"I'll check and see if she's interested in the job." Harbard put the gun back in its rack and looked squarely into his father's eyes. "If you'll excuse me, I'm going to lunch." He brushed past his father, leaving the older man in a fit of rage.

"And this county is going to hell in a hand basket! Whatever possessed me into thinking you'd make a decent lawman is beyond me now!"

Ezra followed Harbard out of the office, slamming the door behind him. The drama played on down Central Avenue and into Josephine's diner, where the matinee abruptly ended when Harbard threatened to arrest his father for disturbing the peace. Temporarily thwarted, yet undeterred in the long-running battle for superiority, Ezra stalked down the road, his mind racing for yet another fight on another day.

The passing of spring into summer healed the wounds of winter. It was a time for renewal and new beginnings, a time for breaking from the past and traveling new paths of life. What was once a reality was now a distant memory. The changing of the seasons stands still for no one, and pauses only long enough for momentary reflections.

Rebecca's hopes and dreams slowly, but surely, became reality. By the end of the year, she was expecting a child. Etta was born in May of 1896, followed two years later by William, and three years after that by Martin.

Of the children, William was most like his father, the similarity noticeable early on. He was aloof, stubborn, and resentful of discipline. The close ties to his father's own personality set up a conflict that intensified as the young boy grew into adolescence. Harbard was as tough on William as Ezra had been with him. He instilled within William a duty to fail, that everything accomplished in life must meet with some exacted cost.

The circle, at last, was nearing completion. As Ezra had alienated himself from Harbard, so Harbard would do with William.

FOURTEEN

THREE YEARS HAD PASSED SINCE Leola and her children left Porterdale, the void of their loss compounded by Rachel's death, her heart broken from the strain of loss. Drastic change entered the lives of many, dispersing them, relocating, returning, starting over, beginning anew. For John and Susie Floyd, the interim period of time brought mixed blessings. They had their fourth child in 1910, a son they named Paul. The welcoming of life, though joyous, was difficult for Susie Floyd, complicated by severe stomach cramps in her seventh month, forcing her to bed.

She hemorrhaged profusely throughout the delivery. Currents of blood soaked through the sheets and towels, flowing onto the hands and arms of Doc Pritchard and his wife, Clara, like currents of crimson streams. Susie Floyd drifted in and out of consciousness, the searing pain hidden behind hallucinations of events long passed. Clara kept a cold compress on her patient's head, holding her hand, praying for relief. As the hours dragged on, the situation worsened, and the room became suffocating with fear.

Clara propped several pillows under Susie Floyd's head to keep her from passing out, shouting encouragement for Susie Floyd to breathe, to push, to survive. But the more Susie Floyd tried, the more intense became the pain. Suddenly, the infant began to emerge, a tiny foot protruded from the birth canal.

Cursing under his breath, Doc reached inside the birth canal, trying desperately to turn the infant. Clara followed his motion on Susie Floyd's belly. They urged Susie Floyd to fight, to endure. Her screams were music to their ears; she was fighting. Finally, Doc felt the head. It moved into place with blessed ease. In what seemed like seconds after ten agonizing hours, Paul was born.

The ordeal shook Doc Pritchard to his core. Clara made him a potion of hot tea and sassafras to calm his frayed nerves. He surveyed the room; blood soaked through the linens as if buckets of plasma had been deliberately poured onto the bed. Susie Floyd rested comfortably, her breathing normal and her pulse only slightly higher than it had been. Clara stayed with her through the night.

The physical and emotional ordeal exhausted Susie Floyd, confining her to bed for several weeks, able to do little more than hold her newborn infant for agonizingly short periods of time. John remained at her side as often as he could, but the burden of her care fell upon the shoulders of Nellie, the eldest, herself a child of thirteen.

Susie Floyd's strength returned slowly, too slowly for her agenda. She forced herself to do as many chores as possible, even though the slightest effort took its toll. She was restless, angry, eager to resume her duties as wife and mother. At times she nearly fainted from the exertion, requiring extended periods of rest that only fueled the fire within her to do more. Nellie worried over her mother, fearful that she would collapse and not awaken. She mentioned her concerns to Doc Pritchard. It was time, he thought, to have a frank discussion with his patient.

"I'm not going to beat around the bush," Doc began. "If you want to see your children grow into adulthood, then you've got to slow down and take it easy for a while. You lost a lot of blood, you're weak, and your body needs time to build itself back up."

"I can't just sit around and do nothing. My family needs me," Susie Floyd pleaded.

"How can you help them if you're dead? I'm telling you, this is serious. You might not wake up from one of those fainting spells."

"Who said I was fainting?"

"That doesn't matter."

"I haven't fainted!" she cried.

Doc shrugged his shoulders. "The choice is yours. You can die today, tomorrow, or the day after. It's up to you."

Susie Floyd visibly shrank from Doc Pritchard's bluntness, beaten by the seriousness of the situation. Pulling the covers around her shoulders, she resigned herself to the inevitable.

"There's something else I want to talk with you about."

"I don't think I'm strong enough to hear any more." Her voice was laced with sarcasm.

"You're strong enough to hear this. Are you listening?" He spoke to her as if she were a child being reprimanded by an angry parent.

"Yes, I'm listening." Her response in turn was childlike, rebuking his tone.

"I don't think you should risk another pregnancy. You'd not only endanger your life, but the life of your child as well. I don't mind telling you now, but I was plenty worried during that delivery. I didn't know if either of you would survive."

"This isn't something I want to discuss right now." She turned away.

"I'm sure it isn't, but I want you to understand what I'm telling you. You might not be so fortunate next time."

Susie Floyd continued her silence, pretending to be asleep, hoping Doc Pritchard would go away. She tried to block his words from her mind; after all, they were only words.

"I'll make sure John knows the seriousness of this matter. You get some rest. I'll check on you tomorrow." Doc Pritchard looked at her tired face, a tinge of sorrow in his heart.

The monotony of the days drove Susie Floyd to distraction. Nellie brought Paul in for short visits in the morning and afternoon, the only part of the day Susie Floyd looked forward to and, ironically, the part she most dreaded. She couldn't bear the thought of being unable to care for her newborn child.

Susie Floyd defined herself by what she did and what she was capable of doing; there was no such word as "weakness" in her vocabulary. She never doubted that she would have less than six or seven children. The thought of having a smaller family was as alien to her as money in the bank.

A year after Paul's birth, she became pregnant again, though she kept the condition to herself. The news would only upset the family and incur the wrath of Doc Pritchard. Undaunted, she determined to present herself as strong and healthy, quite capable of delivering another child.

The cramping and indigestion started earlier with this pregnancy, and with more severity. At times it felt as if her insides were twisting and turning and exchanging places. She briefly entertained the thought that this pregnancy had been a mistake, but quickly pushed it from her mind.

When labor began, Doc Pritchard and Clara prayed silently for mercy. Immediately, however, Doc knew there would be trouble. Susie Floyd bled profusely; the river of blood threatened to suffocate the unborn child if not delivered in time. Sweat poured down Doc's weary face, his heart racing as if he'd run a marathon. The baby was breech.

He looked at Clara with terror in his eyes. They were bound to lose either mother or child or both. The heavy, musky smell of blood and birth fluid spun around the room. Doc doubled over in pain. Clara assumed control, attempting to turn the baby despite the tide of blood hampering her efforts. Susie Floyd's screams subsided to moans and, eventually, to silence.

At last, the baby was delivered, a girl. She was immediately cleaned, her mouth and air passages cleared of blood. She appeared healthy, a miraculous feat considering what she'd been through. Doc Pritchard checked Susie Floyd's vital signs. They were alarmingly weak, the bleeding constant. At half past six, Susie Floyd's heart stopped beating.

FIFTEEN

Finally, summer arrived. The air hung close to the ground, trapping the smells of ripened corn and gardenia blossoms. Along with springtime, it was the season of the year Leola loved the most. The warm weather enticed her to venture outdoors for long walks around the countryside. Budding pecan trees lined the dirt road north of Little Bear Creek, providing homes for hundreds of squirrels that scampered noisily from tree to tree. She watched their playful bickering with glee. It was a cautiously happy time, the first she'd known since Luther's death.

She'd built a fragile stability for herself and her daughters. Though her father was still prone to mood swings and bouts of despair, he tempered his emotions with a newly found respect for his daughter. She worked in the fields at her father's side until he was able to find experienced help, but even then, she continued the work two or three days a week. Hard labor was good for her resolve.

The years of bitterness and abuse were beginning to tell on Elizabeth. She aged considerably, worry lines creased her forehead, dark circles outlined her eyes, denial and acceptance her constant companions. Though she dared not admit at first that Leola and the children brought any joy into her life, their presence was the lifeline she had longed for.

Leola swept the porch on a bright, windy day while Leanice and Lou hosted an outdoor soirée for an assortment of dolls. She felt someone behind her, staring over her. Turning, she saw her mother watching the children with a wistful, melancholic look.

"Is something wrong, Mama?" Leola asked quietly.

"I used to play house when I was a little girl, underneath a pecan tree just like that one. I pretended that I would have many suitors one day, but only one who would sweep me off my feet and carry me away." Her voice trailed off.

Leola studied her mother carefully, never having seen vulnerability in her until this moment.

"I apologize for everything, Leola. I wish you'd had better parents, ones that wouldn't have been afraid to show you love. You were a pretty child, looked just like my grandmother . . . " Her voice faded with emotion.

"Mama, you don't have to—" Leola interjected, but Elizabeth cut her off.

"I want to. Lord knows, you have a right to know." Her face turned soft, the hint of a smile on her face. "When I was sixteen, I was in love with a boy from the church. Hank was his name. Oh, he was a handsome thing, beautiful eyes and the prettiest smile I've ever seen." She paused momentarily, recalling the face she loved to this day.

"He loved me, too, and I wanted to marry him. But Mama and Daddy wouldn't hear of it. They'd already made arrangements for me to marry your father. We're distant cousins, you know, and all our parents could think about was keeping their precious property within the family." Her face tightened, showing signs of anger that lingered within her.

"Mama was so rude to Hank the last time I saw him. It was after church. He and I were talking when she walked up behind me. She told him I was to be married to Zach Cowan, and that any properly engaged young lady shouldn't consort with unmarried gentlemen." Her tone mocked that of her mother.

"She said that deliberately to hurt him. I could see how devastated he was. That killed me, plain and simple. I never saw him again after that day. I heard he died the following year . . . killed himself."

Tears formed in Elizabeth's eyes. Leola choked back tears of her own.

"Hank was my knight in shining armor, and when he went away, so did all my feelings for life. It was unfair of me to take that out on you just because you weren't Hank's child. You were so innocent." Elizabeth wiped tears from her face.

"When you brought Luther home to meet us, I was beside myself with jealousy. You were strong enough to choose the man you loved, and I wasn't. I'm very sorry he was taken away from you, Leola, I truly am." A fragile smile lightened Elizabeth's face as she watched the girls play.

"I can see a father's love in those little girls, Leola. You picked a fine man. Judging from Lou, I'd say he was quite a charmer. She does take after him, doesn't she?"

"Yes, she does."

"I thought so. Leanice is her mother's child and Lou her father's."

"That's what people tell me." Leola looked over at the children.

"Hank would've liked Luther." Elizabeth looked at her daughter, prompting Leola to look up.

"Perhaps they've met in some corner of heaven," Leola said softly.

"Wherever there's joy, and laughter." Elizabeth smiled demurely and rested her hand on Leola's arm.

It was a moment Leola had waited for since she was born, a moment of genuine affection from mother to daughter. All the years of anguish seemed to fade away, leaving behind a mutual feeling of love and loss between two survivors. The sounds of the children's laughter echoed around the yard, encircling Elizabeth and Leola with the promise of new beginnings.

Zach saw the two men approaching from a distance. A cloud of orange dust trailed behind them as they rode toward the house. One of the men looked like Harbard, but the other man was unknown to Zach. He hurriedly made his way to the house and stood by the front porch.

Leola carried an armload of rugs to the clothesline. She, too, studied the men as they turned off the road. She knew one of them to be the deputy sheriff; the other one, at first glance, bore a striking resemblance to Luther's brother, John. She hung the rugs on the clothesline and beat them with a heavy, rounded wire, watching the men from the corner of her eye as they dismounted their horses and talked to her father.

The stranger shook hands with Zach then looked over at Leola. Nervously, she turned her back and vigorously pounded the rugs, stepping between them to block her view of the men. The stranger walked toward her, calling her name as he approached. Through a rising plume of dust, she saw that it was indeed her brother-in-law.

It seemed a lifetime ago since she'd last seen John. But seeing him brought back many memories, and with them a distinct longing to return to the way of life she'd known as Luther's wife. Zach offered Harbard a glass of tea while Leola and John strolled down the road, catching up on times past and present.

"I guess you heard that Mama died." John spoke quietly, his voice lined with sorrow.

"Yes, Susie Floyd sent me a wire. I wanted to attend the funeral, but I couldn't leave the girls alone in new surroundings, you understand." Leola looked at John.

"Of course. We didn't expect you to be there, we just wanted you to know about Mama. She really loved you."

"And I loved her. She inspired me every day that I knew her. She had many burdens resting on her shoulders but never once complained." Leola cried silently.

They walked in silence for several minutes. Leola had the feeling John wanted to talk about something specifically, he was tense, she thought, even sad. Feeling his predicament, she picked up with idle conversation.

"How are Susie Floyd and the children?" Leola asked naively.

"The children are fine. We had two more since you left, a boy and a girl. We named them Paul and Lily." John choked.

Leola placed her hand on his arm as he broke down, stopping by the side of the road near a field of wild dandelions. He tried to hide his tears from Leola as best he could, but the emotions were too strong.

"I lost Susie Floyd six months ago. She died giving birth to Lily. Doc Pritchard told her not to have any more children after Paul, but she wouldn't listen. She convinced me she was fine and that Paul's birth was just one of those rare things that happen from time to time. I knew what Doc Pritchard told her, but she said she knew herself better than he did and . . ." Again, John broke down.

Leola put her arm around him as he rested his head upon her shoulder. She knew his pain, and let him use her strength as long as he needed. Eventually, he composed himself, and they continued walking.

"I've got five children to take care of. Nellie's been doing the cooking and cleaning, and Susie Floyd's sister, Effie, has been looking after the baby. But they need a full-time mother."

Suddenly, Leola realized what was troubling John, what he had been unable to express before.

"I'm going to move the children down here. I think it would be good for us to get a fresh start in new surroundings."

"What about your farm, and your house?" Leola was surprised by the news.

"I sold my share of the land to my brothers, and Bob's family is moving into the house. That money is helping me move down here."

Leola was shocked that John would leave his home, but at the same time, she could understand why he would want to leave a place that held sad memories for him. What she missed least about Porterdale were the constant reminders that Luther had once lived there.

"Do you have something lined up here?" Leola asked without attempting to pry.

"We have some land down here. My granddaddy and Harbard's granddaddy were brothers, and they passed along the land to their sons. But my daddy chose to stay in North Georgia, and Harbard's daddy didn't want it, so they let sharecroppers live there and raise corn." John picked a weed and chewed on its stem.

"I talked to Ezra about the land, and he said I could farm it if I wanted to. It hasn't been touched in over a year." John's emotions settled down.

"The only problem is that the old house has practically fallen apart. But Harbard told me about an empty house only a mile from the farm that I could get for a song. I looked at it today, and I think it'll work out."

Leola nodded her head.

"All that's needed to complete the picture is to find a mother for my children." John blushed. "I know this is sudden but I was wondering . . . well, with you needing a father for your children and me needing a mother for mine, if you'd be interested in getting married and taking care of each other's needs." John looked down.

Leola paused before answering, more out of respect for John's bashfulness than her own need to deliberate his proposal. She stopped next to a magnificent wisteria, which had overtaken the trunk of a dead oak tree. John stood a few feet away, digging the heel of his shoe into the ground. Leola gazed over the climbing purple vine and spoke as if she were addressing it instead of John.

"It's strange, isn't it? How things turn out, I mean. I never thought Luther would be taken away from me so soon. I built my life around him, and then he was gone. And I ended up right back where I started." Leola cleared her throat.

"My girls need stability, as do your children. I think this would be a good solution for all of us. I can't promise to love you like I loved Luther, and I don't expect you to love me like you loved Susie Floyd, but we could have a happy family, I truly believe that."

John looked over Leola's shoulder at the wisteria, as if confirming the proposal and their commitment to family. For the first time in months, he allowed himself to see hope.

SIXTEEN

L EOLA KEPT THE ENGAGEMENT secret after John left, not for concern of the sudden-ness of the proposal or for marrying her late husband's brother, but instead for how her departure would affect Elizabeth. As the date of John's arrival drew nearer, her nervous energies exploded. She busied herself with menial chores, performing the same task over and over again without realizing what she was doing. At night, she could not sleep, tossing and turning until the light of dawn peered over the horizon.

After days of worrying, she took the first step into her new life. She woke the girls early Friday morning and dressed them for a trip into town. They caught a ride with Mr. Sheffield, an elderly neighbor who had a routine of swapping tales with his cronies at the blacksmith shop every week. Mr. Sheffield helped the girls into the back of the cart, all the while complimenting their mother on having the prettiest little girls in the county.

Lou stepped and crawled over Leanice at least a dozen times before they crossed the bridge at Little Bear Creek, intent on seeing and hearing everything along the way.

"Good gracious, Lou. I wish you'd stop climbing all over me. Sit still!"

"I can't sit still!" Lou retorted.

"Why? You got ants in your pants?"

"I'm not wearin' pants, I'm wearin' a dress!" Lou answered with dignity.

"I know that, Miss Smart Aleck! It doesn't mean you have to be wearin' pants!" Leanice shot back.

"I can do whatever I want! Daddy told me, 'pretty is as pretty does.' " Lou made a face at Leanice, complete with a protruding lower lip.

"You're vain, Lou."

"I am not!" Lou was indignant.

"You don't even know what it means."

"I do, too!"

"What does it mean?" Leanice asked.

Lou wrinkled her face as she gave the meaning of the word deep thought, knowing all too well that Leanice had the upper hand.

"I'm not tellin'!" Lou plopped herself down.

"It means you're too proud of yourself, and that's a sin. It says so in the Bible."

"You made that up!" Lou pleaded.

"Did not. Ask Mama if you don't believe me."

Lou quickly stood up and tapped her mother on the shoulder, stepping over Leanice in the process. "Mama, Leanice says I'm vain. Am I vain, Mama?" Lou asked, as only a young child could.

"Of course not. Why would your sister call you vain?"

"I don't know. She said it's in the Bible, and I'm too proud of myself." Lou looked down, adding a sorrowful effect to her plight.

"What on earth is going on back here?" Leola addressed her question to Leanice.

"Lou thinks she can do anything she wants to and get away with it! She won't even sit still. I asked her to stop crawling over me, and she wouldn't."

Leola looked at one daughter and then the other before scolding both of them softly. "You two girls must not be very excited about the surprise I have for you, or you wouldn't be squabbling like this."

"Yes we are, Mama!" the girls replied in unison.

"Then sit still and be quiet the rest of the way." Leola eyed both of them.

Mr. Sheffield pulled the cart into town shortly before eight-thirty. Leola and the girls made their way to the Sheriff's Office, where she found her late husband's cousin.

"Mr. Smith? I'm Leola Smith, Zach Cowan's daughter. We met at my father's house a couple of weeks ago." Leola extended her hand.

Harbard stood and shook Leola's hand. He appeared taller to her than the day he and John rode out to the farm. His massive hand engulfed hers.

"How do you do?" Harbard's manner was polite yet gruff. He motioned for Leola to sit down.

"These are my daughters, Leanice and Lou."

Harbard nodded. "What can I do for you, Leola?" He obviously wanted to move the conversation along.

"I was wondering if I could take a look at the house you showed John. I just wanted to see if there was anything I could do to help make it a home for him and the children when they get here." Leola was careful not to say more than she intended.

The girls were surprised to learn their cousins were moving to Fitzgerald. A nagging feeling of dread intensified within Leanice, certain that something monumental was happening, something that would change the course of their lives.

"Sure. It's not far from here, over on Altamaha Street." Harbard grabbed his hat and gun and led the threesome outside.

They walked two blocks due east of the Sheriff's Office before turning south on Altamaha Street, a dusty road populated with numerous pecan and sycamore trees. The distinct odor of the sycamores reminded Leola of Porterdale. The strong, fresh scent infiltrated the town every summer, filling her lungs with nature's own breath.

Only three houses claimed residence on the wide, dusty road, two on the corner and the other about one hundred yards down the road. All three were two-story houses, but only the farthest one had a wrap-around porch with a swing facing the road. It appealed to Leola right away. Its high-pitched roof and picture windows gave it a majestic appearance. A brilliant vine of morning glories climbed a lattice railing on the west side of the porch.

"This is it. I don't think anyone's lived here in a year or so." Harbard opened the front door and escorted them inside.

The house embraced Leola as if a long-lost friend had finally found her after years of separation. She knew this was meant to be; Luther's hand was guiding her destiny.

"It's a beautiful house. I couldn't imagine anyone wanting to leave here." Leola looked around in awe.

"I've got some business to attend to in town; take all the time you want." Harbard excused himself with a tip of his hat.

"Thank you, Harbard. I hope I didn't trouble you too much."

Harbard nodded and closed the door behind him.

Leola wandered throughout the house as if she had lived in it before. The front door led into the living room; off to the side was the master bedroom. A smaller room with large windows separated the master bedroom from the kitchen.

Leanice stood alone in the smaller room while Lou scurried from one room to the next, exploring every crevice and corner. Leola called the girls into the kitchen.

"What do you girls think of the house?" Leola contained her own excitement.

"It's the biggest house I've ever seen! I wanna go upstairs!" Lou raced toward the stairway.

"Not now, Lou. We'll go upstairs in a minute. What do you think, Leanice? You're awfully quiet."

"It's nice." Leanice's low-key response was typical of her.

Leola slowly walked around the kitchen, building the nerve to tell the girls about John. She admonished herself for being so flustered, but for some reason, at this moment, it was difficult for her to find words. She took a deep breath, and then began. "How would you two like to live in this house?" Leola nearly swallowed the question.

Leanice remained stoically silent. Lou climbed up and down the lower steps of the staircase.

"What about Grandma and Grandpa? Who's going to live with them?" Lou finally asked.

"They have each other, honey. And we'll see them often enough." Leola was comforted by Lou's response, though even more concerned about Leanice. "What are you thinking, Leanice. Is something upsetting you?"

The expression on Leanice's face had not changed from the moment she set foot in the house. It was not a look of joy or of anger, but a look of someone resigned to an ignoble fate. Her eyes looked ahead but did not see, her heart beat soundly but did not feel.

"I only want what's best for you, Mama."

Tears welled in Leanice's eyes. Leola rushed to her side. "What's wrong, honey? Talk to me."

"Is Uncle John taking the place of my daddy?"

Leola put her arms around Leanice, her own heart breaking at the sight of this little girl in such pain and confusion. She called Lou over to them, including her in the embrace.

"I want to tell you something. No matter what happens, you know that I love you, and I loved your father very, very much. A day doesn't go by that I don't think about him and miss him. He will always be part of our family." Leola looked into her daughter's faces.

"Aunt Susie Floyd died a few months ago. And now her children, your cousins, have no mother, just like the two of you don't have a father. So your Uncle John and I are going to be married, giving the two of you a father and his children a mother. This doesn't mean that Uncle John is replacing your daddy. Do you understand me? Your daddy will live in your hearts forever, and he will always be your daddy." Leola looked for signs of understanding.

Leanice wiped the tears from her face, keeping her eyes focused on the floor. Her lips trembled as she tried to hold back a rush of revitalized emotion.

Lou rested her hand on Leanice's head, stroking her long hair. "It's okay, Leanice. You'll always have me to play with," Lou spoke softly.

"Will you still love us, Mama, after we move in with Uncle John?" Leanice finally looked at her mother.

"Of course I will, honey. Is that what you're worried about?"

"I don't want to lose you, too."

"You're not losing me, Leanice. Whatever I do in life, I'll do with my two little girls. Nothing will ever change the way I feel about you and your sister . . . nothing." Leola stroked Leanice's cheek.

The room was quiet; only the sound of a lonely mockingbird whistling into the wind penetrated the silence. Leola kissed her daughters on the forehead, calming their remaining fears.

"Mama, can we go upstairs now?" Lou asked.

Leola looked intently at her older daughter. Leanice approved with a demure smile.

Lou raced happily up the stairs, while Leola and Leanice followed hand-in-hand. The second floor was large, with three good-sized bedrooms, two facing the front and one the side. Lou hopped from room to room, while Leanice looked out the picture window that overlooked the front yard. The view was beautiful. A sycamore tree grew next to the window, its branches just out of reach. Leanice felt comfortable in this room; it filled her with peace.

"Mama, can I have this room?" Leanice's voice was barely above a whisper.

"I don't think anybody would mind. We'll let the girls have the front two rooms, and the boys can have the back room. How does that sound?" Leola smiled.

"I'd like that."

The hurdle she'd cleared with her daughters only cleared the way for the next hurdle. Leola's confidence eroded as she approached her parents' house, wishing the entire situation was over with, that she and John were married and living in their new house. The thought of leaving her mother behind clouded the tenuous happiness of moving forward in her life.

"Did you get all your business tended to?" Mr. Sheffield asked, noticing the inner plight of his passenger.

"Yes, I did." Leola folded her hands.

"I make it a habit to go into town every Friday. It's good to have something to look forward to, kind of breaks up the monotony of life."

"I wish my life was monotonous," Leola answered without thinking. She was embarrassed at having exposed her life to a relative stranger.

"Don't think I've met anyone in this part of the country whose life ain't monotonous. You sure you're from around these parts?" Mr. Sheffield's question was somewhat joking.

"Yes. I grew up here, but I lived for several years in Covington and Porterdale."

"I know that area quite well. My wife, my late wife that is, hailed from Eatonton. Pretty country up that way, especially during the change of seasons when the leaves turn."

His reference to the turning of the leaves changed Leola's frame of mind, replacing the anxiety of the moment with the peacefulness of days gone by. She clearly remembered the crisp, north winds of autumn and the breathtaking artistry of the colorful countryside.

"It's a sight to behold. 'God's handiwork' is what my mother-in-law used to call it. I'd like to see it again someday." Leola's mood was wistful.

"You will if you really want to. A person can do anything he sets his mind to," Mr. Sheffield replied matter-of-factly.

"Do you believe that?" Leola asked with reservation.

"I know it."

The girls stayed awake until late in the night talking about the changes taking place in their lives.

"Who do you like better, Nellie or Ruth?" Lou rolled over next to Leanice.

"I like them both the same," Leanice replied sleepily.

"Ruth laughs more, and she's more fun to play with. Nellie's bossy. She always tells me what to do," Lou stated with certainty.

"That's because she's more mature."

"What's mature?" Lou struggled with the word.

"It means she's more like a grown-up."

"Oh." Lou thought for a moment. "Is Uncle John bossy?"

"Nellie isn't bossy, Lou. She's just more grown up than we are." Leanice turned on her side, away from Lou.

"Is Mama going to have another baby?"

Startled, Leanice quickly turned again and looked at Lou. "What kind of a question is that? You shouldn't be thinking about such things, Lou!" Leanice was indignant.

"Grace McDonough told me that when two people get married they have babies."

"Mama's not going to have a baby."

"But she's marrying Uncle John!"

"Lou, you can't believe everything Grace McDonough tells you. If she told you the world was flat, would you believe her?"

Leanice made her point. Lou thought it over long and hard before making her own decision. "I guess you're right. Mama's not going to have another baby." Lou put her arm around Leanice's shoulder.

A chorus of brown crickets filled the night air with a rhythmic melody. Occasionally, the sound of a barn owl could be heard as it scanned the ground for a nightly meal. A cooling breeze blew in through the open window, temporarily relieving the sticky, humid air on this warm summer night.

Leanice was nearly asleep when Lou spoke again. "Are you gonna miss Grandma and Grandpa when we leave?"

"Aren't you sleepy yet?" Leanice barely opened her eyes.

"I can't sleep."

"Try counting sheep."

"I don't like sheep."

"Then count kitty cats." Leanice yawned deeply.

"Are you gonna miss Grandma and Grandpa?" Lou repeated the question with intensity.

Leanice sighed, knowing she would not get any sleep until she answered Lou's questions. "I guess so. I'll miss Grandma more than Grandpa. He scares me. I feel sorry for Grandma. I wish she could go with us."

"Me too. I don't think Grandpa loves us very much." Lou finally yawned.

"Do you miss Daddy?"

Lou was quiet. Leanice could not even hear her breathe. In a soft, almost inaudible voice, Lou replied, "Uh-huh. I wish Daddy was here instead of heaven. Is that wrong?"

"No. I wish Daddy was here, too. But Mama said he'd always be with us, that makes me feel better."

"Can he see us right now?" Lou asked with wide-eyed curiosity.

"I think so."

"Good-night, Daddy. I love you," Lou whispered into the night air.

"I love you, too, Daddy," Leanice responded before drifting into a deep sleep.

Leola extinguished the lamp by her bed, knowing that tomorrow she would approach her mother.

She rushed into the kitchen ten minutes after Zach left for the back acres, apologizing profusely to Elizabeth. "Let me clean up, Mama. Sit down and finish your coffee." Leola quickly cleared the table after sending the girls outside.

"If I sit down now, I'll be sitting all day long. I've got too much to do today." Elizabeth poured the dishwater.

"Then at least let me wash the dishes," Leola insisted.

"I'll get started on my wash." Elizabeth brought in a metal tub and washboard from the back porch and set them on the counter away from the sink.

"The girls enjoyed their trip into town yesterday."

"I've been wondering what they did that got them all out excited. Lou came tearing in here like somebody'd set fire to her." Elizabeth chuckled as she began the wash. "I thought she was going to bounce off the walls all evening. She is a pistol, that one!"

Leola froze, her resolve having melted away while watching her mother repeat a task she'd performed thousands of times before. The outline of Elizabeth's face, the strength of her hands as she scrubbed clothes, the definition of her life in this simple task tugged at Leola's heart. "We went to look at a house in town."

Elizabeth stopped her washing and faced Leola. "A house? What on earth for? You're not planning on moving, are you?"

"Yes, Mama, we are."

Leola looked away.

"How can you afford to buy a house? Did you get a job?" Elizabeth stood next to Leola.

"No ma'am . . . I'm getting married." Leola's words came out fractured. Elizabeth's mouth dropped open. Leola felt her mother's shock.

"Married? To who?" Elizabeth's voice jumped an octave.

"To John, Luther's brother. That's why he came down here. His wife died a few months ago and left him with five children. He needs a mother for them, and I, well, you know. He's moving down here in another week, and we'll marry then. I took the girls into town to show them the house he was looking at and to talk to them about what's going to happen."

Leola abruptly stopped washing dishes though she held the washcloth tightly in her left hand, afraid to look at her mother, afraid to see the hurt and disappointment in her eyes.

"If that's what you want to do, child, then I'm happy for you. Sometimes we have to do what we need to in this life, rather than what we want to." Elizabeth spoke directly but with feeling.

"You're not upset that I'm marrying Luther's brother?" Leola looked out the window.

"Heavens no, Leola. I think the two of you are doing the right thing. Those children need two parents. As much as I've come to love having you and the girls here, I know this is for the best." Elizabeth patted Leola's hand.

"It makes me feel good to hear you say that, Mama. I've spent all week wondering if I made the right decision. I want my children to have a father, and if it means marrying someone . . ." Leola hesitated.

". . . someone you don't love? I keep telling myself there are worse things in life. Sometimes I can see them and sometimes I can't. I've spent forty years with a man I don't love. I feel sorry for him, and I feel sorry for myself. But you find a way to get by." Elizabeth followed her daughter's gaze out the window.

"How did you do it, Mama? How did you get through all those years knowing that you'd never be with the one person you truly loved?" Leola's voice shook.

Elizabeth was deep in thought, remembering the young girl whose dreams were dashed so long ago. Tears returned to her eyes, the same tears shed that summer afternoon on the grounds of the church.

"You find something to hold on to, something you keep next to your heart no matter what. I will never forget Hank's laugh; it's as clear to me now as it was then." Elizabeth smiled through the tears. "Whenever I let myself hear that laugh, it reminds me what's good in life and decent and pure."

"Does it still hurt? Does the hurt ever go away?"

"Not as long as love is there; it's love that causes the pain. I live with the pain every day because I still love Hank; the pain keeps him alive." Elizabeth's face glowed as she recalled her lost love.

"Did you learn to love Daddy?"

"I could never love him the way I loved Hank; that kind of love only comes around once in a lifetime. I'm sure John's a good man, he'd have to be if he's Luther's brother."

Elizabeth's words gave Leola comfort. She picked up a dish from the sink and continued her chore. "Thank you, Mama. I needed some reassurance. I want to do what's right."

"If it feels right, then it's right. Always listen to your heart, child, it will never lead you astray."

SEVENTEEN

L EOLA CRIED ALL MORNING. When John arrived she gallantly fought back tears, but the redness of her eyes exposed her true emotion. The thought of Luther, their marriage, the happiness of their short time together, clouded her vision, obstructing the view of the present time and the reality of becoming another man's wife. Even this long after his death, she still considered herself Luther's wife; she would always belong to him. It was as natural to her as breathing.

Elizabeth held Leola's face in her hands as John frantically packed the cart, eager to make the appointment with the justice of the peace.

"Be happy, Leola. If anyone in this world has the right to be happy, it's you. I love you, baby." Elizabeth tenderly kissed her daughter on the forehead. As the cart pulled away, Leola turned to look at her mother, heartbroken at the thought of leaving Elizabeth behind.

The justice of the peace performed the ceremony as he would any other official business, sterile and forthright, with a tight lip and toneless voice. The impersonal nature of the event distracted Leola; more than once she neglected to answer "I do," thinking the question was intended for someone else. She felt out of place, as if she had inadvertently barged in on two strangers in the midst of marital vows. There were no flowers or music, only a messy desk and an American flag hanging from the wall.

Though curious about the proceedings, the girls were relegated outside the office, denied entry by the presiding official who cited a statute barring children under the age of sixteen from any public official's office.

"Do we have to call Uncle John Daddy?" Lou asked quietly, not wanting to be overheard.

Leanice shrugged her shoulders. "I don't know. He might not want us to call him Daddy."

"Why not?"

"Because we're not his children."

"We have to call him something!"

"Then ask Mama what to call him." Leanice quickly grew impatient with her sister, though she'd wondered the same thing.

"How come we can't go in there and watch?"

"It's only for grown-ups. Didn't you hear what the man said?"

"No."

"Honestly, Lou, you don't listen very well."

"I do, too." Lou poked out her lower lip.

"Then how come you didn't hear him tell Mama that children aren't allowed in his office?"

"Because I was thinking!"

"About what?"

"What to call Uncle John! Don't you listen, Leanice?" Lou mocked her sister's tone.

Frustrated, Leanice sighed and looked away.

"What will Nellie and Ruth call Mama?"

Leanice did not respond.

"I think they should call her Aunt Mama!" Lou was proud of her deduction.

"There's no such thing as Aunt Mama. Where do you come up with things like that?"

"They can call her Aunt Mama if they want to!" Lou raised her voice slightly.

"Whatever you say, Lou."

John and Leola exited the justice of the peace's office with the same serious expressions that accompanied them inside. The girls followed their mother and new father down the narrow flight of stairs to the waiting cart. John gave a quick tug on the reins, and a white-spotted horse carried the family to their new home.

Leola relished the thought of having her own house again, one that would reflect her personality as lady of the house. There was so much to do: making curtains for the living room, afghan quilts for the children's rooms, and a kitchen arranged just the way she wanted it. Her hopes were high as she entered her new home, ready to meet the challenges ahead, but what she saw unnerved her.

The house was arranged just like John and Susie Floyd's home in Porterdale. The furnishings in the living room were positioned exactly the same, as were those in the master bedroom. The kitchen utensils were stored away as Susie Floyd would have them, frying pans stacked underneath the cupboard, cooking pots to the right. Even the curtains on the windows were made by Susie Floyd. Every room embodied her presence.

The eyes of her stepchildren followed Leola all day long, watching her every move, her every action. They revered their deceased mother; no one, no matter how fit a mother, would ever fill Susie Floyd's shoes.

Nellie led Leanice and Lou to their room upstairs, though it was not the one Leanice wanted. Instead, it was the back room, the one without the nice view. Disappointed, Leanice asked Nellie if she and Lou could have one of the front bedrooms.

"Absolutely not! We already decided who would get each room. And you and your sister get the back one." Nellie's icy tone bit into Leanice's skin.

"But Mama said we could have one of the front ones, because of the pretty trees," Leanice pleaded with Nellie.

"Too bad, we've already unpacked. Besides, this isn't really your house anyway. My daddy paid for it." Nellie looked at her stepsisters with contempt.

Leanice returned Nellie's gaze in kind. Stoically, she picked up her suitcase and marched downstairs, with Lou in close pursuit. Nellie stood at the top of the stairs with her hands on her hips, a contentious smirk on her face. Leanice walked through the house and sat on the front porch with her suitcase in her lap. Lou sat beside her.

"Is that what you mean by mature, Leanice?" Lou asked sincerely yet quietly.

Leanice smiled at her sister's innocence. "No, Lou. That's bossy."

"How long are we gonna sit out here?"

"You can go in any time you want to. I'm staying out here till I'm good and ready."

"Me too. I don't think Nellie likes us very much."

"She likes being bossy better."

Lou watched a yellow butterfly dart in and out of the morning glories that covered the porch lattice, a sight that reminded her of the swarms of butterflies that covered the fields of purple meadow beauties surrounding Hopewell Presbyterian Church every spring.

"How far away is Porterdale?"

"Why do you want to know that?"

"Just because."

"It's a long way from here."

"Could we walk there?"

"No, it'd take until Christmas. But I sure wish we could." Leanice looked beyond the horizon.

Leola glanced out the window and saw the girls on the front porch. "I thought you two would be enjoying your new room." Leola sat beside Leanice.

The girls were silent. Leanice suddenly felt stupid for creating such a fuss over a room. She didn't want to add any more burdens to the ones her mother already had to handle. She wished Nellie hadn't provoked her so much.

"How come you're holding your suitcase, Leanice? Are you going somewhere?" Leola looked with amusement at her oldest daughter.

"No, ma'am. I guess not." Leanice lowered her head.

Noting her sister's plight, Lou chimed in. "Nellie won't let us have the room Leanice wanted. She told us we have to take the back room."

Leola realized that she had not talked with John about dividing up the bedrooms, or that Leanice specifically wanted one of the front rooms.

"Well, I think we can work something out. I'm sure the boys won't mind swapping rooms." Leola took the suitcase and escorted her daughters upstairs.

Nellie was in her room holding her infant sister, oblivious to Leola's presence.

"Nellie, I understand there was a mix-up about the bedrooms. It's my fault, I promised one of the front rooms to Leanice and Lou, but I didn't talk to your father about it. I don't think the boys would mind taking the back room, do you?"

Without responding, Nellie insolently turned her back on Leola and sat on her bed, placing Lily beside her.

"Wilbur and Paul are so young, I couldn't imagine them having a preference for one room over another."

Nellie turned and stared through Leola as if she were addressing a rude neighbor. "We've already made that decision. If Leanice and Lou don't want the back room, they can sleep outside for all I care!"

Leola's eyes flared. She sent her daughters downstairs as she entered Nellie's room and closed the door. "I know this isn't an easy adjustment for you, Nellie; it's not easy for any of us. But I will not allow you to show me disrespect like that. I'm not trying to take your mother's place. I would never do that. But it is my responsibility to be one of the parents of this household, and I expect the same obedience from you that I do my own children. Do you understand what I'm saying?"

Nellie continued playing with Lily.

"Answer me!" Leola's voice filled the house, startling Nellie.

"I heard you!"

"Then answer me when I ask you a question!"

"We don't need you. I can take care of things just fine all by myself." Nellie's tone was goading.

Leola steadied herself. "I appreciate what you've done for your brothers and sisters, Nellie. But they need a mother around the house, an adult. You're just a child."

"I am not a child!"

Leola's temper threatened her resolve.

"Yes you are, Nellie. You're only thirteen, and you've had to assume a tremendous responsibility for someone so young. That's one reason why I married your father, to help him raise the children."

Again, Nellie ignored Leola's presence. Exasperated, Leola picked Lily up from the bed and started to carry her downstairs. Nellie jumped up.

"I was playing with her!" Nellie sniped, as she tried taking Lily from her stepmother.

"She needs her rest. I put her down for a reason, Nellie."

"You can't just take her away like that!"

"Yes I can. I'm her mother now." Leola looked sternly into Nellie's eyes. Rage and resentment emanated from her stepdaughter.

When John arrived home from surveying the property, his tearful daughter besieged him. "Aunt Leola has been awfully mean to us today. She won't let me see Lily, and she won't let us have the rooms we wanted! She changed everything around so Leanice and Lou could have one of the front rooms after we'd already moved Wilbur and Paul in there! And when I was playing with Lily she took her away!" Nellie worked herself into a frenzy.

"I told you things would be different now that you have a new mother."

"She's not my mother! My mother is dead!"

"Nellie, I will not have this. If there's a problem between you and Leola, then we'll take care of it. I do not want you upsetting the other children."

John stalked into the house with Nellie in close pursuit.

"I understand there were some differences of opinion around here today." John's sudden presence invaded the room.

Leola looked up at John, then at Nellie, and back at John. "Nothing we didn't work out amongst ourselves."

"I heard things a little differently."

"Oh?" Leola was not surprised.

"Nellie feels that you were unfair with the children."

"How was I unfair?" Leola refused to give an inch.

"Well, kicking the boys out of their room for one thing, and not letting Nellie see the baby for another."

"I did not kick anyone out of anywhere. I promised Leanice she could have the front bedroom, and I failed to mention that to you ahead of time. That was my fault. I asked Wilbur if he and Paul would mind changing rooms, and he said it was fine with him. And as for the baby, I put her down for a nap because she was getting cranky. I've not told anyone that they could not see her."

"That's not true! She made Wilbur and Paul take the other room! And she took Lily away while I was watching her! She said she was her mother now!" Nellie's face contorted with anger.

"I did not force Wilbur and Paul to do anything, Nellie. And I am Lily's mother now!"

"You are not!" Nellie screamed.

"Do not use that tone of voice with me, young lady!" Leola snapped.

"When the children need disciplining, Leola, I'll handle it!" John's voice rose.

"Then discipline her!"

The tension in the room tore through the three combatants.

"Go to your room, Nellie!"

"But, Daddy—"

"I said go to your room, now!" he barked at her, prompting Nellie to give Leola a look of complete hatred.

John's broad shoulders dropped, as if the world had fallen squarely on top of them. He sat at the kitchen table exhausted.

"I knew this wouldn't be easy, but I sure didn't think it'd get off to such a bad start."

Leola turned away from John, tears filling her eyes.

"Susie Floyd and I had an understanding about things. When she had a problem with the children, I took care of it. She never confronted them. They're not used to a mother who scolds them."

Leola spoke through her tears. "John, I'm going to tell you something that I always want you to remember. I'm not saying this out of disrespect or spite." She paused, building resolve. "I am not Susie Floyd, I cannot do all the things Susie Floyd did just the way she did them. Susie Floyd is dead. Please don't expect me to become her."

John looked down. "I know."

"Everywhere I look in this house, I see Susie Floyd, her presence is all around us. Until I make this our home, her ghost will haunt this family. I know you loved her, as we all did, but we've got to let her go, we can't keep holding on to her memory."

"I'm sorry, Leola. I've been so set in a certain way of doing things, it's hard to break the pattern."

"It isn't easy. At times I find myself thinking that Luther would handle things in a different way, but then I have to remind myself that he's gone."

"Life doesn't cut a person much rope to hold onto, does it?"

"Not always. But as long as there's enough to hang onto, you won't fall."

"Sometimes I feel like I'm hanging on by my fingernails. Just when I think I'm making headway, something comes along to knock me for a loop."

"Adversity builds character."

John chuckled. "If that's the case, I must have enough character for a hundred people."

Leola wiped away her tears as she looked tenderly at John. In his eyes she saw the pain of losing someone once loved.

"I'm sorry about Susie Floyd."

"She was a fine woman. She had a way of making me feel important when I didn't even realize it. She was always trying to please me, and that's what eventually killed her. I just wish . . . "

"Things are a lot clearer when you look back on them. It's what's ahead that's hard to see. Don't beat yourself up about what's already happened, John. If we did nothing in life but worry about where we've been, then we'd never get where we're going. Let it go."

"It won't be easy."

"It never is, but time has a way of softening the blow."

John left the house early, anxious to begin the work that had to be done on his property. He kissed Leola on the cheek and rode away, unaware that Nellie was watching from the upstairs window.

Leola spent the majority of the day rearranging the kitchen and washing clothes, much happier after the talk with John. She fed the children lunch and, at one o'clock, put Lily down for a nap, her crib nestled in the corner of the master bedroom. While Lily slept, Leola busied herself with the enormous wash. At mid-afternoon, she checked in on Lily. The crib was empty.

At first startled, Leola figured that Nellie had taken Lily upstairs with her again, no doubt a show of more defiance. Taking a deep breath to calm her temper, Leola called upstairs but there was no answer. Finally, she ascended the steps and went into Nellie's empty room. None of the children had seen her; Nellie and Lily had vanished. Not since Luther took ill had Leola felt such dread.

She ran throughout the house calling Nellie's name, greeted at every turn by an uncomforting silence. She looked in every room and corner and closet, even searching outside the house, looking as far as she could see down each road but saw nothing. Her heart raced violently. She had to get in touch with John, time a luxury she could ill afford to lose. The more she thought about Lily being without food and proper care, the faster she ran.

She didn't know where to begin looking. John could be anywhere on such an expansive piece of property. She stopped to catch her breath, feeling she might faint otherwise. While looking over the endless acreage on either side of the road, a feeling of futility overcame her.

Following her intuition, she turned east toward the old homestead that sat on the property. The ground was hard and dusty, in places barricaded by patches of thick weeds several feet in height. Leola forced herself through them, the weeds ripping at her dress and cutting her hands as she cleared a path. The hot summer sun beat down unmercifully upon her; sweat poured from her forehead.

She cried uncontrollably, wondering why this was happening, blaming herself for being too tough on Nellie. The weeds grew taller and thicker, a forest of burrs and thorns. She ran into a nest of grasshoppers feeding on the dense vegetation. The disturbance sent the insects into a flying frenzy, swarming around her, hundreds of them flying every which way, landing in her hair, on her face, and on her dress.

Her feet continued moving though she could not see, trying desperately to pull the bugs from her, dozens of them clinging to her hair and neck and face and hands, their scratchy legs fiercely gripping her skin.

As suddenly as they attacked her, the grasshoppers flew away. Out of breath, her mind and body shattered by the assault, Leola continued on her mission, determined to find John. She focused her energies on Lily, which gave her strength. Clearing a pathway through the thicket, she glimpsed the old house. John's tall frame stood next to it.

She called out as loudly as she could, her voice barely carrying through the thick air. John looked up, dropping everything. "My God, Leola. What is it?"

"Lily . . . and Nellie . . . are gone!" Leola clung to John.

"What?" John's mouth dropped open.

"I can't find them . . . I looked everywhere. I'm afraid Nellie took off with her!" Leola gasped for breath.

John couldn't believe what he was hearing. He helped Leola onto the cart and raced for the house.

"How long have they been gone?" John yelled as he frantically searched the house.

"I put Lily down at one and checked on her around two." Leola could barely speak.

The events of the past six months got the best of John. He kicked the door leading from the kitchen to the back porch, splitting the bottom.

"Dammit! I'm going into town to get the Sheriff. All of you stay put!"

John stormed out of the house. Leola comforted the children although she feared the worst herself.

A group of volunteers helped in the search for Nellie and Lily. Sheriff Griner led a group south of the house following Altamaha Street to Ten Mile Road, while Harbard led another group north through town toward Abbeville. The two groups searched until well in the evening; by midnight they called it off until morning.

The strain of the search knotted the muscles in John's neck and shoulders. His head pounded like it could explode at any second. Leola waited up for him. When she saw that he was alone, she cried.

"They'll show up, John. They couldn't have gone too far."

"I cannot figure out why Nellie did this."

"She was given a lot of responsibility when Susie Floyd died. She stepped in and became a mother to the children. And now that I've taken over that role, she feels neglected and unappreciated. I shouldn't have lost my temper with her yesterday."

"It's no one's fault, Leola. We're all victims of circumstance." John sighed.

Leola stroked John's forehead as he cried silently. The night was unforgiving, refusing to relinquish its possessions. Leola prayed continually, asking the heavens to hear their plight. The back porch door opened and closed. John and Leola sprang to their feet.

Nellie held Lily close, both crying and near collapse. John and Leola embraced them warmly, knowing that words were incapable of expressing their relief. A current of healing flowed from one to another, and would bind them together as a family in the years to come.

EIGHTEEN

A<small>T SIXTEEN</small>, W<small>ILLIAM WAS</small> as restless as a gust of wind preceding an afternoon thunderstorm. He was edgy and moody, with a taste for adventure and a driving need to explore beyond the realm of his world. He wanted to be his own man, not the boy in his father's shadow.

Days passed by like years to William, each one longer than the one before. He desperately wanted to find a way out of his father's house, even if it meant living on the streets. He was tired of being punished by his father every time he turned around. There was nothing, it seemed, he could do to make Harbard happy.

William had an interest in mechanics, excelling in detailed, intricate work. He enjoyed taking things apart and putting them back together, once dismantling an old grandfather clock just to see how it worked. The precise detail at which its hundreds of parts ticked and turned fascinated William. He watched the moving wheels for hours on end, studying and mapping the importance of each part.

Harbard ignored his son's mechanical aptitude, scoffing at William's growing fascination with automobiles, which he considered nothing more than a passing fad. He wouldn't let William bring any of his mechanical "doodlings" into the house, which prompted William to argue that his father was a hypocrite, reminding Harbard that he, too, worked as a mechanic at one time in his life.

Tensions between father and son escalated with each day, their shouting matches brutal, as if they were competitors in a slug fest. Though Rebecca tried to keep the peace, her words fell on deaf ears. She shielded her other children as best she could, but the effects of constant battle were far-reaching.

As she always had, Rebecca found solace in her garden, tilling and weeding the ground feverishly even on the hottest of summer afternoons. It was strange for her to seek refuge from a place she so dearly loved, the house where her grandmother once lived. But she felt like a stranger in the house now, as if she had no connection to it whatsoever.

William took off after breakfast each morning, spending most of his time working odd jobs at the blacksmith's shop and the rail yard. Sometimes he'd return home around dinnertime and sometimes he wouldn't, a habit that infuriated his father. On the occasions when the two collided at day's end, sparks flew like fireworks on the Fourth of July.

Rebecca longed for the days when the children were small and meals a time for the family to be together. It seemed like a lifetime ago. As she offered a silent prayer before dinner, William walked in.

Harbard shot a stern look at his oldest son as he took his place at the table. Rebecca held her breath.

"It wouldn't harm you any to let your mother know whether you'll be home for dinner. No sense in cooking for a mouth that won't be here." Harbard baited his son.

"I didn't know until the last minute." William reached for a bowl of peas.

"So you can just come and go as you please, like you were living in a rooming house?"

"I had things to do."

"What things?" Harbard's voice took on a definite edge.

"Hanging around Charley Parramore and drinking whiskey!" Etta chimed in.

William sliced a glance at his sister, his expression suggesting that she refrain from entering the fray. Etta was a strong-willed young woman whose convictions were as righteous as her manner. She never hesitated to point out human faults, especially when they belonged to her brother.

"I've seen the two of you sneaking a bottle of whiskey down the alley between Central and Magnolia." Etta announced.

"You have not!" William barked.

Rebecca held on to the fragments of peace. "Etta, let's not discuss that right now."

"But I did, Mama! They were taking swigs like two drunks in the gutter!"

"Etta, please! Can't we have just one peaceful dinner?" Rebecca pleaded.

The tentative truce lasted no more than a few uneasy moments. "If I ever catch you drinking anything stronger than apple cider, I will lock you up and throw away the key!" Harbard scolded.

"I said I didn't do it!" William sneered.

"I don't believe you!" Harbard's eyes bulged.

Etta glanced at William with a smirk on her face. Martin complained that his stomach hurt.

"Why is it that you believe everyone else in the world but not me?"

"Because I don't trust you!" Harbard glared at his son.

"Harbard!" Rebecca gasped.

William angrily pushed himself from the table. Rebecca threw her napkin onto her plate and followed him out the door.

"William, please don't go. It worries me when you go out like this!"

"I have to. I'm tired of that old man picking on me all the time. And I don't want to upset you anymore." He turned away.

"What upsets me the most is not knowing where you are half the time. Let me talk to your father."

"That doesn't do any good, Mama, and you know it. You've talked to him before and nothing happened."

Although he was right, Rebecca refused to let William leave. "Your father only wants what's best for you, son. He doesn't show it very well, but that's just his way. You are loved, William. I love you with all my heart."

"I love you, too. But I can't live with someone who hates me," William cried.

Stunned, Rebecca hugged William with all her might.

"Your father doesn't hate you. No one in this family hates you; don't ever think that. We will work something out, whatever it takes. I will not let my family be torn apart like this."

Out of respect for his mother, William stayed. For Rebecca, it was a small victory.

Harbard was already in bed when she finished the dishes. She stood over him, his arm draped across his forehead.

"I want to talk to you, Harbard."

"Can't it wait until morning?"

"No, it cannot."

Harbard lowered his arm and looked at her.

"If it's William, I don't want to talk about it."

"I want to talk about it." She emphasized her interest.

"That boy needs a strong hand to guide him. He is headed straight for trouble, and I intend to block his path."

"That boy thinks you hate him."

"Right now, I'm not so sure I don't."

Harbard's comment slapped Rebecca squarely in the face. "How can you say that, Harbard? For God's sake, he is your son! You can't mean that!"

"He needs to grow up, be strong and tough. This isn't an easy world to live in. I've tried to show him a trade, get him interested in becoming a man of the law, but he's so blasted stubborn he won't listen to reason."

"Like father, like son."

Harbard missed the connection.

"He's just a boy, Harbard. He'll grow up in due time. You can't force him to become an adult overnight."

Rebecca walked to the foot of the bed. Harbard sat up.

"These days you have to grow up fast, you got no other choice."

"Let him find his own way!"

"I'm showing him the way!"

"You're driving him away from this family, and I'll not allow that to happen! I've already lost my mother and my father and my brother, I'll be damned if I'll lose my son, too!"

Rebecca stared at Harbard; he'd never seen her so angry. They stood at a crossroad, one that could define their future relationship.

"What do you want me to do, Rebecca? Let him throw his life away on silly dreams?"

"What's wrong with having a dream?" Her manner softened.

"They're not practical." Harbard sank into the bed.

"If you make your dream come true, does that make it practical?"

"I've never seen that happen." He turned away.

"It did for me." Harbard looked at her quizzically. "I dreamed of having a loving husband and a happy home. And that's what I've had for many years."

"That's different. You're not supporting a family," Harbard rebuked.

"Neither is William. He's a child, Harbard. Let him be a child, let him make decisions for himself. If he has a mind to fly to the moon, then let him dream about it. You're suffocating him."

"I know what's best for that boy, and I will make sure he understands that."

Rebecca's shoulders hunched forward; she'd made no progress. Harbard was an impenetrable wall of stubbornness and anger; compassion was a lost concept.

"You must not love me very much."

"Don't say that, Rebecca. You know how much I love you."

"I thought love was what held a family together. This family is falling apart, so there can't be much love within these walls." She was completely deflated.

Harbard had not seen her like this since J.W.'s death. Her pain was his pain.

"I'll see what I can do."

"That's all I ask."

Rebecca sat in the rocking chair next to the bed until well after midnight. The silence comforted her. If only the house could always be this peaceful, she thought.

NINETEEN

THE ATLANTA, BIRMINGHAM AND Coast Railroad snaked its way across the states of Georgia and Alabama from the foothills of the Appalachian Mountains to the coastal town of Brunswick. A major force in the transportation of lumber and agriculture, the AB&C was created by the consolidation of three rails lines in 1903 and the purchase of another in 1904, bringing with the merger a fair amount of prosperity to the small, struggling railroad towns along its route.

For several years, Fitzgerald was a stop along the Tifton and Northeastern Railroad, where heavy pine and cotton were loaded aboard the freight cars for sale to distant markets. Though the rail line was small, it brought steady business and a tenuous economic stability to the two towns. When the Tifton and Northeastern merged into the AB&C Railroad, the promise for prosperity shot as high as the deep blue Georgia sky.

In towns up and down the line, the men who worked the railroad were revered. They were the backbone of the community, the ones who kept the town alive. To teenagers like William, the railroad men were heroic legends, living unconventional lives, traveling the state at all hours of the day and night. It was a world that captured the imaginations of boys like William.

He'd heard tales of intrigue about the men, stories involving back-alley fights, booze, and women, as well as stories about the hard work, long hours, and debilitating fatigue that had the capability of ending careers as soon as they had begun. But William was fearless and daring; nothing, he felt, could be worse than living in his father's house. The day he turned seventeen, William decided it was high time to escape the encumbrance of home.

Bobby Faulk looked William over. The earnestness in the boy's eyes burned with the need to prove something, either to himself or someone else. In his thirty years as foreman, Bobby had seen many a youngster ask to ride the rails, only to be disillusioned by its tough, solitary life. He discouraged as many of them as he could, but more often than not, his warnings went unheeded.

There was a quality about William that was different from the other boys, tough as nails and sincere as the day is long. Bobby was slowly drawn to William's drive and willpower.

"Are you gonna let me ride the rails?" William asked, direct.

"Don't put words in my mouth. You listen, I'll talk."

William moved his chair closer to Bobby's desk, less than two feet between them. Bobby leaned back.

"I've been working this rail line for thirty years. And I've seen a lot of things happen in that time. Grown men, much older than you, have turned their backs and walked away from this kind of life. It's hard, can break a man's spirit easier than snapping a twig."

William did not bat an eye. "I can handle it."

"Sometimes it's just the loneliness that gets to 'em. You might go for days without hearing anything other than the wheels grinding the rails. And once you get where you're going, you've got to load and unload, hitch and unhitch. It's a monotonous life."

"I'm ready."

"I should probably talk to your daddy about this."

"It's my decision, not his. If I can't get on here, I'll find some other place that'll take me."

"I want home guards. You know what those are?"

"It's a worker who sticks with the same line and doesn't jump from one to another when business gets slack."

William's knowledge impressed Bobby.

"I'm a home guard," William proclaimed sincerely.

William looked Bobby straight in the eye without even the hint of reservation. Bobby looked long and hard at William, as if the boy had turned into a man before his eyes.

"I'm breaking my rule for you, William. I used to put boys your age on the rails, but they couldn't handle it, and I took a lot of heat for that. If this doesn't work out, don't go around telling everyone I didn't warn you. We've got to have a clear understanding that you agreed to this knowing everything that's involved."

William stood and extended his hand. "You've got my word."

"I'll put you on next week; you'll work the line to Waycross and Brunswick." Bobby shook William's hand on the deal.

William left the station that day with a solemn demeanor that made him appear older than his seventeen years. He tracked along Main Street, excitement building inside him so much that when he hit Alapaha Street, he turned right and journeyed away from his house into the woods.

When he was out of earshot from the nearest house, he let out a yell that shook the ground beneath him; never had he felt such euphoria. He danced from tree to tree, pounding his fist into the bark to let himself know that he wasn't dreaming. Scooping up a handful of dirt, he threw it into the air, the individual grains of soil scattered about by a gusting wind.

For once, he made it in time for dinner, only to reveal his plans.

"You're too young for that, William," Rebecca responded, as if the topic had never come up.

"Mr. Faulk doesn't think so. He knows I can do the work."

"It's not a matter of doing the work, son. It's a matter of a young boy living that kind of life. There are too many temptations out there. People would as soon take advantage of you as look at you." Rebecca put the subject to rest.

Harbard remained uncharacteristically quiet, secretly thinking this might be just what the boy needed. Where he'd failed in making a man out of William, the railroad might succeed.

"I don't think it's as bad as all that, Rebecca. It'll be good for the boy, give him a chance to grow up, earn his keep, feel like a man."

"What?" She looked at Harbard piercingly.

"I said I thought it'd be good for the boy."

"Good? What on earth is good about a seventeen-year-old boy leaving his home where he has stability for a life on the rails with a suitcase for a companion?"

"It's better than hiding in an alleyway with a pint of whiskey in your hand and mischief on your mind."

"Why are we even discussing this? It's not going to happen." Rebecca dismissed the conversation with a wave of her hand.

"I'm afraid it is, Mama. I start the Waycross and Brunswick run next week."

Etta seized the opportunity to express yet another opinion. "Without even asking for permission? Have you no more respect for our parents than that?"

"I wondered how long it'd take you to bellow in," William taunted his sister.

"You are rude, crass, insensitive, and conceited!"

"Maybe I am, but at least I'm not pious, self-righteous, gossipy, or judgmental!" William shot back.

"That's enough, you two!" Harbard interjected. "If this is what William wants to do with his life, so be it. We'll not discuss it any further!"

Rebecca excused herself from the room in tears. The pain he caused his mother hurt William, but, in his heart, he knew he'd made the best decision.

The Brunswick line arrived in Fitzgerald from Albany, eighty miles to the west, at mid-afternoon. William eagerly waited at the station, ready to prove his worthiness. The four-hour layover allowed the men to load pine and cotton onto the cars, the first of many grueling tasks along the rails. When the AB&C line pulled out, William was aboard, a railroad man giving life to his own legend.

He sat in the workers' car near the caboose, watching the miles and miles of passing landscape as if he had to memorize the placement of every tree, rock, and stream. Gone were the days of innocence and reliance; how far away they seemed, a lifetime ago. In a way, he was angry that he had to make a choice that took him far from home. But, more importantly to him, he was glad to be his own man.

The train pulled into Brunswick at dusk, long enough for the men to unhitch and reconnect a few cars before the blackness of night halted their duties. Most of the men retreated to the decaying line of rooming houses that bordered the intersection of the rail yard and Port of Brunswick, overlooking the stench of industry, black, greasy soot mixed with stale sea water. Life along the waterfront was rough. For a fresh-faced boy from a small town, it was the adventure of a lifetime.

William settled for the night in a two-story house on Front Street. The room was small, hardly worth the twenty-five cents he paid, but clean, and faced away from the street, overlooking a maze of alleyways that seemed to lead everywhere yet nowhere. He unpacked his clothes and neatly folded them onto a chair that sat against a barren wall. After dinner, he ventured into the night.

A couple of men who worked the line out of Albany invited him into a run-down shanty called the Sea Spray Saloon. Without hesitation, William accepted. He'd never been inside a tavern before, but it couldn't be any worse than a hoe-down at McCaffrey's barn. The inside was dank, smelling of stale liquor and wet cigars. A heavy-set man with a bushy moustache stood behind the bar.

"What'll you fellas have?"

The two men ordered shots of whiskey, Kentucky bourbon in particular. The bartender looked closely at William, sizing up the younger man. "How old are you?"

"Twenty-one," William replied, without flinching.

The bartender nodded his head. "What'll you have?"

"What they're having. Only make mine a double."

William downed his drink in one gulp and ordered another, the biting liquor easing his apprehension. As he stood at the bar, inconspicuous, alone, a fancy-dressed woman walked up to him. She appeared to be in her mid-thirties, but it was quite possible that she was much older. Her hair was a reddish-gold color, large bags sunk underneath her eyes. She looked like a woman who'd taken all life had to offer and then some.

"I haven't seen you around here before." Her voice was rough and unfeminine.

"This is my first trip to Brunswick." William barely looked at her.

"Where you from?"

"Fitzgerald."

"Never heard of it. Sounds like one of those Bible-thumping, revival-tent-meeting towns where everybody's high on Jesus and low on tolerance." She stuffed a pinch of snuff into her mouth.

"Yeah, something like that." William looked away.

"You're kinda cute! What's your name?" She put her arm inside his.

"William."

"Hi, William. I'm Claire, but most people around here call me Punkin because my hair is the color of a ripe pumpkin, and I'm sweet as pumpkin pie." She threw back her head and cackled into the air.

William smiled politely, though he hoped she'd go away.

"You don't talk much, do ya?"

"I'm not big on talking, no."

"That's okay, honey. I can talk plenty for both of us. Where you staying?"

William scanned the interior for his buddies, locating them at a corner table playing poker.

"Up the road a piece."

"Well, that don't tell me nothin', baby doll. There's lots of places up the road."

William tried to pull away from Claire's grasp.

"What's the matter? Don't you like me?"

"I gotta go." William managed to untangle his arm, but Claire grabbed him.

"How old are you anyway, boy?" Her manner quickly turned brusque.

"Twenty-one." William looked for the quickest way out.

"Twenty-one, hell! I'll bet you're not even eighteen!" Her voice thundered through the saloon.

"Yes I am!"

"You're nothing but a wet-behind-the-ears mama's boy still tied to her apron strings!" Claire yelled angrily.

William broke from her hold and rushed away. She screamed after him, "That's right, little boy, run back home to mama where you belong! Where all little boys belong! No man would ever turn down Claire Hennessy!"

A group of men laughed as William skulked out of the bar, into the bleakness of an unforgiving night. He went back to his room and looked out the window at the maze of alleyways, crossing here and there and beyond, wondering which path his life would take. Though the glamorous tales of railroad life quickly became a thing of the past, William stuck by his promise to Bobby. He would not back down, but instead, live out the myth of all the railroad men, solitary figures riding through the shadows of night.

TWENTY

For Elizabeth, the years since Leola and the children moved away were filled with loneliness. Although she visited them as often as possible, the chronic sense of melancholy plagued her. She found herself spending much of her time deep in thought, remembering the lost love, recapturing its pain, wondering how things would be different if she had run away with Hank.

Sometimes the intensity of her feelings were so raw she was overcome by hatred and sorrow, haunted by the past, more so now than ever before. Many days she felt she had stepped back in time, reliving those awful days after she last saw Hank. Even her dreams were filled with the elements of change. In a desolate field, she saw a young man standing alone, holding a pistol in his right hand. She sensed his troubled soul, racing to be near him. He raised the pistol to his forehead. She cried out to him, but her voice did not carry. He prayed silently, asking for forgiveness. Slowly, he pulled the trigger. She reached toward him as he fell to the ground.

Elizabeth awoke from these dreams deeply depressed, withdrawing more and more from her everyday life. Zach noticed the change in his wife but dismissed it as easily as he did everything else that concerned her. As long as his routine wasn't altered, Zach didn't much care what state of mind Elizabeth was in.

Early one morning, Elizabeth dashed from the house as Mr. Sheffield made his weekly trip into town, jumping into the cart with him. The trip was unplanned, instinctual, as a newborn gazelle knows at birth that it must run to survive. She didn't know exactly what direction her life was taking, but at least she was moving forward.

She did not return home until Zach had finished working for the day. He was not amused by her absence. Hostility tightened in his jaw, and the familiar build-up to one of his outbursts greeted Elizabeth at the kitchen doorway.

"Where the hell have you been?" His menacing voice scorched her.

"I went into town for something." Elizabeth walked away, but Zach followed like a predatory beast stalking its prey.

"For what?" He slipped up beside her.

"I had a hankerin' to visit Leola and the children, so I did." Elizabeth refused to be intimidated.

"You're lying. I always take you into town to see them. I'll ask you again, where the hell have you been?" His hands gripped her shoulders firmly.

"And I'll tell you again, I visited Leola and the children."

"Don't get smart with me, you pathetic excuse for a woman!" He thrust her against the wall. "I'll get it out of you one way or the other! What's it gonna be?"

Zach stood before Elizabeth, the weight of his body pinning her against the wall. He raised his hand to her face.

"You will not touch me!" Elizabeth spewed at him.

Her defiance stunned Zach. "What did you say?"

"You heard me, you will not touch me." Her voice was calm, lacking emotion.

"I'll do anything—"

"No, you won't. I will not put up with this any longer, Zach. If you want something to beat on, then go outside and hit a tree, hit the side of the barn, hit the sky for all I care, but you will not hit me again . . . ever!" She hissed the last word.

Zach boiled with rage. He slammed his fist into the wall less than an inch from Elizabeth's face. He looked upon her with disgust, veins popping from his forehead. Suddenly, abusively, he kissed her deeply, the force of it nearly bruising Elizabeth's lips. She struggled against him. He again looked at her with contempt. "That's one thing Hank Myers never did."

He smirked and walked away.

Elizabeth called after him, "Hank Myers was a gentleman! And he was more of a man than you could ever hope to be!" She wiped her mouth with the sleeve of her dress.

Zach stopped in his tracks, fighting the impulse to defend his honor. Instead, he walked out the door and into the fields, where he remained throughout the night.

Elizabeth prepared breakfast as if nothing had happened. Zach ate quietly, his motions slower and more deliberate, she thought. Impatiently, she counted the minutes until he was done. When he exited the back door, Elizabeth jumped from the table.

Nervously, yet as excited as a school girl on her tenth birthday, she watched him through the window as he gathered the mule and plow and headed for the back acreage. When he was completely out of sight, she raced to the bedroom and hurriedly packed a few belongings into an old piece of luggage. Her hands had intentions all their own, shaking wildly as she snapped the suitcase closed.

Tearing through the bottom dresser drawer where Zach kept a modest amount of cash, she took only what came with her dowry.

She again looked out the kitchen window, making sure Zach was still in the fields. Spinning around, clutching her belongings, she walked from the kitchen. The sound of a gunshot pierced the air, startling her, the suitcase fell from her grasp. A shadow of doubt surrounded her, nearly eclipsing her resolve to leave. Remembering the day she last saw Hank, the look in his eyes as the rebellion deep inside prompted her to run away with him, she picked up her belongings and ran from the house without once looking back.

She was free. For the first time in her life, she did not have to give an account of her actions to anyone other than herself. She was whole, complete, a person in her own right, not by the right of others. The beginnings of a song crossed her lips, and before she knew it, she was singing.

When she arrived in town, Elizabeth treated herself to lunch at Josephine's. A good meal was in order for the upcoming journey. A few patrons expressed surprise upon seeing her without Zach, their stares and idle remarks ignored. By nightfall, she'd be far from town.

She had two items on her agenda before boarding the afternoon train, two good-byes to say that would propel her life forward. Her mother shared a house with her elderly sister on Pine Street, having moved into town after Elizabeth's father died. When Isabel answered the door, Elizabeth brushed past her, obviously offending her mother by such rude behavior.

"Couldn't you wait for me to invite you inside?" Isabel closed the door behind her.

"I'm in a hurry. Where's Aunt Kate?" Elizabeth set the piece of luggage on the floor.

"She's in her room taking a nap. Why are you carrying that bag?"

"Because I'm leaving; that's why I'm here."

"Leaving? Don't tell me Zach Cowan sold out!" Isabel sat in a chair across the room.

"I'm leaving. Zach's not going anywhere."

"What kind of nonsense are you talking about?" Isabel's voice was sterile.

Elizabeth shook her head and sighed. "That's all my life has meant to you, hasn't it, Mama? One nonsensical charade after another; poor Elizabeth is too stupid to decide things for herself."

The elderly woman shifted in the chair, positioning herself to jump onto the offensive. "Girl, you don't have the sense God gave you when you were born! How could you possibly know what's best for you?"

Elizabeth laughed. "You haven't changed a bit, have you? Still the same old sanctimonious bully who feels the calling to meddle in other people's lives as long as it's in the name of God and family!"

"I will not be spoken to in that manner by the likes of you or anyone else! How dare you bring blasphemy into this house! Get out!" she screamed.

"Not until you hear this! Not until you know and feel the agony you have caused me!"

Isabel looked away.

"Look at me! Do not turn away while I'm talking to you! I want you to see my pain, Mama; I want you to see the forty years of pain you caused me! Do you know what kind of hell you put me through? Do you? Do you even care?"

"Do not curse in this house!"

"Shut up! I'll do anything I damn well please in this house!" Elizabeth started shaking. "Why did you do it, Mama? Why did you send Hank away? You knew I was in love with him! Were you jealous? Is that it? Could you not stand the fact that I wanted to marry the man I loved? The man of my choice?"

"I will not discuss that again, Elizabeth. You know why!"

Elizabeth slammed her hand on the table. "No I don't! Tell me why, Mama! Tell me why you subjected me to this living hell!" She steadily moved closer to her mother.

"You are possessed by a demon! Get out!"

"I am possessed by forty years of terrifying memories, Mama! Forty years of being kicked and beaten and screamed at by a madman! There's your demon, Mama!" Elizabeth stood directly over her mother.

"You don't know what you're talking about!" Isabel tried in vain to hide her shock.

"How could I not know what I'm talking about? I lived it! Every cut and every bruise and every bloody nose, I lived through! Being cursed and shouted at and treated worse than any dog, I lived through! He spat on me, Mama! That crazy man you married me off to would spit on me if I didn't have a meal on the table when he sat his ugly face down at dinnertime!"

Elizabeth pressed on. Her mother cowered at every detail.

"Is that what you wanted for me, Mama? Was it worth my suffering to keep a piece of damnable land within the family?"

"We all have to suffer in this life, Elizabeth. Anything worth keeping is worth the suffering to keep it. You'll see that one day, and you'll thank me!" Isabel begged.

"Thank you? It's all I can do at this moment to keep myself from slapping you!"

Elizabeth saw that she was wasting her time. She abruptly turned and picked up her suitcase.

"Where are you going?" her mother demanded.

"Someplace far away from here . . . as if you care."

Elizabeth walked with determination toward the door. Isabel followed closely.

"How can you turn your back on a legacy like this? I did everything for you, Elizabeth! So that one day all of our land would be yours! That's what Zach brought to your marriage, Elizabeth! Security! You'd never have had anything like that with Hank Myers! He was a nobody!"

Elizabeth turned and looked at her mother through the screen door. "I have spent the majority of my life thinking how pathetic I am. You made me feel that way, Mama, you and your damnable greed. But not any more. You have no power over me. I used to think that every time I looked in a mirror it reflected a picture of what was purely and completely pathetic. But looking at you now, like this, it is not my reflection that I see."

Elizabeth turned and walked down the street as her mother screamed after her, "You're a fool, Elizabeth! You hear me? A fool!"

TWENTY-ONE

L EOLA WAS CLEANING THE master bedroom when she heard the knock at the door, faint yet with purpose. Rolling the bed sheets into a large ball of printed cotton, she wondered who would be calling at this time of day, a Saturday, another working day for most people. Peeking through the lace curtain covering the front door, she was surprised to see her mother on the porch.

"I didn't expect to see you today, Mama. Is everything all right?"

"Everything's fine." Elizabeth set her suitcase on the floor.

Leola noticed the bag. "Are you running away from home?" she asked in jest.

"That's precisely what I'm doing," Elizabeth answered with pride.

"What?" Leola was caught off-guard, upset with herself for making light of the situation.

"I've left your father. It's high time I moved on with my life." Elizabeth smiled wanly.

"Did something happen? Did Daddy—"

"Your father didn't hit me. Although he wanted to, I can tell you that. He raised his hand to me, but I stopped him. I told him he'd never touch me again." Her words filtered the air, strong and proud.

"What prompted this, Mama? Why now?"

"I can't say for sure, Leola. It's just a feeling I have that the time is right. I'm tired of denying myself even a little bit of happiness in this life. I want to be happy again."

Leola's eyes filled with tears. "Where are you going?"

"To Augusta. I wired Uncle Aubrey and let him know I'm coming for a visit. He's the only one of Daddy's brothers I have ever loved and respected. When I married your father, Uncle Aubrey knew how unhappy I was. He didn't like Zach any more than I did. He told me if things ever got bad, I could always come and stay with him and Aunt Gladys."

"Are you coming back?" Leola was breaking.

"I haven't planned everything out just yet." Elizabeth knelt at Leola's side. "Don't cry, baby. Be happy for me, this is good. For once I'm taking care of myself and making my own decisions."

"It's just so sad, Mama. Why does it have to be this way? Why can't we be happy and have what we want out of life?"

Elizabeth hugged her warmly. "It's not always ours to choose what we get out of this life. Sometimes we have to take what it offers whether we want to or not, but we learn from what we're given. It's taken me a long time to learn my lessons, but I'm getting there." Elizabeth cried for herself and her daughter.

"What do you mean about learning your lessons?"

"I've learned to respect myself. All my life everyone else has been making decisions for me, first my parents and then Zach. I got to feeling that I must not be worth much if those around me had to auction me off the way they did. I even started thinking that Hank would've been disappointed in me had we married, and I couldn't bear thinking like that.

"I learned a lot from you, Leola. Lord knows, you didn't have much of a start in life, and how you survived it with as much love as you have with you now is a miracle. I guess Luther had something to do with that, huh?"

Leola smiled.

"When I saw the kind of relationship you have with your girls, it stirred something inside me, something I hadn't felt in a long time. You made me realize just how strong we are, Leola, that we can conquer even the worst things in life. You revitalized me, you gave me the strength to stand up to my life and reclaim what I'd lost many years ago. Thank you, Leola, thank you for showing me the way."

Leola looked deeply into her mother's eyes, seeing her utter joy as she came to terms with the past. She was proud of her mother, and proud of herself for making a difference.

"I've always wanted to tell you something, Leola. But I was ashamed to say anything because of my feelings at the time."

"What?"

"Do you know when I was proudest of you?"

Leola shook her head.

"The day you married Luther. You did something I didn't have the courage to do; you followed your heart. You stood up to generations of tradition and family and property and married the man you wanted to marry. Oh, I was jealous all right, but talk about proud!" Elizabeth's face beamed.

"I'm glad you told me that, Mama. I really am." As Leola looked at her mother, she realized that she would never see her again. A lump formed in her throat. "I love you, Mama."

Elizabeth hugged her daughter with a feeling that eclipsed the years of separation and indifference.

She walked alone to the train depot, leaving the memories of Ben Hill County in a cloud of red dust stirred up by the passing train.

Elizabeth stayed in Augusta one month, remembering how good it felt to laugh and smile and sing again. From there, she traveled to Edgefield, South Carolina, where Hank lived when he died. She stayed at the rooming house his aunt owned, even requesting the very room he occupied. Following the plan her heart mapped out, she inquired about the field where his body was found, getting precise directions from the proprietor.

Around noon the Monday after she arrived, Elizabeth ventured into the field beyond the barn, walking two miles into a clearing in the woods. She looked for three stones placed at the spot where Hank was found by his grieving aunt. Though nearly covered by years of weeds, she found the stones near the center of the oval-shaped field. In them, eventually, staring at their placement, she could see the shape of Hank's lifeless body.

Closing her eyes, alone in the field, all conscious thought erased from her mind, heaven opened its radiant arms of light. The dream returned, Hank before her, tears streaming down his face as he asked forgiveness, the barrel of a pistol between his eyes. He spoke his love for her to the wind, that it would reach her one day on the gentle wings of a breeze. Slowly, he closed his eyes and pulled the trigger. The bullet ripped through his brain, shattering the heartbreak, denying the pain, a stream of blood and matter, love and loss, scattering into the air.

Elizabeth screamed with the ferocity of a thousand mothers who had lost their children, a scream deep from within, primal in its urgency, a scream lasting the forty years she lived without Hank.

All at once, it ended, the screaming stopped as if cut off by a knife. The last breath of air passed through Elizabeth's lungs, its cries reaching skyward, accepted into the marvelous light. She fell to the ground beside the three stones that marked Hank's exodus from this world, remaining there until her body was found, lying peacefully in the field.

TWENTY-TWO

REBECCA WAITED PATIENTLY at the depot, earlier than she needed to be, but there nonetheless when the train arrived. So much time had passed since she'd last seen William, the sporadic trips into town for a couple of hours, hastened words, shallow embraces, a year of life recounted in mere minutes. After the war started, the layovers were even less numerous, distancing families, creating strangers of loved ones.

Everything changed because of the war, The Great War as some called it. The train lines ran on double shifts delivering all the goods and materials they could to help the cause. The grueling schedule worked already tired bodies twenty-four hours a day for weeks at a time. Many of the rail men reached their breaking point, jumping from the train into the stillness of the night, their fates unknown, but to those who remained on board, it couldn't be any worse than working a body to death.

Golden beams from the setting sun touched Rebecca's shoulder as she sat on a small bench underneath the covered portion of the depot, staring at the tracks as they melded into the horizon. She would turn fifty before long, a thought that amused and terrified her. There were times she hadn't expected to live past thirty, yet at other times she felt she could live forever. A tide of memories washed over her, the mother who died at a young age, a father cut down in the prime of life, so distant, so near, so real.

A lonely whistle call announced the train that was bringing her son home. Several people congregated at the depot, all of them looking to the east as the train steamed into view, carrying hope, anticipation, reunion. The ground rumbled as the powerful engine neared. Rebecca turned, facing a stiff breeze from the passing locomotive. Her heart rejoiced. Finally, her son was home.

The small crowd quickly circled the passenger car, anxiously securing positions in hopes of being the first to see and be seen. Rebecca stayed to herself, preferring the shade on the small bench, unfazed by the zealous anticipation surrounding her. This was a moment two years in the making; it would not be rushed.

William exited the train last, his face ruddy, his body ten pounds lighter, though taut and muscular. He walked with the same lazy stride he always did, carrying a dingy jacket over his shoulder, the look on his face telling the story of life on the rails.

"I've been waiting a long time for this." Rebecca hugged William tightly.

"It's good to be home, Mama."

She looked into William's face. "You're tired. When's the last time you got a decent night's sleep?"

William smiled sheepishly. "Probably two years ago."

Rebecca couldn't help chuckling at her son's honesty.

William put his mother's arm in his and escorted her home.

"How long will they let you stay this time?"

William shook his head. "A couple of weeks. But things will be different now that the war's over. It was tough there for a while."

"I can see that from the look on your face. You've grown, William, you're not the headstrong boy who flew out of this town with the wind under his feet."

"It's a hard life, ages a person real fast."

"Do you work with nice people?" Rebecca did not want to pry into William's life, but her motherly instincts would not allow otherwise.

William suppressed the impulse to laugh at his mother's innocence. "It's a whole other world, Mama. Not one that any of us has ever seen."

Rebecca accepted the invitation to proceed further. "What do you mean?"

William thought carefully. "The people I met aren't exactly the kind you'd find in church every Sunday."

Rebecca's eyes grew wide. "You didn't get yourself in trouble, did you? There are all sorts of riffraff out there who'll take advantage of a young boy."

"I know that, Mama. I didn't get into any trouble."

"Oh, William, this is exactly what I was afraid of. You weren't meant for this kind of life. I didn't raise my children to live this way."

"I didn't do anything wrong, Mama."

"All that loose living and fancy women and curse language, I shudder just thinking about it. I can only pray that you kept your distance from that sort of thing."

"It's not as bad as all that."

"And I hear the drinking that goes on is an absolute abomination." Rebecca winced.

"Gee, Mama, the way you make it sound, every town we pulled in to was either Sodom or Gomorrah. Most places along the line are just like Fitzgerald, small towns with only one hitch for a horse."

"Atlanta's a big city." Rebecca would not concede her point.

"What do you want me to do? Sign a written oath that I was on my best behavior?" William half-joked.

"I'm sorry. It's just that I worry about you. Times are hard, and people will do desperate things to try and better their own lives."

"I know." William spoke with a resigned familiarity.

He couldn't tell his mother everything he'd witnessed—the drunken brawls over a game of cards, the prostitutes roaming the streets and bars in search of a quick dollar. Nor could he tell her that his own vices were lured from their hiding places by the rigors of life on the rails. He drank to escape the loneliness, and loneliness was his constant companion. Sometimes he drank for days at a time, unable to distinguish one town from the next, one carload of cotton from another.

There was an emptiness in his life, a gray void that dared him to concede that he needed affection. He always had the love of his mother, but he needed more than that, someone to love him above all others, someone with whom he could share the good in life as well as the bad. What he wanted, needed desperately, was a companion who would always be there just for him.

"Have you given much thought to settling down?"

Rebecca's question caught William off-guard, making him wonder if she could read his thoughts. "Sort of, but it's not easy to meet someone when you spend the majority of your time on a train headed for one town or another."

"You should go to church with me Sunday. You just might meet someone who has a proper upbringing."

William blushed. He'd not been inside a church since he started his life on the rails. "I'm not looking to find someone right away, Mama. They say love comes knocking at your door when you least expect it."

"Never hurts to help it along a little bit."

William looked at her coyly. "Sounds like you've already picked someone out for me."

"Not necessarily, but there are several good prospects in the homemaker Sunday school class." Rebecca winked at him.

"Why this sudden interest in my social life?"

"It's important to have a family so you won't be alone in life. When you get older, you'll have someone to take care of you; it isn't natural growing old alone. When your grandmother died, she was surrounded by her family; she went to heaven knowing she was loved."

William felt a tinge of guilt at the mention of Nancy's death.

"I'm sorry I didn't make it to Grandma's funeral. I tried, but it was impossible to get away."

"I know, son. She went so suddenly, it took us all by surprise."

"How's Daddy taking it?"

Rebecca became pensive, looking down, then away from William, tears filling her eyes. "I've never seen your father so hurt by anything. He just fell completely apart. I think a big part of him died with her."

William put his arm around his mother's shoulders.

"She was always there for him, picking up the pieces after Ezra tore him down. She pulled both of us through the tough times after Daddy died. She was our rock, the steady influence that kept us from falling apart. And now, without her, we've got to learn how to walk through life all over again."

William had never known his father to have a vulnerable side, having only seen the rough exterior of a man forced into maturity before his time. When they reached the house, William slept solidly through the afternoon and into the next day.

Harbard was serving two prisoners their lunch when William arrived. A narrow hallway separated the outer office from the jail cells. William waited, stoic, apprehensive, unsure what kind of reaction he'd receive from his father. When the door opened, his heart jumped, his eyes fixed upon the door.

Harbard stopped dead in his tracks.

"Your mother told me that you'd put on some muscle." Harbard placed the empty trays on a table underneath the window.

William managed a half-smile. "One of the benefits of hitching cars and unloading bales of cotton every day."

"I've seen many young boys become men overnight; the rails will do that."

William suddenly became self-conscious, unable to think of more he could say to his estranged father. Harbard sat behind his desk and looked up at William; his face was different somehow, almost serene, peaceful looking.

"I wish I could've been here for Grandma's funeral." William looked away from his father, ashamed.

"It's all right, son. We all understood."

Again, there was an awkward silence, a fragmented space of regret and forgiveness between them.

"Mama's death had a big impact on me. I never thought of what life would be like without her. I remember how hard your mother took her father's death, and now I know what that feeling is like."

"It's not always easy to feel someone else's pain." William's words surprised even himself.

"I guess we're both experts on that."

Harbard looked directly at William; he nodded silently.

"Your grandmother left something for you." Harbard reached in his pocket and pulled out Ezra's gold watch. "She wanted her first-born grandson to have this. It was Daddy's pride and joy after he retired."

William studied the watch carefully. It had a large, round winding knob on the top that, when pushed down, popped open the face. He put the watch to his ear and listened to its precise ticking, imagining to himself the thousands of tiny parts spinning and turning inside.

"Thank you, Daddy."

The emotion of the moment grabbed them, as if Nancy had purposely planned this to bring father and son together. William didn't want his father to see the tears in his eyes, a weakness that might make him less of a man. As he turned to walk away, Harbard called after him.

"It's good to see you, son. I'm happy things are working out for you."

He walked out of the office a different person, no longer the boy who ran from his problems, intent on finding a means of escape, but, instead, a man who faced his troubles, carving out a life for himself.

As he hurried down the sidewalk, William noticed a flurry of activity on the grounds of Town Square. A hand-painted sign reading "Bake Sale to Benefit Arbor Baptist Church" was placed next to a large booth.

In the midst of the circle of women was a teenage girl with dark hair and an angelic face perfect in shape and complexion. Her soft smile made her even more radiant, the tilt of her head a movement as graceful as a swan in flight. If ever he'd pictured an angel on earth, this was it. So taken was he by her beauty, William momentarily forgot how to breathe.

Hesitantly, he approached the booth, keeping a watchful eye on the pretty girl who, by this time, had turned her attention to a pesky family of blowflies whizzing and whirring over the meringue-topped pies. He stood over the row of frosted cakes, opposite her, lavishing attention over a red-velvet cake with pecan and butter frosting.

Her lack of attention to him irritated William. An inkling of doubt trickled down his spine, his ego briefly entertaining the notion that he wasn't good enough for her, his appearance below standard. He all but abandoned the hope of gaining her attention when a soothing voice interrupted his burgeoning doubts.

"You must have a fondness for red velvet cake."

Confused, William looked up. "Excuse me?"

"You've been staring at that particular cake for ten minutes. I said you must really like red velvet cake."

"Oh, yeah, I do. It's my favorite."

"It's yours for seventy-five cents. All proceeds will help us build a new sanctuary for the church."

Though distracted, William tried to be polite. "Sounds like a worthy cause. How much are the pies?" William eyed the beautiful brunette.

Leola followed his eyes. "Fifty cents apiece, or you can get two for eighty-five cents. That's a real bargain if you've got a sweet tooth."

"How 'bout if I bought the red velvet cake and a chocolate pie? What kind of bargain would I get?"

The woman studied William with amusement. "A dollar and fifteen cents. You must have more than one sweet tooth."

William shook his head. "Supporting the church would make my mother happy."

"Who's your mother?"

"Rebecca Smith."

The woman cocked her head to one side. "Are you William?"

"Yes, I am. Who are you?"

"I'm Leola Smith. My husband and your father are cousins. I haven't seen you in quite a while, you've grown."

Leola called over to Lou.

"Lou, this is William Smith, a distant cousin of yours. This is my daughter, Lou."

She was even more beautiful than he had imagined. William muttered a greeting unintelligible even to himself, then looked away, certain of having made a fool of himself.

"It's a pleasure to meet you." Lou's voice was strong and self-assured.

"What are you doing with yourself these days, William?" Leola asked.

William cleared his throat. "I work for the railroad, as a home guard."

Leola nodded her head, impressed with the young man's ambition. "Maybe we'll see you in church Sunday."

"Yeah, maybe. I've got to run. It was nice meeting you both."

William quickly scurried away, his growing embarrassment following like a long, dismal shadow.

Leola called after him, "William! You forgot something!"

Lou giggled openly as William retrieved his purchases, silently cursing himself for being such a transparent fool, his masquerade as shallow as his concern for the church.

Reaching the security of home, William placed the cake and pie upon the kitchen table then closed himself in his room, relieved that the house was empty, its silence inviting him into a world of daydreams.

TWENTY-THREE

THE TRAIN WHISTLE BLEW for the third, and final, time. Bobby checked his pocket watch, a scowl on his face. William was late, uncharacteristic of the young man who for four years followed every rule as if his life depended upon it. Bobby sighed then gave the signal to the engineer. William sauntered up to the train as if he had all day to board.

"Cutting it a bit close, aren't ya?" Bobby checked his watch again.

"A bit." William tossed his bag aboard an empty cargo car as the train struggled to gain momentum.

"What's gotten into that boy?" Bobby asked no one in particular.

The train pulled away, grinding the rails, heading for another round of small towns, hard work, and chronic loneliness. William sat on the ledge of the car, his legs hanging over the side of the open door, staring blankly at the passing countryside, looking like he'd lost his best friend.

Riding the rails had lost its appeal for him, the long distances an intrusion, the time away from home a nuisance. Even the rhythmic grinding of the wheels upon the tracks no longer soothed his wandering heart. The thought of hitching and unhitching cars, loading and unloading cotton and pine was an annoyance beyond definition. Everything about the job bothered him, nothing more so than being away from the girl who played with his heart.

As the last rays of daylight relinquished their hold to a graying sky, the AB&C line continued its eastward journey toward Brunswick. William had not moved from his vantage point, locked in his own world, his mood devoured by the constant longing for Lou.

"So this is where you've been hiding yourself!"

The voice came from above, an odd angle for sure considering he was riding in an empty train car. William looked up, seeing Earl's head jutting from the top of the car.

"What the hell you doing up there?" William looked at Earl incredulously.

"We thought you'd bailed out and jumped the track, so I've been hopping cars looking for you. Gimme a hand, will ya?"

Earl grabbed the edge of the car at the top of the open door and hung down. William grabbed him by the waist and pulled him inside.

"Whew! I've been up there nearly an hour. Fightin' a steady wind that long can sure tire ya out!"

"You know I'm not stupid enough to jump. What made y'all think I would do that?"

"Nobody's seen ya, we figured you disappeared into the woods somewhere and set out to tangle with a black bear!" Earl gave William a mischievous smile.

"I think you fellas need to find yourselves something else to speculate on." William's tone was flat.

He turned from Earl, his face expressionless and surly. Earl stepped back mockingly, as if he was expecting William to punch him.

"Watch out! Mighty Bob Fitzsimmons is in the ring! He starts with a left, then a right, then another left, and a combination of lefts and rights!" Earl danced around William, dodging imaginary blows.

"Knock it off, Earl. I'm in no kind of mood for your foolishness." William resumed his seat in the open door.

"Damn! I can't even get a laugh out of you! What's up, William? You're as grumpy as an alligator in a dry stream bed." Earl sat next to William.

"Ain't nothin' up with me. You just got an overactive imagination, you know that?"

"It don't take any imagination to know what's up with you, buddy."

Earl pulled a flask from the front pocket of his overalls, downing a healthy swig before offering it to William.

"What do you mean? That it don't take any imagination?" William accepted the flask and downed a mouthful of Tennessee's finest whiskey.

"Only two things in life can make a man as grumpy as you are. One is a lack of money, and the other is a lack of affection. And seein' as how we're both keepin' our heads above water these days, I'd say it's the latter of the two." Earl took another swig.

"A lot you know. There could be a hundred reasons why I'm grumpy. I could just be a natural born bastard, for all you know. When did you sneak off to college and get so smart?" William grabbed the flask.

"I've seen guys in your state of mind too many times. One day on top of the world and the next so far down in the dumps you'd have to reach up to touch bottom. It's got to be a woman—happens every time."

Earl attempted to take the flask away but William held to it tightly, almost downing the remaining whiskey in one swig. The high-octane elixir lightened his mood, lowering the resistance that guarded his wounded soul. Folding his hands behind his head, he leaned back, kicking his feet into the stiff wind, deeply inhaling the cool autumn air.

"I hate this job, hate everything about it. Don't stay in one place long enough to sneeze, can't put down roots anywhere, and sure as hell can't find the right woman."

"Aha! I knew it! You can't put one over on Earl Pomeroy! I knew it was a woman as sure as I'm sittin' here!" Earl rewarded himself with the last of the whiskey.

"I didn't say it was a woman. It's women in general. They act like they're too good to give you a second look. Get themselves all prettied up and then want nothing to do with ya."

William sat up and stared straight ahead, the passing silhouettes of trees and overgrowth blurred into a dismal painting. Suddenly, he sprang to his feet. In what seemed like one movement to Earl, William jumped up, grabbed the top of the open doorway, and hoisted himself atop the car.

Earl looked up at him. "What are you doing up there, you idiot? You're drunk!" Earl saw double images of William.

"Ain't no woman ever gonna catch me. I'm free as the wind! I don't need nobody for nothin'!"

William took off down the length of the car.

"That idiot's gonna kill himself!"

Earl struggled to the top of the car, his head beginning to reel from the whiskey. Out of the corner of his eye, he saw William running across the next car toward the caboose, yelling as loud as he could into the twilight.

Shaking his head in disbelief, Earl followed his buddy from car to car, jumping over the hitching spaces in between, caught up in the moment, feeling as carefree as a high-flying kite on a windy day. The danger of falling between cars and being crushed by the churning wheels never entered his mind.

A stiff wind challenged William's every jump, making the effort all the more exciting. Out of breath, he made the final leap atop the caboose, collapsing onto his back as he landed. He stared at the darkening sky for several minutes, laughing devilishly to himself, thinking what a fool he'd been for doing something so dangerous.

Earl finally caught up with him. "You are one crazy son-of-a-gun, William! I'm surprised both of us didn't break our fool necks doing something so stupid!"

"You gotta admit it was fun!" William remarked with impish glee.

"Fun, hell! It was bald-ass stupid! What'd ya do it for?" Earl breathed heavily.

"You really wanna know?"

"Yeah! I didn't go chasing after you for nothin'! We could've been killed, drunk as we are!"

"I did it for the sheer hell of it. Nothing more, nothing less."

Earl plopped down next to William, wondering what was going on in his friend's mind. A sly grin overcame William's countenance.

"I sure would like to get a look at that gal one day. She must be something special!" Earl breathed.

Before long, Earl dozed off. William stared at the night sky, the smile still etched on his face as he created Lou's face from the specter of shining stars.

The line pulled into Brunswick just after dawn, the port calm and quiet, not quite awakened by the early light bouncing off the Atlantic. A few men waited by the docks when the train arrived, eager to load it up with a shipment of bananas and coffee beans so they could begin the voyage back to Cuba.

William and Earl slept soundly, unaware that the train had reached its destination until the cars rattled to a complete, if not jarring, stop. William's head pounded unmercifully, his mouth dry and stale, his stomach churning, his face green and sweaty. Slowly, the memory of the previous night's escapade returned. The sobering reality of what he'd done did not improve his mood.

He nudged Earl awake, surveying the situation below him. A group of co-workers spotted them atop the caboose.

"What in God's name are you two doing up there?" shouted Roger Whittle.

"Rounding up buffalo! What do you think?" William shot back.

"Get on down from there! We got work to do!"

Though agitated and nauseous, William climbed down from the caboose to begin the daily grind. The sudden movement sent a rush of nausea up his intestines. In a sudden and violent rush, he purged himself of the night's bingeing. The other men laughed at him, all except Earl, who turned green himself.

The working day was made longer by the dull, throbbing headache that stayed with William. Hour upon hour, load upon load, it insinuated itself further into his scalp, down his neck and into his shoulders. As soon as the train was loaded, he checked into the same boarding house he always did and took a long, comatose nap, awakened at eight o'clock sharp by a disgustingly cheery knock on the door.

"Nothing better for your ailments than the hair of the dog that bit ya!" Earl waltzed in.

"That dog should be shot." William returned to bed.

"On the contrary. A couple of belts are just what the doctor ordered. We'll have some dinner then check out what's happening over at the Sea Spray."

William's eyes furrowed at the mention of the Sea Spray Saloon.

"I don't want to go there."

"Why not? The bartender is generous with the drinks, and you can find plenty of action, if you know what I mean." Earl winked at William to accentuate his point.

"Let's just find a place to eat then worry about the entertainment later."

"Whatever you say, partner, but snap to it, time's a wastin'!"

Earl decided they should eat at the boarding house; it would save time and he'd already given the proprietor two dollars for an extra seat at the table. He made quick work of the turkey and dressing before nagging at William to hop over to the Sea Spray. His contagious enthusiasm amused William.

They quickly made their way through the maze of alleyways that led to the small taverns at the fringe of Brunswick's waterfront district. Earl led the way, eager for an evening of poker and, if he played his cards right, romance at the Sea Spray Saloon. The city was full of weekend revelers, electrifying the night air, the taste for adventure as full as the salty breeze that swept through the alleyways. Earl brimmed with excitement. This would be, he felt, an evening to remember.

When they reached the Sea Spray, Earl burst through the door like he'd been shot out of a cannon. William hesitated at first but then thought of Lou, the memory of her, the possibility that he might never see her again. His face dropped, his mood swinging from amusement to melancholy. The dark feelings of loneliness clouded his soul. He entered the tavern with a look that dared anyone to bother him. Earl was already at the bar downing his second shot of whiskey, making small talk with a petite brunette.

"I'll have a whiskey . . . double," William ordered.

"There you are, partner! What happened to ya?" Earl slapped William on the back.

"Nothing. Guess I'm just not as anxious as you," William replied coldly.

"Listen, this here's Velma; she and I got a lot in common. We was both raised in the Methodist Church."

William looked at Earl with annoyance. "Well praise be to God the Father above! Somebody call the justice of the peace, we got ourselves a match made in heaven! Two Methodists swilling sour mash whiskey on a Saturday night!"

Earl threw back his head, cackling at William's dry response. He slapped William on the back again, further antagonizing his disposition. William cut him a nasty look, but Earl shrugged it off with another round of drinks.

As William turned to polish off his drink, he caught Velma's stare. She looked at him with a half-smile, her eyes burning into his. She was a young girl, probably his age or slightly younger, her lips full and pouty, her large brown eyes sorrowful. She spoke in a husky, provocative voice.

"You never did introduce me proper to your friend."

"Oh, I'm sorry, Velma baby, this is the best friend a fella could have on the rails, William Smith."

"How do you do, William?" Velma extended her hand.

"Pleased to meet you." William quickly shook her hand and backed off.

"This your first time at the Sea Spray?" Velma cooed.

"I've been here once." William looked away.

"That's funny. I've never seen you here before, and I'm on this stool practically every night of the week."

"It's been a while." William downed his second drink.

"I've seen this one here plenty of times, usually drunker than a skunk and losing his shirt in a poker game." She winked at Earl.

"See how well she knows me?" Earl cackled again.

"Yeah." William looked at Earl glumly.

"You know me better than I know myself, Punkin." Earl slurred his words.

"Don't call me that! There's only one Punkin at this dump, and it ain't me!" Velma declared.

William's ears perked up; he looked directly at Velma.

"Punkin still comes here?" His voice echoed his surprise.

"As long as there's a breath of life left in her."

"So why aren't we graced with her company tonight? Somebody let the air out of her lungs?" William asked sarcastically.

"I should say not! She's right behind you and wondering just who the hell you are!" Claire's raspy voice filled the air, and her cheap perfume drowned the thick blanket of cigar smoke.

William hastily ordered another double.

She had not aged well. Her face was heavily lined, the bags under her eyes more pronounced. She looked as though she'd lived her entire life in the last four years. When she saw William, she instantly recognized him. A wry smile overcame her face.

"Well, well, well. If it isn't Mr. Small Town America. How's life treatin' ya, Billy boy?" Claire sauntered over next to William.

"You two know each other?" Velma asked in surprise.

"Oh, hell yeah! We go way back, don't we, baby?" Claire purred in William's ear.

"Yeah." William downed the double shot of whiskey and ordered another.

Claire wrapped her left arm in William's and stroked his hair with her right hand. "How 'bout buying Punkin a drink, good lookin'?"

Earl nudged William suggestively, nodding his head toward the door.

"Two double whiskeys," William ordered begrudgingly.

"Thanks, baby. Now what were you kids talking about?"

"I was telling William how much Velma and I are alike," Earl announced proudly.

"Oh, yeah. I can see the resemblance, only she got the looks in the family," Claire retorted dryly.

Earl cackled wildly, losing his balance in the process, stumbling back then forward, his eyes glazed over, a wicked smile across his face. He put his arm around Velma's shoulders and whispered into her ear. After thinking for a moment, she nodded in agreement.

"We're taking off! Gonna look for the gateway to heaven!" Earl winked at William.

"Don't look too hard, you may never find it."

Claire tapped her empty shot glass and smiled at the bartender.

William nodded to Earl, the look on his face imploring Earl to stay. Velma pushed him along before grabbing William's arm and whispering into his ear. "Next time, it's you and me, sweetheart."

Velma helped Earl out of the tavern, leaving William alone with Claire, a fate he did not enjoy. He ordered one drink after another until he was comfortable enough to let Claire take him back to the boarding house.

He could barely stand, let alone walk. Claire shouldered the bulk of his weight as they traveled the alleyways up to the house. He began singing *Amazing Grace,* his mother's favorite hymn. Claire laughed at him, trying to join in though she didn't know the words. They stumbled through the alleyways laughing and singing, William's head spinning in a slow-motion dream.

Claire put her hand on William's mouth as they reached the boarding house. He pushed it away; the smell of her perfume agitated his stomach. Staggering inside and up the stairway, falling back two steps to every one they ascended, William laughed out loud. Claire again put her hand to his mouth.

"Don't do that! You're making me sick!" William barked.

"Shut up, idiot," Claire whispered forcefully. "You'll wake up the whole house!"

They finally reached William's room. Claire fumbled through his pockets for the key.

Once inside, William spun around several times like a top, laughing and singing. Claire grabbed him by the waist, staring into his eyes. William wobbled unsteadily, the room spinning like the inside of a tornado. He didn't know where he was or who he was with. He looked at the dark figure in front of him, seeing only the silhouette of a small-framed woman.

"Lou? Is that you?"

He made fun of the rhyme, repeating it over and over.

Claire unbuttoned his shirt. "I'm whoever you want me to be, honey," Claire replied huskily.

Her voice unnerved William. He felt a sudden rush of nausea gushing up his throat from the pit of his stomach. He pushed Claire aside and knelt next to the bed, heaving violently on the floor. Claire looked at him in disgust.

"Good Lord! What a waste."

She helped William into bed, being sure to place him on his stomach and remove his shoes. Before she left, she took two dollars from his wallet for her troubles.

"Thanks for a great time, little boy blue. Sleep well."

TWENTY-FOUR

Hurry up, Leanice! We're gonna be late!" Lou rushed from the bedroom in a state of panic.

"There's plenty of time. What's your hurry?" Leanice sighed.

Lou's patent leather pumps clanked rhythmically down the stairway. Leanice sighed again, flustered by her sister's vibrant energy. She dreaded the trip to Lake Beatrice.

In a custom dating back further than anyone could remember, the single, young women of Arbor Baptist Church prepared box dinners for the church's summertime social gatherings. The lunches were put on display and then chosen by the available bachelors, matching the preparer of the meal with the young man who chose it. For young women as socially outgoing as Lou, it was an occasion filled with excitement and expectation.

Lou fretted over her box dinner for hours, nearly worrying her mother to death in the process. The kitchen was in total disarray, with greased skillets here and there, two large bowls of flour on the kitchen table, and enough spoons scattered around to supply a small army.

When Lou finally decided upon a dinner of fried chicken with field peas and okra, Leola looked toward the heavens and gave thanks. Her kitchen had never been so messy with so little to show for the effort.

Lou flew into the kitchen from the stairway. "Maybe I should make some rice to go with the okra, and I could stew some tomatoes, too. Okra always tastes better when it's cooked with stewed tomatoes."

"Good heavens, Lou. Don't you think you've done enough damage for one day?" Leola replied with a touch of exasperation.

"It's got to be good, Mama. Otherwise nobody's gonna want it, and I'll be sittin' by myself with all the other old maids!"

"You're hardly an old maid, Lou. I don't think eighteen makes you over the hill."

Lou poured water into a pot and scooped half-a-cup of rice from a glass container.

"Lou, you're not serious about making rice and stewed tomatoes, are you?"

"Of course I am."

"Child, there's not enough time for that now. We're leaving in ten minutes. That rice won't be anywhere near set up by then!"

Lou poked out her lips. "I guess I'll just be an old maid then!"

Leola sighed loudly. "Honestly, Lou, you're going to make an old lady out of me before my time. There's absolutely nothing wrong with your dinner, and I seriously doubt that your entire future rests on a side dish of rice and stewed tomatoes."

Leanice walked down the stairs as Lou grudgingly put away the rice and poured out the pot of water. She wore a simple, blue print dress and her hair was pulled back into a tight bun, making her look older than her twenty-one years.

"Leanice, I'm hard-pressed for figuring out why you chose to wear that dress when you have prettier things to wear." Leola packed her daughters' box dinners into a basket.

"I like this dress, Mama. It's comfortable," Leanice answered demurely.

"It might be, honey, but, quite frankly, it's not that becoming on you. Your lavender dress with the little bows on the ends of the sleeves is real pretty. Why don't you wear it?"

Leanice looked at the floor. "Why do I have to go to the picnic anyway, Mama? You know how much I don't like being around crowds of people. It makes me nervous."

Lou offered her perspective. "What are you so nervous about? It's just like going to church on Sunday, it's the same people."

"I don't want to go."

"No one is forcing you to go, honey. But I do think you should give it a try. You never know if you're going to like something if you don't at least give it a shot."

"There're always more dinners than there are boys, and I'll be one of the girls left out. It's humiliating."

"If you take that kind of attitude with you, it'll certainly happen. I have every confidence that my dinner will attract someone's attention," Lou boasted.

Leola was quick to put Lou in her place. "That's not what you were saying ten minutes ago, when you nearly went hysterical over stewed tomatoes and rice."

"It doesn't matter what Lou makes. Frazier Morris knows which dinner is hers." Leanice walked to the counter.

"No he doesn't!" Lou spoke defensively.

"You always use the same plate so he knows which one is yours. If I uncovered your dinner right now, I'd find a blue plate with a chipped edge and a small crack running from it shaped like a Y."

Leanice opened the box despite Lou's objections. Leola laughed to herself at the unfolding drama.

"Just as I thought, the blue plate with the chipped edge."

"Lou, have you been cheating all this time?" Leola scolded Lou mockingly.

Lou's face turned red. She flew over next to Leanice and covered her dinner. "So what if I am! Frazier likes me, and I like his company. What difference does it make if he knows which dinner is mine?"

"Why, Lou, I do believe you're blushing! How long have you been sweet on Frazier?" Leola couldn't resist the temptation to tease her youngest daughter.

"Can we please leave? We're gonna be late!"

Lou grabbed the basket and walked outside with a scowl on her face. Leanice dropped her head and followed.

"Lord, how did I wind up with two daughters so completely different?" Leola asked with amusement.

A group of tall pine trees provided a canopy against the hot sun, sheltering the tables where the young bachelors would dine with their dinner companions. Wagons and horses encircled the area, small children ran from one place to another, their squeals delighting the ears of parents and onlookers.

As John pulled the cart next to the church building, Leanice's face tightened. Leola carried the dinners to the designated tables, as was the custom, Leanice close by her side, barely able to acknowledge those around her. Lou eagerly joined the group of young women gathered next to the table.

She scanned the edge of the lake where the young bachelors were kept while the box dinners arrived, a mischievous smile on her face. Frazier stood beside a tree with his hands in his pockets. His tall, slender frame easily set him apart from the other young men.

He turned and looked at Lou then tipped his hat to her, their signal that everything was following the usual plan. When all was in place, the women notified the men and the young bachelors were led to the table. After several minutes of inspection, the bachelors drew a number from a hat, delineating their order in picking dinners.

The waiting maddened Lou, her desire to spend the afternoon with Frazier on the line, hoping against hope that he had drawn a low number. Her fondness for him appreciated after their first date, his manners courtly with just enough of a childish quality to have fun. She bit her lip as the first number was called. Martin Smith, Rebecca's son, stepped forward. Lou pouted.

Martin was pale and thin, his frail appearance advancing his years. Quiet and nervous, he rarely ventured beyond his parent's home, only partaking in such occasions when convinced to do so by his mother. All eyes were upon him, the weight of expectation sagged upon his shoulders. He quickly narrowed his choices to two dinners, one of which was Lou's. She held her breath, crossed her fingers on both hands, and sent up a quick prayer. After hedging from one dinner to the other, Martin finally chose the ham dinner with mashed potatoes and gravy.

Lou heaved a sigh of relief, uncrossed her fingers, and smiled at Frazier, who winked in return. The head of the women's Sunday school class called for the preparer of the meal to identify herself. A nervous silence filled the air when none of the girls claimed her date. Martin self-consciously stood in the middle of the circle, his pale face pink with embarrassment.

Again the call was made, lingering in the air, hollow, echoing through an empty canyon, a lonely call unanswered. Finally, Leanice stepped forward. Trembling visibly, she and Martin sat together, neither looking at the other, not even a stolen glance, conversation adrift on the clouds in the sky above them. Leola's face lit up like a field of fireflies; maybe, hopefully, Leanice could break free from the lonely world she had created for herself. If nothing else, at least, this one afternoon could be a small step in a new direction.

The next number was called. Lou tensed, again biting her lip. Frazier stepped forward, presented his ticket, and browsed around the table. He looked seriously at a couple of dinners, particularly eyeing a plate of fried fish with grits and hush puppies. Lou hated it when he teased her like this. Discretion was one thing, but carrying it too far only made her impatient.

He leaned over the plate of fried fish then reached for it, but his attention was caught by a plate of fried chicken. He stood over it, smelling the tempting, crispy aroma. Lou was beside herself, ready to jump into the middle of the circle and pop Frazier on the head. He glanced back over at the fried fish dinner, moved toward it, and then picked up the plate of fried chicken.

"You should be on the stage with all your dramatic training!" Lou sat indignantly at the end of a long table.

"I was just trying not to be too obvious," Frazier complained.

"You were being mean. I'm beginning to wonder if you even like me. How do I know you're not just performing on stage when you tell me that you enjoy my company?"

Frazier squirmed, unsure how he could work his way out of this predicament. "You know how much I like you."

"I don't know anything of the sort, Frazier Morris! If you really liked me, you wouldn't tease me so mercilessly! A real gentleman would act with tact and sensitivity." Lou's eyes flashed coyly.

"I'm sorry, Lou. I didn't mean anything by it. Why are you being so critical all of a sudden? Are you sweet on someone else?" Frazier grew suspicious.

"No. I just want to know where I stand with you. If I'm wasting my time on someone who isn't serious, then I'll find someone who is."

"Gosh, Lou. I sure think you're reading an awful lot into this. I'm only eighteen, you know. It's not like I'm ready to settle down and have a family right away."

"I didn't say anything about settling down. I just want to know how you feel about me." Lou picked at a piece of fried chicken.

Frazier's patience wore thin. "You're infuriating, Lou. How many times do I have to tell ya that I like you?"

Lou thought for a moment. "At least fifty!"

She looked at Frazier with a half-smile. He nodded his head, smiling broadly as he looked into Lou's face, captivated by her beauty.

Leola tried to keep herself from watching over her daughters too much, realizing at some point that she'd have to cut the apron strings. For all practical purposes, they were well past the stage of needing constant motherly attention. She looked toward the lake, where Paul and Lily played with the other children at water's edge without a care in the world. Their innocent play reminded Leola of a time when her own girls were small and how Luther would take them to Chastain's Pond on a hot, summer afternoon. She missed Luther this day as much as any other since he died.

"I don't think Martin and Leanice have said more than two words to each other since they sat down." Rebecca sat down next to Leola.

"I think it's been even less than that," Leola exclaimed.

"I feel sorry for them. They look like they're so out of place here. And for the life of me, I can't figure out why." Rebecca spoke wistfully, barely above a whisper.

"Leanice has been like that since she was a child, almost like she was afraid of entering this life and what it had to offer. When her father died, she withdrew even more. I often wonder what she would be like had Luther lived."

Tears formed in Leola's eyes. "As a mother, you never really know what's going on in a child's mind. They can look happy and content on the outside, but inside they're scared and lonely."

"It's not easy raising children," Rebecca said. "You try to do what's best for them, protect them from the bumps and bruises of life, and give them all the love and support you can. But then you have to set them free, and that's the hardest part of all."

TWENTY-FIVE

THE CLOCK IN THE SMALL ROOM off the kitchen ticked louder than usual. Leola even heard it while she cleaned the bedrooms upstairs, ticking past seconds and minutes that turned into hours, spilling into every room of the house, tapping her shoulder, into her subconscious mind. She tried her best not to think about the exact time of day but it was useless. Leanice had been gone three hours.

Ever since the picnic at the lake, Leanice appeared both troubled and distracted, oftentimes seeming lost, not knowing where she was or where she was going. The days slipped by like breadcrumbs that were swept off the floor, useless and cluttering, no real purpose other than to be wiped away. Leola worried about her daughter, as was her right, attempting to draw her out, discuss what was bothering her, but all she met with was a wall of silence.

It was shortly after two in the afternoon when Leanice came home. The sound of the front door closing sent Leola racing into the living room from the kitchen. "Where in the world have you been? I've practically worried myself into a sickbed wondering where you were!"

"I'm sorry, Mama. I told you I was going into town."

Leola backed off, defused by Leanice's nonchalant reply. "Yes, I know, but it's not like you to go off by yourself for such a long stretch of time."

"I had some things to see about, that's all," Leanice answered calmly.

"Did you go shopping?" Leola prodded.

"No, ma'am. I went into town to look for a job." Leanice walked past her mother.

Dumbfounded, Leola followed. "A job? Why didn't you tell me that?"

Leanice poured herself a glass of water. "Because I wanted to do it by myself, and I didn't want anyone teasing me about it."

"Tease you about it? Leanice, we wouldn't tease you about anything you decided to do."

"You know what I mean, Mama. I'm not like Lou, or anybody else for that matter. Nobody's as shy as me or as nervous as I am, and nobody thinks I can do anything for myself. So I wanted to prove to everyone, including myself, that I can."

Leola beamed. "Honey, you can do anything you set your mind to. It doesn't matter if you're shy or outspoken, short or tall, black or white. If you want to accomplish something in life, you'll find a way to do it. Did you find a job?"

"I start work tomorrow at Halperin's Dime Store. I'll be waiting on customers when they're ready to pay for their purchases."

Leola hugged Leanice tightly. "I'm so proud of you. I have often worried about letting my daughters grow up, thinking that I always had to be there to show them the way. But I don't have to worry anymore, my girls are young women who can find their own way."

Leanice and her sister still shared a room, even though Nellie, Ruth, and Wilbur had left the house to begin families of their own. They actually preferred it that way and they weren't ready to put an end to the comfort of having the other so near.

Lou stretched out on the bed, the blue tint of moonlight spilled into the room. She was as curious about her sister's new job as Leanice was about Lou's boyfriends. "Are you nervous about tomorrow?" Lou asked.

"A little. I'll start to thinking that I won't be able to do the job and then they'll fire me and I'll be a burden on everyone for the rest of my life."

"You're not a burden, Leanice. Why do you say that?"

"Because I don't want to have to depend on anyone other than myself. I know it might be hard to believe, but I don't want to be afraid of living. The picnic at Lake Beatrice last week made me realize that." Leanice yawned.

Lou propped herself on her elbow, looking through the blue haze at her sister. "How so?"

"I've got to find out who I am, what I'm capable of doing, and what I'm not capable of doing. I know I'll never be an outgoing person. Poor Martin nearly starved the other day from a lack of conversation."

"A person can change, Leanice. Just because you're uncomfortable around someone one day doesn't mean it'll be that way every day."

"But it will be. I know that. There are some things about ourselves that we know will always be there. It's a part of yourself that you can't explain. I will always be by myself, but I'm learning that it doesn't mean that I have to stop living."

Lou mulled over Leanice's words, the sadness they conveyed, thinking how much of life she would miss without a husband and children. But she understood her sister's point. Having her own family was a part of Lou that had always been there. One thing she realized at that moment, more than ever before, was that she would always be there for her sister.

"Do you think you'll get married?" Lou asked quietly.

"Maybe, but if I don't, it won't be the end of the world. What about you and Frazier? You two seem to be having a high old time."

Leanice faced her sister with a renewed interest in the conversation. Lou crossed her eyes and contorted her face. "Frazier is fun to be with and he looks good, but he's very immature. He cuts the fool all the time. I can't get a serious conversation out of him to save my life. I can't see him wanting to settle down for a long time."

"Are you that ready to get married?" Leanice asked with some surprise.

"I think so. I want to have children and my own house to fix up the way I want it. I don't want to have to do something the way someone else tells me to do it."

Leanice giggled out loud. "Uncle John?"

"Who else?" Again, Lou rolled her eyes. "I don't know how Mama puts up with it. He's always telling her to do something this way or that way because Aunt Susie Floyd did it like that. I would be pulling my hair out."

"I feel sorry for Mama. Things would be so different if Daddy were still alive."

"Do you still think about him?" Lou asked.

"Every day. I miss him as much now as I did when he died."

"Me, too. Do you remember when he'd take us into town for ice cream on Saturday afternoons?"

"And then we'd stop at Chastain's Pond to go swimming. Mama would nearly have a heart attack thinking we'd wander in too far and drown. Remember how she used to yell at Daddy any time one of us went underwater?"

Lou couldn't stifle a hearty laugh. "Lord, yes. Her face turned red and she screamed like she'd just seen the devil himself walk right into the middle of prayer meetin'."

Leanice buried her face in the pillow so her laughter wouldn't wake up the others. "And Daddy would get that expression on his face like he didn't know who that crazy woman was carrying on like that. And he'd dive underwater and swim way out in the lake, just to make Mama scream even more."

Both girls laughed until their sides hurt, something neither had done in a long time. The memories of their father carried with them a peacefulness that reached beyond the dimensions of time.

Leanice awoke early the next morning, too excited to sleep past five o'clock. She changed outfits several times, worrying that she didn't have the right clothes for work, then settled on the lavender dress with the tiny bows on the ends of the sleeves, the one her mother liked. She wore her hair in a loosely wrapped bun with ringlet curls along the sides of her face.

Leola did a double take when Leanice entered the kitchen. It was like looking into a mirror twenty years ago. "Don't you look stunning!" Leola held her daughter by the shoulders.

Leanice smiled self-consciously. "Thank you, Mama."

"I'm very proud of you, Leanice. Make sure after each working day that you're proud of yourself, too. Promise me that, okay?"

"I will, Mama."

Leola kissed her daughter on the forehead and went about the business of getting through the day.

Shortly after three o'clock, a frantic knock pounded on the front door. Leola was in the middle of scrubbing the kitchen floor and lost her balance as she scurried across the slippery surface. A man with a worried look on his face stood at the door.

"Are you Mrs. Smith? Mrs. Leola Smith?" He was short of breath.

"Yes, I am." A sense of dread infiltrated her.

"I'm Cale Garber, Sarah's son."

"Oh, yes. I remember now. You worked with my father."

"Yes, ma'am. That's why I'm here. Mama sent me. Your daddy had an accident a couple of weeks ago. We didn't think it was too serious at the time, but then his leg turned green, so we called the doctor. He said it was gangrene and there was nothing he could do. Mr. Zack took a turn for the worst last night. That's why Mama sent me."

With mixed emotions, Leola rode with Cale to her father's farm; a million images flashed before her, a little girl crying in the loneliness of her room, a mother afraid to breathe. Almost every image of her father contained an element of anger and pain that made her stomach turn. She felt faint, choking on the silent screams of a little girl terrified into obedience.

The cart rounded the bend into the last stretch of the road, exposing the house that once haunted her. Vines wrapped around the exterior, consuming it, making the little house look more like a large, unkempt shrub.

Cale escorted Leola inside. A wave of melancholy assaulted her as she looked over the furnishings that her mother had worked so hard to keep clean. The echoes of a broom rhythmically sweeping the floors sounded in the hallway. Leola cried as she pictured her mother's small frame tirelessly working its way around the house.

"I know how you must feel, Leola. I lost my daddy two years ago. It hurt so bad, I didn't think I could take it."

Cale wrapped his burly arm around her. Leola couldn't bear to tell him that she was not crying for her father, but for the pain she and her mother endured at his hands.

"Mama's with him. She said it wouldn't be fittin' for a human being to die alone. He's in his room." Cale pointed toward the side hallway.

Leola forced herself to walk solemnly to the back room. Her hand gripped the doorknob, though she could not turn it, the effort futile, as if the knob had burned her hand. Cale stepped forward and slowly opened the door.

Sarah gave her a compassionate hug, smiling warmly, then left the room, closing the door behind her. Leola faced her father, the man who brought such fear into her life, the larger-than-life father who terrorized a little girl. Then, he looked as though he were seven feet tall, but now, on his deathbed, he was a mere shell of the towering man she'd known.

She sat in the chair next to the bed, staring blankly at him. The sight of her father evoked little emotion within Leola, other than the sadness of a life so misspent.

He slept most of the time she was there, unaware that his only child, the one who so cursed his life, had returned in the end. He struggled to open his eyes, turning his head slightly toward her. A hint of recognition shone on his face and what looked like a brief, pitiful smile. His eyes closed, and the last breath left his body.

The saddest part of all, Leola thought, was that no one would truly grieve her father's death.

TWENTY-SIX

Etta angrily watched from the bedroom window as her mother weeded the vegetable garden. The scorching heat spared no one, inside or out, as it crept into every breathable space, draping itself over everything within its reach like a twenty-pound sack of damp flour. Etta fanned herself rigorously, her temper rising as high as the noontime temperature on a hot southern day. The indignity of being ignored grated on her remaining untested nerve.

Rebecca chose to work in the garden despite her daughter's vociferous tirade to the contrary, which the neighbors down the street heard with distinct clarity. No matter how angry Etta became or how loudly she argued her point, Rebecca was not swayed. Agitated to the point of distraction, affronted by the insult to her nursing career, Etta placed her hands on her hips, shook her head side-to-side, and yelled out the window.

"How much longer do you plan on being stubborn? That's all this is about! You wouldn't have stayed out there this long if I hadn't told you not to go out there in the first place!" Etta barked one last time.

Rebecca continued tilling the ground as though she had fully expected another outburst. Without breaking stride, she answered calmly. "I'll be done soon, Etta. I'm not pushing myself to do too much."

"You're pushing yourself into an early grave, that's what you're doing! You're going to have a stroke and drop dead right there on top of your precious turnips!" Etta sneered.

Rebecca stopped tilling momentarily and wiped her forehead. Taking a deep breath, she surveyed the progress she'd made. "If it'd make you feel any better, you can bring me a glass of cold water," Rebecca called out.

"I oughta bring out a net and drag you back inside. You belong in a home for crazy people since you're acting so crazy!" Etta slammed the window shut.

Rebecca merely shrugged her shoulders and sighed to herself. As headstrong as Etta was, there was no point to be made by arguing with her.

Etta handed the glass of water to her mother, snatching the hoe from Rebecca's hands. "Give me that blasted thing! I'll finish tilling the ground myself!"

"I don't want you doing that, Etta. This is my job to do, and I'm going to do it." Rebecca spoke softly but with authority.

"Mama—"

"Etta, listen to me. You're making this very unpleasant. I enjoy doing this. It gives me a sense of peace, and I need that. It's good for me. I've been working this garden since before you were born, and I'll continue working in it as long as the good Lord lets me.

"Everyone needs one thing in their life that no one can take away from them. Most people find it in their work, whatever that may be. You know how much you like working at the hospital and being with your friends there. It's something that's uniquely yours, and you wouldn't want anyone telling you that you could no longer do it, now would you?"

"I'm not saying you should give this up!" Etta replied defensively.

"You have a fit every time I do a little work in this garden, whether it's hot, cold, warm, or just right. I want you to stop that, Etta. If you don't like me doing this, then just turn your back and keep silent."

Rebecca handed Etta the empty glass and returned to her chore. The searing heat prompted more frequent breaks than usual, the thought entering her mind that perhaps it was too hot to continue on. Rebecca arched her back, stretching out the sore muscles after stooping for such a prolonged time. Her eyes closed tightly as she faced the sun.

A warm breeze washed over her, accomplishing little more than moving the intense heat from one spot to another. As she opened her eyes, the shadow of a man flanked beside her, at arm's length. She did not feel threatened in any way, only thinking it odd that someone would sneak up behind her without making his presence known.

"Sure is a scorcher today. Hasn't been this hot in at least five years. I don't mind it so much myself, but it sure is hard on the turnips." Rebecca spoke into the stifling air.

The man did not answer, prompting Rebecca to tighten her grasp on the sharpened hoe.

"Can I help you with something?"

"You can start by giving me a big hug," the man finally answered.

Rebecca's face brightened, even more brilliant than the sun, recognizing the voice immediately.

"Why didn't you tell me you were coming home?" She threw her arms around William.

"I didn't want to give you time enough to wonder whether you wanted me home or not." William smiled coyly.

"Oh, William, stop that! You know you're always welcome in your own home." Rebecca looked him up and down. "You're still too skinny; I'll have to do something about that. How long are you here for this time?"

William grinned slyly. "As long as you'll have me. I asked to be transferred to the stockyard, and Bobby said it was fine with him. I'm home for good, Mama."

"Hallelujah, son. Hallelujah!"

It was still hot after sundown, so much so that at best a glass of iced tea was little more than lukewarm. Rebecca used a white lace hand fan to keep cool as she and Harbard sat on the swing in the breezeway. William opened the screen door, sitting in its place with one foot propped against the doorframe.

Rebecca studied him carefully, knowing something was on his mind by the way his lips pursed together.

"How are things down at the rail yard?" Harbard asked. "I haven't talked with Bobby lately. Virgil and I have been tracking down 'shiners the last couple of weeks."

" 'Bout back to normal." William flicked a beetle off his leg.

"I imagine it got kinda rough there for a while, what with the trains running double time and all. I don't envy you that."

"I wouldn't want to go through it again anytime soon," William replied wearily.

"Why any civilized human being would want to go to battle with another is purely beyond me. It's hard enough getting by each day without having to fight someone to prove it." Rebecca aired her philosophy.

"Wars are fought over small matters," Harbard said. "If everyone would just let everyone else be, there wouldn't be any wars. But people aren't contented unless they're sticking their noses in where they don't belong. It's just the nature of the beast. No one's truly happy with what they've got, they always want something more." He sipped his tea.

William ran his left foot up the doorframe and kicked the side of the steps with the other. He was a million miles away.

"Is something bothering you, son?" Rebecca asked.

William looked away. "Nothing I can't work out myself."

Rebecca glanced at Harbard, who silently discouraged further interrogation.

"We're having a picnic on the grounds after church Sunday if you're interested, William." Rebecca cast the bait.

"I don't know, maybe."

"Sure will be lots of good food there. I tried to talk Etta into taking a box dinner, but she wouldn't hear of it. She said it was a disgrace to put girls on display like that." Rebecca shook her head. "That girl's as headstrong as a mule."

William shunned the idea of matchmaking-by-dinner, but in the back of his mind he clung to the hope of seeing Lou once again.

A string of wispy clouds, looking like puffs of cotton tied together by a narrow rope, lazily filtered past the midday sun. William stood nervously with the other bachelors down by the lake, his hands in his pockets, staring over the calm waters as the ladies of the church set the large cedar table with the box dinners.

His heart skipped a beat when he eyed Lou amongst the young women. Her soft blue eyes sparkled in the light of midday, her skin as soft and pure as finely combed cotton. She scanned the group of bachelors, purposely ignoring Frazier, disenchanted by his frivolous nature.

William studied the dinners carefully, hoping that fate, if not intuition, would lead him to Lou. Narrowing his choices to fried catfish and meatloaf, he reached for the catfish, his hand upon the plate, when, as if guided by an invisible force, he chose the meatloaf dinner. Lou stepped forward, her eyes meeting his, completing the dream he'd held for two years.

TWENTY-SEVEN

T HE SETTING SUN CAST LONG, billowy shadows across the yard, dancing from side to side in the evening breeze. John focused his attention on the corner of Altamaha and Lee Streets, his jaw clenched and set, a hard look of irritation casting his face into a deep scowl. He'd been fixed in that position for an hour, growing more agitated the longer he waited. A noisy group of passing children did not interrupt his stare.

"I thought you were inside taking a nap," Leola called from the doorway.

"Can't sleep," John snapped.

Leola knew that tone of voice all too well. John had worked himself up about something, but she was not really compelled to find out what it was. She stepped out onto the front steps, in front of John, basking in the glory of the last rays of daylight. "It's such a beautiful afternoon, I feel like going for a stroll. You want to join me?"

"I aim to stand right here for a spell." John did not even bother to look at her.

Leola studied her husband carefully. "Do you want to let me in on what's got you so riled up?" Leola treaded lightly.

"It will be sundown shortly, and Lou is still off gallivanting with that boy. It's high time she got herself home. It's not proper for a young girl to be out past dark."

Leola nodded in an understanding manner and looked toward the junction of the two streets. "I wouldn't worry too much about it, John. Lou's a good girl. She's been raised in the church, knows what's right and what's wrong. She'll be home soon," Leola replied confidently.

"All the same, she shouldn't be out past dark. Doesn't matter how good she is. What I'm concerned about is that boy and what's on his mind!" John spat onto the ground.

"William's a nice young man. Knowing his parents, particularly his father, I don't think he'd do anything improper."

"A father's influence on a young boy isn't the same after the boy becomes a man. And that boy rode the rails for a number of years. I don't trust boys who've lived that kind of life."

Leola looked at John quizzically. "What do you mean by that?"

"I mean that any boy who's been living on the fly like he has and consorting with God knows what kind of people is not a suitable match for a girl like Lou. She shouldn't become involved with someone like him, and you shouldn't let her."

John's manner was condescending. Leola felt her temper rising. "I can't tell my daughters who they can date and who they can't date. That's a matter of the heart, and you can't tell the heart what it feels."

"It is the responsibility of parents to steer their children toward the path in life that's best for them. Children cannot know what's best for them because they're not experienced enough. They need the guidance of someone older and wiser."

"I think Lou's mature enough to make decisions concerning her own life."

"I don't. And you're wrong for letting her. Susie Floyd wouldn't allow it, and neither will I!"

This latest comparison to her predecessor unnerved Leola. "Susie Floyd did not give birth to my children, John. She does not know everything they've had to face in life. She wasn't there after their father died. She doesn't know what went on in my father's house while they lived there. I know my children better than anyone, and when I say they can be trusted, that means you better trust them."

Though agitated to the point of distraction, John refused to reply. Leola's forthright response surprised him, and what surprised him even more was that she didn't agree with him. He spat into the ground once again.

"I've tried my best to do things the way you wanted them done, John, even though I wanted to scream every time you said that Susie Floyd would do it like this or that. But when it comes to my children, I will not let a dead woman tell me how to raise them. Nor would I let the memories of Luther raise your children. I don't want you saying anything ugly to Lou when she gets home, you hear?"

John glared at Leola, but she did not back down. With a grievous sigh, he marched into the house, slamming the door behind him. Leola shrugged her shoulders, turned toward the setting sun, and took a nice, leisurely walk.

The shimmering light reflected off the lake like thousands of sparkling diamonds, dancing briefly upon the gentle ripples as William skipped stones across the water's surface. In the distance, a mourning dove cooed its lonely song, echoing against the tranquility of a lazy afternoon. Lou leaned against a sturdy pine tree.

She watched William with amusement as he attempted to skip a stone across the lake. He was determined to make it work, refusing to give up until he'd accomplished the feat. He made several stones skip four times, but each one plopped underwater before the fifth skip. Frustrated, he threw the remaining stones into the water.

Stalking the shoreline, he feverishly searched for the perfect stone, one that was smooth on all sides and flat rather than round. He threw the round, jagged stones he found into the pond, cursing them under his breath. He was consumed with the need to impress Lou in all that he did, and since he'd already bragged about his ability at skipping stones, there was no way he could let her down.

"If I can find the right stone, I'll make this work," William huffed as he dug into an embankment at the water's edge.

"What makes one different from another?" Lou asked.

"The round ones don't skip well. A flat stone will bounce across the entire lake, especially when the water's as calm as it is today."

William's face shone as streams of sweat trickled down his cheeks, his determination contagious. Lou joined in the search, intrigued by William's indomitable spirit and unfaltering attitude.

While William looked in a narrow inlet, Lou searched along the dirt road that led down to the lake. She picked up anything that vaguely fit the description, hoping one of the stones would do the trick and save William's pride. He was like a little child, she thought to herself, desperately seeking the approval of those around him.

She examined the stones she'd collected and picked out the flattest and smoothest of the bunch. She looked at it closely, holding it up against the sky to see the detailed, smooth contours of its surface.

"What you got there?"

"Take a look at this. You think it'll work?" Lou handed the stone to William.

He rubbed it between his fingers, testing its feel in his hand. "Now that's what I call a skipping stone!"

William looked at her with a broad smile. "You just might have saved my reputation, Lou."

She followed him down to the edge of the lake, his infectious enthusiasm stirring excitement within her. Dipping the stone in the water, he washed off the excess dirt; its surface gleamed brightly, a perfect specimen. He held the stone firmly between his thumb and index finger, showing Lou how he would flick his wrist just as he released the stone to make it spin.

"If you get this thing spinning just right, it'll shoot off the surface of the water like a bullet out of a rifle."

Lou watched eagerly, captivated by William's attention to detail. He waited for the precise moment when not even the slightest breeze caused a ripple upon the water.

He cocked his right arm behind him, held it for a fraction of a second, then slung it forward, releasing the stone with a flick of his wrist. He and Lou watched anxiously as the stone skipped on the lake once . . . twice . . . three times . . . four

. . . five . . . six . . . seven. Seven skips! William jumped into the air, whooping and hollering like he'd just hit a home run to win a game of softball.

There was something charming about William's childlike glee over an event as simple as skipping stones. In him, Lou saw images of her own father.

"I've never done seven before! That's a record I might not break for a while. And it's all because of you. Thanks, Lou. I'm glad you didn't give up on me."

William placed his hands on Lou's shoulders, looking into her eyes, into the innocent pools of purity, a love unconditional. He stroked her hair; it was soft to the touch, as fine as corn silk. This was a fantastic dream, one from which he never wanted to wake. Lou smiled at him tenderly and stepped into his embrace. He held tight to her, instilling the sense of security she had longed for since her father's death.

William thought about his days riding the rails, the endless stops along the line as well as the frequent drinking binges. It all seemed so long ago, as if it never really happened. How strange is life, he thought, that two people can find each other despite the separation of time and distance.

They held hands as they left the lake, strolling casually toward the car, hoping their time together would never end.

TWENTY-EIGHT

U NCLE JOHN SURE WAS UPSET with you this afternoon," Leanice whispered into the darkness.

"What about?" Lou asked.

"You and William being gone so long. I heard him talking to Mama."

"I told him we'd be home before dark! What's his problem?"

"You know him. He told Mama that if Aunt Susie Floyd were alive, she wouldn't let a daughter of hers stay out so late in the day." Leanice mimicked his voice.

"When is he ever going to get off that train? Aunt Susie Floyd's been dead for years, and he still throws her memory into Mama's face every chance he gets. What did Mama say?"

"Oh, she lit into him. Told him that she can't tell us who to date, and he can't either."

"Good. I'm glad she stood up to him. I don't want her suffering because of me." Lou turned over facing Leanice.

"There's something else I should tell you, but you've got to promise me you won't get mad."

"What is it?" Lou asked.

"You've got to promise."

"I promise, cross my heart and hope to die. What is it?" Lou's impatience overshadowed her curiosity.

"Uncle John doesn't like William. He said that any boy who's worked the rails can't be trusted. He doesn't think you should get involved with him."

Lou's temper flared. "Well, what does he think he's going to do about it? He can't forbid me to see William. My daddy wouldn't do that!" She paused to catch her breath. "Besides, it's too late to tell me not to get involved with William."

Leanice shot a look at Lou, catching her silhouette against the window. "Do you love him?" Leanice whispered.

"I think so. I know that I've never felt this way about anyone before. I've certainly never met anyone like William. In some ways he's very strong, and in other ways he's just like a little boy. He'll set his mind to doing something, and he won't give up until he does it. I like that about him, it shows character." Lou smiled in recollection of the afternoon.

"What if Uncle John refuses to let you see him?" Leanice asked pensively.

"If William feels as strongly about me as I do him, that won't be a problem."

"What do you mean?"

"We'll get married," Lou answered decisively.

Leanice was silent as the repercussions of the situation became apparent. She hadn't thought seriously about losing her sister until this very moment.

John was up early the next morning, having tossed and turned all night trying to figure out some way to keep Lou and William apart. He was as much concerned for his own pride as he was for his stepdaughter's well-being. The thought of losing control of the situation angered him.

He jumped up from the table after breakfast, informing Leola that he was going into town. His eyes sparkled, his smile mischievous, the stride in his step buoyant, practically lifting him off the ground. Leola let him be, grateful that his mood had changed.

He walked around the market trying to look as interested in cantaloupe as he possibly could, squeezing and sniffing the ripening melons, all the while scanning the interior for Frazier, though there was no sign of him. John had little patience for delay. The succulent smell of freshly cut watermelon did not alleviate his mood.

"Hi there, Mr. Smith!" Frazier called to John as he ran into the market.

John breathed a sigh of relief. "Hello, Frazier. How's the world treating you?"

"Keepin' busy today. I've already made five deliveries, and it ain't even ten o'clock yet!" Frazier's smile was as big as his broad shoulders.

John returned the smile. "Glad to hear it. Everybody should be so busy."

"What can I help you with? Those are mighty good cantaloupe you're looking over. They came straight over from Abbeville, so did the watermelons. Nobody grows 'em sweeter or juicier than Old Man Comstock." Frazier rearranged some of the picked-over vegetables.

"Nothing I like better than a good slice of watermelon. Those we had at the picnic last week sure tasted good."

"Yes siree. We supply watermelon for all the church picnics. Do it every year," Frazier boasted proudly.

John treaded slowly, setting his plan into motion. "Say, I don't remember seeing you at the last picnic."

"Oh, I was there. It was the first time I didn't get to pick out Lou's dinner plate. William got to her first, and I wound up with Ruth Taylor."

"That's right, I forgot about that. Lou was mighty disappointed. It's always a highlight for her when the two of you get together."

Surprise registered on Frazier's face. "I didn't think she really cared one way or the other. She looked like she was having a good time with William."

"Nah, she was just being polite, didn't want to hurt his feelings. That's the kind of girl Lou is, very sweet and considerate, sometimes too much for her own good. As pretty as she is, the young fellows flock around her. And because she's so sweet and friendly, some young men can misinterpret her intentions."

"Oh, I know that all too well. There's not a prettier girl in the county, and I'd venture to extend that compliment statewide!" Frazier blushed.

John casually moved further into his plan, sizing up a healthy looking watermelon as he took another step. "When's the next picnic? Has the church put in an order for watermelons?"

"Not that I know of. The one we had last week might be the last for the summer."

"Hmmm. It'd be a shame to let these melons go to waste. I tell you what, why don't you drop a couple off at the house late this afternoon and stay for supper? And throw in a cantaloupe, too."

"Sure thing, Mr. Smith. And thanks for the invitation. I accept with gratitude."

John walked away from the market on a cloud of air, proud of himself for pulling off such a compelling performance.

The dinner table was set as usual, but with two places on each side and one on each end. When Lou entered the kitchen, she noticed the extra place setting next to her. "Are we expecting company?"

"I suppose. John said to set out an extra plate for dinner." Leola added a ham hock to a boiling pot of black-eyed peas.

"Who's coming over?"

"I don't know, he wouldn't say. Sometimes John doesn't feel the need to explain."

Lou helped her mother by slicing a loaf of bread and putting it on the table with a bowl of home-churned butter.

John rushed in from the back porch. "Has the delivery gotten here yet?"

"What delivery?" Leola looked over her shoulder.

"I had a taste for watermelon tonight, so I'm having a couple sent over. Where are the children?" John was bursting with nervous energy.

"Upstairs. Why?" Leola took note of his frantic behavior.

John called to his children. "Paul! Lily! Get yourselves ready for dinner!"

"Why are you calling them now? For heavens sake, John, Leanice isn't even home yet!" Leola didn't like being hurried while cooking.

"I just want everything to be ready when our company gets here." John glanced at Lou before closing himself in the washroom.

She watched him warily, curiously alarmed by his bubbling enthusiasm. If Lou learned anything from her mother, it was that backing down from adversity would only create more adversity.

The children raced down the stairs and took their places at the table as Leola placed the fried chicken on a large serving plate. Lou chipped away at a block of ice, filling glasses with the pieces.

"Why is there another plate at the table?" Lily asked.

"Because your father invited someone to eat with us," Leola answered.

"Who?"

"I don't know, sweetie. He wants to surprise us."

"I hope it's Miss Turlington. I like her," Paul stated.

Leola patted him lightly on the head. "Good for you, Paul. I don't know too many boys who like their teacher well enough to invite her to dinner."

"She lets us do fun things in class. And she's pretty."

Leola couldn't help herself from laughing.

"What's so funny?" John sat at the table.

"Paul was hoping that you'd invited Miss Turlington over for dinner."

"The guest we're having for dinner is someone your sister will enjoy seeing."

"Who'd want to see Lily?" Paul asked disdainfully.

"I have lots of friends! More than you!" Lily replied defiantly.

"I was talking about your other sister." John looked at Lou as she set the glasses on the table.

She returned his glance with a mock smile. "Me? Who would I want to see? Unless it's William. Did you invite William over for dinner?"

John's face dropped, his mood shifting midstream. He snatched the glass from Lou's hand as she attempted to set it in front of him. Leola watched him intently, a growing suspicion engulfing her.

"Where do you want these, Mr. Smith?" Frazier followed Leanice into the dining room, carrying two large watermelons.

"Set 'em over there, son." John directed him to a large table freshly coated with white paint.

"These were heavier than I thought. I kinda worked up a sweat on the way over."

"Have a seat, son. Lou, pour our guest a glass of tea." John directed Frazier to the seat next to Lou's.

She poured Frazier's drink with an overabundance of graciousness, determined to outwit her stepfather regardless of where its outcome might take her. Leanice sensed the tension between them and glanced over at Lou, silently communicating her support.

"Frazier tells me that we've probably seen the last picnic of the summer. I seem to recall that we always had one more just before the change of seasons, into the second week of September."

"I don't think so, John. That's close to Lou's birthday, and I don't remember there being one that late," Leola answered quickly, hoping to keep the conversation in calm waters.

"Well, that might be. I can barely remember the last one we had. In fact, I didn't remember seeing Frazier there at all. I'm so used to he and Lou being together."

Leola looked anxiously around the table. "Eat some more peas, Lily."

"I don't want any. Can I be excused?" Lily asked.

Leola excused her from the table, aware that tempers were on edge.

"I know Lou was disappointed the two of you couldn't be together at the last picnic, Frazier." John ventured forward.

"That's the way it happens sometimes. William beat me out fair and square." Frazier shrugged his shoulders, smiling sheepishly.

"I don't think Frazier suffered too much. He and Ruth looked to be having a good time together." Lou playfully nudged Frazier with her elbow.

"Ruth's a nice girl, but you're a better cook." Frazier blushed openly.

John nodded his head subtly, convinced his plan was taking root. He steered the conversation even further, arrogantly pursuing his selfish cause. "Nothing a man appreciates more than a wife who's a good cook. Three square meals a day, that's what I say. You live a long life if you have a healthy appetite."

"Oh, I agree." Frazier wiped his mouth.

"Lou's a fine little cook. Her mother taught her very well. Isn't that right, Lou?"

"Uh-huh. Mama taught me how to cook, sew, make tatting, stand up for what I believe in, and always follow my heart."

Lou looked directly at John, her expression sincere but not aggressive. Leanice giggled to herself. Leola prayed that things would not get out of hand.

"I agree with that, too," Frazier said. "A person should never do something unless it feels right." He dipped more peas onto his plate.

"Sometimes the heart needs guidance, though. It doesn't have the capacity to think and reason like the mind. And what better teacher is there for the mind than experience?" John lured Lou into a debate.

"Feelings are what join two people together. And feelings are a result of the heart, not the mind," Lou replied.

John put down his knife and fork. Leaning on his elbows, he clasped his hands together over his plate, like a preacher preparing for a lengthy sermon. "Feelings can often cloud a person's judgment, Lou. And when that happens, you can't see what's truly there, what the other person is like, because the heart is impulsive."

Lou stood her ground, fending off his rebuttals with kindness and logic. "The mind helps you choose friends. Because of it, you figure out what they're like and then decide if your common interests can form a friendship. I suppose that's how you decided that Frazier would be a good friend, and why you invited him for dinner. But love is another matter altogether. Only the heart can tell you who to love."

John's face turned beet red, as though he'd suddenly been stricken with a paralytic malady. Lou felt his anger wrapping around her, pulling tight. John looked away, biding his time until he could explode.

Frazier left without realizing the powder keg of emotions underlying the gathering.

"I want to talk to you, young lady . . . alone." John framed the doorway leading into the kitchen.

Lou placed a stack of plates into the cabinet. "What do you want to talk about?" Lou asked naively.

John didn't answer, the permeating silence speaking for him.

Leola was turned away from John. She spoke to him as she scrubbed the last plate. "Whatever you have to say to Lou you can say in front of me, John. There are no secrets in this house."

"This concerns Lou and me, nobody else."

Leola turned to face John, wiping her hands on a dishtowel. "If it concerns my daughter, then it concerns me. What's on your mind?"

John put his hands on his hips, nodded his head, and laughed sarcastically. "If you want me to fight both of you, then that's fine by me. Why not bring Leanice into the fray as well. Have a seat, Leanice. You might enjoy this."

John stood in the middle of the kitchen, his hands grasping the back of a chair. He stared at Lou, his voice controlled.

"How dare you embarrass me like that in front of company? How dare you challenge me the way you did, twisting and turning words and meanings when I was trying to make a point? If your mother didn't raise you any better than that, I will begin that process today and make sure you know how to show respect for your elders!"

Leola faced John from the other end of the table. "I don't know what point you're trying to make, but there is nothing wrong with the way I've raised my children. What are you carrying on about?"

"I know what it is," Lou spoke up. "He invited Frazier over hoping that I'd forget about William. He planned the whole thing, but I didn't fall for it. That's what he's mad about."

"I invited Frazier over because he's a nice young man. This has nothing to do with William," John replied.

"Of course it does. You don't like William, and you're trying to keep me from seeing him."

"I never said that!" John's voice rose.

"Yes you did," Leanice joined in. "I heard you and Mama talking yesterday. You said William was not the sort of boy Lou should become involved with."

"And what were you doing? Spying?" John snapped at her.

"I was in my room and the window was open. I couldn't help hearing what you were saying," Leanice defended herself.

John knew he'd been caught. He picked up the chair then slammed it back onto the floor. "So what? So what if I did say that! There's nothing wrong with expressing an opinion! I am looking out for her best interest! William is not the boy for her, and I forbid her from seeing him again!"

Lou stepped forward, undaunted. "I will continue to see William whether you like it or not."

"You do and I will disown you!"

"You can't disown her! You're not her natural daddy!" Leanice spat the words from her mouth.

John spun around, menacingly pointing his finger at her. "I will disown whoever I please. This is my house and my family. I am your father now! I will tell you what to do, how to do it, and when you can do it! I want that understood by all of you."

He looked at each of them, defying either one to challenge him.

Leola locked herself into his stare, refusing to let him intimidate her. "When I agreed to marry you, John, I said something that I wanted you to remember, but, apparently, you didn't. I said that I would not try to replace Susie Floyd in your children's lives, and that you shouldn't try to replace Luther in my children's lives. If you want to run Paul and Lily's lives, that's your decision. But if you do, I can guarantee they'll only grow to resent you. However, when it comes to my children, I will be their judge and jury. And if I say that they can see whoever they want, there'll be no more discussion of it. You will not chastise this child anymore. If you disown her, then you disown me and her sister as well."

John rattled the chair in his hands, his pride threatened, then stormed out of the kitchen, growling like an angry bear with a burr in its paw. Stubbornly, he refused to condone Lou's affection for William and, in so doing, permanently strained his relationship with Leola and her children.

TWENTY-NINE

RALPH PREFERRED WORKING the fields by himself. He was a quiet man who enjoyed the simple things in life, quiet walks along the creek, fishing in the pond not far from his home, watching the sun set over the crops he tended to with the utmost care. He had lived his life much the way he wanted, free of stress and confrontation. But all that changed when he married John's daughter.

Ralph and Nellie moved into the small house on John's farm. Though it took some fixing up, they turned it into a comfortable home. Ralph repaid his father-in-law from his share of the profits off each crop. It wasn't a bad arrangement for Ralph, but all the same, he liked to keep his distance from John.

Their working philosophies could not have been more diametrically opposed. John wanted his workers close to him so he could watch over them, instructing them by the minute on the most efficient way to pick cotton. He was quick to point out faults but slow with any praise. Though Ralph had built up some immunity to John's idiosyncratic behavior, there were days when his mood swings were impossible to ignore.

Ralph worked the front acre while John made his weekly trip into town. It was a warm Saturday morning, the rows of cotton plants dry after a week with no rain. This suited Ralph fine. Bone dry cotton was much easier to pick, pulling apart from the open pod with only the slightest tug, sparing the need to grab underneath the pod where the sharp burrs grew.

He had cleared a quarter of an acre by the time John pulled up, surprising even himself with the amount of work he'd accomplished as he dumped the frothy balls of cotton into the large bin. John stormed over to him like he was a conquering explorer staking his claim to a new world. He grabbed one of the burlap bags and slung it across his shoulder, almost hitting Ralph in the face.

"Tell me where to start!" John growled.

Ralph continued his chore, knowing that his father-in-law was in a rare mood. "You can start on the back acre. I haven't picked it yet."

"Is that where you left off?" John glanced over the field.

"No. But it's as good a place as any to get started."

"I'm gonna start where you left off. There's no sense in picking a field without an orderly plan. You should know that by now! Where do you want me?"

"Down by the group of pecan trees." Ralph slurred.

"That's all you had to tell me."

John's testiness rolled right off Ralph's back, though it would be hard to ignore his verbal jabs all day. He didn't know precisely what had inspired John's outlook, but he did have a sneaking suspicion it had to do with the wedding.

John was all thumbs, picking at the cotton like it was glued inside the pod. He cursed himself every time he cut his hands on the thorny burrs, anger seething inside, threatening to erupt, his curses more frequent and vociferous. The more furiously he picked, the deeper the bolls cut into his hands.

He struggled with one plant after another until finally his temper got the best of him. Snatching an entire plant out of the ground, roots and all, he slung it through the air. "Damn you!" John screamed at the plant.

Ralph watched as the innocent plant landed about twenty feet away. If he was at all amused by John's actions, it did not register on his face.

"What are you looking at?" John snapped at him.

"Nothing of any interest to me." Ralph went about his chore.

Frustrated that he couldn't engage Ralph in an argument, John angrily kicked the ground, sending a plume of dirt into the air.

"I don't suppose Nellie could bring some gauze out here to wrap my hand with." John stood over Ralph.

"She's not home."

"Not home? On a Saturday? Where else would she be?" John asked incredulously.

Ralph thought a moment, purposely stalling, knowing that his reply would antagonize John even further. He moved down the row he was working on, out of the direct line of fire. "She went to Lou's wedding."

John's face turned as red as his bloodied hand; his teeth gnashed together like he was grinding rocks. When it appeared he would burst into a fireball of contentiousness, the sound of church bells wafted over the fields of fluffy white cotton.

Leola's mind wandered throughout the ceremony, her thoughts flipping from one thing to another, momentarily settling on the parallels between her marriage to Luther and Lou's marriage to William. Neither of them had a father to walk them down the aisle, yet both took advantage of the opportunity to marry the man they loved, despite the objections of others.

She was angry at John for ruining this day, but she wouldn't let that spoil Lou's wedding. She watched her daughter carefully, wondering if she had any second thoughts about marrying William. She was only eighteen, still a child in Leola's eyes, but had the maturity of someone twice her age. Her manner was sincere, her voice strong as she declared her love for William. Leola knew there was nothing to worry about; her daughter had made the best decision for her life.

She knocked on the dressing room door as Lou changed into a short-sleeved cotton dress for the long trip to Miami.

"I told myself I wouldn't cry, and I almost made it until I started thinking about your father and grandmother." Leola dried her eyes with a lace handkerchief given to her by Luther.

"Oh, Mama. Don't cry, you'll get me started." Lou hugged her mother.

"I'm sorry. The last thing I want to do is make you cry on your wedding day. I've had a lot on my mind today, and everything kinda caught up on me all at once." Leola calmed herself and helped Lou clean up the room.

"I wish Daddy could be here. I've thought about him so much today. But I've also felt very close to him, like he was watching over me and wishing me happiness."

Leola carefully folded Lou's gown and put it into a large box. "You are so much like your father. I can see the resemblance more and more every day. He was a spiritual person, always looked for the good in other people. He was kind and sensitive, not much of a churchgoer, but he practiced the principles of love and humanity every day of his life. You inherited his spiritual quality and his love of life. Leanice is like me, reserved and quiet, not very sure of herself. But you're just like Luther, confident and head-strong, willing to take on anything life has to offer.

"If he were here, I know what he'd want to tell you. I can't say this as good as he could, but I'll give it a try. Always remember who you are and where you come from. If you hold onto that knowledge, you'll never lose your way in life. That is the anchor that'll keep you safe in any storm."

Leola cupped Lou's face in her hands. "You are Lucy Margaret Smith, nicknamed Lou, daughter of Luther and Leola Smith, loved dearly by your parents, sister, family, and all those who know you. This is your heritage, something you will pass along to your children and grandchildren in the years to come."

Leola tenderly kissed her daughter on the forehead and left the room to gather with the other guests outside.

A shower of rice cascaded upon the couple as they climbed into the back of a wagon. Lou tossed the bouquet to Leanice and waved good-bye to her mother.

Harbard kept the horses at a steady pace. Lou brushed a handful of rice from her hair, tossing it playfully at William. He peeked at her, self-conscious, unsure, much as he had on their first date, blushing profusely as he looked away. His shyness endeared him to her even more than before. Behind his rough exterior lived a sensitive little boy.

They reached the depot a half-hour before the train was due. Harbard hitched the horses, while William settled the tickets with the teller. Lou fantasized about the trip to Miami, curious as to the look and feel of the mighty ocean she'd only read about in school, its romantic lure, the moonlight strolls along the beach, the palm trees swaying in rhythm to the concerto of the wind.

William helped his father unload the baggage. Harbard was quiet; he stood before William as the last of the baggage was unloaded. "I hope you'll be happy, son. That's all anyone can ask for in this life."

"I am happy. Lou's made me the happiest man in the whole wide world."

"There's a lot that goes with being married, William—responsibilities, commitments, expectations. It takes a lot of work to even come close to satisfying everything."

"I'm used to hard work. I've been at it since I was seventeen, and it hasn't scared me off yet," William replied with self-assurance.

Harbard nodded his head, proud of his son's confidence, despite its youthful innocence. William would learn things in his own time and in his own way, Harbard thought, much the way he had.

"Good luck to you, son. I wish you and Lou every happiness." Harbard extended his hand.

A distant whistle announced the train's arrival. Harbard unhitched the horses and steered the small wagon back to the church. William watched his father drive away. He hardly seemed like the same man with whom he'd fought so bitterly long ago. Perhaps Harbard had mellowed in his golden years, or perhaps, William thought, he himself had grown up.

Lou was fast asleep when the train pulled into the Miami station after midnight, her head resting on William's shoulder. He roused her with a gentle kiss on the forehead. A myriad of bright lights, shining and glaring from every direction, shone against the silhouette of tall buildings outlining the clear, moonlit sky.

She thought for a moment that she'd somehow landed on another planet, having never seen, nor even imagined, anything like this. Her mouth dropped open in disbelief. William laughed at her wide-eyed fascination. The grandeur of the city amazed her. Everywhere she looked there were people milling about and roaming in and out of a sea of buildings.

Automobiles rushed up and down the street like a swarm of bees around the hive, horns blaring and motors racing as everyone appeared to be in a hurry to get to the same place. She clung to William's arm as he retrieved their luggage.

"For heaven's sake, Lou. I can't carry all these bags with you wrapped around me like a plumber's wrench."

Lou picked up a bag with her right hand, the other still firmly gripped to William's arm. As they approached the street, they noticed a man standing next to an automobile holding a sign that had William's name written on it.

"What in the name of glory is this all about? How does he know who I am?"

"I don't know, but whatever you do, stay away from him. Lord only knows what he wants. He could be some kind of crazy person for all we know," Lou whispered.

"There has to be a simple explanation for it."

William walked toward the man but Lou pulled him back. "Don't William! You could get yourself killed!"

"It's okay, Lou. Nothing's gonna happen right out here on the sidewalk with all these people around."

William approached the man with Lou in tow. "I couldn't help noticing your sign. It's got my name on it."

"Are you William Smith?" the man asked with an air of pretentiousness.

"That's what I just said," William answered flatly.

"I was hired to chauffeur you and your wife to the cottage where you'll be staying."

The man handed William an envelope. He opened it and started laughing. "It's from Uncle Dex. He says this is part of our wedding gift. This man will drive us to his cottage." William blushed sheepishly as the man put their bags into the automobile.

The ride through town both amazed and frightened Lou. From her perspective it looked as though every oncoming vehicle would crash directly into them. The driver made a sudden eastbound turn onto a smoother, less congested highway, leaving the city and all its commotion behind them. They passed through majestic rows of swaying palms, the slightest scent of salt in the air. Lou breathed it in vigorously, intoxicated by the smell of the ocean. The sound of waves crashing on shore soothed her mind. Closing her eyes, she felt as if she were as light as air.

The car pulled up to a small cottage constructed of stone and concrete. Two sabal palms guarded the front entrance on either side, a row of pink oleander lining the side of the cottage facing the road. Less than one hundred yards away, the mighty Atlantic caressed the sand in ceaseless, perfectly constructed waves. This was the romantic paradise Lou imagined. Impulsively, she ran to the water's edge and waded in its warm bath, feeling thousands of tiny grains of sand wash under her bare feet.

The sea breeze embraced her, soothing and maternal, its whistling song a melody of enchantment. She gazed at the stars, pushing all thought from her mind, listening only to the calling of the waves. William watched her from the cottage, as mesmerized by her presence as the first time he saw her. Every move she made was magical, the sound of her laughter rapturous. He could watch her for hours, completely entranced at the mere sight of her. She quickly turned and ran up the beach to him, as if he had beckoned her to him.

She jumped into his arms. He held her tightly, kissing her with a passion he'd never known. He could not imagine loving someone more than he loved her.

THIRTY

"Hᴇʟʟᴏ ᴛʜᴇʀᴇ! Aɴʏʙᴏᴅʏ ʜᴏᴍᴇ?" Roy pounded on the cottage door. Lou peeked out the window at the young man dressed in a nice gray suit, a pair of suspenders with shiny silver clamps outlining his chest. His thick, dark hair was slicked straight back, revealing a deeply tanned face.

"My, my. William was right on target. You sure are pretty! It's nice to meet you. I'm Roy Smith, your husband's cousin. Welcome to the family."

Roy shook Lou's hand and walked inside, his forthright nature catching her off guard. She expected someone more reserved and mannerly, someone who waited to enter until invited. Roy's father, Harbard's younger brother, moved to Florida's southern coast before the boom transformed the area from a tropical paradise into a concrete goliath. Roy was a city boy to the core, a trait Lou found somewhat grating.

"Won't you have a seat?" Lou offered him a chair across the room by the window overlooking the ocean. He stared at her, captivated by her appearance. Though dressed simply, with only a necklace for an accessory, she looked elegant. Roy's fervent attention made her uncomfortable. Blushing, she looked toward the hallway.

"I'm sorry. I don't mean to stare," Roy blurted out. "You're not what I expected. What I mean is, when William said you were pretty, I expected someone average, you know. I figured he was exaggerating, but I can plainly see that he wasn't. You're about the prettiest thing I've ever seen. How did an old dog like William snag a girl like you?"

Lou shifted in the chair, unsure what to say in the face of such praise. "We sure do thank your father for letting us stay in this cottage. It's lovely."

"Ain't it though? This used to be a completely isolated spot before everybody and their mother started moving down here. All the snowbirds from up north who vacation here during the winter have been staying longer and longer, and now they won't leave! That really irritates some of the locals, but not me. It means more business for our shop. I've been trying to get that hard-headed husband of yours to come down and go into business with us. It's perfect for him. And a pretty gal like you would fit right in with Miami society."

Roy jumped up as William entered, anxiously greeting the cousin he hadn't seen since childhood. "How you doin', you old hammer knocker?"

"Making ends meet and puttin' a little in the bank. How about yourself?" William asked.

"Fine, fine. Business is good. We're expanding this year, adding two more garages. I was just telling your pretty wife that I've been trying to knock some sense into your head and get you into the business." Roy flashed one of his million dollar smiles.

"The railroad's treating me well, the pay is decent, and the benefits are fair. The best part of all is it's security. I don't have to go out and get the work, it's already there."

"Ah, the hell with that, Billy. Nothing beats working for yourself, investing in your own future, nobody telling you how much you can earn in any one year. It's capitalism at its best, baby. Get in while the going's good!" Roy sounded to Lou like a fast-talking insurance salesman.

"I'll decide how good it is when I see this eating establishment you've been crowing about." William slapped Roy's arm.

"Oh, you two'll love it. There's nothing like this place in that one-horse town you live in. It's called the Royal Palm Court, looks right out on the ocean, has a fancy dining area and a huge dance floor with a flowing fountain right in the middle of it. Makes you feel like you're dancing under a waterfall." Roy took Lou's hand and escorted her to the door. "Gotta move fast, Billy boy. A lady this beautiful will have a full dance card this evening."

William shook his head. Roy was still the same high-spirited boy from fifteen years ago, though now with a big city attitude.

The automobile Roy drove was much sportier than the carriage-like sedan that picked up the couple at the train station. His was sleeker and fancier, which came as no surprise to either Lou or William. The car fit Roy's personality like a glove, brash and arrogant. William looked it over with a tinge of jealousy. It was as close to perfection as he'd seen in an automobile.

"Not bad, huh?" Roy cocked his head.

"It's a beauty all right." William hated giving his cousin the satisfaction of his admiration.

Roy walked around the car, pointing out its features as if he were selling it himself. "Brand new, straight from the factory. 1922 Haynes Sport Sedan; six-cylinder, aluminum body, spacious trunk, rear protection bar—never know when someone's gonna try and plow into you—individual steps for each door—the ladies love that—windshield wings trimmed in Spanish leather, interior trimmed in leather, and the best part of all, top up or top down." Roy motioned the raising and lowering of the convertible top.

William whistled in spite of himself.

"Maybe this'll convince your husband that I've been right all along." Roy winked at Lou as he helped her into the back seat.

"How much did this set you back?" William asked as he sat next to Lou.

"Twenty-two hundred dollars and worth every penny. In this town, how you're seen is just as important as where you're seen."

Roy hopped into the front seat. As he pulled the automobile onto the highway, William's imagination ran wild. The grandeur of the vehicle made his head spin: the comfort of the leather seats, the slick feel of fresh paint on the body, the attention to detail and design. Maybe Roy was onto something, maybe he was right after all.

He looked at Lou wistfully, almost apologetically, wondering if she could truly be happy with him the way things were, wondering if he'd ever be able to give her everything she deserved, everything he wanted to give her. In his estimation, she could have the world at her feet, and he was only a speck of dirt beneath her stance.

Roy stopped in front of a posh apartment building, white stucco with a ceramic roof, to pick up his date. She was older than him, probably in her late twenties or even thirty. When Lou first saw her, she thought the girl must be a fashion model who just stepped off a runway in Paris. She wore a tight-fitting gold lamé dress with a matching cloche all but hiding her dark blonde hair. The metallic gold shoes with stiletto heels made her walk with an exaggerated swagger.

From a distance she looked like one of Mack Sennett's beauties, tall, glamorous, every inch of perfection. But when she stepped into the car, it became apparent that the generous layer of makeup she wore helped define her beauty. Underneath the facade, her features were rather harsh, her face wide and square, and her eyes set deep behind a prominent nose. She hardly looked like the same girl who sauntered down the sidewalk.

Roy opened the door and held her hand as she stepped into the automobile, a look of slight disdain on her face, as if the automobile, or its company, was beneath her status. Roy introduced her as Gayle Mattison, the daughter of a prominent Miami family. She barely acknowledged the couple behind her, waving the back of her hand at them while puffing away on a cigarette held by a six-inch black holder. It seemed as if the presence of other people annoyed her, that somehow they stole a portion of the spotlight reserved only for her.

William rolled his eyes as he stared at the back of her gold lamé head, furrowing his brow at her haughty nature. He turned to Lou and whispered in her ear, "They're a perfect match. He's beauty, and she's the beast!"

Lou stifled a laugh, tapping William on the leg.

Roy fawned over Gayle as if she were a visiting crowned head of state. His attempts at humor fell on deaf ears, but he managed occasionally to elicit from her the droll laughter he found so fascinating. He could never match her socially, which was the main reason she liked being around him. She had the upper hand, the one who mattered when they went out on the town.

The drive through downtown, overlooking the Intracoastal Waterway, was a golden spectacle. The reflection of the tall buildings rippled over the water, while pleasure yachts sailed past into the setting sun. A flock of pink flamingos settled gracefully at the water's edge, preening their majestic feathers into beautiful plumes of puffy pink.

As Roy pulled into the circular drive of the Royal Palm Court, Gayle slowly came to life. Her shoulders raised, her head tilted slightly backward, her entire presence turning stately, superior. It was the act she put on every weekend, the one that set her apart from the rest. She stepped from the automobile lightly, as though she would break something if she should step normally. For the first time since they met, she got a good look at Lou.

She studied her closely, sizing up the young girl whom she considered a rival. A subtle, jealous, haughty sneer overcame her face. Unlike herself, Lou was a natural beauty who wore only a light base of powder, a hint of rouge, and lipstick. Her skin was flawless, her eyes like two radiant sapphires. Though plain, her dress looked exquisite on her youthful frame. For all her jewelry and expensive clothes, Gayle was no match for Lou's simple beauty.

A fifteen-member orchestra provided background music as the patrons dined on Maine lobster, filet mignon, and Atlantic swordfish. Lou read over the menu as if she were studying a textbook filled with complicated mathematical equations. Its exotic offerings baffled her. She was uneasy in this atmosphere, an outsider who sensed that Miami's society could see she didn't belong.

"What looks interesting to you, dear?" Gayle's voice lilted through a fog of cigarette smoke.

Lou peered over the menu. "I don't know yet. Everything looks so . . . unusual."

Gayle snickered, condescending, eyeing Lou callously, her smile wicked, poisoned. "Unusual to whom, my dear? Men from Mars? Don't tell me you've never tasted broiled lobster simmering in lemon butter sauce. Or fresh asparagus tips covered in creamy hollandaise."

"Well, no I haven't." Lou was flustered.

"Oh, my dear, you have lived a deprived life, haven't you?" Gayle purred.

Lou stared back at her, wounded, remembering all that she had been through in life. She did not have the advantages that some had, but she never lacked for anything either. Her mother's words were with her.

"I wouldn't necessarily call it deprived, as you say. I may not have some of the things you do, but I do have something that is much more important to me than nice clothes or expensive homes or fancy cars. I have the love and support of my family, and that's something all the money in the world couldn't buy."

Gayle did not bat an eye. "I'm not putting you down, sweetheart. You've misinterpreted my meaning. I think everyone in the world should taste the advantages of life that only so few of us are granted. I wasn't singling you out in particular. It's a disgrace all the way around that the little people have to work so hard their whole lives to make a decent living, and before they know it, their life is over."

Gayle acknowledged a couple at the next table. William glared at Roy, his face fixed with anger. Roy nervously shrugged his shoulders. William turned to Lou. "Would you like to dance?"

Gayle quickly grabbed William's arm, as if she was preventing him from jumping into a fire. "Oh, darling, no, no, no! You'd be committing a serious faux pas to dance now. Dancing isn't permitted until eleven o'clock. The band takes a break precisely at ten-thirty for one-half hour, and then they play music one can dance by."

"So what is this music they're playing now?" William asked with mounting agitation.

"That's dinner music, darling. It compliments the conversation, stimulates discussion. Think of it as a monochord, keeps the pianist in correct timing with the piece of music." Gayle took a sip of wine.

William found her explanation ironic. With Gayle looking down upon him and Lou all evening, it would take an earthquake to stimulate any conversation.

Lou contented herself by observing the magnificent hall. Crystal chandeliers hung gracefully overhead, while pristine marble columns defined the perimeter of the dance floor. In the middle stood the fountain Roy mentioned, a magnificent piece of craftsmanship: tiny dolphins circling higher and higher, each one chasing the tail of the one before it until the last one reached for the sky.

The guests at the tables around them reeked of money. Diamonds, pearls, and emeralds were the order of the evening, long gowns and tuxedos abounded. As Lou admired a woman in a turquoise evening gown, she got the distinct impression that someone was watching her. Looking sharply to the right, she noticed a man staring at her, not at all self-conscious that he'd been caught.

At the end of dinner, during the half-hour when the band took its break, the man approached the table. He was large in stature though meticulously dressed. His sideburns were long and full but neatly trimmed. Gayle extended her hand to him, which he kissed delicately. "Why, Addison Davis, I thought you were seeking your next fortune on the other side of the continent."

"I seek fortunes wherever they happen to be. And there's as much fortune in one place as there is another." He glanced at Lou.

"You remember my escort, Roy Smith. And these are his cousins William and Lou Smith from . . . oh dear, now don't tell me, was it Hogsbelly . . . or Possum something?" Gayle asked not so innocently.

"Fitzgerald, Georgia," William replied.

"Oh yes. All those small towns sound the same." She smiled superficially at William then turned to Addison. "So tell me, darling, what are you doing back in Miami? You haven't finished your motion picture, have you? Addison went to California to finance a picture with none other than Gloria Swanson."

"Yes it was completed last month, should be distributed very soon now. I came back to Miami to look after the business. Advertising is my first love, you know. The motion picture business is indeed a goldmine. One day there'll be a screening house in every town across America. But for now, advertising's the name of the game."

"Addison creates advertisements for some of the biggest names around. He worked with John Jacob Astor to publicize this hotel and has made it the most successful enterprise on the entire Atlantic coast. Everything he touches turns to gold." Gayle took on even more airs if possible.

"Including you, my dear!" Addison teased.

"Addison, you're such a bad boy," she purred. "Addison asked me to pose for some of his advertisements, that's how we met. He always keeps an eye out for a pretty face."

"Precisely, my dear, that's what brought me to your table. When I saw this beautiful young girl from across the room, I told myself that I had to get her on film." Addison looked directly at Lou.

"Me?" Lou asked, surprised.

Gayle's face turned hard as stone. "I hardly think he was referring to your husband, dear!"

"Have you ever modeled before?" Addison asked, drawn into Lou's beauty.

"Well, no. I live in a very small town . . . " Lou offered.

"With a face like yours, you could grace any magazine cover in the country. There are plenty of pretty young girls out there trying desperately to make something of themselves, but it's the rare few who have the natural beauty to make it happen. And you, my dear, are one of the chosen few."

Lou looked into William's eyes, hoping he would know what to say, uncomfortable at the attention focused upon her. He looked at her as he had Roy's automobile: Things of such complete beauty were unattainable. He didn't want to stand in her way, to be the tie that bound her to the only way of life he knew.

"Thank you for your interest, Mr. Davis. But we're only going to be in Miami a few more days. The only thing I want out of life right now is a family. I guess I'm not glamour girl material." Lou held William's hand.

"Ah, but you could change your mind, there's lots of money to be made. You could support a family very well on what some girls make."

Again Lou looked at William, but his face was vacant.

"I'll give you my card. Contact me when you make a decision."

Addison returned to his table. Lou held the card in her hand, embarrassed by the attention lavished upon her, downplaying the situation, laughing self-consciously at the thought of being a model. "I'm no more a model than the next person." Lou blushed.

"But you are, Lou," Roy stopped her cold. "He's right. You have that special beauty that so few girls possess. You'd be a natural in front of the camera."

Gayle stared through Roy, her eyes burning with animosity.

William's demeanor sunk into the pit of doubt, his face sad, his feelings of inferiority compounded by this turn of events. He placed Lou on such a pedestal, it was becoming increasingly difficult for him to reach her. She was a bird of paradise, soaring away from him for the sun.

The evening ended abruptly when Gayle became incapacitated by a relentless headache, depriving the newlywed couple of an opportunity to dance beneath the cascading waterfall.

It was only eleven o'clock when Roy dropped them off at the cottage. Lou noticed William's mood and playfully tried coaxing him into a walk along the beach, but he feigned exhaustion.

"What's wrong, William?"

"Nothing. I'm just tired. It's been a long day."

His explanation was weak.

"Is something upsetting you?"

"No, I'm fine. I hate to see our honeymoon come to an end, that's all." William looked at the ground.

"How about a swim? I promised myself that I'd take at least one dip in the Atlantic Ocean and I haven't done it yet. You want to join me?"

Lou's sincerity made William kick himself for doubting her, for thinking that she would so easily walk away from him. She ran from the cottage directly into the water, tossing a towel onto the beach, diving head first into an oncoming wave. The warm water invited her in. William watched from the shore, wading no further than ankle deep. The pull of the tide was strong. He cautioned Lou about swimming too far.

She was not afraid of the ocean, naively unaware of its sometimes-unforgiving nature. The gentle waves beckoned the child in her to swim and play undaunted, like being with an old friend, safe and comfortable. She lost track of how far out she was, the tide surreptitiously pulling her further from land. William called out, warning her to swim closer to shore, his voice edged with concern.

The ocean's spell lured her into the deeper waters, the cushion of sand no longer beneath her feet. Disoriented, frightened, she swam blindly in every direction. Her arms cut into the water furiously, helplessly, the receding tide maliciously pulling her away. Groping for air, she swallowed a mouthful of salty water for every breath she took.

Desperate, she managed to scream for William. He ran into the water like a man possessed, taking on the ocean as if it were a mud puddle in the back yard. Lou slipped underwater, exhausted from battling the waves and tide. William cut through the waves, looking desperately for her, terrified when he couldn't find her. He screamed her name into the windswept air. There was no reply.

His mind burst into a million thoughts, his heart pounded wildly. He couldn't see her. The vastness of the ocean overwhelmed him. He cried out savagely, cursing the heavens, begging them to take him instead of his beautiful wife. He screamed again as loud as he could and then even louder. Lou's name bounced across the waves, hollow, without reply.

She was nearly unconscious, less than ten feet from him. Her consciousness slowly slipped away, her body numb. A bright light flashed before her, and she could see her father's face, still young and handsome. He smiled and then embraced her as he had when she was a little girl. She put her arms around him, to embrace his light, but he pushed her away, telling her to go back, it wasn't her time.

She snapped into consciousness, aware of the danger she was in. Thrusting her head above the surface, she cried out for William. He swam to her, battling the pulling tide with all his might. Wrapping his arms around her, he held tight, refusing to relinquish her to the mighty ocean.

Lou collapsed on the beach, coughing deeply, purging the salt water from her lungs. William held her as she bent forward gasping for air. So close had he come to losing her, grateful tears streamed from his eyes. When she caught her breath she fell back into his arms, facing the ocean, distrusting its innocent call, fearful of its awesome power.

THIRTY-ONE

S IX MONTHS PASSED AND John had not spoken to Lou. A consuming anger over her marriage to William prevented even this mildest of civilities. He ranted and raved to anyone who would listen but soon found that his audience had lost interest in the tired old recording, spinning itself over and over on the same tune. Aggravated, but not undone, he vented his frustrations the only way he knew how, readying his land for the next planting season.

The cotton crop was coming off a banner year, yielding over two hundred pounds per acre, netting a tidy profit for a small farm. With cotton prices still on the upswing after the war, John was eager to expand his operation, moving up a rung on the ladder of cotton operations in South Georgia. He had his eye on fifteen acres of land to the south of his property line, recently available after a foreclosure. It was a gamble to invest so much in a larger enterprise, but John was determined to see it through.

He wasted no time. The opportunity arose, and he grabbed it, working out a loan with the bank, putting his house up as collateral, and signing a five-year note, confident he could pay it off early. After struggling for a decade to make ends meet, John was ready to reap the rewards of his hard work.

Ralph didn't question the purchase of the land. In fact, he saw it as a golden opportunity for their operation to grow and become more profitable. But he was uneasy with John's plan to seed the land exclusively with cotton. There were rumors that a plague from the west was threatening the cotton fields of Georgia, a threat Ralph took seriously.

For years, agriculturalists had been warning cotton farmers about the "winged demon" spreading eastward from the southwest, first appearing in Texas thirty years before, in 1894, and steadily moving to the east at a rate of nearly one hundred miles per year. In its wake, the small, snout-nosed beetle wreaked havoc in Mississippi and Alabama, wiping out thousands of acres of cotton and forcing hundreds of farmers into the vast pit of bankruptcy.

During the Great War, the production of cotton skyrocketed. Market prices jumped dramatically, and with it the amount of acreage devoted to cotton. By 1918, Georgia's farmers were putting over two million bales of cotton into the marketplace, creating extraordinary wealth. Cotton alone brought one-half billion dollars into the state's economy, and word of the boom spread like wildfire. Even sharecroppers were benefiting from the wealth.

Acres that once had been planted with corn and tobacco were turned under in favor of cotton. In the ensuing mania to cash in on the craze, five million acres of Georgia farmland turned to the cash crop. John was infected with the fever, eagerly pouring all of his resources into the pool of cotton profits.

He purchased an additional mule and plow, giving him two working units in all, then hired a sharecropper from Queensland to work the third unit for the duration of the cotton season, which ran from March until September. Hopes were high and prayers whispered as the men began the arduous task of preparing the acreage for seed.

The land had to be plowed under and then harrowed with a spike-toothed revolving grater to aerate the soil. Ralph and Obadiah Foster, the sharecropper who some called Reverend because he preached most every Sunday at a black Episcopal Church in Queensland, guided the plows through the thick underbrush, while John followed with the harrower. Despite its unkempt appearance, the ground was soft and fertile. The plows ripped through the soil with surprising ease. As the rich, dark earth spun through the harrower, John began counting his profits.

It took the better part of two weeks to plow, harrow, and fertilize the additional acreage. Though exhausted, the men were then faced with the task of clearing the dead stalks from last year's cotton crop on the original land. With an average of five thousand plants per acre, the process would take away valuable time. With only one mechanical stalk cutter to work with, the rest had to be cleared by hand, a backbreaking, grueling process. The more they cleared, the more there appeared to be. While one man operated the mechanical cutter, the other two knocked plants down with big sticks.

Calluses and festering blisters covered the men's hands, but they pushed forward, never complaining, keeping their eyes focused upon the rewards John promised them. In the second week of March, they began mounding rows of dirt, the final process before seeding. Ralph and Obadiah worked in spite of the pain from the festering blisters that covered their hands. They wrapped them in bandages, which, nonetheless, were soaked in blood by day's end. Nellie worried over them constantly, oftentimes taking a pan of warm water into the fields so they could soak their hands and then rewrap them in fresh bandages.

"I do thank ya, Miz Nellie. My wife appreciates the way you take care of me." Obadiah soaked his hands in the warm water, which felt as if it were a tub of acid upon his seared hands.

"Think nothing of it, Reverend Foster. Annie Lee is a fine woman, and I know she'd do the same thing for Ralph." Nellie cut a swath of the cloth to wrap around Obadiah's hands.

"That she would, Miz Nellie. She considers us all to be one big family." Obadiah wrapped his hands in the swatches of cloth.

"In the struggles of life we are all family," Ralph said, wiping his face with a towel Nellie handed him. "I just hope this crop can bring a little prosperity into all our lives."

"Mister John says this will be the best crop ever. He sure sets mighty big stock in this season. Says cotton prices will bring in a better price than last year."

"I hope he's right, Reverend. Otherwise we might be eating dust and skunk-weed all winter."

Ralph's sense of foreboding remained steadfast, gnawing away at the hope he clung to, afraid that all of their hard work would be in vain. He desperately wanted to change John's mind, to make him see that they were taking a sizable risk. But he knew how stubborn John could be. Seeding would begin before the end of the month.

"Those south acres are begging for seed." Ralph wiped his brow with the sleeve of his shirt at day's end. "That soil's as rich and dark as any I've seen. You could throw nickels out there and grow money trees."

John spoke decisively. "It'll get us two hundred pounds easy. Hell, I might get my money back on that loan off one crop! We'll start planting next week."

Ralph looked out over the empty fields, squinting into the fiery sun. "I've been reading in the paper lately about more and more farmers turning to peanuts instead of cotton. It's returning a fair price, and there's oil mills around the state now that are buying 'em up as fast as you can get 'em to market."

"Peanuts will never bring what cotton does. We'll make twice off cotton what we'd make off peanuts."

Ralph pumped water from the well using his wrist, letting it pour over his bleeding hands. He pulled away the raw skin, leaving burning patches of bright pink. "There's a risk that goes along with growing cotton these days. We need to think about that. They've been telling us for years that the boll weevil is coming this way, and it's already been reported in some parts of Georgia."

John was indignant. "Poppycock! That's nothing more than scare tactics used by state officials to keep smaller farmers like myself from jumping aboard the bandwagon. All they're trying to do is create a monopoly on the market. They want to keep the big guys in business and weed the smaller ones out."

"What benefit is there to doing that?"

"A purely selfish one. State legislators will support anybody who'll line their pockets with cold hard cash. Money does a heap of talking in this world, Ralph. You can't believe everything you read or hear just on face value."

"But production on cotton has already started going down. Last year there was a fifteen percent loss because of the boll weevil."

"See! They've already got you believing that and scared silly to boot! You're ready to run for the high ground with your tail between your legs. You've gotta be smarter than they are. Outsmart your opponent before he outsmarts you!" John was pleased with his debate.

"I don't see it that way, John. They said how bad it got in Mississippi and Alabama. The federal government wouldn't lie about a thing like that just so a few Georgia legislators could profit under the table. This is serious business, and I'm not willing to risk everything I have for this."

Ralph's statement struck a tender nerve in John. "I'm the one who stands to lose on this deal! All of this property is mine. The house you live in is still mine. I put up my own house as collateral so our families wouldn't have to scratch and sweat and bleed our entire lives just to stay one step behind everyone else. Do you think I would have gone through all of this if I thought for one second that we could lose everything? Give me more credit than that, Ralph. I know what your concerns are, but I don't think there's that much of a threat. The same federal government you spoke so highly of also told us that a way to control the boll weevil has been found. If those damnable pests find their way to our cotton, we'll fight 'em! Let's not have this discussion again. We're sticking with cotton, and we'll begin planting next week."

John abruptly walked away, having won the argument and putting to rest any fears that might interfere with his plans.

On schedule to the day, seeding began the last Monday in March, the entire family recruited to help. Using long sticks to poke holes in the ground two feet apart, a handful of seeds were dropped into each hole. Weather conditions were perfect for seeding, moderate rain and warm. By the end of the week, with seeding finished, John gathered the family together and led a prayer of thanksgiving, praising God for the good fortune He had bestowed upon them.

THIRTY-TWO

FIELDS OF YOUNG COTTON spread as far as the eye could see. For John and his family they were fields of gold, harboring everything they owned and everything they stood to gain. The afternoon rains that gave the young plants their life were the blood that coursed through the veins of the family. So much rested on the tender, vulnerable cotton plants, so much could be lost if they failed to produce.

After working valiantly to prepare the soil for seeding, the men took a needed break as the seedlings pushed their way above ground. John took this time to make a trip into town. He scheduled a meeting with Jasper Sidwell, a cotton buyer whose business dealings stretched from the coast of Georgia to the plains of Alabama. John sold his last cotton crop to Jasper and earned a fair price in the sale. This season, he planned on striking an early deal, promising a premium product and lots of it.

He strode into the two-story building on Grant Street with the air of a business tycoon. On this occasion, and in a small way, maybe he was. At the moment he was sitting upon thirty acres of ripening cotton at five thousand plants per acre. He was on top of the world, and he wanted Jasper to know why.

"Is it July already? I could've sworn we just celebrated Easter." Jasper rose and extended his hand.

"It's still the month of April, Jasper. I'm making my call early this year." John's handshake was more vigorous than usual.

"Things looking good, I take it?"

"Better than good. This is going to be the best crop ever. I bought the old Nicholson property, fifteen acres of the blackest, richest dirt you'll find anywhere in this county. Plowed it, seeded it, and now I'm sittin' back and watchin' it come up like somebody lit a fire underneath it. I got thirty acres of cotton to put on the market this year. Just wanted to make sure we were still doing business together."

"That's a mighty big undertaking, John. What kind of overhead are we talking about?" Jasper leaned back in his chair.

"Not much. I bought another mule and plow, extra seed and fertilizer, and hired out a sharecropper. But I'll make all that back and then some, the way this crop is looking." John leaned forward, accentuating his confidence.

"If I didn't know you any better, John, I'd say you're optimistic," Jasper teased, knowing all too well that his friend was as down-to-earth as he was.

"For once I feel like I got cause to be. Things are looking good, the weather's holding out. I feel like the good Lord is smiling upon us this year. This could be the crop that finally puts us ahead."

Jasper opened a desk drawer and pulled out a loose-leaf report. He thumbed through it, stopping on the page with the latest market prices. "These just came in last week. Cotton's trading at seven-and-three-quarters a pound. If you can pull in two hundred pounds per acre, you got yourself a pretty good profit."

John practically sneered at the deduction. "I pulled in over two hundred pounds last year, and that wasn't particularly good soil. What I'm working with this year will bring in even more than that."

Jasper nodded his head, aware of the bountiful pride John took in what he did. "Then I'll see you in August with a heap of cotton to put on the market."

John walked down Grant Street with an arrogant stride, as if he was privy to some secret information. It was a glorious day, the air fresh and crisp with the faint, sweet smell of budding gardenias. As he passed the barbershop, John treated himself to a shave and haircut before going home.

A merry whistling tune breezed through the air as Leola hung clothes on the backyard line, its bright melody catchy and uplifting. Curious, she peered around the dangling sheets, but seeing no one, she returned her attention to the clothesline. The whistling got louder and louder; somebody definitely was approaching. She peered around the sheet again, coming nose to nose with John. Startled, she lunged backward, losing her balance as she tripped over the empty basket and fell to the ground.

John broke into a hearty laugh, hardly amusing his wife.

"Aren't you going to help me up?" She reached out her hand.

John pulled her up, trying to suppress his laughter but unable to do so. "You looked just like one of those spinning tops the kids used to play with."

"I thought you went into town." Leola brusquely brushed herself off.

"I did. I finished my business, got a shave and haircut, and then came home. It's almost noontime. I've been gone all morning."

"Guess I lost track of time. I've got a pot of stew warming on the stove. It should be ready."

Leola picked up the basket and started for the house. John remained where he was, looking up at the clear sky, lost in thought. Leola searched the heavens, squinting in the bright light, trying to see what it was that captured John's attention. She wandered over next to him, trying to pinpoint the exact location where he was looking. "What are you looking at?" she asked with frustration.

"It's a beautiful day, isn't it? Why don't we ride out to the farm after lunch and take a look at the crop. We'll start chopping out the excess plants in a few days."

John walked past Leola and into the house, leaving her searching the sky, perplexed as to what he saw.

John was in a strange mood as they rode down Altamaha Street—optimistic, cheerful, and full of conversation. Whatever brought this on had Leola's full blessing. After the upheaval of Lou's wedding and the ensuing acrimony, she sometimes wondered if John was capable of happiness anymore. She hadn't seen him like this since Susie Floyd was alive.

"One of these days I'm going to break down and buy me one of those automobiles." John guided the cart slowly.

Leola glanced at him sideways. "Just don't expect me to ride around in it. They scare me. The way people tear all up and down, a person can get killed walking across the street. I prefer the old ways myself. A horse and buggy can get you where you need to go as good as any automobile."

"Times are changing, Leola. You'll have to live with progress one day."

"Not if I don't want to. I can live the rest of my life the way I always have and not feel like I'm missing anything."

John grinned. "You're a stubborn woman, Leola. Wouldn't you even like to have a telephone? You could talk to anyone in town whenever you felt like it. For instance, if you wanted the recipe for the preacher's wife's custard pudding, you could call her up without having to wait until Sunday."

"I will talk to anyone I need to in due time," Leola countered. "I don't think I'm so hard up for good custard pudding that I need to be calling across town for the recipe."

"How about a washing machine? It'll save wear and tear on your hands."

"It can't clean clothes any better than a scrubbing board."

John grew flustered with his wife's refusal to indulge him. "Honestly, Leola. I'm trying to tell you that we'll have a little extra spending money after this crop comes through. And I thought we should get something we could use."

"I can't think of anything I need, John. Spend it on what you like, or put it in the bank and save it for a rainy day if you want to. I've been poor all my life, and I'll go to my grave being poor. I've never wanted anything more out of life than a little corner of space where there's some peace and happiness."

Leola's sentiment touched John. She was one of the most selfless people he'd known. Pulling on the reins, he steered the mule into the sloping fields of cotton. "I guess you're right. We should store it away for a time when we really need it. But it sure is nice to be in a position of dreaming about things we could own."

Ralph and Obadiah hoed weeds in a distant field. The care they gave the crops impressed Leola; the energy of their work invigorated her with the hopes and aspirations all of them had riding on this year's crop. She was as happy for them as she was for John and herself. It would be nice, she thought, to see each of the families prosper.

The warm, sunny days and afternoon rains continued into May as the first squares began forming, followed by the three triangular-shaped leaflets of the cotton plant, as well as the flower bud itself. In three weeks, the fields would become awash in pale yellow as the blooms opened up. This was the critical stage in the development of cotton. When the blooms turned purple and fell off the plant after three days, the infant boll was left behind. Green and tender, the boll housed the growing cotton lint.

Farmers all over South Georgia nervously watched the skies, praying for warm temperatures and dry weather. Too much rain and cooler weather could not only prolong the development of cotton, but also serve as a breeding ground for the deadly boll weevil. The forty-five-day period between the tender boll and the ripened cotton could make or break an entire planting season.

A cool wind blew into the area in early June, followed by gray skies and pesky rains that lingered for weeks. Weeding and cultivating were limited because of the soggy ground. A minute uneasiness subtly gnawed at John. He became impatient with the gray, wet weather, which stubbornly persisted day after day. He held his tongue, however, refusing to lose his composure and anger the God whose blessings he so desperately needed.

When the rains ended, the men resumed their work, plowing in between the rows, filling dirt back onto the base of each plant. Though the bolls were expanding with the growing cotton, it would be another three weeks at the earliest before they hardened and split open, exposing the mature balls of cotton.

Ralph awoke earlier than usual one morning after a night of troubled sleep. He'd heard through the grapevine that the rains and cooler weather had given birth to an infestation of the boll weevil in Dougherty County, eighty miles to the west. He made a pot of coffee and sipped a cup on the back porch, watching the blackness of night give way to the glow of dawn.

As Nellie started breakfast, he ventured outside, walking through the field closest to the house. After inspecting the ripening bolls and finding nothing out of the ordinary, he scolded himself for being such an alarmist, thinking that John had been right all along—this crop was blessed. Relieved, he walked back toward the house.

Just as he passed the last row of cotton, a flying insect landed on his cheek. It was unlike anything he'd seen before. The snout-nosed bug did not resemble the cotton flea hopper or the cotton aphid, both common pests of Georgia cotton. The longer he looked at it, the more it resembled the drawings he'd seen of the boll weevil.

Suddenly, the insects were everywhere, jumping from plant to plant, appearing out of thin air, multiplying by the second, whizzing around Ralph by the thousands. Quickly, he snatched a young boll from the plant in front of him, eyeing it closely, looking for the two small holes burrowed in its side where the female weevil lays her eggs. Frantically, he picked through dozens of bolls, all of them infected.

The once promising harvest turned black before his eyes, all around him, the fresh cotton lint rotting in its deathly shell. Shaken by the discovery, he stumbled into the house, fearful of confronting his father-in-law with the news.

John arrived promptly at seven o'clock, full of energy as always and ready to tackle another day cultivating the fields. Ralph met him in the tool shed, his face tight and drawn.

"A sleepyhead this morning, huh? I can't remember the last time I beat you to the tool shed." John's voice echoed.

Ralph did not respond. He stood like a pillar of granite, emotionless, unflinching.

"What's wrong, Ralph? You look like you're taking sick. What is it, son? Is it Nellie?" John became alarmed.

Ralph merely shook his head and looked out over the fields. John's face went numb, his eyes fixed on Ralph. He knew what his son-in-law could not say.

"No! I will not accept that!" John shouted.

He stormed to the fields, his pace quick and determined. If there were boll weevils in his crop, he would get rid of them by sheer force of will. He had not come this far to be put asunder now. He bolted into the first row of cotton, daring the flying insects to come near him.

The young bolls Ralph had picked littered the ground around him. John, too, noticed the two holes in their side. He ran to another row and then another and another until he was in the next field and the one beyond. At first he cursed under his breath, vainly swatting at the winged demons.

He surveyed the acres and acres of cotton surrounding him, all at once feeling the months of hard work creeping into his bones, aging significantly in a matter of minutes, the weight of the universe on his shoulders. A rising anger built deep from within and exploded into a fury he screamed at the sky.

"Why are you doing this to me? What is it that I have to do in this damnable life to get ahead? Shed my blood? Here! Take all the blood you want!" He exposed his wrists to the sky. "Better yet, strike me down with lightning! If you want to see me suffer so much, go ahead and kill me right here and now! I can't take any more of this!

"You're supposed to be a loving and caring God! Well, where the hell is that? I'm not seeing any of it! You encouraged me along, making me think things were going to work out, and then you go and pull something like this! If you are a merciful God, then why did you lead me on this way? In the name of heaven! Why?"

John fell to his knees, beaten and destroyed, convinced that God and the heavens had abandoned him.

THIRTY-THREE

THE BOLL WEEVIL INFESTATION crippled cotton farms all over the state. The grossly proficient beetle multiplied into the millions in one growing season alone. Wave after wave of infant and mature beetles ravaged the cotton fields, destroying the immature cotton bolls and, with them, the lives of those who depended upon a healthy crop.

Overnight, John's world, as well as that of thousands like him, collapsed. The drive that pushed him for so many years, the drive to expand and become a bigger player in the cotton market, deserted him, wounding his pride irrevocably. The optimism he felt while planting his crop vanished, replaced, instead, by a dark, consuming bleakness.

He stood to lose everything he owned. In debt up to his ears and with word of the infestation all over the county, the bank wouldn't loan him any more money to save his house or farm. He was a risk, his hands tied to the thirty acres of dying cotton and, with it, his willingness to fight.

Leola knew the resignation on his face, the lethargy of spirit, the way she felt shortly before Luther died. It hurt her to see John so distraught, so beaten, his hopes and dreams dying inside the infected bolls. Once more, she had to stare her old acquaintance fate square between the eyes and see her way through these troubled times.

"There's got to be some way to kill these things. Aren't they like cotton aphids? Won't sulfur kill them?" Lou poured her mother a cup of coffee.

"If there's anything we can do, I sure don't know what it is," Leola sighed. "John's as tight-lipped as an old spinster on her niece's wedding day."

"It's not as simple as killing cotton aphids," William said. "From what I understand they're almost impossible to get rid of once they've infested a crop. They can wipe out an entire acre of cotton in a matter of days."

Leola rested her head in her hands, deflated by the ugly reality. "I can't take much more in the way of hardship in this life. It seems like everything is stacked up against me. Every time I turn around there's another tragedy standing there ready to take the place of the one before." Her eyes filled with tears.

"There's one thing that might work. I was talking with Bobby Faulk about it the other day. Calcium arsenate. The Agriculture Department is shipping it around the state by rail. It'll be passing through here in a couple of days." William spoke solemnly.

"Why didn't you say something earlier?" Lou jumped with excitement. "That's the answer to our prayers right there!"

"There's a catch to this stuff, Lou. It's expensive, and it takes a lot of work to keep it on the plants. Whenever a good rain comes along, it's got to be reapplied. And it won't do any good for the bolls that are already infected."

"I've got some money saved up," Leanice added.

"And I could get a loan from the bank to help with the cost," William offered.

"I don't think John will take to this idea. He won't accept charity from anyone." Leola dried her tears.

Lou spoke in a business-like manner. "It's not charity, Mama, it's necessity. If this crop fails, you could lose the house, your land, and Nellie and Ralph's house. There isn't anything charitable about this. We've got to do whatever it takes to save as much of this crop as we can."

"How will we know what to do with this poison once we get it?" Leanice asked. "It won't do us any good if we don't know what we're doing."

"They've got farm bureau agents traveling with the trains to explain how to use it," William replied.

"Lord, I don't know what we're going to do if this doesn't work. Everything we own is tied up in those fields."

"We'll make it work, Mama." Lou held her mother's hand. "If it takes all of us working twenty-four hours a day to see this crop through, then that's what we'll do. You've shouldered the burden for us so many years, it's time you let us take on some of it."

William injected the reality of things to come. "This won't be an easy task by any means. I don't know if we can even pull it off. The first bolls are probably all wiped out, and by the time the second and third bolls blossom, the number of weevils will have increased a thousand times over. We're fighting an opponent that has all the advantages. We can't delude ourselves into thinking that we can get two hundred pounds of cotton out of each acre. We'll have to take what's left over."

Tears burned in Leola's eyes and rolled down her cheeks like streams of boiling water.

"Don't cry, Mama." Leanice picked up her mother's withering strength. "Even if the bottom does fall out, we'll find a way to make ends meet until you and Uncle John get back on your feet again."

Leola smiled through the tears, remembering something she was told many years before by a saintly woman. She dried the tears, her resolve rebuilding itself with the help of her daughters.

"I don't want any of you overextending yourselves financially on this poison. We'll get what we can afford and make do with it. When this crisis comes to an end—and it will, all things do—I will find a way to pay back each of you. It may take a while, but I will."

At noon on Friday, Leola met Lou at the train depot. William waited for them on the platform with three of his co-workers, ready to unload the poison for those who could afford it. A group of cotton farmers and their families soon gathered. Their solemn faces reflected the turmoil that was ruining their lives, their bodies bent from the weight of devastation.

Many looked as though they hadn't slept in days, their eyes glazed over by shock and futility. Lou noticed a young boy standing in front of his mother, no more than her age when she was uprooted from her home in Porterdale and moved to Ben Hill County. His small, frail body reminded her how impressionable a child is to sudden change.

She felt sorry for him. He would be forced to mature beyond his years as she had when she lived with Grandpa Cowan. He looked up at her, and she smiled softly, his sad little face brightening momentarily before being pulled away as the group prepared to meet their salvation.

William reached into his vest pocket and pulled out a white envelope, discreetly handing it to Leola, whispering in her ear so those around could not hear. "This is the money I got with the loan, one hundred dollars. How much do you have altogether?"

"Leanice gave me thirty-five, and I scraped up five on my own. That's one hundred forty," Leola replied softly.

"Okay. Don't let on how much you've got right away. They might try and short-change you. Let everyone else set the price. Once these people find out how expensive this stuff is, they'll work the price down. Wait until it's set before you purchase anything."

William tipped his cap to her and led his co-workers to the "Peddler Cars" at the end of the line, beyond the edge of the platform.

Several men, all dressed in suits and ties, stepped from the train onto the platform, their smiles affected. To those old enough, they were reminiscent of the carpetbaggers who descended upon the South during Reconstruction. One of the men stepped forward to address the assembled group.

"Good afternoon, ladies and gentlemen. We come to you today in the belly of hard times. Many of you, like your fellow farmers across the state, are standing on the edge of the biggest crisis in your lives. The situation is serious, and it will only get worse with time. We've seen people like you all across the great State of Georgia and, like you, all of them confused and afraid. The boll weevil has invaded your fields as well as your lives and livelihood. Some of you may face foreclosure on your home and property if the plague isn't stopped. We bring to you this very day, hope, a poisonous powder that can help save your cotton.

"No doubt, some of you have considered plowing under your cotton and replanting with peanuts or cow peas. And some might turn to raising cattle. If you can absorb the loss of your cotton without any repercussions, then I say go ahead. But I would venture to guess that most of you could not absorb that kind of loss. That's why we're here, offering each of you a solution to the boll weevil."

The man looked imperiously over the crowd.

"I've heard this stuff is expensive," a voice called from the crowd. "None of us here have much money."

"Expensive is a relative concept," the man boldly replied. "Is there a price too high to save your crop, your home, your property?"

"You bet your life there is! We're dirt poor!" another person responded.

Someone else raised his concern. "If I go any more into debt, I'll owe the bank all my kids *and* grandkids!"

A few knowing chuckles rippled through the crowd.

"I understand what you're saying, people, believe me, I do. Let me show you what I'm talking about."

The man led the group to the cars where the twenty-pound bags of poison were stored. William and his men, having opened the doors, stood nearby. The man pulled a mason jar filled with a gray, powdery substance from the car.

"This is calcium arsenate. It was developed by entomologists at the United States Department of Agriculture. It will stop the boll weevil dead in its tracks. The government pays the developers and manufacturers for this product and, in turn, sells it to the states. We then sell it to farmers for the purpose of saving their crops."

"Stop beatin' around the bush and get to the point. How much does it cost?" one man asked.

"Calcium arsenate is sold in twenty-pound bags. Each bag will dust approximately one-half acre. The cost is ten dollars per bag."

A loud cry erupted from the crowd as if it were a single beast injured by gunfire. The moans of concern echoed in unison, each person out yelling the other.

"That's highway robbery! At that price those bags should be filled with gold dust!"

"We've been breaking our backs for years making this state a pile of money on cotton. We should be given this stuff for all that hard work!"

"I'd have to buy twenty bags for my ten acres. Where the hell am I gonna get two hundred dollars from?"

"I say five dollars a bag and not a penny more!"

The man from Atlanta tried to calm the crowd, raising his hands, asking for quiet, but the debate raged on. Leola and Lou held close to each other, the tension escalating around them. William pushed his way through the crowd and stood behind them. A couple of farmers rushed the open car, reaching for the bags of poison. The men in suits blocked their way.

A skirmish quickly ensued, fists were thrown and bodies shoved around. William pushed Lou and Leola out of harm's way then jumped into the middle of the fracas with his co-workers, trying to quell tempers on both sides. A swinging fist caught William square on the temple, stunning him. Lou rushed over as he fell back, shielding him from the fight. Leola watched in horror as one of the men in suits fell on Lou, pinning her to the ground.

Suddenly, two gunshots screamed into the air in rapid succession. The fighting stopped abruptly. Heads turned toward the sound. In its wake stood Harbard, stoic, calm, and fearless. He leisurely walked through the gathering, his rifle resting upon his shoulder, speaking to those he knew and nodding his head at others. When he saw William on the ground holding his head, he paused, extending his hand to lift him up.

"Looks like you took a nasty lick to the head, son. You okay?"

"Yes, sir." William leaned on Lou.

Harbard turned to the crowd, his tall frame towering above them. "Somebody mind telling me what's going on here?"

The man from Atlanta brushed himself off, regaining his composure. "Only a minor difference of opinion, sir. Quite understandable, considering the circumstances. We've seen this across the state. People are desperate."

"Uh-huh." Harbard wasn't convinced. He eyed the crowd one by one, his manner menacing. "Seems to me you boys could find a better way of conducting business. You're giving our visitors here a bad impression of our town."

William's head pounded, his legs weak and uncertain. But he stood his ground at Harbard's side.

"I sure hope I don't find out who gave my son this shiner. That'd be at least three days in jail for public brawling, not to mention the personal score I'd have to settle."

The men from Atlanta offered to bury the hatchet and move on, keeping on schedule for another stop in Ashburn before day's end. Their spokesman addressed the crowd. "We'll strike a deal with all of you. Seven dollars a bag, that's as low as I can offer."

Some dissention peppered through the crowd, agitated grumbling from one to another. Harbard stared them down. A few families dragged away home, more defeated than before the trip into town. Those who remained bought what they could and received instruction from the agriculturalists. Leola purchased twenty bags, which William and Harbard loaded onto a wagon.

"William told us about John's crop. Rebecca and I would be happy to help out. I suppose you'll start dusting first thing in the morning, the sooner the better. We'll be there, might even bring Etta if she's not tending to someone." Harbard extended his hand.

"I appreciate that, Harbard. We could use all the help we can get. I look forward to seeing Rebecca, though I feel guilty about it being under these circumstances."

"Rebecca's happiest when she's working outdoors in the sunshine and fresh air. Besides, we're family, and this is what families are supposed to do."

Leola grasped Harbard's firm handshake as if it were the lifeline keeping her from drifting out to sea.

Shortly before dawn, Leola and Leanice walked past the railroad tracks to Merrimac Drive, where Harbard and Rebecca were to meet them. It was a warm, humid morning. The moist air clung to their faces and arms as they waited, the backs of their dresses sticking to them like wet towels after a hot, steamy bath. Leola wiped at the beads of sweat covering her face, wondering if their effort would be in vain.

William explained the procedure for applying the poison. Each plant had to be meticulously dusted, applying the poison on every leaf, as well as in and around the base of each flower, giving special attention to the young bolls just beginning to sprout underneath. It would be a painstaking, backbreaking, lengthy process, nearly fifty thousand tender plants to be dusted by hand.

Obadiah brought his wife to help with the work. Annie Lee was a tall woman whose faith was as strong as her willingness to help others.

"I can't thank you enough for helping us out, Annie Lee. It seems like adversity brings people together." Leola hugged the Reverend's wife.

"I'm glad to be of help, Miz Leola. My husband said you needed all the hands you could get and I got two strong hands. And what's more, I never been afraid of hard work. It's good for the soul, just like the Good Book says." Annie Lee's simple faith inspired the workers for the task at hand.

With the help from Obadiah and his wife, the family took to the fields, wearing gloves to limit their exposure to the poisonous dust. Leola brought extra hand towels to cover their mouths and noses.

As the blood red sun made its initial, fiery appearance over the horizon, they began their arduous work.

Harbard positioned the wagon carrying the bags of poison between two fields. They divided into two groups, each charged with dusting one acre and then moving on to the next. Rebecca and Leola worked side by side, carefully dusting each leaf and flower base.

Their work was slow and tedious; they'd barely dusted one-quarter of an acre by mid-morning. The blazing sun was their enemy, beating unmercifully upon them, its accomplice the humid air, drenching the hand towels they wore around their faces. Even the periodic breaks brought little reprieve, only long enough to stretch out the stiffness of backs and hands while guzzling down water that Nellie brought in abundant supply. While Leola took a momentary rest, she noticed a wagon galloping clumsily over the hill. She heaved a lengthy sigh, prompting Rebecca and Nellie to look behind them.

"Is that Daddy?" Nellie strained to look.

"I'm afraid so," Leola replied.

"He sure looks like he's in a hurry," Rebecca observed.

"I have no doubt that he is," Leola answered wryly.

John raced out to the fields, crashing through cotton plants like they were made of paper. William and Harbard watched from the other field.

Nellie stuck by her stepmother. "Don't let him intimidate you, Leola. You know how Daddy is. He'll blow his stack and then cool off, just like a tea kettle."

John approached Leola and stood before her, his breath heavy from the long walk. He glanced sideways at Rebecca and Nellie.

"What's going on here, Leola?" John placed his hands on his hips.

"It should be fairly obvious, John. We're dusting the plants with calcium arsenate, trying our best to save what we can," Leola answered forthrightly.

"Who paid for it? It's not cheap!"

"William and Lou paid for most of it. I told them they'd be reimbursed when I could afford it."

Ralph walked up and took a glass of water from Nellie. "Why didn't you tell me about this, Ralph? This is my land and my cotton! I have a right to know what's going on!" John was more hurt than angry.

"Ralph didn't know anything about it until this morning, John. This was all my idea. You haven't been in any shape this week to talk to, let alone make any decisions as to what should be done, so I took matters into my own hands."

"We're only doing what we think is right," Ralph spoke up in defense of Leola.

John surveyed their work, nodded in the direction of Harbard and William, then, quite humbly, realizing they were helping him stave off impending disaster, set aside his pride.

"I thank all of you for taking an interest and being here today. I guess I kinda lost my way there for a while. If someone will show me what to do, I'll start in the next field."

John worked with the energy of two men. It took four days, working in shifts as their time allowed, to cover the ten acres. The remaining twenty were left untreated, at the mercy of the boll weevil. If the rains returned, their exhausting work could be wiped out in one afternoon thundershower. But it was a chance they had to take.

John and Ralph inspected the fields daily; only a smattering of puffy white cotton balls dotted the acreage. The sight tore at John's pride. He swallowed bitter tears thinking of the boastful promises he made to Jasper. As June gave way to July, a hot, dry wind blew over the fields, kicking up the topsoil as it raced through the rows of cotton.

The plants thrived under the dry conditions, the cotton bolls hardening and splitting open. A sea of white cotton balls waved lazily in the breeze. The searing temperatures and dry wind were the death knell of the boll weevil, killing the prolific pests almost as quickly as they appeared. Yet, their effect upon John's cotton crop was devastating. The ten acres treated with calcium arsenate yielded one hundred and twenty pounds per acre, the untreated fields less than eighty.

At the end of the cotton growing season, there would normally be anywhere from ten to twenty wagons lined up outside the weighing station, waiting their turn to enter the huge clapboard building with the season's crop. On this day there was not a wagon in sight. John pulled directly into the building, puzzled but not entirely surprised by the lack of activity.

It was cool and dark inside the airy structure; several light bulbs hung from electrical cords draped from the rafters high above, providing the only light. The creaking sound of the wagon and the horses' hooves upon the dry ground echoed against the vast walls. John felt as though he'd entered a tomb.

He stepped out of the wagon and hitched the horses to a nearby post. The office door was closed, as were the doors that led out of the weigh station. The large, iron hook that weighed the bundles of cotton was still. John called out, but no answer came back.

Frustrated, he walked outside the building, looking in all directions for signs of life. The eerie stagnation made him uneasy. A lone voice caught his attention.

"Strange, isn't it? Less activity than you'd see at a graveyard." Jasper stood atop the stairs that led from the office to the weighing area.

"I thought I'd gotten my days mixed up. This sure looks like a Sunday."

"Carl and the boys went into town to eat. They haven't had any business in two days. The infestation hurt everyone real bad, wiped out most."

Jasper walked down the stairs, his hands in his pockets.

"It sure didn't do me any favors. If it weren't for the poison Leola bought, I'd be wiped out, too." John spat at the ground.

"How'd you make out?" Jasper asked tentatively.

John shook his head wearily. "Didn't bring in a third of what I could have. This is the worst crop I've had in a long time."

"At least you had something to bring in. Most people around here couldn't even fill a five-pound bag. You're one of the lucky ones."

"Hmph! Lucky? If this is what constitutes luck, give me a dark cloud any day. I stand to lose my land, house, everything. All because of a little luck." John's voice was edged in sarcasm.

"I'm sorry, John. I didn't realize things were that bad."

"It's not your fault, Jasper. No one could've predicted things would turn out the way they did. I took a chance on something, and I failed—just wasn't meant to be. My biggest fear now is that I'll lose the house. I put it up as collateral on the land, and if I can't meet the note on the land, I'll lose the house, too."

"I could put in a good word for you at the bank, John. I know most of the members of the board. They know you're a good customer of mine and a hard worker. I'm sure they'll give you an extension on the loan."

"I appreciate that. But banks operate on money, not promises. I'll think of something."

John walked away, his shoulders hunched over.

Jasper mulled over John's predicament, then caught up to him. "I don't know how receptive you might be to this idea, John, but if you want to sell off the acreage you bought, I know someone who'd be interested in buying it. I used to do business with a fellow over in Tift County. He switched from cotton to dairy farming a few years back, and I know he's looking for grazing land. That'd get the lien off your house anyway."

John stared at the ground, unblinking, his thoughts bitter as he recounted all his plans, now stolen from him by the forces of nature. "I guess that's the best thing to do. At this point, I'd be happy just to get back what I paid for it. At least then I'd be back where I was before. That might not be the best place to be, but it's a step ahead of where I am now."

Jasper patted John on the back as they walked inside the weigh station.

After his crop was weighed, the net total barely reached twenty-eight hundred pounds. John turned away from the men, refusing to let them see the disappointment in his face. He left the building as quietly as he'd entered, his spirit broken but his dignity intact.

With production of cotton at an all time low across the South, market prices inched upward. Jasper secured eight-and-a-half cents per pound for John's crop. With the two hundred fifty dollars he earned, John barely broke even, a godsend considering where he was the month before. He never again tried to expand his farming operation, choosing instead to accept his lot in life, a small-time farmer in a small South Georgia town.

THIRTY-FOUR

THE BOLL WEEVIL PLAGUE CAME to an end as abruptly as it began. Its brief foray into Georgia ripped apart the lives of farmers across the state, leaving in its wake a mountain of foreclosures and bankruptcies. The losses incurred by small farmers were eventually, painstakingly replaced, though the scars lived with the victims forever. The one constant that weathered the storm of destruction was family. The fight against a common enemy strengthened ties and healed old wounds.

The following summer Lou gave birth to a son, whom she called Junior. He was a happy little boy who boasted an ever-present smile and hearty laugh. His grandparents doted on him with unashamed pleasure. He was his mother's greatest gift.

Lou's dream of marriage and family made her life complete. Trouble seemed as far away from her as the distant planets, out of reach, too far away to touch her perfect world.

She didn't notice the subtle changes taking place within her husband, the feelings of inferiority that ate at his self-worth. Sometimes he didn't answer when she called him, or he lost patience with her over little things. Her presence, it seemed, annoyed him.

In the spring of 1926, as Junior began to walk, life within the household turned upside down. William's moods swung in all directions, his words edged with resentment, his manner distant and aloof. He preferred the company of his drinking buddies rather than his family. At first, he stayed out late a couple of nights a week, drinking whiskey until midnight, then stumbling home drunk and in a nasty mood.

Lou sheltered the family from William's caustic behavior, absorbing the thrust of his brief tirades, the caustic words he threw at her that, in truth, were meant for himself. As his insecurities deepened, William's drinking spiraled out of control.

The stability he longed for while riding the rails slowly lost its appeal. He wanted the excitement of a new challenge, something other than the constraining duties of husband and father. He needed the chance to excel, to prove to himself once and for all that he could succeed. But more so, he had to prove himself worthy of Lou.

In April, Junior came down with a severe cold. His deep, hacking cough reminded Lou of the haunting sounds her father made shortly before his death. She tended to him night and day, refusing to leave his side, ignoring William's late-night escapades.

Leanice stopped by the house every evening after work. Her sister looked worn and nervous. It was completely out of character for her to be so listless.

"What's wrong, Lou?" Leanice asked as she stood at the back door.

"Nothing," Lou replied defensively. "Why do you ask?"

"You look tired, you need some sleep."

"Raising a baby isn't easy, especially one who's been as sick as Junior."

Leanice looked hard at her sister, seeing through the facade she attempted to create. "I have a feeling there's more to it than that."

Lou's eyes darted away. "Everything's fine, Leanice. Honest."

Leanice knew better. "I wish you'd let Mama and me help out while Junior's sick. Mama's got plenty of time on her hands, and I can take off from work anytime. You don't need to work yourself down till you're sick, too."

"I don't want you missing work because of me, Leanice. And Mama's done nothing her whole life but raise children. I'm not going to ask her for help, it's my responsibility. Besides, Etta will be home soon, and if anyone can nurse Junior back to health, it's her."

Leanice lingered for a moment then opened the door, turning to Lou as she walked down the steps. "You let me know if you need anything. Don't be too proud to ask. Pride is a fine thing to have, but it should never stand in the way of need. I'm just a stone's throw away, holler if you need me."

Lou smiled wanly, though she could not bring herself to ask for help.

When Etta returned home from a weeklong stint tending to the sick around the county, she immediately tended to Junior. Etta had changed little over the years, still as headstrong as ever. No one was more qualified than her, she reasoned, to take care of her sick nephew. She picked up her medical bag, packed an overnight case, and descended upon William's house.

"Where's Junior?" Etta asked in a professional tone.

"He's in his bed," Lou replied weakly. "Thank you, Etta."

"Don't thank me just yet. Wait until Junior's better, then you can thank me."

Etta lumbered into Junior's room and closed the door. Lou breathed a sigh of relief. Etta was just the spark to ignite William's hostilities, and if anyone could stand toe to toe with William during his drunken outbursts and come out on top, it was Etta.

Lou nervously watched the clock as she prepared dinner, knowing Etta would become suspicious if William wasn't home soon. She looked out the dining room window after setting the table.

"Junior's sleeping soundly. What can I do to help with dinner?" Etta walked into the dining room.

"It's almost ready, Etta. There's nothing more to do."

Lou closed the curtain and walked into the kitchen. Etta followed closely.

"What were you looking at out the window?"

"Nothing. I thought I heard thunder, so I checked to see if a cloud was coming up." Lou stirred the black-eyed peas simmering on the stove.

"I didn't hear anything in the way of thunder." Etta peered out the kitchen window. "And it sure doesn't look like rain."

"Oh, well, maybe it was a train whistle or something."

"A train whistle at six-thirty? There aren't any trains that come through here at this time of day," Etta replied with certainty.

"Maybe it was just my imagination. Go ahead and fix yourself a plate." Lou tried to divert Etta's attention.

"Shouldn't we wait for William?"

Etta's question knifed through the air.

"I think he's working late tonight. They were behind schedule all last week." Lou quickly prepared a plate for Etta.

"I can do that. Don't wait on me like I'm an invalid!" Etta tried to grab the plate.

"Now go and sit down, Etta. You've had a long day. I don't mind doing this one bit."

Lou practically pushed Etta out of the kitchen. Uneasiness circled them as they ate, pausing momentarily over the table as a dark cloud expanding with showers of doubt. Lou ate quickly, hoping Etta would follow her lead and retire early. When darkness fell, however, Etta's curiosity gave way to suspicion.

"Shouldn't William be home by now? They sure can't work after dark!" Etta's impatient voice penetrated the silence.

"Maybe they've got lanterns to work by," Lou offered weakly.

"Well, that wouldn't help them see any better! For what they're doing they need full daylight. He should be home by now. With a sick baby to look after there's no excuse for him being this late."

Etta was well on her way to a bona fide snit. She folded her arms and rested them upon her chest, staring at the living room door. Her aggravated silence deafened the room. As the clock struck eleven, the back door opened and closed, followed by the sound of footsteps clumsily making their way into the kitchen.

Etta rose from the chair as if cued for her entrance onto the stage. The scowl on her face barely measured her disdain. She marched into the kitchen, where she found her brother bent over the sink drinking water directly from the faucet.

"It's about time you decided to bring yourself home. Where have you been all evening?"

Despite his intoxicated state, William recognized his sister's accusing voice all too well. He lifted his head and wiped his mouth, addressing Etta while facing the wall.

"When did you fly back into town? I didn't see your broomstick parked by the back door."

"Still the same unrighteous heathen you've always been. Don't you know you've got a sick baby in there?"

"Don't you know when to mind your own business?"

"That baby is my business! And he should be your business, too! I sure hope Mama hasn't seen what's going on here."

William spun around, losing his balance, stumbling into the stove. "Don't you go telling Mama anything! What I do in my house is my business!"

"You're drunk."

"And you're ugly. So what's your point?"

"My point is that you are an unfit father and an unfit husband. Here you come straggling in late at night after carousing around doing Lord knows what while your baby's sick in his bed and your wife's worried sick. What's the matter with you? Where's your sense of responsibility? You oughta be taken out back and horsewhipped!"

William glared at Etta, pointing his finger in her face. "If you so much as lay a hand on me—"

"William! That's enough!" Lou spoke up. "Etta was good enough to come over here and look after Junior, the least you can do is thank her."

"That's right, take her side. You never back me up in anything. Nothing I do around this place is ever good enough for you." William leaned back into the corner of the room.

"That's not true, William, and you know it. I've always supported you in everything you've done. And I've backed you up in ways you don't even know about. I've kept this behavior of yours from the family. I've covered for you and made excuses for you so everyone thinks you're a dutiful husband and father. But I will not do that any more if you continue to behave like this." Lou spoke through rising tears.

Etta shook her head, the look on her face conveying her contempt. "Get out of here. Go outside and sleep on the ground with the other dogs!"

"Who do you think you are? Kicking me out of my own house! You're the intruder here! You go outside and sleep with the dogs, if they'll have you!"

William smirked at his sister, his drunken eyes threatening her. Etta stepped back, suddenly afraid of her brother's alcohol-induced demeanor.

She'd never encountered William in a frame of mind like this. Lou stepped in front of Etta.

"Get out of the house, William. I don't want you in here when you're acting like this. Go outside and sleep it off."

William looked at her without expression. Lou swallowed hard, determined to hold her ground.

"Why in hell did we ever get married? You don't love me. You only married me to get away from that overbearing father of yours. You needed a way out, and I was just the meal ticket you were looking for. What a chump I am. I let a pretty face and a few soft words trap me in a marriage and family I never wanted."

Lou gasped, openly shocked by William's words. Fiery tears misted her eyes as she avoided William's stare. He remained in the corner, motionless, like a defeated boxer in the last round of a brutal match.

"Why don't you get it over with and divorce me? Free yourself of the shackles I've put on you. Find someone who can support you, someone who can give you what you want out of life. What about the guy in Miami with the camera? He seemed to think you were something special. You could be a rich girl, Lou. Fancy cars, fancy clothes, fancy men to escort you everywhere you go. Put your beauty to good use. You'll never be happy with a grease monkey like me. Leave, Lou. Take the baby and get out while you can. I don't want to be married any more."

Lou ran from the room, William's words chasing her as a bully chases its victim. She burst into her bedroom and threw herself on the bed, her sobs digging into the depths of her soul.

Etta turned to William. "You are a disgrace to this family, William Smith! A drunken, idiotic disgrace!"

William slowly sank to the floor, too intoxicated to hold himself up but aware enough to realize that he'd maliciously ruined his life.

THIRTY-FIVE

L OU POURED HERSELF A CUP of coffee, her worn face reflecting the long, restless night. Junior was in high spirits, chattering to himself endlessly as he ate a good-sized breakfast of oatmeal and bananas. Lou put her hand to his cheek and smiled at his enthusiasm. "Someone's feeling better today."

"His fever's gone, but he'll have a cough for a while." Etta fed him a spoonful of oatmeal.

Junior let out a loud squeal as if confirming Etta's prognosis, prompting both women to laugh. The levity of the moment broke the tension.

"I'm sorry about last night, Etta. I don't know what's gotten into William."

"It's not your place to apologize, Lou. And certainly not to me. William's the one who should be apologizing, and that'll never happen."

"I've been racking my brain trying to figure out what's got him so cross. If it's something I've done, I sure wish he'd tell me."

"It's not you, it's him. William's mad at himself, and he's taking it out on you."

"What's he mad at himself for?"

"I don't know. William's always kept to himself. Mama's the only one who could reach him, get him to open up and express himself. But after last night, I can't say who he is or what he's about. I've never seen him like that before."

Lou sat back in her chair. "Me neither. He's nothing like the man I married."

Etta fed Junior the last of his oatmeal. "I think you should leave William." Her words surprised herself as much as they did Lou. "It doesn't have to be forever, but I think you should leave him for a while anyway. Once he sees what a mess he's made of things, he'll straighten up. But the longer you stay, the more he'll think he can get away with."

Etta's suggestion did not surprise Lou. "I've thought long and hard about that, Etta. But I don't know if I can. I don't want to hurt him."

"Think of what's best for you and your child, Lou. Do you want Junior growing up around this? Watching a drunken father berate his mother? And maybe even himself one day?"

Lou's heart sank, as she lost herself in a million different thoughts. "Where would I go? I can't move back home with Mama and Uncle John. They have enough to worry about without me adding to their problems."

"You can stay with Mama and Daddy and me. As much as I'm away on calls, the house won't be crowded, and you know Mama would love to have you stay there. And William wouldn't dare do anything stupid in front of her or Daddy."

Lou fought the notion to leave with every ounce of fiber in her being. But she couldn't stay and subject herself and Junior to William's antics. "I'll start packing some things. I don't want to be here when William gets home," Lou stated wearily.

"It's for the best. At least for the time being."

"I love William with all my heart, but I hate him, too. I hate him for putting us in a fix like this. I hate him for forcing me to make decisions that I don't want to follow." Lou quickly excused herself from the table, holding on to her tears.

They left the house shortly before noon. Etta led the way down Main Street, huffing and puffing as she carried her own bags under one arm and Lou's under the other. Lou held Junior close to her, not once looking back at the little house that at one time held such promise for happiness.

Rebecca was just sitting down to lunch when she heard someone entering the front door. She listened intently. Perplexed, she called out Harbard's name as Etta entered the kitchen. "What are you doing back so soon?" Rebecca asked.

"I've got something to tell you, Mama."

The frankness of Etta's reply throttled Rebecca. "Oh my Lord! It's the baby! Something's happened to Junior!"

"No, Mama. Calm down. Junior's fine."

"Thank God. I was thinking he might have contracted influenza."

"Mama, Lou and Junior are in Martin's old room. They're going to be staying with us for a while."

Rebecca was puzzled. She started to speak, but Etta cut her off.

"William's drinking again. Apparently it's been going on awhile, but Lou's been covering for him. Last night he was so drunk and hostile, he even scared me. I told Lou if this is what his behavior's been like, then she should leave. So I invited her to stay here."

Though saddened, Rebecca agreed. "You're right. No child should have to see that, and no woman should put up with it. I wish I knew what was going on inside that boy's head. He's got everything he could want, but he's bent on destroying it! How's Lou?"

"Shaky. She didn't want to leave, but then she didn't really have a choice. I think she'd appreciate a shoulder to lean on."

"Of course. I'll go to her now."

"I'm going into town. I told Lou I'd tell her sister what was going on so she could tell Leola. I don't know what to tell you to do if William comes by."

"Don't concern yourself with that. I can handle my son."

Rebecca was not afraid of William; he wasn't the sort of man who would physically harm anyone. But he angered her, and seeing the sadness in Lou's face angered her even more. She held Lou's hand, looking deeply into her agonized eyes, reminded of a day many years before when she, too, needed a shoulder to lean on.

"Have I ever told you about my father's death?"

Lou solemnly shook her head.

"My daddy was shot and killed by a moonshiner. He'd gone with Harbard's daddy to check on a still they'd heard about, and they were ambushed. That was a very bad time for me. I'd already lost my mother, and when Daddy died I shut down. I couldn't get out of bed, I didn't want to eat. I didn't want to live anymore. Harbard was so worried. He couldn't reach me, nobody could.

"Then one morning Harbard's mother showed up. She was a godsend. She sent Harbard to work and took over the house, cleaning the rooms and cooking the meals, doing what I was incapable of doing at the time. I remember hearing her sing as she worked. I got out of bed and looked out the window at the garden Daddy loved so much. I was mad at Ezra for asking Daddy to go with him and mad at Daddy for going. I was afraid to tell Nancy how mad I was at her husband. I didn't want to be disrespectful of her. But I didn't have to tell her anything, she knew. And she wasn't judgmental or angry with me. She didn't try to change my feelings.

"She just wanted to let me know that she was there for me. Whatever I had to say, she'd listen. She pulled me through that time by showing me how much she cared. I'm here for you, Lou. I care for you and I love you. Whatever you're feeling toward my son you can tell me. It will not upset me nor hurt my feelings. Tell me what you want to say."

Lou burst into tears. "I don't understand why he's so angry. What have I done to make him so mad?"

"It's not you, honey. William loves you deeply, that's something you can bank on. I can't say that I know exactly what's going on with him, but I'm sure he's angrier with himself than anyone else. William has always had the need to prove himself, his father made him that way. Harbard never gave William much encouragement. They had terrible arguments. Oh, it made me sick to watch them tear into each other the way they did. I don't think William has gotten over that. He wants to give you the moon and stars, Lou. And if he feels like he hasn't, then he'll punish himself and all those around him until he does. I'm not trying to excuse his behavior any, because there's no excuse for it. And when he comes around here, and he will, I'll tell him as much."

"Why does he even think that I want the moon and stars? I've told him over and over again that all I want is a happy and healthy family. I don't need a fancy house or fancy clothes. I'm happy with the way things are . . . or were."

"William idolizes you. He has never felt about someone the way he feels about you. He wants to give back to you everything you've brought into his life, and in his mind that means the fancy house and clothes and things like that. Believe it or not, William's a very sensitive boy when he's sober. He'd do anything within his power to make you happy."

Lou blushed meekly. "A simple hug would be nice."

"He'll come around." Rebecca squeezed Lou's hand. "Now eat something. A healthy appetite is a sure sign of a happy mind."

Rebecca watched over Lou as Nancy had done for her. It made her feel good to complete the circle, to give to someone else the same attention and love that was given to her. She built a wall around Lou, one that made Lou feel safe. She vowed to protect her, even if it meant turning away her own son.

As she predicted, William showed up at the house that evening in an agitated state, the smell of alcohol on his breath. He called Lou's name repeatedly from the front porch, waking the entire household. Harbard was livid. He swung open the door, nearly pulling it from the hinges. Rebecca ran after him, jumping in front of William.

"Harbard, I can handle this! Go inside please and see to Lou and the baby."

Harbard hesitated but did as Rebecca asked, giving William a long look before leaving.

"Call me if he gives you any trouble."

Rebecca kept her back to William, so angry with him she didn't even want to look at him.

William was oblivious to her anger. "I want to see my wife."

Rebecca spun around, her face hard and vicious. "Do not speak to me, do you hear? Not one word!" She moved closer to him. "I will not have you showing up at my house in a drunken fit like this! You're being disrespectful to everyone, including yourself. No, you may not see your wife tonight. And if you don't straighten up, you may never see her again. Go home, William. Go home and think about how you want to live the rest of your life. If this is the way you want to live it, then do it to the fullest. But don't expect me or anyone else in this family to support that decision."

"But Ma—" William interjected.

"I told you not to speak and I meant it! Go home! And don't come back until you're sober!"

William cowered before his mother.

The following morning Rebecca woke early, having paced the floor half the night. She looked around the yard, hoping William followed her advice and stayed at his house. At her feet, outside the screen door, a bright assortment of colors caught her eye. A bouquet of red and yellow zinnias accompanied by a note addressed to Lou. Rebecca carried the bouquet inside and placed it on the kitchen table.

"What's this?" Lou asked.

"It was on the front porch." Rebecca kissed Junior on the cheek and held out her arms. "I can feed Junior his breakfast if you want some time to yourself. I've made his oatmeal. It's cooling on the counter."

Lou read over the note. "Whatever William has to say to me he can say to everyone. I'm not the only injured person here. I'm sorry you had to face him last night."

"I didn't mind. In fact, I'm glad I got to talk to him. It gave me a chance to tell him what he needed to hear." Rebecca fed Junior a teaspoon of oatmeal.

"And did he listen?" Lou cracked.

"Oh, I think he did. I can get my point across when I want to." Rebecca smiled.

"Looks like we're going to have company tonight."

"Oh?"

"William wants to talk. Do you mind if he comes over?"

"That's your decision, honey. William is always welcome in my home, as long as he conducts himself appropriately."

"I don't know what to say to him. I can't just excuse everything he's done and pretend that it never happened. He hurt me, and it's going to take a while to get over that. He has to change his ways."

"So why don't you tell him that?" Rebecca replied.

When William arrived at the house his father met him at the door. Harbard was stiff yet cordial, inviting William inside before excusing himself to another room. William sat on the couch, wringing his hands, his forehead damp with fear. He jumped to his feet when Lou entered the room, his courtly manner revealing his penitence. He struggled for words. Lou waited patiently until he found them.

"I couldn't blame you if you never forgave me. I said some nasty, hurtful things, and I'm sorry. I was drunk. I didn't know what I was saying, and I didn't mean any of it. I'm a fool, a stupid fool. I'll do anything you want, Lou. I'll crawl on my hands and knees, beg like a dog, whatever it takes to get you home."

"All I want to know is one thing, William. Why?"

William slowly shook his head. "There's not a simple answer to that. My whole life I've been taught to fail, to expect the worst out of life. And I guess I learned that lesson better than any other. I've never given myself an even break, and I have the tendency to take that out on everyone around me. When

I first met you I couldn't believe you'd even give me the time of day. I figured you were too stuck up to spend time with the likes of me. But you did. And ever since then I've been trying to prove my worthiness, to give you the kind of life you deserve. When we went to Miami and I saw how well Roy and them were doing, I wanted that for you.

"You're special, Lou. Sometimes I wonder if you know how beautiful you are. That advertising man saw it right away. He offered you a way to the top. All I can offer you is a humdrum life in a two-bit town. You could've married anyone you wanted, Lou. And chances are you'd be a lot better off than you are now."

Lou was even more perplexed by William's explanation. "William, when did I ever tell you that I wanted or even expected a certain standard of living? I've never known anything in life but struggle and hard times. And I haven't complained about that. As long as I have my family around me, those that I dearly love, I'm happy."

"I know. But wouldn't it be nice to live a little better? From year to year rather than day to day? I want the best for you and our family. If I don't give it a shot now, I'll always wonder, what if I had?"

Lou saw the determination in William's face, the need to prove himself as a husband and father and, most importantly, a man. She didn't want to stand in the way of his dreams. It was only fair, she thought, to let him reach for the stars and find his place in the sun.

THIRTY-SIX

M OVING? WHERE?" Leola asked, stunned.

"Homestead, Florida, where William's Uncle Dex lives."

Leola sat back in her chair, catching her breath. "What in the world prompted this decision?"

Lou looked askance, away from her mother's eyes. "William's cousins have been after him for years to go into business with them at their auto shop. They're doing great business, and William feels like it's time to make the move. I've got to support him in this, Mama. It's important to him."

"I understand that, Lou. It's just kind of a shock. It'll take some getting used to, not seeing you or my only grandchild."

Leola was so overcome with emotion she excused herself from the room and hurried to the back porch.

Lou followed. "It's not like we won't ever see each other again, Mama."

"I know, baby. It's just not easy to let go of your children. It was hard enough when you got married, and now this. One day you'll understand what I mean. Your father keeps coming to my mind. I can just hear him telling me, 'Now, Leola, you've got to let the children lead their own lives. You can't keep them tied to your apron strings forever.' He was so practical. He could see through anything, get right to the heart of the matter. There's not a day goes by that I don't think of him, and miss him. That's how it'll be when you leave. But at least I'll know you're walking the face of this earth somewhere, and I can see you again and hold you in my arms."

Lou rushed into her mother's embrace, resting her head upon Leola's shoulder. "I'm gonna miss you, Mama."

"Always remember how much I love you, baby. When you feel the warmth of the afternoon sun embracing you, think of being in my arms, that's how much I love you."

Lou clung to her mother as long as she could, wondering where she would find the strength to let go.

When the day of their departure arrived, William moved around the house with lightning speed, packing belongings in the car and pushing Lou to hurry along. He was manic, ready to hit the road and get on with their new life; sentiment only wasted precious time. Lou, on the other hand, asked Leanice to be with her up to the end. William had to bite his tongue while they dawdled over possessions and retold stories.

"Come on, Lou. We need to get going. I want to reach Daytona by nightfall."

"I'll be there in a minute, William. You said you wanted to leave by eight, and it's five till. A few minutes one way or the other isn't going to hurt any."

Exasperated, William scooped up Junior and took him to the car.

"I wish Mama was here."

"You know she couldn't bear it, Lou. Just thinking about you leaving makes her cry. She's got to keep herself busy so she won't think about it. She was washing windows when I left." Leanice giggled.

"At eight o'clock in the morning?" Lou cackled aloud.

Though they were laughing, it was nervous laughter, the kind of laughter that masks an otherwise unpleasant moment. They weren't ready to part. Though they knew for days the time was ever near, it was always one day away, or one hour away, a buffer of time both women needed to cope with the thought of losing one another. William honked the horn impatiently.

"I guess I'd better get out there before he leaves without me."

Lou looked into Leanice's eyes, the enormity of the loss falling upon her like stones from heaven. Other than her honeymoon, she'd never been separated from her sister. Leanice was the other half of herself, the mirror who constantly reflected the image of who she was. Lou dissolved into tears, gripping Leanice with a hug that would last until they were together again.

As the car pulled down the highway she watched her confidante and closest friend until she disappeared beyond the reaches of the horizon. Somehow, someday, she knew they would be reunited again.

The long, arduous drive to Homestead tested Lou's resolve. The oppressive heat clung to her, the stagnant air suffocating, the intermittent sea breeze being the only thing that kept her from collapsing. The moisture stuck to her skin like a coating of cheap, runny lotion. The sticky, humid-laden air irritated Junior's frail body. He bounced from the back seat to the front, unable to sleep yet too tired to stay awake. If there was a place where the earth ended and weary travelers fell over the end, this was it.

The house Uncle Dex picked out for them was only two blocks east of his home. It was a small, wooden house on a corner lot, clean, and with a well-kept lawn. A group of sabal palms towered above alongside the road, swaying peacefully in the breeze. A wrap-around porch greeted them at the front door, complete with two hanging ferns.

The interior, though small, was well kept and airy. A series of shuttered windows faced the porch from the living room and lined the side of the house overlooking the street. Beyond the kitchen was a Florida room, an enclosed back porch with huge, double-paned windows that opened by turning a lever.

Though sparsely furnished, the house came with two beds, a kitchen table with chairs, and a sofa.

"Not bad," William observed as he walked through, "not bad at all. I think we're gonna like it here, Lou. I have a good feeling about this place."

Lou smiled and agreed tenuously. But she couldn't shake the strong feeling that nagged at her, a feeling of impending disaster.

William went to work right away, leaving most of the unpacking to Lou. The chore of setting up house took her mind off the family she left behind. But as the days turned into weeks, she found herself in an unsettling position, in unfamiliar surroundings without her mother or sister. She was lonely. And with each passing day she became lonelier. The little house was her home, as well as her prison.

The move to Homestead made a new man out of William. He was happy, secure in himself as the provider and head of the household. The change in him was a complete turnaround from the nights of boozing and carousing. As much as Lou was happy for him, she began to believe that her feeling of disaster was nothing more than her intense desire to return home. The more comfortable William became with his new life, the less chance there was of ever returning to Fitzgerald.

Roy and Uncle Dex often joined William for lunch. Even though Roy put on airs, he was entertaining and always kept the conversation moving. He could eat as fast as he could talk, which was no small feat.

"Like I always say, the way to a man's heart is through his stomach. I'm telling ya, Lou, if you ever decide to dump this guy, I'm waiting in the wings!"

"I'll keep that in mind." Lou blushed.

"How's the house treating you?" Uncle Dex asked. "It's not a bad little starter home. Once you get comfortable with the business you might think about something larger, especially if you want a bigger family." He preened his teeth with a toothpick.

"It suits our purpose just fine. I talked to a man about putting a new roof on it. Other than that, we're satisfied," William stated.

"I noticed that when I first looked at the house, but it'll last until next storm season."

"Storm season?" William asked.

"Aw, Daddy, don't scare 'em with that. Daddy worries this time every year about the storms. Why, I don't know. We've lived here fifteen years and have never seen a bad storm. Nothing worse than any afternoon gully washer we saw in Georgia." Roy spoke with authority.

"A person can never be too cautious. I've heard about these storms—wind so strong it can knock a fella off his feet and rain so thick you can't see your hand in front of your face," Uncle Dex rebutted.

"You're a doomsayer, Daddy. We've never gone through anything like that. What makes you think we're going to be blown off the face of the earth?"

"I didn't say that. I only said it's a good idea to be prepared."

"Prepared for what?" William asked with rising curiosity.

"Hurricanes," Uncle Dex replied. "They come out of the ocean, big, ferocious storms. The old-timers here are afraid of them. That's why you see so many homes built on risers, to keep the water out. And the storm shutters keep things from blowing through the windows. You might want to check their condition before next year."

William and Lou struggled to grasp the notion of a storm so strong it could wreak such catastrophic destruction. What Uncle Dex described to them sounded like Armageddon.

"Maybe I should get the man working on the roof right away," William stated.

"Don't let Daddy scare ya, Billy," Roy said. "It's the middle of September. Storm season is winding down. Wait till the first of the year. You'll get a better price in the off-season."

"I'm not trying to scare anyone, Roy. I wish you'd stop saying that. I only want William and Lou to become knowledgeable about hurricanes, just in case. I didn't say we were going to have one. Better prepared than not, I always say."

"So should I wait on the roof or what?" William asked.

"It'll do for one more season."

The first week of September was even hotter and more humid than the day they drove into Homestead. Clear skies allowed the sun to beat upon the land without remorse, making furnaces out of the insides of houses. When she could stand it no longer, Lou dressed Junior in a pair of shorts with a loose-fitting shirt and walked into town.

She carried him close to her, shading him underneath the wide-brimmed hat she wore. He smiled as he looked around at the alien surroundings, oblivious to the scorching heat. When they reached the highway, Lou turned north, in the direction of an ice cream shop William had taken them to the previous week. Junior's eyes brightened when he saw the colorful canopy hanging over the storefront. He clapped his hands together and squealed with delight.

The store was owned by a widower in his late fifties who lived in the back of the building. He was a congenial fellow who never forgot a customer or a customer's order. He kept a radio playing on a shelf above the cash register, tuned to a station that carried the news.

An elderly man sat on a stool behind the proprietor. His deep wrinkle lines and coarse skin accentuated a hard life. He stared at Lou with an unnerving scowl.

"Good afternoon, ma'am. I recall seeing you and this little fellow in here last week," the proprietor said with a toothy grin.

Lou broke from the old man's gaze. "Yes, my husband brought us in on his day off."

"That's right. He works down at Dex's automobile shop. If memory serves correct he had a scoop of strawberry and you and the little one shared a chocolate sundae. Would you like the same, or would you like to try something different? Our root beer float is awfully good this time of year," he boasted.

"That does sound good. We'll have the float."

Lou purposely avoided the old man, sitting at a table directly in front of one of the rotating fans bolted into the wall, as far from him as she could get.

The two men bickered over the last year each remembered it being this hot in September. When the older man called the proprietor a stupid imbecile, the conversation ended.

A deep, male voice reported the news over the radio, his words resonating through the heavy air. After he announced the weather report, a thundering silence shattered the room.

"Did I hear him correctly?" the older man asked.

"That depends on what you heard, old man," the proprietor responded coolly.

"He did say hurricane, didn't he?" His question was more of a statement.

"That's what he said."

The old man nodded his head fearfully. "Lord, have mercy upon us."

Lou froze in mid-bite. The fatalistic tone of the man's voice fed upon the fear already nibbling inside her.

"It's not the end of the world, Mac." The proprietor scooped himself a cone of chocolate ice cream.

"Isn't it? How many of these things have you been through?"

"We had one about twenty years back. Nothing much to it, a little wind and rain. I've seen thunderstorms with more punch."

"Don't underestimate their power. The weaker ones make you complacent. It's when you've been through a bad one that you know what hell on earth is all about."

"And you've been through hell on earth, I suppose?"

"Yes, sir. I can honestly say that I have."

"Where was this, Mac?"

"Galveston, Texas, 1900, the eighth of August. I was working in the harbor as a longshoreman, been there a few years, maybe six or seven. It was hot as blazes that week, we all near about got sunstroke. I think it was a Saturday that the sky started to darken and a wind came up out of the water. It was a relief to us right then, the first breeze we'd felt all week. We kept working even when it started raining. It felt good. I was on the dock operating a pulley system we used to unload ships. A big freighter pulled in the day before from Cuba, loaded with sugar cane. The crew told us something about a storm over the water, but their English was so bad we couldn't understand 'em all that well, so we didn't pay it much mind. We didn't have radios back then, no warning if a storm was out there, no warning where it might hit, how bad it was, all we had was word of mouth. I wish to God we had understood what those fellas were trying to tell us."

The old man's words trailed off, constricted by the agony of memory. Lou turned to him, her eyes transfixed by the horror on his face.

"You all right, Mac?" the proprietor asked.

"All those people, screaming, crying, holding on for dear life to anything they could grab. I can still hear them, see them. We wanted to pull them to safety, but the wind . . . the wind blew so fierce, straight from the mouth of hell."

The proprietor tossed out his ice cream cone, having lost his appetite. Lou felt her stomach churning.

"The wind picked up, gradually at first, and then with great fury. People scattered everywhere. My buddy and I hopped aboard the freighter. Some of the crew helped us on board. They were scared. They'd been through this monster over the water. Some went down into the belly of the ship to ride out the storm. We stayed on the steering deck. The wind was like nothing I've ever seen. Huge waves, one on top of the other, sailed right on through the harbor and onto the island. The ship we were on rocked back and forth like a toy boat in a tub of water. We were tossed about like rag dolls. The water was rising fast, first over the lower docks and then the higher ones. It kept pushing forward until it burst over the top and raced into town. That's when we started seeing 'em, by the hundreds. People from town, my friends and neighbors, being swept out to sea.

"I thought the world was coming to an end, another flood like in the Bible. We tried to help them, but it was all we could do to hold on and not go crashing through the windows into the water. They all had the same look on their faces. It wasn't shock, really, or fear. It was beyond that. They knew they were going to die." The screams of the dead rang in his ears, the faces of death and dying clouded his vision. "Before it was over I didn't much care if I lived or died. It was well into the next day when things settled down. None of us could move. My arms were hurting real bad from hanging on for so long. When we finally walked out on the deck and looked around we got sick to our stomachs at what we saw. Dead bodies everywhere, floating in the bay like dead leaves from an old oak tree. Had we known how many people died we would've gone mad right then and there. Six thousand people lost their lives that day, and those of us that survived would never again be the same."

Lou exhaled, unaware she had been holding her breath. The proprietor glanced at her. The old man's recollection scared both of them to the core. Their minds spun on all cylinders, each of them wondering what was lurking over the warm, tropical waters of the Atlantic.

THIRTY-SEVEN

WILLIAM WAS TAKING forever to get home, Lou thought. Every noise sent her running to the back door, her nerves on edge, the feeling of foreboding stronger than ever. She could not shake the old man's tale or the look of horror etched upon his face.

When William finally walked in the back door, she jumped on him. "Did you hear the news? There's one of those hurricanes out there!"

William paused. "Good afternoon to you, too."

"We heard it on the radio this afternoon. I took Junior to the ice cream shop. I think we should leave, William. Right now!" Lou pleaded.

"Leave? What are you talking about, Lou?"

"Get out while we can. I'm afraid of this thing, got a bad feeling about it. Ever since we left home, I've had this sense that we're in danger."

"There's nothing to worry about, Lou. You're overreacting."

Lou followed William to the bathroom, shadowing him while he washed the day's grease and grime from his hands and arms. "I'm not overreacting. I'm thinking about our safety. You don't know what this thing is capable of doing."

"And you do?" William dried his hands.

"There was an old man at the store. He told us about a hurricane that hit Texas while he was living there. It completely destroyed the town. Six thousand people died that day, most of them swept out to sea."

William paused. Though awed by the story, he brushed it off as an old man's ramblings. "He was probably exaggerating, Lou. You know how old people are. They tend to distort things they can't remember. I doubt it was as bad as he said." William's bravado lacked conviction.

"You didn't see the terror in his eyes as he told the story. You didn't see the tears streaming down his face as he relived that awful day. There was no distortion in his mind. He knew what he'd been through."

"So what are you suggesting we do? Pack up everything and move back to Georgia? We just got here, Lou. We haven't even been here six months yet. You want me to leave my job, leave our home, and move back to a place where I don't have a job and we have no home? That's crazy, Lou." William masked his fears behind logic.

"What's more crazy? Moving back to a place that provides safety or risking our lives here on something we know nothing about?"

William's cheeks turned red, his temper getting the best of him. "I will not be intimidated by some damnable storm. We are staying here and that's all there is to it. We didn't pack up and move out of Fitzgerald every time we heard a clap of thunder or saw a flash of lightning, did we? There's nothing that storm can do to harm us. Now let's just drop the subject, okay?"

Lou brusquely turned and walked away. Time was running out, she felt, and there was nothing she could do to stop it.

On the morning of September seventeenth, Lou glanced over the front page of the newspaper, immediately turning her attention to a small article about the hurricane. The report stated that it was not expected to hit Florida but, instead, would veer south and threaten Cuba. Lou heaved a sigh of relief then laughed at her misguided sense of doom.

At mid-morning, she watered the ferns on the front porch. The sky was clear, a few high clouds blew in from the east. A sudden surge of tropical air swept over her face. She breathed in its moist, salty fumes. It was a beautiful day and, undoubtedly, the nice weather would continue into the weekend.

William came home for a quick lunch then hurried back to the shop, anxious to complete a repair job that was taking longer than he anticipated.

"Don't wait up. Dex is treating us to a steak dinner after work tonight, had the best month of business ever!" William kissed Lou on the cheek and ran out the door. She was glad that he had not given in to her sense of doom.

The lilting winds of afternoon gave way to the unsettled breezes of evening. A restless wind blew in from the east, winding its way down streets, in between the tall buildings, through the graceful fronds of the sabal palms. Its innocent playfulness teased the diners, gamblers, and moviegoers who were setting out on their Friday night traditions, inviting them in, beguiling them with its cruel touch.

Lou worked on a tatted doily while Junior slept soundly. A burst of wind skirted the house as it raced through the neighborhood, consuming fragile limbs and late summer flowers. The fern baskets swung wildly in the heightening wind. Lou set them inside as another blast of wind shot through the door, fighting its way inside as she struggled to block its entrance.

She gazed at the ominous sky from the living room window. Restless clouds boiled like a teapot, rotating counterclockwise. The wind blew even stronger, ripping the fronds from the palm trees. Large raindrops began beating against the house like giant marbles, followed by torrential sheets of rain that blew in circles around the house. Lou woke Junior and held him in her arms. The screaming winds tore at the small-framed house.

Junior sensed his mother's fear and began crying. The assault upon the house was deafening. At times it seemed the battering winds would lift it right off its foundation and scatter it away. The storm shutters beat against the windows like warning drums before battle. Lou tried to push the maddening noise from her mind but couldn't. She was trapped inside the belly of this indiscriminate beast, wondering if she and her son would die together.

The living room began vibrating; the curtains and hanging light bulbs swayed back and forth in unison as the rumbling wind passed through the house like a freight train on a cross-country run. A booming explosion preceded the loss of comforting light, invading the house with the abandoning darkness of a crypt on a moonless night. The roof popped and cracked under the stress of nature. Lou sprinted from the living room into the kitchen as the roof collapsed upon the couch.

The screaming winds tore through the living room and down the hall, into the kitchen, seeking, searching, sparing nothing in their path, bringing with them the driving, pelting rain. Junior cried hysterically. Lou fell apart, crying through her tears, begging the God she believed in to spare her and her child.

She backed into the pantry, stooped below the lowest shelf, and closed the door. The wind and rain intensified their assault. The pantry door rattled, the murderous wind trying to push its way inside. Lou held Junior tight, her legs pressed against the door. They could barely breathe. She felt water at her feet, leaking in underneath the door, inch by inch.

Oh, Mama. I wish you could hear me. I wish you could hold me and comfort me and tell me everything's going to be all right. I don't want to die, Mama, not now, not like this. Please pray for me, Mama, pray for my son. I'll see you again one day. I love you, Mama.

The rains pounded furiously upon William's car, pelting the windows with unashamed brutality, the vengeful winds buffeting the sides, pushing the car across the road. For all he knew he was traveling directly into the ocean, into the teeth of the monstrous storm. People on the streets gripped onto lampposts and trees, trying in vain to hold on against the powerful winds. Some were tossed about like paper dolls, blown into the night, never to be seen again.

William cursed himself for not leaving sooner. If anything happened to Lou or Junior, he'd never forgive himself. He pressed on, driving blindly, hoping either instinct or sheer luck would get him home. A ferocious gust of wind rocked the car from side to side, tipping it onto two wheels, spraying a giant palm across the road, inches from the car.

Miraculously, the house appeared out of the mayhem. William pulled the car around back, using the house as a shield. With a momentous effort, he pushed open the car door. The wind blew through him, knocking him off his feet, the stinging rain pelting his body. Gasping for breath, he grabbed the railing and pulled himself up.

He felt he'd been in a boxing match with a much stronger and seasoned opponent, holding his own but the worse for wear. Each time he got up another blow struck him down. Crawling on his knees, he reached the door. Wind-blown possessions greeted him inside the house, as if possessed by demons, pictures and papers flying through the air, chairs moving of their own accord, windows shattered, a sea of water rising at his feet.

His heart leapt into his throat. He ran through the house, terrified, looking for his family. A gaping hole in the ceiling of the living room ushered in the elements, chunks of plaster and cement littered the room. Rain and wind poured through the open wound. He screamed Lou's name. Under the overturned couch, he found Lou's framed picture of her mother and sister.

He went out of his mind, looking in closets and under beds, his cries lost in the howling wind. One of the large palms snapped like a twig and fell across the yard, brushing the side of the house.

Where are they? They've got to be in the house! Oh Lord, help me! Please help me!

The winds howled unmercifully as the eye wall of the hurricane neared. William ran blindly from room to room, opening doors, screaming Lou's name. He made his way into the kitchen, feeling his way for the pantry door. Lou and Junior huddled together underneath the collapsing shelves. A silhouetted hand pulled them out and held them close.

"We've got to get out of here!" William screamed. "We'll be safer at Uncle Dex's house!"

William took Junior from Lou's arms and led them to the Florida room. Holding onto Lou's hand with all his might, he led them outside. Lou pulled back. "You've got to, Lou! We'll die if we stay here!" he screamed

"We're going to die anyway, William!"

"No we won't. I will not allow it!"

William's fortitude helped Lou move forward. The screen door crashed helplessly against the house, breaking free and tumbling down the street. Lou held onto the railing for dear life. The relentless winds made it difficult to breathe. William fought with the car door while Lou clung to the railing. Junior buried his head underneath his father's chin.

With a violent and angered pull, William opened the door. He pushed Lou inside and handed Junior to her; they were near the point of collapse.

Lou slumped in her seat, resting her head against the window. Her face was numb, her thoughts dulled by the prospect of death. William started the car and slowly pulled away from the house. The saturated ground nearly ingested the vehicle, as if the earth intended to open up and swallow them whole.

The car bounced across the road like a rubber ball, spinning from side to side, tossing them back and forth, slamming them into the doors and dashboard. Raindrops pelted the car like bullets hitting their target. Junior screamed; Lou tried comforting him but was too weak to fight. In the blackness of night, besieged by the wrath of nature, the little car drove into the clutches of hell.

Through luck or divine fate, they reached Dex's house. The winds hit their peak, gusting upwards of one hundred seventy-five miles per hour.

Lou crawled up the front steps on her hands and knees, the winds arrogantly whipping through her clothes and body, stripping her dignity. William clutched Junior in his arms as Dex and Roy ran to their aid.

"Good Lord! What are you doing out in this storm?" Dex screamed.

"We had to get out of the house. The roof collapsed!" William answered breathlessly.

"Have mercy on us all! Get 'em some towels, Roy," Dex yelled as they all stumbled inside the house.

"What is this?" William asked incredulously.

"It's what we fear the most, the unknown. I've never seen anything like this in my life, and I hope never to again."

Roy rushed in with towels. "We've got some bathrobes if you'd like to get out of your wet clothes. But the way that wind is blowing the roof could fly off at any time!"

"Maybe we'd better go to the back room. It might be safer there." Dex led them to the large kitchen. Through the window they watched as palms, oaks, and pines snapped in two. Part of a tin roof flew past like a piece of paper, a garage apartment across the street leaned sideways before collapsing. Water flowed into the house from every direction. It looked to them like the end of the world.

The eye of the hurricane crossed over Miami. Its calmness deceived the shocked survivors into staggering from their hiding places, into the streets, into the imminent fury of the storm's eastern side. The unbelievable destruction was shocking. Highway 1 was a war zone, downtown Miami a pile of wet, musty rubble. Some ran to their homes, only to find mounds of twisted debris.

Before anyone had the chance to internalize what had happened, the storm's parallel side slammed onto land. Terrified residents scrambled for cover, some only able to crawl underneath the ruins of their demolished houses. Those who wandered too close to shore were washed away into the raging ocean.

As the eye moved overhead, Lou relaxed. Her muscles ached. She slowly rolled her head from side to side.

"I gotta go check on my house!" William bolted upright.

"Wait until tomorrow, son. There's nothing you can do about it now. Get a good night's sleep here and then face it. We've all been through enough trauma for one day."

William wiped his hand across his face. "Everything we own is in that house. I've got to do whatever I can to save what's left. I can't let Lou down any more than I already have. I should've listened to her. She was scared, but I wouldn't listen."

"Don't blame yourself. We can't pretend to have more knowledge than the forces of nature. If you knew what was to come, you'd be taking credit for being smarter than all the elements of the universe. And as much as I admire your intellect, I don't think you're that smart." Dex grinned.

Lou made sandwiches of ham, tomato, and lettuce. The weary group sat around the table, too tired and shaken to converse. The silence was refreshing, the howling wind gone forever. They were glad it was over, giving nervous thanks for being spared, blessed to be alive.

A sudden gale rocked the house. Pictures fell from the walls, drawers flung open. William grabbed Junior. Lou covered her face. They cowered in a corner of the kitchen. The wind screamed even mightier than before. Again, the beast swung its brutal arm over them, tightening its grip, refusing to let go.

Lord, help us, they thought. Lord, help us!

THIRTY-EIGHT

T HE SUN AWAKENED FROM its slumber, rising lazily over the horizon, its glaring light exposing the crumpled wreckage that once was Homestead. The picturesque little town, once breathing with vitality, now lay in a broken heap, strangled on its fallen palms and pines. Debris was everywhere, cars overturned, business signs smashed upon the streets, houses flattened or knee deep in water, every structure touched by the storm. Warily, still distrusting the will of nature, residents pulled from their hiding places only to be greeted by the shock of devastation as they began sorting through the fragments of their shattered lives.

The hurricane cut a swath of destruction from Miami to the Gulf Coast, sparing nothing in its path. Its incredible storm surge contaminated drinking water, the ferocious winds cut off electrical power and, with it, South Florida's connection to the rest of civilization, their plight unknown. For all they knew, it might take days or weeks or even months before anyone knew what had happened to them.

William woke early, having slept no more than an hour, the fate of his home weighing heavily on his mind. He snuck out of the room, intent on seeing his house, or what was left of it. Dex greeted him in the kitchen.

"You couldn't sleep either?"

"I'm worried about the house, worried about it all night. I don't want Lou to see it yet, until I get a chance to clean things up some."

"Why don't I go with you? Might be better if you had company."

"I can handle it."

"I was thinking we could drive into town and see what's still standing. We're going to need some ice to keep what food we have from spoiling. We don't have any electricity. And we're gonna need drinking water. The tap water's no good."

"We might have something over at the house, that is, if it's still there." William tried to make light of the situation.

"It'll be there. If this house made it through those winds, then that one did, too. They're built the same, the only difference being that old roof. Whatever happens, you've got a place to stay." Dex patted William on the back.

The neighborhood had been transformed into the war-scarred battlefields of Europe. William and Dex could only look in stunned silence at the severity of destruction.

William trembled in the wake of his house, tears rushing to his eyes.

"I don't think I can go in there, Uncle Dex. I thought I could but not now. Everything we have—" William cried openly.

"It'll be all right, son. Whatever's lost can be replaced. If you don't want to do this now, I can go in and have a look around."

"I don't like crying. It's weakness. I'll go in."

"There's nothing weak about crying, William. The biggest weakness we have in this life is our unwillingness to show emotion. We were born with feelings and sensitivities for a reason. To shut them off goes against our natural being."

"I might need a shoulder to lean on." William dried his tears.

"That's what I'm here for."

Dex entered the house through the back door, and a stream of water gushed from the Florida room, soaking his shoes. William braced himself. Nearly a foot of water covered the interior, the walls completely soaked through. The stench of stale water and plaster burned their eyes. In the kitchen, cans of food littered the countertops, the pantry's shelves in a broken heap on the floor. The stove was ruined. William leaned on the counter, steadying himself.

Dex walked down the hallway past the bedrooms. Except for the water, they were in remarkably good shape. Overall, Dex had a good feeling about saving the little house. The two ferns sat in the corner of the hallway where Lou placed them the night before. He chuckled to himself; they survived the storm with little injury.

Wooden beams spread about the living room like a pile of matchsticks, roofing tile littered the floor and walls, the roof, essentially, lay in a broken heap square on the living room floor.

"That wipes us out," William stated bitterly as he looked out the ceiling at the tranquil sky.

"Sure is a mess, all right." Dex cautiously looked over the fragile remains of the roof. "I'm worried about the rest of it caving in. The stress on it has to be taking a toll."

"Why not? Might as well go ahead and get it over with. Bring the whole damn thing down."

"I know it looks bad, son. But we'll work through this with everyone pitching in to help."

"What am I gonna tell Lou? She didn't want to move down here in the first place, but I'm the one who talked her into it. I said this would be the start of a new life for us, and now look. Our lives are nothing more than a busted roof and broken dreams."

"This isn't your fault, William. It's a circumstance beyond your control."

"It is my fault. Lou never should've married me. I've done nothing but bring bad luck and hardship to her. I should stay here and let the rest of the roof fall down on top of me. That'd be the best thing I could do for her."

"Don't talk like that. You can't take responsibility for everything in life. Unfortunate things happen to all of us. You overcome them and move on. Let's ride into town and see what we can find out."

Dex nudged William along.

The center of town suffered destruction beyond description. Its buildings were crushed and demolished, one on top of the other like a stack of fallen dominoes. Storeowners picked through the rubble, while police officers gallantly patrolled the streets against looters. Water was knee deep in some places. William parked the car outside the downtown area where the water level was slightly lower.

"We need wading boots," William groaned.

"Look at this." Dex looked around in awe. "The ocean must be trying to reclaim the land."

"What are we gonna do?"

"Let's find out what's going on."

Dex rolled up his pant legs and stepped out of the car. William reluctantly followed. The ice cream store tenuously stood in broken rubble, its proprietor in the midst of the wreckage, his demeanor as broken as the building around him.

"Hard to believe, ain't it? One day everything's going along just fine, then the next—"

"Everyone's been touched by the storm, Tom. Some of the houses along Palm and First Streets aren't even there anymore," Dex stated.

"This will ruin me. I've been standing here like a zombie all morning. Hell, everybody is walking around like they're half dead, in shock, probably wishing they were dead. We can't get word out. Telephone and telegraph lines are down. Who knows how long it'll be before anyone knows what's happened to us." Tom shook his head.

"If it comes down to it, I'll drive into Miami and call the governor myself. Have you seen Tate around this morning?" Dex surveyed the scene.

"He and a couple of commissioners went by here about an hour ago. It looked like they were headed for the courthouse," Tom responded.

"Take it easy, Tom. We'll see what we can do."

Dex and William waded into the heart of downtown, past the demolished storefronts and vacant stares of their owners. It was just as Tom described. They were zombies, not knowing what to think or what to do.

The courthouse escaped the storm largely unscathed. Its two-story, white marble exterior stood proud amidst the destruction around it, gleaming in the early morning sun. Dex opened the front door and called out. He was greeted by a stern voice.

"Go away! No one's allowed in here today except city officials!"

"That you, Tate?" Dex asked.

"Dex?"

Tate entered the large foyer from a side office. He was a big man, well over six feet tall, and rather young to hold the position of mayor. Though he ran things his way, he remained indebted to those who helped get him elected. And Dexter Smith used quite a bit of influence to get Tate elected.

"Good to see you, Dex. We took quite a beating yesterday." Tate half-smiled.

"I'd call it a knockout myself."

"Worst hurricane this area has seen in a long time. Electricity's out, drinking water is no good, houses are gone, people are missing by the hundreds, most folks don't have anywhere to stay. I got part of the police force going door to door telling people not to drink the water, and the rest patrolling the streets. We're trying to set up shelters in the few buildings that made it through. We even thought of asking anyone whose house is still standing to open it up to their neighbors. We're in a bad fix, Dex, really bad."

"I can drive over to Miami and get the word out," Dex offered.

"From what I understand, Miami is worse off than we are. We'll have to start rationing what we've got and share the rest. If you can spread the word around about the drinking water, I'd appreciate it. And tell people as soon as we hear something from the governor and get some relief supplies in we'll let them know. Most of all, try to keep them calm."

"It's done."

Dex strode out of the municipal building on a mission. He and William drove through several neighborhoods with Tate's message. They went as far as they could without depleting the car of gas.

By late afternoon, slowly but surely, neighbors were helping neighbors, opening their homes and sharing their resources until relief arrived.

"Where have the two of you been all day?" Lou asked.

"We went into town to see if we could get some ice or food but there's not much out there. The whole town's wiped out." William carried a bag of canned goods he salvaged from his house.

"How's our house?"

William somberly nodded his head. "We brought these things over. It might be a while before help gets down here."

Dex opened the door. "Tate said it could be a couple of weeks, maybe even longer. We've got to band together with our neighbors to get by."

Lou was heartsick. She didn't want to leave William in the midst of the tragedy, but she wasn't sure she had the desire to stay either. The howling winds blew away her pride, the prospect of death made her long for her family.

William began working on their house despite the unstable roof, mopping as much of the water as he could from the floors and removing the fallen beams and chunks of plaster. The more he was able to do, the better he felt about saving the house. He wasn't willing to give up on Homestead just yet.

On the third morning after the hurricane hit, and against William's wishes, Lou walked to the house. The floor in the Florida room was drier than she expected, though standing puddles dotted the room. Large stains on the walls were still moist. William cleaned the kitchen admirably, but the effects of water and wind damage were evident. Lou felt a lump growing in her throat.

She stopped in the entranceway to the living room. It was worse than she imagined. A slimy combination of plaster and water covered the walls and floor. The stench was awful, like a forest floor covered in wet, rotten, moldy leaves.

William walked in as she started to cry. "Lou! What are you doing here? I told you not to come over yet!"

"I had to see for myself what was going on. I had no idea it would be this bad."

"It's getting better. In a few days I'll have the house cleaned up real good. It won't look so bad then."

"I'm trying to keep a positive attitude about all this, William, truly I am. But I don't know if I can ever get over it."

"You can, Lou. It'll take time, but you can. We've been through the worst of it."

"Have we? We're down to our last gallon of water, and we've eaten nothing but crackers and canned beans for three days. Sometimes I wonder if anyone outside of here even knows what's happened to us. We could go on like this indefinitely, and I just don't know if I have the strength to do that."

"Relief's on the way. We should be getting help any day now. Things will get better. All I'm asking is that you be strong just a little while longer," William pleaded with Lou.

She was torn between her duty to him and her desire to leave Homestead. "I'll do my best."

When relief finally trickled in, residents stood in line for hours in the hopes of getting fresh water and food. Many were still in shock, unwilling to grasp the magnitude of their losses. Neighbors and strangers exchanged stories of hardship and hunger. They had all become allies in the aftermath of the hurricane's devastating fury. When supplies ran out, those who were first in line shared what they had with those in the rear.

The trucks came in every day after that, bringing with them everything from food and water to clothing and bedding supplies. Lines formed early in the morning and often lasted until late afternoon. The entire family went into town each morning to get what they could, each standing in a different line for hours on end. The waiting was tedious, though necessary. A cool wind blew in from the east, the only saving grace under miserable conditions.

Lou waited three hours before reaching the front of the food line. She held a bag large enough to carry a week's supply of provisions. Volunteers from Sebring handed out bread, peanut butter, corn, tomatoes, and dry cereal. The people in line around her were unusually quiet. Maybe it was the stress of the situation catching up to them, or something more sinister.

Slowly, the news filtered up and down the line. Ships were reporting another hurricane just north of Puerto Rico moving in a northwesterly course, putting South Florida in jeopardy a second time. Most in the line shook their heads in disbelief, others laughed timidly. A disquieting pall fell over the battle-weary residents of Homestead. Lou graciously accepted the provisions and walked away.

The following morning she again went over to the house, knowing William would put up a fight, but she was prepared. The house was empty. She went into the bedroom and began pulling clothes out of the closet and tossing them onto the bed. William appeared in the doorway as she pulled out her last dress.

"What are you doing?"

"I'm going back home," she answered without disturbing her chore.

"How come? I thought we'd talked this out."

"That was before I heard about another storm out there."

"You can't just up and leave like this, Lou, without even talking it over with me. I went into town to talk with a man about repairing the roof. I'm trying my best to get things back together. I asked you to be patient until then."

Lou pulled a suitcase from the top closet shelf and packed her dresses. "I know, William. And I've been as patient and understanding as I can be. I've gone without food and water so my son could eat. I've stood in lines for hours on end to keep us from starving. I was nearly killed by something I still don't understand, and now you're telling me to be patient so another storm can finish us off?" She closed the suitcase, deflated by her emotions. "My patience blew away with that storm, William. I can't go through another one."

William couldn't blame her for feeling the way she did, but he was terrified of losing what he worked so hard to create. "What about me? I can't just go off and leave things the way they are. I owe Uncle Dex better than that. He's been very good to us."

"I'm not trying to be ungrateful or unappreciative, and I will make certain he knows that. But you don't understand how much that storm affected me. Being that close to death made me realize that I don't want to die without seeing my mama again. I need her. And I'm not going to wait around for this other storm to keep me from seeing her."

Lou's mind was made up. Reluctantly, William resigned himself to the inevitable.

"It's going to take me a while to wrap things up before I can go back. Why don't you stay with Mama and Daddy until I get home? And we'll start over . . . somehow."

William took Lou and Junior to the train station, free passage having been offered to all those who wanted to leave the stricken area, as well as the hellacious memories, behind. He was ill at ease, estranged from his wife, their show of affection more an obligation than an emotional release, neither completely sure what the future held for them. William backed away as the engine pulled the line of cars from the station, feeling once again that he'd let his wife down.

THIRTY-NINE

WITH THEIR EXPERIENCE IN Homestead behind them, William and Lou renewed their ties to Fitzgerald. William went into business for himself, earning a steady, and sometimes profitable, income as an auto mechanic. Lou gave birth to a daughter in the summer of 1928 and became pregnant again the following summer. As she saw it, their return home was blessed. Everything fell into place without much effort, as if designed by fate.

William found a house directly across the street from his parents. Originally a two-bedroom structure, it had been converted into a three-bedroom house with an addition to the back. A large dining room adjoined the living area, and two bedrooms fed off from either room. Two full-sized cedar trees stood at both ends of a front porch that extended across the entire face of the house, sheltering it from the hot summer sun.

Though he still had occasional binges of self-doubt, William curtailed his drinking markedly, keeping his insecurities in check, learning to deal with them in solitude. There was closeness in the home that, for a time, seemed impenetrable.

In the fourth month of Lou's pregnancy, an event beyond the control of small-town, working-class people threatened to destroy the balance in their lives. Lou was shelling a bowl of snap beans when a furious knock rattled the front door. The urgency of it made her jump.

"Leanice! What in the world?" Lou asked.

"I ran all the way from the store! Where's William?" Leanice gasped for breath.

"Out in the shop. What's wrong? Is it Mama?" Lou panicked.

Leanice shook her head. "There's a run on the bank! People are lining up to get their money out! You'd better get down there as quick as you can!"

"How can there be a run on the bank?"

"The Stock Market crashed! Banks are closing up all over!"

Lou ran to the garage. William was replacing sparkplugs under the hood of a Dodge Touring Car. "The bank's going under! People are getting their money out!"

"What?" William asked, confused.

"The Stock Market crashed! Leanice said there's a crowd of people at the bank trying to get their money out!"

William turned white as a sheet, the repercussions immediate and vicious. He sprinted past Lou and Leanice, running down the street like an athlete in training for the Olympics. A discontented mob milled around the bank, faces long and grim, voices rising in defeated anger, calling for bank officials.

William tried working his way through the crowd, but those in line weren't willing to give an inch of the space they'd fought to gain, one step closer to redemption, one step further away from disaster. Hostilities ran high, desperation prevalent. The crowd surged forward, squeezing those in the middle, intending to burst into the bank. The doors would not budge.

"Why won't they open the doors?" William asked a man next to him.

"People are panicked. Everyone wants their money. Bank officials are scared. They done gave out all the cash they had on hand. The rest is gone. They lost out just like the rest of us. Problem is, most people here don't want to believe that. They want their money."

William studied the man. "All of us here are plain out of luck?"

"That's about the size of it. We can kiss that money good-bye, never see it again," the man lamented.

Dispassionately, William watched as the mob pushed against the doors. "What good is there in beating a dead horse? He's dead just the same."

He put his hands in his pockets and walked away, morose, impassive. The volatile crowd beat against the doors, their pathetic cries shrinking in the face of disaster.

The impact of the crash hit everyone, but some harder than others. Those who didn't have much to begin with barely noticed the difference. Those who had a lot to lose faced the sobering, even suicidal, prospect of bankruptcy. Others, like William, caught in the middle of ruination and normalcy, had to struggle to keep afloat. The meager emergency fund he kept at the house wasn't nearly enough to support a family of four with another one on the way. Somehow, and at this point he didn't even know how, he'd have to find a way to make ends meet until times got better.

Business at the shop dropped off significantly. As money became a scarce commodity, William bartered his skills for food, clothing, and, on occasion, medicine for the children. Times were tough and becoming even tougher, bills piled up while the pantry turned bare. William shouldered the sole responsibility of providing for his family the best he could; accepting charity was altogether out of the question.

When he wasn't working he was out looking for work, sometimes being away for twenty-four hours at a time, down into Irwinville and Ocilla, over to Abbeville and Rochelle, wherever his work took him. Day after anxious day, he collected and counted the few coins and dollar bills he earned, barely enough to survive, but enough to keep his family from starving, a day's labor for a few coins. Slowly, methodically, bit by bit, dollar by dollar, he was killing himself.

Necessity hung over Lou so heavily she thought the sheer force would collapse her onto the ground. It bothered her, angered her, forced her to do something she despised. The weight of it suddenly became so unbearable she lost her temper, snapping at the nothingness in front of her.

"Good heavens, Lou. What are you so angry about?" Leanice asked as she sipped a glass of homemade lemonade on the porch.

Frustrated, embarrassed, unapologetic, Lou responded. "Nothing, nothing at all. I'm not angry, it's just . . . I don't know, nothing." There was a genuine sadness about her, the softness of her face edged with melancholy. "I hate this Depression. I hate what it's doing to people. I hate what it's doing to us." She paused, a hint of bitterness in her eyes. "I'm worried about William. He's running himself ragged trying to keep a roof over our heads and food on the table. We'd be doing fine if we hadn't lost the money we had in the bank. Sometimes I wonder why the good Lord is putting us through all this. He knows how rough it's been on us in the past, and now it's getting even worse."

"He never gives you more of a burden than you can handle, Lou. And even then, He puts others around to help when you need them. We're all in this life together, and it's important that we help each other out."

"He also gave us pride. And William's got more than his fair share of that. He won't accept help from anyone."

"He's not the only one who's prideful, Lou."

Lou looked askance, knowing she'd been caught. "So we're both a little prideful. It's not a bad thing, really. I guess neither of us wants to become a burden on others."

"Asking for help isn't being a burden. And besides, how often do you ask for help?"

Leanice saw the turmoil her sister was going through, the angst of wanting to do something but afraid to take the first step. "I never put much stock in banks. I don't like the idea of strangers handling my money. I cash my paycheck, give Mama and Uncle John money for room and board, and keep the rest in my lingerie drawer. I've got a nest egg stashed away."

Lou pretended not to hear, the thought of asking for money all at once inappropriate and crass. "I should wake up the children. If they sleep too long in the afternoon, they won't sleep any tonight."

"You're as stubborn as a mule, Lou. I know how you feel about being helped, but did you ever consider how it would make me feel to be able to contribute to others?"

The love Lou felt for her sister at that moment knew no bounds. She looked at her with admiration and respect. "I love you with all my heart, Leanice. You're the most caring person I know. And I appreciate what you want to do, but I can't take your money. You've worked hard for what you have, it's yours, you earned it. Do something with it that makes you happy."

"I'm trying to, but you won't let me. Giving this to you would make me happier than anything I could buy. I don't need the money. I don't have a family of my own, I don't like to travel, I'm very content with my life and what I have. It would do a lot more good for you to have the money and make some use of it. Please let me do this. It'll make me feel more like a part of your family. I want your children to grow up happy and have everything they need. I don't want them to suffer the way we did."

Lou thought back to her childhood days with Grandpa Cowan, remembering with clarity the anxiety he brought into their lives. They were at the mercy of circumstance, much like her family was now. Only this time, she had the opportunity to change her destiny. "Mama did the best she could with what life gave her. She made the best out of a bad situation and sacrificed so much so we could have a better life than she did."

"I wish she'd had someone to turn to for help. I can't even imagine what she went through after Daddy died. She had to face the world alone with two small children to raise. I don't want your family to go through anything like that, Lou. I really don't."

Tears came to Leanice's eyes, tears of sorrow for the hardships in her life yet tears of happiness for the many blessings she could count.

"I will make this up to you one day, Leanice. When everything's back in place as it should be and we're on our feet again, I will repay you."

"You've already paid me, Lou, by letting me be a part of your family. You don't know how it makes me feel to belong to something as wonderful as this. It's worth more than all the money in the world."

Lou reached over and held Leanice's hand. They sat in silence, the power of their bond unbroken, strengthened by the many adversities in their lives. The golden light of afternoon slowly faded into the twilight of gray.

FORTY

L OU SPENT THE MONEY SPARINGLY, knowing that William kept track of every penny he earned and where every penny was spent. If there was too much to show for the household account, he'd surely know about it. She kept the money inside a jar placed on the back shelf in the pantry, a lining of white paper concealing the contents.

"What's this?" William asked, his voice flat, the jar and its contents spread out in front of him

Lou stopped in her tracks. "Looks like money to me." She strode past him, an air of nervous indifference around her.

"I thought it was mayonnaise. I went to make myself a sandwich, couldn't find any mayonnaise so I went looking for some and, lo and behold, look what I found. Must be my lucky day." William sarcastically played with the money, letting the numerous coins filter through his fingers. "I can't begin to suppose where all this money came from. Do you know, Lou? Do you know where this little fortune came from?"

"It's not yours?" she asked innocently.

"I don't have a habit of keeping money in a jar in the back of the pantry. No, it isn't mine, so it must be yours or the children's. Why have you been squirreling away money, Lou? You got some plans I don't know about?" William's tone was laced with accusation.

Lou took offense to his insinuation, whatever it might be. "If you're calling me a thief or suggesting that I'm using that money for my own gain, then let me stop you right there. You ought to know me better than to imply that I'm capable of doing something underhanded."

"Then how do you explain this? How come I didn't know anything about it? If your intentions were honest, then you wouldn't have anything to hide, now would you?"

Lou's back arched. "Don't you ever accuse me of being dishonest with you! I've done nothing but stand by you and protect you since we got married. Who was it that kept your drinking from the family? Who went with you to Homestead so you could pursue a dream? If I happen to have a little extra spending money around the house, it's to take some of the burden off you. I haven't spent any of that money on myself, if that's what you're wondering. I spent it on food and clothes for our family." Lou ran out of breath.

William backed off slightly but persisted with his inquisition. "That doesn't explain where it came from."

"It came from Leanice! Are you satisfied?" Lou lost her composure. "I didn't ask her for it, she offered. She's got a good savings, and she wanted us to have what we needed."

William quelled his anger, tempering the explosion with false gratitude. "I see." He put the money inside the jar. "Give this back to Leanice and tell her thank you, but we don't need it after all."

Lou steeled herself for a fight. "I'm not going to do that, William. We need this money. It's helped us get by this past year."

William pushed the jar toward her. "Take it back . . . today. I do not need Leanice's charity."

"It's not charity, it's necessity. These are hard times, and you're worrying yourself into an early grave trying to support us. This money should take some of that worry off your shoulders. Can't you see that?"

"I do not need this money. Take it back."

"Maybe you don't need it, but your children do! I have as much at stake in this family as you, William. I'm a partner in this marriage, so my opinion counts for something. I'm not going to take food out of my children's mouths or clothes off their backs because you're too stubborn to admit that this Depression is more than we can handle!"

William grabbed the jar and threw it into the corner of the room, smashing it against the wall. He jumped to his feet, sending the chair sprawling behind him. "I will be the one responsible for supporting this family! Not your sister!" he growled.

Lou backed off. William's demeanor reminded her of Grandpa Cowan's frequent outbursts that terrified her as a child. "She's just trying to help, William," Lou answered meekly.

"Why is it that everyone in the world is under the impression that I need help? 'Everyone help William, he's such a lame-brained fool!' " he mocked the words.

"No one's saying that but you, William. Accepting help from others doesn't mean you're a failure, it only means that you're human like the rest of us," Lou reasoned.

Fearing his volatile temper would get the best of him, William stormed from the house, slamming the door behind him, a swirl of anger pushing through the room. Lou went to the corner, picked up the money, and placed it inside the lining of her winter coat.

William was gone all day, finally stumbling home around midnight, drunk and singing a catchy tune. He was disheveled, his shirt unbuttoned. Lou heard him trying to open the door and confronted him on the back porch. "Where have you been all this time? I've been worried sick!"

"Don't be angry, Lou. I'm not angry. See how I'm not angry? I wouldn't be singing if I were angry." William spoke like a child being scolded by his mother.

"Look at you. You look like something that fell off the back of a freight train."

William conscientiously checked himself over, slicking back his hair. "I don't know, Lou. I think I look damn good for a man approaching his fortieth year." William belched loudly. The smell of stale whiskey made Lou recoil in disgust. "Come on, baby. Don't spoil the mood I'm trying to create here."

William put his arms around Lou's waist and tried to kiss her. She fought him. He persisted, tightening his grip on her. His whiskey-laden breath made her nauseous. The more she fought, the more forceful he became. For a split second, she was afraid of him. They struggled, knocking over the ironing board. Lou pushed William against the wall. "Get out of this house! And don't come back!" Lou railed at him.

William stared at her arrogantly, brutishly. "And where would that leave you if I didn't come back? Would you go rushing back home to Uncle John and your precious sister? You only married me to get away from John. All you wanted was my money, free room and board for the rest of your days off the sweat of my brow. That's not such a bad deal. Maybe I should try that sometime."

Lou chuckled incredulously, tired of the same old accusations that sounded like a phonograph that skipped over the same place again and again. "Don't you ever get tired of that song and dance routine? You've thrown that in my face how many times over the years? Do you really believe that? I want to know. Do you think I married you just to get out of Uncle John's house?"

William fidgeted in the face of Lou's questions. In his heart he knew that she truly loved him but he was too stubborn to let go of the one upper hand he had on her. "Yes."

His answer cut through Lou's heart. She felt hurt, betrayed, unloved, and unwanted. He wounded her deeply, so much that she couldn't speak, and barely with the strength to remain standing.

William reached out to her but pulled away, ashamed by his brutality. He desperately wanted to recant his answer, to declare his absolute adoration for her. But he couldn't, it was useless. There was too much between them now, too much had been said. He limped out the back door, into the stillness of a bleak, starless night.

He lived in the shop for days, taking meals at his mother's house. Rebecca scolded him soundly. "I don't know what to do with you, William. You are intent on destroying everything close to you—your wife, your children . . . your mother. I'm not going to stand idly by and watch you do that. I worked too long and too hard on you, encouraging and protecting you."

"It don't matter now, Mama. Nothing does," William sulked.

"You go over there and apologize to her! Get on your hands and knees and beg her for forgiveness!"

"It's too late for that."

"It's never too late, son. Certainly there's nothing you could've done to keep her from accepting an apology."

William dropped his head and cried. He sobbed deeply and loudly, giving his soul over to pure emotion. "I was drunk. I didn't know what I was doing. Oh God! I wish I could take it back. Please help me, Mama! Please!"

Rebecca put her hand to her mouth and dropped into a chair. "My God, William. What have you done?"

"I was out of my mind drunk, mad at her for something that wasn't her fault! I hate myself!"

Rebecca didn't know what to do or say or feel. She looked at William as if he were a stranger, as if she had not raised him. He was lost to her, adrift on a sea of anger and uncertainty that kept her at bay. William calmed himself enough to tell her what happened.

Rebecca merely shook her head. "If I didn't raise you any better than that, then I don't know who you are. No son of mine would ever do anything like that. I can't tell you how much this hurts me, William. It's breaking my heart. Maybe this is my fault, maybe I wasn't there for you as much as I should have been." Rebecca cried.

"Don't go blaming yourself, Mama. It's not your fault. It's this damn Depression. Everything was going fine until it came along. Something that happens two thousand miles away is destroying our lives."

"It's not the Depression. Not all of it anyway. There's something inside you that propels you to drink and escape from whatever it is that possesses you. This same sort of thing happened before the Depression. You've got to confront what that is before you go blaming something else."

William sat quietly, searching his soul for an answer he already knew. "I'm not good enough for her. She deserves better than I can give her."

"That is nonsense, William. She loves you more than she loves herself. And for some reason you've got this blind spot that prevents you from seeing it."

"I know. And I really fixed it this time. She'll never speak to me again."

Rebecca leaned over and lifted William's face level with hers. "You look me in the eye and promise me you'll never do anything like that again. Ever!"

"I won't, Mama. I swear. I love Lou with all my heart. If I do it again, I want the heavens to strike me down."

"Do not disappoint me."

Rebecca led William across the street, sitting him down on the front porch as she called for Lou. "William has something to say to you."

Lou ignored her husband. "He's already said everything he has to say to me."

"I don't blame you for being angry, Lou. What he did was hateful, mean, selfish, and criminal. I'm not sure I'd take him back myself. But in his own way he does love you. And I suspect that he loves you more than he could ever express to you. That's why he acts the way he does, because you mean so much to him and he doesn't feel like he's giving you enough in return. He's mad at himself, not you."

"We've been through this before, Rebecca. William says he's sorry and he won't do it again, but then he does. Why should I believe it's different this time?"

"Because . . . if he ever steps out of line again he knows I'll disown him. And his father will come after him with a shotgun and a pair of handcuffs." Rebecca glared at William.

Lou remained aloof, unmoved. "Then he'll have to prove that to me. I don't want him in the house. If he loves me, then he'll wait until I'm ready, even if it takes six months."

"William?" Rebecca expected an answer.

"I'll do whatever it takes. I don't want to lose you, Lou. I love you."

"I hope you do, William. I really hope you do."

FORTY-ONE

SEPTEMBER 26, 1942, WAS A BIG day for Rebecca, her seventieth birthday. It seemed impossible to her, an illusion, everything that had happened in her life was just below the surface of her skin, as real and close as ever. Though the years had rushed by like a speeding locomotive, always in a grand hurry to reach its next destination, she had remained the same. When she looked in the mirror she saw the lines and wrinkles and gray hairs of old age, but her spirit was still as young as the little girl who sat upon her daddy's shoulders as they explored the forests near her home.

She awoke in an unusual mood, the memory of her parents fresh on her mind. They haunted her, as if gathered around, looking over her shoulder, visible if she turned fast enough. It was an odd feeling, a wonderfully, comforting, odd feeling.

Harbard made plans to honor her birthday, going so far as to hire a woman to come into the house and cook the meal. Rebecca silently pitched a fit, and when she could stand it no longer, the indignity of having someone cooking in her own kitchen, she donned a hat and shawl and went for a walk.

She turned onto Main Street from Alapaha and passed through downtown to Lemon Street. The air was laced with the smell of acrid smoke from outdoor incinerators burning the day's trash. The smell reminded her of her childhood and the many mounds of smoldering trash piles in the backyard. Her father's voice came to her, his love embracing as she strode past the railroad tracks, a short distance from her destination.

On a high, sloping meadow outlined with magnolia trees and dotted with brush cedars, Evergreen Cemetery kept a watchful eye over the town. Its inviting solitude provided peace for many, a place where the living and dead reunited on the earthly plane. Given the way her day started, beckoned by the love of her parents, it was only natural that Rebecca should end up here.

A hammock of pine trees bordered the cemetery's south side, outlining the plot where her parents were buried. Rebecca stood at the foot of her mother's tombstone, the dates of her life nearly obscured by the passage of time. She was sad, not having had a mother as she grew into womanhood, but sadder more for a mother's life cut short before it had a chance to begin.

The rush of emotions swept through her, so sharp and deep, a sudden pain knifed down her right arm, followed by a feeling of light-headedness, as if she'd stood too fast and lost her balance. Her eyes lost focus, blurry objects spun around in mid-air. Her breathing was erratic, the top of her head numb. She was frightened and alone. Silently, she panicked.

As quickly as the spell struck it went away, leaving her exhausted, unable to move for the better part of an hour, hoping her strength would return. When she tried to stand it was a monumental chore, her weakened body unresponsive to her commands, her right leg and arm stiff. The walk home was endless.

Harbard greeted her on the front porch. "I was contemplating whether I should hop in the car and go looking for you."

"I didn't mean to be gone so long. I went for a walk and lost track of time."

Harbard helped her up the steps, noticing her unsteady gait. "Are you all right, Rebecca?" he asked.

"I'm fine. I just walked further than I intended and it left me winded."

Harbard took her arm and helped her inside. "Perhaps you'd better lie down before everyone gets here."

"I think I will. Fetch me a glass of water if you will."

Rebecca took to the safety of her bed. Her weary body responded exultantly to the comfort. Harbard brought her a glass of water and sat next to her.

"Feel better?"

"Much better. I overdid it. Sometimes I forget that my body isn't as young as my mind is." Rebecca took a sip of water.

"You're not getting old, Rebecca. You're maturing a little."

Rebecca chuckled. "I'm getting old, Harbard. Plain and simple, I'm an old woman."

Rebecca looked at Harbard lovingly. She stroked the side of his rugged face, it reflected the years of hard work and struggle. There was a mellowness to it now, an acceptance of things he could not change.

"Do you remember when we got married and moved into this house? You were working at the rail yard, and you'd come home at the end of the day looking like you'd jumped into a barrel of grease."

"I remember." Harbard held her hand.

"Those were happy times, weren't they?"

"Still are."

"I miss those days. Your mother came over nearly every afternoon. We'd work in the garden and make bread together. She was like my very own mother."

"She was a special lady."

"After Daddy died she was my rock. I will always love her for that."

"She loved you too, Rebecca. She thought the world of you. And she knew how happy you made me."

Rebecca forced a smile. She stared at Harbard for a long time without speaking, unable to bear the thought of leaving him behind. "I love you, Harbard. You're the one constant in my life that I could always depend on. I'm glad I married you."

Harbard kissed the back of her hand and held it to his heart as Rebecca drifted off to sleep. "You nap for a while, sweetheart."

Rebecca slept solidly; Harbard let her rest long after the family arrived. When she awoke, she was embarrassed at having held up the party. "Why didn't you wake me, Harbard?"

"You needed the rest. And we couldn't start the celebration without the guest of honor."

Fan-shaped cloth napkins delicately adorned each place setting. The crystal and china sparkled, the silverware perfectly arranged. A centerpiece of pink and white gladiolas cast a dancing shadow upon the wall by the flickering candlelight. Harbard put his arm around Rebecca and kissed her on the temple. "Happy birthday, darling."

"It's beautiful, Harbard."

After dinner, the adults adjourned to the breezeway while the children went off by themselves to catch fireflies and search for crickets. Having turned eighteen, Junior joined the adults, his outline in the doorway reminiscent of his father many years before.

Though they talked of simple things, their minds were fixed upon events occurring across the ocean, the unrest in Europe, the ascension to power of a man who threatened the fragile peace set in place after the Big War. His fiery speeches alarmed them, his benign face insulating a diabolical mind bent on destruction.

"I listened to President Roosevelt on the radio the other night," Harbard slowly began. "He said the situation in Europe is getting worse. Hitler's gaining ground every day. He'll have half of Europe under his control before long."

"And we'll be sending more and more of our boys over there. Mandatory draft is what they're saying," William added.

"This thing is spreading far and wide." Harbard sighed.

"Lord, what is wrong with people these days?" Rebecca fumed. "They're all half crazy. Fighting and shooting at one another. We went through one of these things already. Why couldn't we learn from that?"

Harbard chuckled at Rebecca's temper. "Not everyone learns things as easily as you, dear."

"Doesn't take a genius to figure out that killing innocent people won't solve anything."

"A madman can't figure things out, Mama," Etta scoffed. "That's why he's a madman!"

Junior listened intently while his mother fidgeted nervously. The thought of her son being drafted terrified Lou.

"Will I be drafted, Daddy?" Junior asked.

"In time you will, son," William responded. "Unless the war ends quickly."

Harbard stretched his legs. "That's not likely to happen. We made a pact with the Brits and the French. The President's not going to back down on that. This thing's gonna drag on for a while."

Junior was quiet, deep in thought as he contemplated his future.

Rebecca still fumed. "If they want to settle this thing, why don't Hitler and Churchill duke it out behind a barn somewhere instead of sending so many young boys to their deaths?"

"That would make too much sense," William answered.

"We're gonna keep right on till there's not a one of us left alive, and we still won't be satisfied," Etta offered.

"All those young lives wasted on something so stupid," Rebecca replied bitterly.

Lou had heard enough. All the talk about doom and young boys dying was more than she could handle.

William started after her, but Rebecca called him off. "Let me, William."

Lou was on the couch, her face in her hands. Rebecca sat next to her, holding her close.

"This is so unfair! Why do they have to take my baby from me?" Lou cried.

"It's okay, honey."

"First that blasted Depression almost destroyed us, and now this war is going to finish us off! I don't know how much more I can take." Lou rested her head on Rebecca's shoulder.

"It doesn't seem fair, does it? But keep in mind there's a million other mothers out there who feel the same way you do. It's one of the compromises we have to make for our time here on earth."

"What do you mean?"

"We were never promised a perfect life. There are as many hardships as there are triumphs. You have to take the bad with the good. If Junior does go off to war, that doesn't necessarily mean something's going to happen to him. Keep the faith, Lou. Pray for him. Pray every night and day, every waking moment."

"I don't want to lose him," Lou sobbed.

"Pray for strength and mercy. What man tears down God builds from the dust."

"I'm not as strong as you."

"You have strengths inside you that you aren't even aware of yet. Don't give up on yourself, Lou. If you do, then you're giving up on your child, too."

"I'll try, Rebecca. But it won't be easy."

"Nothing worth having in this life is easy. Fight for him, Lou. He won't leave you if you believe in yourself and your God."

Rebecca held Lou close.

"I want to believe, I'm trying to. But I can't help feeling what a travesty this whole thing is. Where is our God while all this is going on? Why doesn't He put an end to it? I've lived my whole life in the belief of a kind and loving God. What is kind and loving about war?" Lou broke down again, bothered by her wavering faith.

"He loves us enough to put us in charge of our own destiny. What we do with it is up to us. And if we create war, then we have to suffer the consequences. You're right, it isn't fair to people like you and me who ask for nothing more than the happiness of our families. All we want are the simple pleasures of life."

"That's not asking too much, is it?" Lou asked.

"Of course not. And you can have it if you want it. God listens to those who ask His help. We may not be able to control the destiny of world events, but we can control our own destiny. Don't be afraid to ask, Lou. There's a mighty power in your spiritual being."

One month after she turned seventy, Rebecca died in her sleep. A massive stroke ended her life, sending her spirit into the bright light with the knowledge that she'd found her way home.

FORTY-TWO

JUNIOR WAS DRAFTED IN THE spring of 1944. He was nineteen, a high school graduate with plans of attending law school. The letter arrived on the first day of spring, the day of nature's rebirth, a day that could possibly hold his death sentence. He held the unopened envelope in his hand, staring at it, hoping it was a cruel mistake. When he found the nerve to read it, he memorized every line, every word.

He agonized over what to do. The reality of warfare invaded his senses. Visions of combat clouded his mind, the newsreels at the local theater playing before him. Airborne bombs exploded around him, hand grenades burst at his feet. The rapid fire of a machine gun whistled over his shoulder.

William was in the shop working on one of three cars waiting for repair. The tinkering sounds calmed Junior, familiar and secure. He dragged himself outside, clutching the letter in his hand. William noticed him leaning against one of the massive garage doors, a resigned look on his face.

"What's wrong, son? You look like you just lost your best girl."

Junior handed the letter to his father. William wiped the grease from his hands and read it over slowly. "Dammit!" He mumbled. "Have you told your mother?"

Junior shook his head. "She's not home yet. I don't know what to tell her, Daddy. You know she'll fall apart when she finds out."

"Let me tell her." William angrily wadded the letter into a ball and threw it against the wall. "Dammit!"

He screamed louder. The outburst shook the walls. "What in the hell is wrong with this world? Nobody can get along, people fighting each other left and right! And who pays the price for it? Little people like us, that's who! Where is the fairness in that?" William slammed the hood closed.

"I'm scared, Daddy."

"I am too, son."

William stared long and hard at Junior, wishing that he could turn back the hands of time, realizing how ineffective he'd been as a father. The years of anguished drinking put a barrier between him and his children. They didn't know what to expect out of their father from one day to the next. For years his mood swings and erratic behavior let them down. It was well past time, he felt, to become a father.

"What's wrong?" Lou asked as she walked into the living room.

"Sit down, Lou," William answered.

She refused. "No. Tell me what's wrong."

"I really think you should sit down."

"No. If it's that bad, then I won't sit down. It can't be bad if I'm standing. Tell me it isn't bad, William."

"Lou—" William began.

"Don't tell me! Whatever it is, I don't want to hear it."

"Junior's been drafted, Lou."

The directness of the reply stabbed her in the side. She fell against the wall, her body numb and limp. Though she felt she couldn't move, she found herself running out of the house and down the street. She wanted to scream, but her lungs refused.

William pursued her but she kept running, all the way past the railroad tracks to an open meadow. She fell to her knees, dissolving into tears. William sat next to her, catching his breath. He pulled her to him. "It'll be fine, Lou. It will."

"How can you say that? You don't know!" Lou heaved.

"You're right, I don't know. None of us do. We don't know what will happen. It's out of our hands. All we can do is believe that everything will turn out for the best."

"You sound like your mother," Lou exclaimed between sobs.

"I reckon I do. Mama put her faith in God above all else. I've never been much of a religious man, you know that, but at this point I don't know where else to turn."

Lou eyed him suspiciously, a smirk on her face. "Don't tell me you're converting, William Smith."

"I didn't say that," William retorted, returning Lou's smile.

"Why, I might just get you into church after all."

"Don't go expecting something like that."

"We could use another man in the choir, especially a baritone."

"Stop it, Lou."

He held her tight, catching her gaze, enchanted by her eyes. "I love you, Lou. We will get through this together. No matter what happens, we still have each other, we will be there to lift each other up, to embrace one another, to laugh or to cry, to believe . . . together."

He kissed her tenderly, recapturing the feelings he had for her the day they married. She rested her head upon his shoulder, finding comfort in their bond.

Junior boarded the bus for Columbus at eight o'clock Monday morning. Lou fought back tears as he said good-bye. Her baby was leaving her for the first time in his life, a man amongst men, all headed for an uncertain future.

Her heart broke, though she had to let go, realizing at this moment what her own mother felt when she went away and what Rebecca felt when William went away. It's what all mothers feel when their children leave the security of home.

"You be good, you hear? Don't let anyone turn you away from your upbringing." Lou fixed Junior's collar. "Remember who you are, son. And keep with you the knowledge that you are loved."

"I will, Mama. I'll write to you as often as I can," Junior responded.

William grabbed Junior's shoulders. "I'll miss you, son. Things won't be the same at home without you. Do as you're told, be prompt, ambitious, eager, let 'em know that you're good enough to be an officer, okay?"

"Yes sir, Daddy."

"Let's go, son," the bus driver intoned. "If you're going to Columbus, you've got to board now."

Junior hugged his parents and boarded the bus. Lou forced a brave smile, but emotions smothered her. She buried her face in her hands.

The days turned into weeks, which in turn gave way to months. An end to the war was nowhere in sight. Headlines in the local paper screamed of casualties and deaths as Allied troops tried to take control of Europe. Over two thousand Allied soldiers were killed as a massive offensive effort began on the shores of France. Another forty thousand were wounded over a seven-mile area as troops pushed toward the heart of the country.

Early in 1945, four thousand died and another twenty thousand were wounded in the Pacific front as the Marine Corps suffered its worst casualty count ever during the battle for Iwo Jima. The numbers were staggering, the effects far-reaching as town after town, city after city, state after state came to know loss.

Lou fell into a deep depression, her prayers for a quick end to the war unanswered, her faith stretched beyond its limit. Days passed when she would not emerge from the house, closing herself off behind the darkness of curtains, unwilling to live yet unable to die. Like many mothers, she was another casualty of the war.

She obsessed over the war's progress, reading every newspaper and magazine she could find for the latest details. She rarely slept and wouldn't eat, her beautiful face pale and sad, her blue eyes dull and lethargic.

Nobody could reach her, not even the two teenage daughters who needed their mother. She would be satisfied with nothing less than an end to the war. Her maniacal devotion to Junior's memory tore the family apart. Anne, the oldest, kept to herself as much as possible, insulating herself from her mother's unyielding grief. But Susie was too emotionally charged to distance herself that way. She was caught in the vortex of pain spiraling around her mother.

One afternoon she burst into the store where Leanice worked, tears streaming down her face. Leanice embraced her. "What's wrong, Susie?"

"I can't take it anymore, Aunt Leanice. Mama is sick, all she does is sit on the couch and stare out the window. Something bad is happening to her. I don't want Mama to die!" Susie sobbed in halting dialogue.

Leanice calmed her niece, drying her tears. "There, there, Susie. Your mama isn't going to die. Come with me. I'll see what I can do." Leanice took Susie by the hand. "Cover for me, Myrtice. If D.R. asks where I am, tell him there's an emergency in the family and I'll explain later."

"Don't worry about him none. I can put that sourpuss in his place." Myrtice winked.

Lou was on the couch just as Susie described. Leanice ripped open the curtains and turned to her sister. "Get dressed, Lou. Take a bath and get dressed. We're going for a walk," Leanice stated categorically.

"I'm not going anywhere but here, Leanice," Lou replied.

"Oh yes you are." Infuriated, Leanice pulled Lou from the couch. "You are going to bathe, fix your hair, put on some powder and rouge, and get some sun on your face. I'll wait until you're ready."

Leanice forcibly led Lou to the bathroom, pushed her inside, and closed the door. "I'm going to stand right here. There's no use in stalling. I can be just as stubborn as you." Leanice blocked the door for an hour, waiting for Lou to emerge.

"There, you look better already. Now go put on something decent and grab a sweater, it's a little windy today."

Lou did as she was told, her motions robotic. The brightness of the clear April day temporarily blinded her, accentuating the pout she'd had since childhood when things didn't go her way.

Leanice chuckled at her. "Heavens, Lou. You look just like you did when you were ten years old and Nellie wouldn't let you play with Ruth's dolls."

Lou resented the intrusion into her grief.

"It's such a pretty day, isn't it? Makes a person glad to be alive. Have you noticed how sweet the air is today? The wind is carrying the scent of gardenias and sassafras. Take a deep breath, it's wonderful."

Lou ignored her, much to Leanice's increasing impatience.

"Listen, Lou. You know how much I love you. There's nothing I wouldn't do for you and your family. But you have got to snap out of this. We're all concerned about Junior, but making ourselves sick over it isn't going to bring an end to the war. You've got two growing girls at home who need their mother. And if you can't be there for them, then I'll find someone who can. Maybe they should come stay with Mama and me for a while."

Lou reacted abruptly, like she'd been slapped in the face. "I can raise my girls, thank you very much!"

"Then do it! Be their mother again, Lou. You've been neglecting them, and they're worried about you. All of us are."

"I can't give up on Junior," Lou implored.

"No one's asking you to," Leanice countered.

"He needs me."

"And so do your daughters. Susie came to the store this afternoon. She was crying, crying because the mother she loves so much has gone away. And the mother who replaced her hardly speaks and doesn't hug her the way she used to. You can't stop living because of this war, Lou; it's not fair to the girls. They're young and they need their mother. We can all share the burden of worrying about Junior. That's not something you need do all by yourself."

They continued walking down Central Avenue against a stiff breeze. Lou faced it, letting it wash over her. "I remember breezes like this down in Homestead when I'd take Junior into town for ice cream. William was working long hours then, six days a week, and Junior was my closest companion. Sometimes a big wind would come along, and he'd let out the biggest squeal. He loved that. I leaned on his company so much. I guess I always have. To me, he'll always be that little boy waving his arms in the breeze."

Lou stopped, closing her eyes in the remembrance of things past. "I can still see him, that wonderful, boyish smile, his nose and forehead turning pink in the sun. He's my baby, and I'll never let go of him."

Leanice suddenly felt ashamed of herself, unaware, until that moment, how deep Lou's devotion was to her children.

"I'm glad you made me do this, Leanice. You tore me away from my self-pity and told me what I needed to hear. Rebecca once told me that nothing in this life is promised, and I never really believed that until now. I've always wanted things to work out just right for my children so they'd be happy. But you can't guarantee happiness, can you?"

Leanice looked at Lou with the utmost respect. It was like her sister was emerging from a cocoon, shedding the naivete of the past while embracing the uncertainty of the future.

"I have to accept whatever happens. I cannot change it. If something happens to Junior, then I'll love him even more for what he has done for his country and what he has done for me. He has brought such joy and happiness to my life, and for that I am eternally grateful."

The sparkle returned to Lou's eyes.

The war in Europe mercifully ended. Allied forces made a last push into Germany during the late spring of 1945, overtaking the remnants of the retreating German army, uncovering the horrors of a regime gone mad. The news of concentration camps and mass murder shocked the world. Newsreel images of the survivors sickened the hearts of decent civilization. It was appalling and unreal, signaling the end of an innocent age and the heralding of a bleak future.

Lou got down on her knees and prayed for forgiveness. After reading and seeing accounts of the Holocaust, she realized how selfish her actions had been. There were those who suffered far greater than she, indignities she could not begin to fathom. She gave thanks for everything she had. Hers was a life unscathed by the insanity of hatred and ignorance. She was blessed with simplicity.

FORTY-THREE

THREE SLICES OF SWEET POTATO PIE were missing when Etta checked the refrigerator. She knew it was coming. Harbard had a habit of taking food down to the jail on weekends for his prisoners. His generosity with her cooking unnerved Etta. She didn't want her culinary efforts going into the stomach of some common criminal. But there was nothing she could say or do about it. Harbard did whatever he pleased, despite her protests to the contrary.

He'd become even more stubborn in old age, if that was possible, working whether he felt good or not, and on most days, in his own mind, he felt fine. In a year's time, he would celebrate his fiftieth anniversary on the job, a feat unparalleled in Ben Hill County's history. He planned on retiring at the end of 1952 and taking it easy for a while. He was seventy-seven years old, and his reflexes weren't as sharp as they were in his youth.

Etta nagged him constantly about retirement, unable to understand for the life of her why he wanted to keep working. "You're an old man," she'd say, "too old to be running off after some chicken thief!" To which Harbard replied, "Maybe I am old, but I can assure you that the chicken is glad I'm still doing my job." His flippant attitude riled Etta into distraction. She often warned him that he was playing with fire and that one day, if he was not careful, he would be badly burned.

Harbard waited outside the jail cell while the three prisoners finished their meals. They were harmless folk; one was drying out after an all-night binge, while the other two were cooling off after a public brawl over a woman of questionable repute. Even so, Harbard kept himself out of arm's reach. He jingled a pocketful of change, the clinking noise reverberating through the cells, sounding like a myriad of coins tap-dancing down a flight of stairs.

"If you boys feel the need to visit here next weekend, I can promise each of you the tastiest slice of pecan pie you'll ever put in your mouth. My daughter-in-law is making it to celebrate my forty-ninth year on the job."

"Forty-nine years?" one of the men asked. "You that old, Mr. Smith?"

Harbard chuckled. "That old and then some. I've been locking people up in this jail since way before you boys were born. I even locked up your daddy, Ernest. And for doing the same thing you did, fightin' over a woman."

"I wouldn't have to be fightin' at all if some back-stabbin' polecat had kept his paws to himself." Ernest spit through the cell at his rival.

"Knock it off, Ernest. You want me to add another day to your sentence?" Harbard collected the plates.

"If it meant not having to look at his ugly mug, I wouldn't mind it!"

"Fine by me," the other man stated, "that'd give me an extra day with your woman!"

Ernest slammed his open hand into the cell bars, seething with rage. "I'm gonna kill you, Hal!" he screamed.

Harbard turned. "Shut up! Both of you! If I hear so much as a peep out of either one of ya, someone's gonna be sleeping under the jail tonight!"

When Harbard was serious he could still bore holes through a person with a single glance. He meant business, and both boys knew it.

Virgil Griner, the Sheriff of Ben Hill County, sat with his feet propped up on his desk when Harbard entered the office. "I thought you'd be gone for the rest of the day," Harbard said.

"Me, too. I got sidetracked. Saw that Ford station wagon out on the highway again. I doubled back and followed him for a while. Think I spooked him. He headed straight for home. Didn't turn off the highway, didn't head into town. Went home like any good ol' boy would do who was totin' a load of shine in his car with the Sheriff on his tail." Virgil smirked.

"You think he's our man?" Harbard asked.

"I know he is. What else would he be doing on the Ashton Highway as much as he is? And don't tell me it's just coincidence that there's a still right off the highway next to the county line and he just happened to be riding by."

"How come you didn't stop him?" Harbard placed the dirty dishes into a bag.

"I didn't actually see him come up off the old county road onto the highway. For all I know, he could've been out for an innocent Saturday afternoon drive." Virgil glanced over his shoulder at Harbard. "And if you believe that, I got a parcel of land down at Ocmulgee Swamp you might be interested in."

Harbard rubbed the side of his face. "What do you want to do about him?"

"Why don't we take a little trip down the Ashton Highway in the morning? Park the car in that clearing just east of the county road and see if Mr. Spires pays us a visit."

Virgil folded his arms across his chest, the wheels spinning inside his head, formulating a plan to catch the suspect red-handed. Harbard circled the next day's date on his calendar, August 26, 1951, a reminder to let out his prisoners before he and Sheriff Griner went looking for Allen Spires.

Etta awoke earlier than usual, just in time to see Harbard leaving the house. It was Sunday, and she expected him to transport her to church, as was the routine every Sunday. He wouldn't say why he was leaving the house so early or when he'd be back.

"Well how am I supposed to get to church?" Etta pouted.

"Get a ride with Junior and Lou. It won't kill you to vary your routine, Etta."

Harbard closed the car door and drove off.

Etta watched from the doorway, muttering to herself how unappreciated she was.

Harbard sent his prisoners on their way before Virgil showed up. Ernest was still cranky and started to go after Hal, but Harbard put an end to his foray with a slap to the side of his head. Checking over his rifle thoroughly, Harbard inserted two bullets into the double barrel and dropped two more into his coat pocket, in case they encountered any trouble with Mr. Spires.

Virgil parked the Sheriff's car in the clearing to the east of the county road as planned. The car was invisible to anyone passing from north to south toward the highway, a stand of pines and thick underbrush blocking its presence. The Sheriff and deputy waited in silence, neither daring to speak for fear of tipping their hand. Harbard's senses were on full alert. If anything was stirring in the woods around them, he'd know it.

The crescendo of a lone cicada's song spilled into the air, its piercing buzz rising and falling with the gentle breeze. The presence of the early morning sun was partially obscured by the pines and thick brush. Harbard checked his watch. It was eight-thirty. They might have to wait all day for Spires, if he was to pass by at all.

A car engine slowly cranked, sputtering a few times before kicking into gear. Sheriff Griner rose in his seat, his fingers teasing the ignition. Slowly but surely, an automobile made its way down the dusty road. Harbard remained stoic, his eyes fixed between two pines. The car neared. Their anticipation grew, neither of them willing to breathe. As the car crept past, Harbard got a good look at the driver. It was Spires.

The suspected bootlegger pulled his old station wagon onto the highway and headed east toward town. Sheriff Griner let him travel about a mile down the road before emerging from the clearing. Spires was in no hurry. With a cargo of moonshine in the tail of his car he took it slow and easy. The officers approached the suspect's vehicle at a leisurely pace.

Harbard rolled the window down as Sheriff Griner made the initial move to overtake Spires, pulling onto the left lane. Spires caught a glimpse of the Sheriff's logo on the side of the car as it sped alongside. He checked over his shoulder. A barrel of shine was exposed despite the tarp clumsily tossed over it. "Shit!" Spires cursed.

He stepped on the accelerator, and the old station wagon jerked forward like a racehorse out of the gate. The race was on.

"He spotted us! Hang on!" Virgil yelled over the accelerating motor.

Spires drove like a bat out of hell, swerving over into the left lane, bumping the Sheriff's car onto the dusty shoulder.

"He ain't going down without a fight!" Virgil yelled as he battled the steering wheel.

"I could shoot out one of his tires!" Harbard screamed back over the howling wind gushing into the car.

"Too risky! He's going too fast. Might spin out of control!"

The vehicular dance continued down the highway for several miles, Spires outracing the Sheriff toward town. Virgil had to act fast. He didn't want to risk running the high-speed chase through the middle of town.

A little ways down the road he saw an approaching car. His brain spun into action. "I got a plan! Hold on to your liver!"

He stepped on the gas, the front fender of the Sheriff's car nudging Spires's bumper. Timing was critical. Just as the westbound car passed, Virgil swung the car into the left lane, giving Spires little time to react.

"Here we go!"

Spires glanced in his rearview mirror. The officers were nowhere in sight. Sweat streamed down his face, his hands glued to the steering wheel. Harbard leaned out the window next to Spires. "Pull over!" he screamed.

Spires swerved toward the officers. Harbard quickly ducked back inside as Virgil made a severe cut to his left to avoid a collision.

"We gotta play hardball!"

Virgil cut sharply to the right, bumping the side of Spires's car. Spires momentarily lost control on the right shoulder, sending a twisting cloud of dust spiraling upward. Virgil bumped him again. Harbard motioned for Spires to pull over but he would not concede. Spires bumped them again. Virgil sped up, pulling slightly in front of Spires. He edged over, daring Spires to hit him. Spires had nowhere to go but off the road. He screeched to a halt. Virgil stopped just ahead of him.

As the stir of dust settled around them, Harbard warily stepped out of the car, clutching his rifle in his left hand. "Turn the engine off!" he ordered.

Spires sat motionless, his car idling in high gear.

"Turn it off, I said!" Harbard reiterated.

Reluctantly, Spires turned the ignition.

"Throw the keys out the window!"

Harbard stood tall, his lanky frame towering above the car. Spires deliberated, his mind spinning at the speed of light. A .38-caliber pistol lay concealed on the seat next to him. When he threw the keys out the window, he carefully grabbed the gun.

Harbard slowly approached Spires. Sheriff Griner backed him up. "Step out of the car slow and easy." Harbard eyed him closely.

Spires opened the door. Harbard was less than six feet away, his rifle pointing at the ground. Sheriff Griner stepped out of the car and rounded the trunk. A group of black crows bickered noisily above them. Spires slid out of the front seat, his body protected by the open door. Suddenly, brutally, he aimed the pistol directly at Harbard.

"Please don't shoot," Harbard uttered as the shot rang out.

The single bullet tore through Harbard's chest, piercing his heart. He fell to the ground. Sheriff Griner tried to take cover, but Spires emptied the remaining rounds into him, striking his right arm, chest, abdomen, and right leg. He fell across the trunk, sliding into a kneeling position against the rear bumper, his face pressed against the shiny black metal.

A deadly silence screamed through the air, the bodies of the Sheriff and his deputy motionless and bleeding. Spires picked up his keys and drove off, leaving the two bodies at the mercy of the elements.

An old man down the road heard what sounded like gunshots as he weeded his garden. His house was less than half a mile from where the cars came to a stop. Upon seeing the flash of smoke, he ran into his house and told his daughter to call the Sheriff's office. He picked up a rifle and raced to the scene.

The black station wagon cruised down the highway barely above the speed limit. The old man got a quick glimpse of the man in the driver's seat. He was wearing a white shirt and a straw hat. A late model car pulled up seconds after the shooting, and a young man jumped out of his car.

"What happened?" Alvin asked.

"They were shot! I saw it happen!"

The older man raced up the road.

"Get me to the hospital. I'm hurt bad," Sheriff Griner moaned.

"My God! It's the Sheriff!" The older man panicked.

"Help me get him into my car!"

They picked him up gingerly, struggling to get Virgil's large body into the back seat of Alvin's car.

"How about the other one?" Alvin asked.

The older man bent over the still body. "It's Harbard Smith. And he don't look too good!"

"You stay here with him. I'll take the Sheriff to the hospital and send someone for him."

Alvin pushed the car as fast as it would go, spraying loose rocks and dirt in his wake. An older model station wagon was just ahead. He did not notice the man in the white shirt and straw hat as he roared past.

"The Sheriff's been shot!" Alvin yelled at two officers in front of the police station. "I'm taking him to the hospital! Another man is seriously injured out on the Ashton Highway, a few miles east of the county line!"

Dried pools of blood darkened the hot pavement, red splatters dotted the rear and passenger's side of the Sheriff's car. Harbard lay still, his head propped upon a blanket. The elderly man and his daughter sheltered the body against the blazing sun.

The arriving officer and the old man lifted Harbard's body into the police car. The vehicle sped into town as fast as it could go, but it was too late. Harbard died instantly, his heart shattered by an assassin's bullet.

FORTY-FOUR

WORD OF THE MURDER SPREAD like wildfire in a field of dried weeds. Mayor McDonald immediately ordered the formation of a posse to search for the man fingered by a dying Sheriff as the triggerman. The primary search area centered upon the Ocmulgee Forest, which bordered the Ashton Highway, not far from the shooting site. The forest was a dense tangle of tall pines and oak that blocked the sun, creating a canopy of darkness. Some days, visibility was reduced to three or four feet, even at high noon. Deeper into the forest, in menacing wait, was the Ocmulgee Swamp, a quagmire of stench and rot. Trailing someone in the swamp was the undoing of many a lawman.

Mayor McDonald called Dave Paulk, clerk of the city. Dave was a longtime neighbor of Harbard's and good friend to William. He and his wife Birdie played cards with William and Lou every Thursday night.

Birdie listened to Dave's end of the conversation with the Mayor as she dressed for church.

"Harbard and Sheriff Griner have been shot," Dave stated as he hung up the phone.

Birdie gasped. "Oh Lord! How bad is it?"

Dave shook his head. "It doesn't look good."

"Who did it? What happened?" Birdie put her hand to her chest.

"I don't know. The Mayor asked me to get William and Etta to the hospital as quickly as possible." Dave put on his hat.

"I'm going with you." Birdie followed him out the door.

Etta huffed and puffed as she strolled up the sidewalk. Though she'd only walked across the street to William's house, she appeared as though she'd run to Wilcox County and back. She had a way of accentuating her trials in life, and the fact that her father left her stranded on a Sunday morning was, to her, a definite cause for drama.

"What are you doing here?" William asked blankly as he let Etta in.

"Well, I'd think even you could figure that out. It's Sunday morning, I'm wearing church clothes, isn't that obvious enough for you?" She lumbered past William.

"I figured that much. But what are you doing *here*?" William grunted, returning her attitude in kind.

"Daddy had to go off somewhere this morning and left me stranded. I thought I could catch a ride to church with Junior and Lou."

"Take the load off." William offered Etta a seat. "What did Daddy have to do so early on a Sunday morning?"

"I have no idea. All I know is that he left me high and dry knowing full well that I had to get to church."

"Well, it must've been something really big to miss an important engagement like that," William scoffed at her.

"Once a heathen, always a heathen. And just look at you, not even dressed to show respect for the Sabbath."

William buried himself behind the morning paper, ignoring his sister's invitation to do battle over religion. A knock at the door broke their stalemate.

"That's probably Daddy now, come to escort the forgotten princess to the ball," he mocked. William opened the door.

"I'm sorry to bother you so early in the morning, William," Dave began, "but I'm afraid I've got some bad news for you. Your daddy's been shot. He's at the hospital. You and Etta need to get over there right away. Birdie and I can give you a ride."

A puzzled look overcame William's face. The mere thought of his father being shot did not make any sense to him. In his mind, Harbard was invincible, indestructible. He may not be as quick on the draw as he once was, but his aim was still deadly.

"Thank you, Dave. But we'll get there." William spoke though he could not hear his words.

He sped through the intersection of Main Street and Central Avenue, oblivious to the stop sign posted there. For once, Etta did not point out his latest fault. She sat in a dazed silence. It did not occur to either of them that their father could be dead.

A uniformed police officer motioned William into the emergency area of the two-story brick hospital. A small group of city officials waited for them in a room at the foot of a flight of stairs, their faces grim.

"Good to see you, William. Why don't you all have a seat," Mayor McDonald took over the situation.

"It's that bad?" William guessed.

"Please, have a seat," the Mayor reiterated. He again motioned for William to sit, but every fiber within William's body fought the gesture.

"What happened?" William asked bluntly.

"I'll be honest with you, William. This morning Sheriff Griner and your father went after a man they suspected of bootlegging. They pulled him over on the Ashton Highway, and he shot both of them. We don't know all the details just yet. Virgil was shot four times, and his condition is serious. He could only tell us who shot them before he passed out. They're taking him to Atlanta this afternoon for surgery." The Mayor paused.

"What about Daddy?" William reluctantly asked.

"I'm sorry, William, Etta. Your father was killed."

Etta fainted at the news, nearly hitting the floor, but Dave and Birdie broke her fall. William dropped into the chair he had so steadfastly refused.

"We have a posse out looking for the man. I'm sure he'll be found soon," Mayor McDonald offered in assurance.

William heard nothing. He did not even feel Lou's arms around his shoulders. His only thought at that moment was avenging his father's death.

"Who did it?" he finally asked.

"A man named Spires . . . Allen Spires. He's an axe-handle maker."

William thought for a moment then shot up and flew toward the exit. Two men grabbed him.

"Don't, William," the Mayor said. "It's not going to help matters any by going and doing something foolish. We'll find this man. And when we do, he'll be brought to justice."

William wrestled against the men ferociously, so deep was his desire to find the man who killed his father.

Luck was on the side of Allen Spires, from the moment he shot the two lawmen to his escape into the Ocmulgee Swamp. A coordinated search required two-way radios for communication, something the county's law enforcement vehicles did not have. A call was made to Cordele to send over a radio-equipped vehicle, but it broke down while en-route to Fitzgerald, as did the second one sent to replace it. The search was delayed by half a day, allowing Allen Spires a generous head start into the dark corners of the swamp.

Spires went directly to his house from the murder scene, frantically restocking his supply of ammunition, taking what little cash he had, and beginning his flight from the law.

He headed west on the Irwin County Highway toward the small town of Arp. Once he was beyond the city limits, he picked up speed and raced toward freedom. He had not grasped the gravity of what had occurred until this moment, as he drove away from his home and family. He felt nauseous, briefly pulling over to the side of the road to purge himself. His forehead dripped with nervous perspiration. What had happened to trigger his violent outburst? Why had he shot both men?

There was no time for second-guessing. He drove farther down the highway, his increasing fear turning into paranoia, convinced that patrol cars were stationed in the thick woods surrounding the highway. He felt their eyes upon him, ready to spring into pursuit and shoot him down in a cloud of smoke as he

241 — Nathan Hipps

had done to the two lawmen. A car approached from the west. Spires swerved onto a dirt-covered country lane.

He drove recklessly, in a vain attempt to escape the demons tormenting him. He jerked the steering wheel into a left turn, nearly overturning his vehicle and clipping another car also turning onto the dusty road. Speeding down the lane, he suddenly turned again, steering himself directly into a pine tree. Cursing himself, he slammed the car into reverse and backed up to the narrow lane, passing the other car once again.

Changing course, he turned east, toward town, then veered north on the Arbor Church Road. It was almost noon; the search for him must be in high gear. He drove several miles north to an oak ridge across from the old Players Cemetery, near Reubens Lake, a black settlement on the northern edge of Ben Hill County. He pulled into the thicket of oak, partially obscuring the car's presence behind a maze of low-hanging limbs. Clutching the revolver in his left hand, he set off on a course deep into the woods.

He traveled south and then east, half running then walking a two-mile distance until he came across an old house on the lake. He watched it from the security of the forest while catching his breath. His stomach growled, as the smell of frying chicken whetted his appetite. He hadn't eaten since sunrise. Sliding the revolver inside the back of his pants, he approached the house.

A middle-aged black woman answered the door, a bandana wrapped around her head and a grease-stained apron across her waist. She eyed Spires suspiciously, wondering what a white man was doing this deep in the woods.

"What you want?" she asked with caution.

"Pardon the intrusion, ma'am," Spires tipped his hat. "I was fishing down at the lake, and I got separated from my friends. I was wondering if you could tell me how to get back to town."

She looked at Spires uneasily. "How come you don't know that? You not from around here?"

"No, ma'am. I'm visiting from Valdosta."

The woman did not believe Spires. A nervous tick belied his story. "Follow that trail to the cemetery and then go past it to the road. Then turn right. It's about eight miles from there."

"Thank you kindly, ma'am."

Spires again tipped his hat to the woman and turned to leave though he was desperately hungry. The woman watched from the doorway. Spires stopped and turned back around. "That sure is a far piece to travel on a empty stomach. I don't suppose you could spare me a piece of chicken, could ya? I'll pay. I got fifty cents."

She looked at him impatiently. "Wait here."

The woman closed the door then returned with a piece of chicken and a scoop of rice. Spires took a few bites of the dinner then handed the plate to her. He thanked the woman, paid her the fifty cents he promised, then left. He followed the trail until the woman's house was no longer visible, then turned south into the heart of the swamp.

A radio-equipped car from Cordele finally arrived at four in the afternoon, followed thirty minutes later by another from the Georgia Bureau of Investigation out of Macon. Up until then, the search for Spires had been unorganized and unproductive. Sightings of the 1942 Ford station wagon were slow in finding their way to the roaming posse.

At five o'clock in the afternoon, a telephone call came into the Sheriff's Office from the woman at Reubens Lake. After hearing accounts of the murder on the radio as well as a description of the suspect, she knew she had come face to face with a murderer. A group of officers met the woman at her home, listening with rising interest to her account of the man in the white shirt and straw hat.

"He wasn't right. Kept fidgetin', lookin' round like somebody be after him. He axed for something to eat but didn't eat nairy a bite. Look to me that he was in a hurry to get somewhere."

"Did he say where he was going?" Deputy Ellis asked.

"Said he was headin' to town. I tole him how to get there."

"Did you see which way he went?"

She pointed to the trail. "He followed the trail till I couldn't see him no more. What he did after that, only he and God know."

The posse followed the trail to the highway where they split into two groups, one traveling north and the other south. The thick underbrush revealed little in the way of clues, holding fast to its grip on the secrets of the swamp. As the light faded and the shadows of dusk grew longer, the northbound group stumbled upon Spires's car. They radioed the other half of their search party and combed the immediate area until the blackness of night ended their mission.

They returned to the oak ridge the following morning with two bloodhounds from the GBI. The dogs picked up a scent that led the posse south and east to the old Players Cemetery. There, however, the dogs stopped, confused by the scent leading in two directions where Spires backtracked after leaving the house on Reubens Lake.

One trail led back to the woman's house, the other went deep into the swamp. The dogs lost the scent completely where the water deepened. The deputies from the GBI shook their heads in defeat. The swamp was Spires's biggest ally, and they knew he was using it to the fullest advantage.

Rumors spread countywide as unverified sightings flooded the Sheriff's Office for days following the fatal shooting. Investigators and volunteers were sent on one wild goose chase after another. Patience ran thin amongst the ranks of volunteers and law enforcement officials; they needed a substantial break in the case to quell the rising concern amongst the townspeople. No one would feel safe until Allen Spires was behind bars.

Deputy Ellis took a call from a resident in Abbeville early Tuesday morning. A man fitting Spires's description asked him where he could find the nearest store. The man was hungry, the caller explained, and needed something to eat. Dogged by a backlog of unverified sightings, Deputy Ellis started to log in the information when the man said something that caught his attention.

"He asked if I could spare him a glass of water. Said he had some kind of medication to take."

"Did he say what the medicine was for?"

"I recollect him saying it was for a heart problem."

Deputy Ellis excitedly motioned to one of the GBI agents.

"How long ago was this?"

"Inside an hour, I reckon," the caller replied.

"You stay put and we'll be there directly."

The GBI agent radioed the search party near Bowen's Mill. With a fresh lead such as this, every man and every second was needed.

The posse convened at the caller's property. The man pointed to the area where Spires emerged from the woods and to the area where Spires returned. The dogs quickly picked up a scent that led to an abandoned house on the Old Abbeville Road. The posse circled the house. Deputy Ellis and the GBI agents covered the front. When all the men were in place, Deputy Ellis called to Spires, "We've got you boxed in, Spires. There's nowhere to run now. Come out peacefully, and there won't be any trouble."

His request met with stone cold silence, and the echo of his voice bounced off the exterior of the dilapidated structure. He called out again. Still, there was no reply. He nodded to one of the agents, who fired a single shot through a front window.

"We're prepared to take you by force if necessary, Spires. Make this easy on yourself, you're outnumbered twenty to one."

The GBI agent fired another shot through the front door. The three lead men held an impromptu meeting, deciding to storm the house and take Spires by force. Deputy Ellis led the way. Slithering around the pines and overgrowth, he expertly made his way to the front porch, where he waited for the GBI agents to catch up.

Spires was dangerous, even more dangerous since he'd been on the run for two days. One of the GBI agents slipped off to the rear of the house. As part of a prearranged plan, he would fire two shots into a back window, hopefully diverting Spires from the front. Deputy Ellis and the other agent would then storm the front door and make entry. Both men breathed deeply, waiting on the gunshots. As the second rang out, they burst upon the door.

It crumbled beneath their weight, spilling them onto the floor. The deputy's shotgun accidentally discharged as he lost his grip on the handle. The GBI agent fired a round on impulse. The men surrounding the house quickly convened upon it, expecting to find Spires holed up in some corner like a wildcat backed against a riverbank. Instead, they found only their two comrades. Allen Spires was nowhere in sight.

Several days passed without any reported sightings of Spires. Despite the many hours of searching and chasing, law enforcement officials had nothing to show for their efforts. As far as they knew, Spires could be hundreds of miles away or right under their noses. He was winning the battle, and the longer he remained free, the more ridiculous they looked in the eyes of the public. They were fighting fifty square miles of swampland against a man who knew the area like the back of his hand.

One week after the shooting, Sheriff Griner died in an Atlanta hospital, prompting Governor Herman Talmadge to post a reward of $500 for the capture of Allen Spires.

Distraught, angered, the officers were desperate for a break. One afternoon, a cousin of Spires offered to mediate, thinking that his cousin might be hiding out in an uncle's cabin down the river. The GBI agents were leery of the offer, fearing it was a plan to allow Spires to escape. They asked for the location of the cabin, but the man refused, promising that his intent was legitimate.

Reluctantly, the agents agreed. They'd had no luck up to this point, so there was no reason not to let this man try. Hopes were high as the arresting team waited his return. He showed up two days later, empty-handed. Grim faces and cursed cries met with the news. They were back to square one, which was, in effect, nowhere.

FORTY-FIVE

S PIRES SLEPT RESTLESSLY ON A makeshift mattress of pine straw and oak leaves, and the mosquitoes drove him from the swamp when night fell. He was awakened every hour or so by the creatures of the forest as they stalked their prey by the light of the moon. He was delirious, sleep a luxury he could ill-afford to indulge. The putrid smells of the swamp, its rotting vegetation and dying flesh, glazed over him. He tried washing the smell away, but it had become part of him.

He returned to the river swamp each morning for water and a quick bath, then searched for food in beds of wild sugar cane and occasional pear trees. As he stooped over to cup a mouthful of water, he caught a glimpse of his reflection. With his hair wildly sprayed about his head and his face covered in whiskers and mosquito welts, he looked ragged and old, like some prehistoric caveman. He'd lost weight. His cheeks sunk under his eyes. Nineteen days he'd lived on the run. He could endure no more.

When the sun rose full into the sky, he started making his way downriver, figuring he was a half-day's travel from Jacksonville, Georgia. The miles passed by like inches, so ready was he to leave the unforgiving swamp. He ran when he could, stopping infrequently to sip water. He pushed himself though his body needed rest. There was no turning back, however; he had to keep going. He followed the river south where it flowed under Highway 441, climbed the embankment, and slowly walked toward town.

His body balked, having reached and surpassed its physical limits. Dark spots appeared before his eyes, his breath quick and uneven. The combination of hunger and sleep deprivation exhausted his energy. He stopped at a house along the way and rested on its front porch. The occupants, an elderly couple, watched the stranger from the front window. He looked to them as if he might be sleeping.

"Are you all right, sir?"

Spires sprawled out on the porch. The hard floor felt good. He could sleep forever. "Could you do me a favor, please?" Spires asked.

"If I'm able, I will."

"Do you happen to have a pencil and scrap piece of paper?"

"Yes."

"Could you bring them to me, please?"

The old man brought the pencil and slip of paper to Spires, laying them on the floor next to him. Spires scribbled something on the paper, then folded it several times so the man couldn't read it.

"Would you mind taking this into town and giving it to your sheriff? I need help. I'll wait right here." Spires handed the note to the elderly man.

The couple delivered the note and, as promised, Spires waited on the front porch. He was immediately handcuffed and taken to jail, where he slept for the remainder of the day and through the evening. He was then taken to Cordele, where he awaited extradition to Ben Hill County.

William couldn't wait to confront the man who murdered his father. He camped out on the doorstep of the jail, determined to be the first person Spires saw when he returned to town.

Deputy Ellis took note of William's impassioned presence. "How long do you intend on showing up here loitering by the door?"

"Until I see Spires," William answered perfunctorily.

"Go home, William. You can see Spires in due time. There's nothing to be gained by hanging around here all day."

"There's more to be gained than you know anything about. Was your father gunned down in cold blood? Do you know what that feels like? To know that the low-life piece of scum that murdered your daddy is alive and well and still walking around? He will get no peace while I'm around. I owe that to my daddy."

The deputy reluctantly nodded William inside.

"I don't know exactly when they're bringing him in, could be today or tomorrow. I feel for what you and your family are going through, William, but I can't allow you to hound this office every day looking for Spires. I can't take any risks for his safety."

"There's no risk to his safety from me. I just want him to know that I'm here, and watching him, every move he makes. I want to make him uncomfortable. I want him to know that somebody's eyes are upon him so he's looking over his shoulder every minute of the day. I don't want him to have a minute's peace as long as he lives."

Deputy Ellis pulled a ring of keys from his pocket and unlocked the gun cabinet. He took a rifle from the case and proceeded to load it.

"You see this, William? I will not hesitate to use this against anyone who threatens a prisoner. I'm bound to this by my duty as a law enforcement officer. I don't like what Spires did any more than you. Between you and me, I hope the bastard gets hanged for what he did. But until he goes to court and faces a jury, he's my responsibility."

"There's nothing to worry about where I'm concerned, Frank. I just want to see him squirm around like a worm on hot pavement."

"Make sure that's all you have in mind."

"It is."

Captain W.A. Jones delivered Spires to the Ben Hill County jail two days after his surrender. The clean-shaven criminal was met by a crowd of curious onlookers, his wife and daughter at his side. In handcuffs and leg shackles, Spires limped past the crowd, bowing his head from their angered stares. Some jeered him while others merely shook their heads in disbelief. Spires was not the salivating, rabid monster they wanted him to be. He was an ordinary man who appeared no more harmful than any of them.

William waited for the fanfare to die down before seeing Spires. Deputy Ellis led him into the cell area. William stood in the middle of the floor, staring at Spires with all the loathing he could summon. He found it hard to believe that this simple, undistinguished man gunned down the most efficient lawman the county had ever known.

"I hope you rot in hell for what you've done." William spat contemptuously as he left.

True to his word, William visited Spires every day, haunting him, staring at him, hating him. Even when the trial date was pushed back six months, William kept up the tribute to his father.

Spires's defense team asked for a delay in the trial, citing the lack of necessary preparation time to meet the October term of court. When Judge Wendell Horne denied their request, they lodged a motion for a change in venue, claiming bias in the jury pool. After two days of testimony, including Spires's own daughter, who stated that her father had been treated fairly while in jail, their motion was denied.

Under Georgia law, the defense had six days in which to file an appeal on the change of venue motion. From there, the request went on the calendar of the Court of Appeals, eliminating any possibility of a trial during the October term. Though they won this early battle, it would be an uphill fight. The evidence against their client was overwhelming. Bullet fragments pulled from Harbard's body matched those from Spires's gun. Witnesses saw him leaving the scene. And worst of all, a dead man's words implicated their client as the murderer.

Christmas came and went. Harbard's absence left a void that precluded celebration. Etta took his death very hard. The last conversation she had with him tormented her day and night. She couldn't sleep for fear of reliving that final day in her dreams, yet it was all she thought about while awake. Lou felt sorry for her, rambling around that old house by herself without anyone to comfort her.

"You have to stop being so hard on yourself, Etta. You had no way of knowing what was going to happen. And it's not like your father went to his grave thinking you hated him. He knew how much you loved him."

"When he drove off that morning, the last thing I remember thinking was how inconsiderate he was, leaving me without a ride to church. He was doing his job, but all I could think about was myself, my inconvenience. And when I think how he was lying out there on that road . . ." Etta dissolved into tears.

Lou embraced her. "Don't torment yourself, Etta. We can't help what happened. All we can do is make our peace with it and go on with our lives."

"I can't make my peace with it. I can't find peace with myself. I am a selfish person," Etta sobbed.

"Oh, Etta. You are not selfish, what a ridiculous thing to say. Look at all you do for other people. You've nursed others back to health all over this county, giving up so much of your time to help the sick."

"But I couldn't be patient with my father on the day he died. That's all that matters now."

"I can't tell you how to feel. That wouldn't be right. It's not for me to suppose things for you. I can tell you, though, that you are a good person, and well respected in this community. Your father was proud of you, and he loved you with all his heart. Remember the lifetime you had with him, not the last day."

Lou left it at that. Etta would have to find inner peace on her own.

The trial was delayed once more as the Court of Appeals heard arguments for a change in venue. Again, witnesses were called to testify that no bias existed in Ben Hill County. The Court of Appeals agreed with the original ruling, finding no sign of bias. After seven months of heartache and delay, the family finally had a trial date with Harbard's executioner.

The Ben Hill County Courthouse stood majestically against a picture perfect sky, a line of magnolia trees lazily swaying in a cool, spring breeze. The two-story marble building encompassed an entire city block on North Central Avenue. Court records and documents were housed in the basement, while administrative offices occupied the first floor. The courtroom was located on the second floor, overlooking the Standard Supply Company.

The large room had recently been refurbished. The judge's desk and jury box were done in dark mahogany, while the spectators' benches glistened in waxed cherry wood. Cleaning crews scrubbed the marble floors to a sparkling finish. It was as if the courtroom had been prepared for a visiting dignitary rather than an accused murderer.

Spires's family sat on the bench behind the defense table, across from Harbard's family. The courtroom was filled to capacity. Those who couldn't find a seat waited in the hallway for a recess, hoping to steal a place while others stretched their legs. The fervor generated by the trial created the biggest event the town had ever seen. The advent of radio and live reports via telephone made Fitzgerald the center of a growing fascination with instant news as thousands tuned in for the latest developments.

William dodged questions from overzealous reporters as he made his way into the courthouse, their dogged determination all the more reason for him to keep silent. He would do his talking after Allen Spires was convicted of murdering his father.

At five minutes until ten, all interested parties and spectators had been admitted into the courtroom. All except one. Allen Spires was not present. A buzz of curiosity spread through the room, from row to row, spectator to spectator.

Whispered theories suddenly quieted as Allen Spires entered the courtroom.

William's jaw dropped, his mouth hung open in disbelief. Prosecutor Harvey Jay could not believe what he was seeing, immediately turning to confer with his colleagues. Allen Spires was wheeled into the courtroom on a hospital bed and placed next to the defense table, directly across from the jury box.

Prosecutor Jay petitioned Judge Horne, requesting a conference at the judge's bench. He accused Defense Attorney Watson of deceit.

"This is a deliberate, malicious attempt to sway the jury," the prosecutor whispered, "and I protest vigorously, your Honor."

"Your Honor, Mr. Spires is a sick man. He has a heart condition and is very weak. We were advised that he would be best suited in a hospital bed, for his comfort only," Watson countered.

"Do you have medical confirmation on this?"

"Yes, sir, I do."

"Bring it to me."

Judge Horne looked over the diagnostic report submitted by the defense. Prosecutor Jay voiced his dissention.

"We should be allowed to have Mr. Spires examined by a physician as well, your Honor. That is, if Mr. Spires is actually that bad off. I don't recall him needing a hospital bed while in jail. Why did the defense not inform us of this before now?"

"Mr. Spires has had this condition for a long time, your Honor. This is not something we made up at the last minute. That should be obvious from the doctor's report."

"Gentlemen, I'll be the arbiter of what is and is not admissible in this courtroom," Judge Horne declared. "If Dr. Walters states that Mr. Spires should not exert himself and would be more comfortable on a bed, as he does in this report, then I have no reason to doubt that."

"But your Honor, what about our right to have Mr. Spires examined?" Prosecutor Jay demanded.

"Mr. Jay, if you can find a doctor who can perform an examination and get a different finding than the one I have before me, I'll stop seeing Dr. Walters myself for fear of malpractice. Request denied! We will proceed with the trial," Judge Horne ordered.

Though temporarily thwarted, the prosecution moved ahead with what it felt was an airtight case. Calling only five witnesses, their most damning testimony came from Sheriff Virgil Griner himself. In a sworn statement taken before he died, Sheriff Griner identified Allen Spires as the man who murdered Harbard Smith and then wounded himself.

The defense team knew it was backed into a corner. They did not deny that Spires had shot Harbard Smith and Virgil Griner. This was admitted. What they challenged was the point of provocation. While damning, they felt Sheriff Griner's testimony was not beyond reproach. They presented a theory that Spires acted in self-defense.

Spires was questioned from the hospital bed. He answered slowly, forcing himself to speak above a whisper, taking frequent breaks in his responses to catch his breath. The jurors had trouble understanding him. Judge Horne ordered the bed wheeled closer to the jury box. William's stomach turned. Spires was milking his illness for all it was worth. When asked by his attorneys why he shot the two men, Spires answered in a brief statement.

"I thought I had the right to defend myself. I didn't know what would happen next."

The courtroom settled into an uneasy silence as Prosecutor Jay began his cross-examination. Rising slowly from the prosecutor's table, he deliberately took his time, savoring the moment he had awaited for seven months. He had Allen Spires exactly where he wanted him.

"Mr. Spires, you stated that you did not know what would happen next. Is that correct?" He approached the jurors, his hands in his pockets.

"Yes. That is correct."

The prosecutor baited the witness. "Mr. Spires, had you ever seen the Sheriff's car prior to August 26, 1951?"

"I'm sure I had," Spires answered.

"Is there something that distinguishes that car from any privately owned vehicle?"

"What do you mean?"

"Anything you might have noticed that would identify it as an official vehicle?"

Spires hesitated. "It has an emblem on the side, if that's what you mean."

"That's exactly what I mean, Mr. Spires. So you were aware when these two men chased you, bumped your car, and pulled you over that they were in an official car?"

Again, Spires hesitated, glancing at his attorneys. "I did not see it while they were chasing me, no."

"That may be. But when they pulled you over, and your car was facing them, could you not see that emblem?" Prosecutor Jay faced the jury.

"I might have seen it, but things happened fast. I did not know what they wanted." Spires wheezed for air.

"Are you all right, Mr. Spires?"

"Yes, sir. I do as well as can be expected."

"Mr. Spires, prior to August 26, 1951, had you ever seen Harbard Smith or Virgil Griner before?"

"Yes."

"And did you know them to be the Deputy Sheriff and Sheriff of Ben Hill County?"

"Yes." Spires squirmed.

William grinned wryly.

"So, Mr. Spires, if you knew them to be law enforcement officials, why were you so concerned about what would happen next? Don't they have the right, the duty, to stop citizens whom they suspect of criminal activities? Is that not their job as Deputy Sheriff and Sheriff?" The prosecutor's voice boomed through the courtroom.

Spires cowered. "I did not know what they wanted with me."

"Is that any reason to gun down two law enforcement officials?"

"Objection!" Defense Attorney Watson screamed.

"I withdraw the question, your Honor," Prosecutor Jay acquiesced. "Mr. Spires, did you give the Sheriff and his deputy ample time to tell you what they wanted before you shot them?"

Spires knew he was losing the jury, as well as any credibility he might have had. He panicked, closing his eyes, praying that everyone would go away and leave him alone. More than anything, he wished the events of August 26, 1951, had never occurred.

"Well, Mr. Spires?" Harvey Jay asked triumphantly as he stood over the hospital bed.

"I don't recall," Spires answered, defeated.

"Did they threaten you, Mr. Spires?"

"I don't recall."

"I see. The Sheriff and Deputy Sheriff pull you over, you shoot them, but you don't recall if they explained why they pulled you over or if they threatened you? Is that correct?"

Spires barely breathed. William looked upon him in disgust.

"Yes. That is correct."

"I have no further questions, your Honor."

The jury was charged with its duty and sent out for deliberations. The trial lasted a mere two days, an anticlimactic ending for those who expected a legal spectacle. For all the drama of the shooting, manhunt, and surrender, the trial failed to provide a chilling closing chapter.

The jurors deliberated an hour before sending word that a verdict had been reached. William held Lou's hand. Etta clutched a handkerchief in one hand and a Bible in the other. Judge Horne asked to see the verdict, then handed it to the bailiff. Etta held her breath.

"We the jury hereby find the defendant, Allen Spires, guilty of murder in the first degree."

The packed courtroom greeted the news with a smattering of applause and a genuine sense of relief and vindication. Etta sobbed openly for her father. William looked at Spires, catching his eye after the verdict was read. He nodded smugly at Spires, then watched as he was wheeled from the courtroom to spend the rest of his natural life behind bars.

FORTY-SIX

PINK AND WHITE AZALEAS covered the yard in an explosion of color, bumblebees darting in and out from flower to flower. The camellia bushes were heavy-laden with an overabundance of red and pink buds. And the dogwoods created a canopy of soft, white lace down the street. Leola soaked in the feel of early spring, fanning herself as she rocked back and forth in a heavy wicker chair. It was mid-afternoon, her favorite time of day.

After seventy-nine years of living, she found enjoyment in solitude. It became her passion, her best friend. She relished moments to herself, taking pleasure in the simplest of events. She had time to think, spending much of her days looking back on her life and remembering the one man who still charmed her heart.

If anything, she thought about Luther more than ever. He was with her; she felt his presence. Sometimes it was so intense she could smell his scent and hear the sound of his voice. He followed her everywhere. Fifty springtimes had passed since she last saw him, though the picture of his face was as fresh and clear as yesterday.

She missed everything about him. He was her life, and when he died he took with him a piece of her soul. The longing to be near him intensified with each passing day.

As the chimes of the Methodist Church acknowledged the three o'clock hour, Leola looked toward Lee Street. Mr. Ball, the letter carrier, rounded the corner on schedule and made his way to her house.

"Good afternoon, Mrs. Smith. Looks like we got ourselves another picture postcard day. Have you ever seen such a beautiful spring as this one?" he asked enthusiastically.

"It ranks up there with the best. But then I love springtime. All of them look good to me."

He handed Leola three envelopes. "I'll agree with you there. This is the best time of year. All this beauty makes a person feel that much more alive, wouldn't you say?"

"Nothing gives me as much pleasure these days as sitting here on the porch and taking in this beautiful sight. How could anyone not be appreciative of a gift like this?"

"Well you know how people can be. They'll always find something to complain about."

Leola shook her head. "On a day like today, I'd be awfully hard-pressed to find something I could complain about."

"I'm with you on that one. Have a good afternoon, Mrs. Smith."

"You too, Melvin."

Leola glanced at the envelopes. One was addressed to Leola Cowan Smith, postmarked Covington, Georgia. She had not heard from her upstate relatives in quite some time. Eagerly, she ripped open the envelope.

The letter was from Will, one of Luther's nephews, informing Leola that his father, Bob, had passed away. Bob was the brother closest in age to Luther, and the one who favored him most. He was a handsome man, with prominent Irish features like Luther, but not as striking as his little brother. Leola had always liked Bob. He had protected her and the girls in that little house so long ago. He was quick-witted and laughed heartily. He was a dedicated family man who devoted his life to his wife and ten children.

The news of Bob's death saddened Leola. So many of the people she knew from Porterdale had passed on or moved away. As she sat on the porch, recalling those long ago days in north Georgia, she realized why Luther had returned to her.

"I want to take a trip to Porterdale," Leola stated.

"What brought this about?" Leanice asked as she put away the dinner dishes.

"Nothing in particular. I got to thinking how long it's been since I was last there, probably twenty-five years or so. John took me up there one fall to see the leaves turn, remember that?"

"That was 1928. Lou had just given birth to Anne and couldn't go."

"You're right. I wanted her to go and see all her relatives on Luther's side. I feel like we've lost contact with them, and I don't want that to happen. They were so good to me when your father died. I couldn't have made it through that time without them. I need to see the place where your father was born and grew up, where he and I met and married, and where he was laid to rest. I don't want to go to my grave without seeing it again."

"Mama, don't talk like that. You're healthier than any of us." Leanice went about her chore, ignoring Leola's insinuation.

"I've lived a long life, and my body is tired. I'm not going to see many more springs and summers, Leanice. A person knows when their time is near, and I've made my peace with that. The happiest times of my life were spent in Porterdale, and I want to go there one more time."

Leanice was uneasy with her mother's comments. "If you want to go to Porterdale, why don't you just say so? We can plan a trip up there for a few days. I wouldn't mind seeing it again myself. And we could get Lou to go with us this time."

Leola smiled wanly, knowing full well that her daughter was purposely avoiding the subject of death. She respected her feelings enough to leave it alone.

"I like that idea. It would mean a lot to your father if we visited him as a family. I can just see him smiling from ear to ear like a child at a county fair." Leola paused in recollection as Leanice sat beside her.

"I never stopped loving him. That plague may have taken him from my arms, but it didn't succeed in taking him from my heart. Your father was a special man. Everyone adored Luther Smith. He had that quality about him so few have. He just drew people to him. He was honest, personable, funny, and handsome. My goodness, but was that man handsome?"

Leanice giggled at her mother's girlish honesty.

"He was by far the most handsome man in the county, and the most handsome man I've ever seen. Why, he could charm the leaves off a tree with that smile of his. He had a little bit of rascal in him."

Leola caught herself and laughed out loud. "Well, I've become what I said I never would, a babbling old woman droning on endlessly about nothing."

"No you're not, Mama. I'm enjoying this. You haven't talked about Daddy this much in a long time."

"It's not always easy to talk about losing someone you loved as much as I loved your father. But that doesn't mean I don't think about him. Your father has always been in my heart. Every morning when I wake up he's the first thing I think about, and when I go to bed I always tell him goodnight and that I love him." Leola found herself wrapped in the warmth of Luther's love.

"When we first moved in with Grandma and Grandpa Cowan, Lou and I talked about Daddy a lot. We wondered if he could hear us when we talked to him."

"Your father has been with us all along. He's not the type to let go easily. And it's out of respect and love for him that I want to be near his resting place."

Leanice was troubled, quiet as she sipped a cup of coffee.

"What's troubling you, Leanice?" Leola asked.

"Nothing, Mama."

"I know better than that, child. A mother always knows when one of her children is troubled. That look on your face says it all. I haven't seen that expression since the day we first looked at this house."

Leanice blushed. "I can't hide anything from you, can I?"

"Of course not. I'm your mother," Leola answered proudly.

Leanice struggled for words that could adequately express her thoughts. "I remember the day we looked at this house and how upset I was. I thought Uncle John was taking my daddy's place. And you told me that could never happen. Daddy would always be my father," Leanice stammered.

"That's correct. And it's still true. Nothing will ever change that."

"But I wondered, on occasion, well, you and Uncle John were married so long, if you loved him like you loved Daddy."

Leola looked deeply into her daughter's eyes, her face aglow.

"I will never love anyone the way I loved your father. John was a good man, a hard worker and provided well for his family. I loved him for that. But I was not in love with him. Nor was he in love with me. We were two people in need of help, and we were able to help and support each other and our families. A person only finds true love once in a lifetime."

Leanice smiled. She would find a way to get her mother to Porterdale.

William did not bat an eye when Lou asked him to take them to North Georgia. He changed the oil, replaced the air filter, and cleaned the car to a shiny finish both inside and out. His meticulous approach to the trip amused Lou, reminding her of the young man who took the task of skipping stones across Lake Beatrice so seriously. With all the dignity of a hired chauffeur, he made the three-hour drive a comfortable trip.

Though only six miles separated Porterdale from Covington, the two towns were worlds apart in outlook and personality. Covington became a modern city with a wealth of shops downtown and enough parking spaces to accommodate every customer. Urban sprawl crept along the borders of its city limits, bedroom communities sprang up in once desolate fields. An eagerly anticipated interstate highway was under construction that would provide a direct route to Atlanta.

As much as Covington embraced its growth-oriented future, Porterdale clung to the ways of its past. The same covered sidewalks that lined downtown at the turn of the century still stood, though weathered by time. Bumpy, cobblestone streets twisted and turned through the town; the years of wear and tear had rearranged the red clay bricks. The abandoned cotton mill cast a ghostly presence over the Yellow River. The only sign of modernization was a new concrete bridge spanning the river, replacing the wooden one that collapsed under its own weight.

Leola's face brightened as the car pulled onto State Road 26, she was home. Though pristine asphalt covered the clay roads she remembered, and telephone lines criss-crossed the sky, she recognized the hilly, tree-lined terrain of her youth. In her mind, she pictured horse-drawn buggies lazily making their way into town, couples walking by arm in arm, a lace umbrella sheltering them from the sun. And at the top of the hill, a handsome young man with the bluest of eyes.

With his hands in his pockets and his hair slicked back, he nodded at her as they passed, a friendly smile on his face. She watched him forever, standing underneath a sprawling oak. He waved to her, and she waved back. She knew where he was, where he'd been all this time, always around her, never too far away.

As they passed over Snapping Shoals Creek, Leola asked William to look for the Hopewell Church Road. The sloping meadow was as wild and untouched as the day she married Luther, the purple meadow beauties in full bloom. Leola walked to the grove of crepe myrtles where Luther's family was buried. She stood at his grave, smiling through bittersweet tears.

"I know you can see me, Luther. I'm an old woman now, not young and pretty like I once was. But I know that doesn't matter. What matters is that we'll be together again, and I know that time is coming soon. I'm looking forward to being with you again, Luther. You've kept me waiting fifty years, fifty years of missing you. I don't want to wait much longer."

Leanice and Lou respectfully gave their mother time alone with the man she loved. They could not begin to know her pain, the longing to be with him after so many years. When they stood at her side, they felt his presence, and knew that he'd heard the prayers of two little girls who missed their father.

Leola left the cemetery with a sense of reconciliation. The peace that had eluded her at last found its way into her heart. She understood why the people of Porterdale acted as they did so long ago. They were afraid, consumed by their own mortality. They were no different than herself or Luther. Their actions were human, and she was human, and Luther was human.

She spent her remaining days in complete bliss, knowing that her reunion with Luther was soon to come. As she sat on the porch one summer day, enjoying the peace of mid-afternoon, she closed her eyes and slept. Luther was before her. She went to him, embracing his love with all her heart.

At Leola's funeral, Susie read a poem that her grandmother wrote expressing her grief over Luther's death.

And in the end do we find
the meaning of life we have lived
only then do we see
what was always meant to be

We were parted so soon
from this world we call home
for the moment we have been
knowing, we will meet again